CW01291007

THE COWBOY AND THE HOODLUM

Also by Jackie North

The Farthingdale Ranch Series

The Foreman and the Drifter

The Blacksmith and the Ex-Con

The Ranch Hand and the Single Dad

The Wrangler and the Orphan

The Cook and the Gangster

The Trail Boss and the Brat

The Farthingdale Valley Series

The Cowboy and the Rascal

The Cowboy and the Hoodlum

The Love Across Time Series

Heroes for Ghosts

Honey From the Lion

Wild as the West Texas Wind

Ride the Whirlwind

Hemingway's Notebook

For the Love of a Ghost

Love Across Time Sequels

Heroes Across Time - Sequel to Heroes for Ghosts

The Oliver & Jack Series

Fagin's Boy

At Lodgings in Lyme

In Axminster Workhouse

Out in the World

On the Isle of Dogs

In London Towne

Holiday Standalones

The Christmas Knife

Hot Chocolate Kisses

The Little Matchboy

Standalone

The Duke of Hand to Heart

THE COWBOY AND THE HOODLUM

A GAY M/M COWBOY ROMANCE

FARTHINGDALE VALLEY
BOOK TWO

JACKIE NORTH

Jackie North
MM Romance Author

The Cowboy and the Hoodlum
Copyright ©2023 Jackie North
Published May 31, 2023

All rights reserved. No part of this book may be reproduced, distributed, or transmitted in any form or by any means, electronic or mechanical, including photocopying, recording, or any information storage and retrieval system without the written permission of the author, except where permitted by law.

For permission requests, write to the author at jackie@jackienorth.com

This is a work of fiction. Names, characters, places, and incidents are a product of the author's imagination or are used fictitiously. Any resemblance to people, places, or things is completely coincidental.

Cover Design by Cate Ashwood

The Cowboy and the Hoodlum/Jackie North

ISBN Number:

Print - 978-1-942809-80-7

Library of Congress Control Number: 2023909142

This book is dedicated to...

Those who know that there are all kinds of love in the world, and that there is nothing more beautiful than the giving and receiving of it...

...and to those who look to the stars.

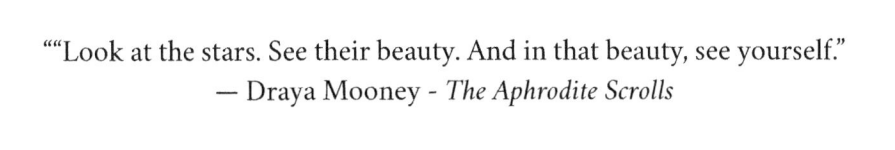

""Look at the stars. See their beauty. And in that beauty, see yourself."
— Draya Mooney - *The Aphrodite Scrolls*

CONTENTS

1. Jonah — 1
2. Royce — 13
3. Jonah — 21
4. Jonah — 29
5. Royce — 41
6. Jonah — 49
7. Royce — 61
8. Jonah — 71
9. Royce — 81
10. Jonah — 87
11. Jonah — 97
12. Jonah — 103
13. Royce — 109
14. Jonah — 113
15. Jonah — 117
16. Royce — 127
17. Jonah — 137
18. Royce — 141
19. Jonah — 149
20. Royce — 157
21. Jonah — 165
22. Royce — 173
23. Jonah — 179
24. Royce — 185
25. Jonah — 193
26. Royce — 203
27. Jonah — 207
28. Jonah — 215
29. Jonah — 223
30. Royce — 233
31. Royce — 241
32. Jonah — 247
33. Jonah — 255
34. Jonah — 263
Epilogue - Jonah — 269

Epilogue - Royce	279
Jackie's Newsletter	291
Author's Notes About the Story	293
Royce's Favorite Poem	295
A Letter From Jackie	297
About the Author	299

CHAPTER 1

JONAH

Sitting across from Beck at a metal table in the prison's visiting room was vastly different from talking to Beck from behind a wall of glass using the prison's phone system. Without the glass and the phone as buffers, Beck's energy came through like a blast from a fire hose with zero filters, his dark eyes intense, teeth clicking together as he spoke.

"You should have made a run from this place ages ago, Jonah," Beck said, shaking his head, running his fingers through his dark oily hair like some mafia don wannabe. "And I don't know why you're not planning on taking off from this work camp the second you get there. Hell, I'll pick you up and we can be on our way, back to how it used to be."

Jonah knew he shouldn't be as surprised as he sometimes was at Beck's energy and insistence on how things should be, but he was. Beck was always focused on some dreamy, smoke-scaped yesteryear, back when they were young dogs carving out their territory, looking down at everyone else, those rule followers, those model citizens.

It had been good, back in the day, when Jonah and Beck had decided their practically preordained jobs working at the dog food factory weren't enough, and that their special gift with engines and cars was the way to go—more specifically stealing cars and stripping them for parts in the back end of the legit auto shop that Jonah's uncle owned. In time, the chop shop grew, and though they never made a ton of money, at least they were independent.

Those were heady times and what Beck was always on about, even if he didn't say it outright: *Let's go back to the way it was. When we were hotshots. When we could fuck any hole we wanted, when we wanted it.*

It wasn't that Jonah didn't get jazzed about working with cars, he *loved* cars, loved making them purr, loved finding just the right part for some car owner, or finding someone who wanted that stolen Volvo and would pay for those numbers to be filed off. With the two of them working together, nobody else could compete, simply because from stealing hubcaps to hot wiring cars to stripping them, they had no competition. Not in the whole of Denver, not anywhere. Jonah was at the top of his game, exceeded only by Beck.

But over time, being the best of the best, king of the stolen cars, master of filing off VINs, had become a tad boring, at least to Jonah. Because, alas, there were always more cars to steal and break down, more parts to sell, more buyers who simply wouldn't go anywhere else.

Jonah wanted to deal in something special, but his customers wanted cheap Subarus. And on it went like that. Day after day. For years.

Maybe that sense of boredom was what had tripped him up and landed him in jail. Somewhere, in some bar, or maybe on YouTube, he'd heard about ghost plates, a way to fix the license plate so that if the driver ran a red light, or sped through an intersection without slowing down, or simply did what he pleased—because life was too short to get stuck behind an old grandma driver, right?—he would not get caught.

Hell, a guy paid his taxes, his bills, he deserved to go as fast as he wanted, where he wanted, when he wanted. And Jonah was all for that. Maybe it was himself he'd been trying to set free, except now he was in jail and less free than he'd ever been.

Or maybe more free, since listening to Beck during his once-a-week visits to the prison—with or without the shield of glass—and on the prison phone for ten straight minutes every Saturday afternoon, was a time-limited prospect. On the outside, he would have listened to Beck yammer on about the good old days for, well, days.

It wasn't that he didn't love Beck, because he did. But in the year before he'd gotten arrested, something had changed in Jonah's mind over time. While he didn't know what had changed, or what he was looking for, doing the work he and Beck did had become quite intensely boring.

They'd fucked that one time, when the cash had rolled in especially well, a celebratory weekend-long jizz fest. Beck had started it, being rough, then curling beneath Jonah's body in Jonah's bed in their shared apartment above the back half of the garage because he wanted *Jonah* to get rough.

Jonah had done as Beck seemed to need, though it had quickly become overly intense, but not really interesting. Beck beneath Jonah, his eyes begging Jonah to fuck him hard, and harder still, until the headboard left marks on the cheap plaster, and they both were covered with sweat, the sheets soaked with fluids that made it uncomfortable to sleep on and sticky besides.

"It's hard to escape a state-run prison, Beck," said Jonah, as patiently as he could. "Plus, you never brought me a cake with a file inside, and you know why?"

"Why, Jonah?" asked Beck, and Jonah had to keep from rolling his eyes because Beck sounded like he actually believed that cake-with-file-inside was a *real* thing rather than a cartoon thing.

"Because they've got metal detectors that they use on visitors, that's why."

"I could have tried it if you'd wanted me to."

Christ, Beck was just about pouting because in his mind, Jonah had never given him a chance to help Jonah escape, as if he should have. This idea, of course, took Beck on a well-marked path to the other idea, that of springing Jonah out of the Farthingdale Valley parole program just as soon as humanly possible.

"Text me your location when you get there," said Beck. He tapped his finger on the top of the metal picnic-style table as if he could conjure a kind of digital map that they could both examine and memorize. "I'll be waiting in—what's the town's name? Farthing. I'll hang out in Farthing till you give word."

Beck was a city boy, born and bred just blocks north of Colfax in Denver, and so was Jonah. They'd met, years before, on the steps outside the lunchroom of the junior high they'd both gone to. Seventh grade was, so it seemed, a time to prove one's manhood, even if one was only twelve years old. A couple of gangster wannabes had jumped Jonah when his back was turned, and he'd gone down, fast and hard, his head banging on the blacktop, gravel digging into his right arm.

Out of the ring of gawping kids had come Beck, slender, agile, dark-haired, and full of fury at the fact that two boys had ganged up on Jonah. He would have stood back and just watched with all the other kids, had there only been one boy but, as he'd later explained to Jonah, *I couldn't stand that there were two mothafuckas on ya*, which was why he'd jumped into the fray.

Having Beck as his very good friend, his best friend, was well worth the beating. Years later, Jonah had gotten a tattoo of a blue heron on the wing to cover up the scars after Beck's Auntie Lynette had dug the gravel out, but in the meantime, he had Beck. Who was not only loyal, having Jonah's back from the day of the fight on, he'd given Jonah his first leather jacket, hurriedly stolen from a church yard sale. Plus, he was hella smart and knew things that he'd learned while hanging around his Auntie Lynette's bakery in the wee hours of the morning.

Jonah wouldn't trade Beck for the world. But the problem with Beck's plan was that they both had breathed city air from the day of their births, knew every inch of its roads, where the best coffee could be had for almost nothing. If Beck waited in Farthing dressed as he was, all in black, with leather boots on his feet, and a motorcycle jacket, winter or summer, Beck would stand out in a small town in Wyoming and the local law would know something was up.

Jonah would stand out as well, whether or not he was wearing his non-prison clothes, a less in-your-face version than what Beck wore,

THE COWBOY AND THE HOODLUM

but still black, still a lot of leather. He had a long black, white, and blue tattoo on his left arm of a blue heron in flight, kind of hard to miss.

When Jonah had been arrested, he'd been wearing all of that, down to the leather boot and boot knife that Beck had given him on his last birthday. All of which was in lockup until release day, which was tomorrow.

Whether his boot knife would be in evidence when they handed him his gate money remained to be seen. Regardless, once dressed in his own clothes, Jonah would be casting a very dark shadow across the landscape, and he probably would have been glad to let Beck haul his ass across the Wyoming state line to Colorado. Back to Denver and home to the apartment above Good Deal Auto Repair on Dayton Street.

That might have seemed a good option two years ago when he'd been arrested, because being behind bars had never been part of the plan when he'd driven up to Cheyenne with a trunk-load of plastic license plate covers so opaque and milky that no security camera or high-speed detector could register them.

The plate covers had been a new layer to the ghost plate game, a little more down market from the privacy flip-and-hide plate covers Jonah had gotten from China and sold for twice what he paid for them. The plastic plate covers required no electricity, just a Phillips head screwdriver, nimble fingers, and about two minutes. Those, as well, he'd been planning to sell for twice what he'd paid.

He'd been planning to use the money from the ghosts plates to buy Beck a new set of whitewall tires for his beloved green Pontiac, and to make up for being shitty to Beck that year. But he'd no sooner made it past the Welcome to Wyoming sign, pulling into the Ranchette's Stop 'n Go to meet the buyer, when he'd gotten pulled over for speeding, of all things. And him without a ghost plate!

The two county sheriffs had taken one look at Jonah's tattoo, easily seen as he'd been wearing his tightest black t-shirt, his leather jacket on the seat beside him. His hair, at the time, had been long, curling around his ears in its usual defiant way.

All of that and, yes, his attitude, had gotten him welcomed to step out of his car, a year-old BMW MC CSL, which had been painted a dull smoke gray to avoid attention but which, in the middle of the tawny, lion gold fields of the high prairie stuck out in all kinds of unexpected ways.

Another car had shown up with two more county sheriffs in it. And a discussion was had, at which point they'd all determined they had probable cause and opened the trunk. Voila! Behold, three boxes of plastic plate covers from China with no import tags of any kind.

Plus, Jonah had forgotten the little box of plate flippers, and that baggie of pot he'd been planning to smoke with Beck when they celebrated his birthday. It was as they smoked that Jonah'd planned to present the whitewall tires to Beck, but at the moment, this kind of information would only make Beck mad all over again. *Why'd you do a fuckin' dumb thing like that just to buy me tires!* Beck would demand. *I c'n buy my own tires, you idiot.*

There had been no return to Denver for Jonah, and he was summarily arrested, booked, tried, and thrown in jail because, evidently, illegal imports, along with illegal attempts to circumvent you from getting tickets, the law in Laramie County was not for play play. And while Jonah's sentence of twenty-four months had turned into twenty months, time spent behind bars in the middle of nowhere was not for the faint of heart.

Still, he'd managed to get put in the same cell as a gangster wannabe by the name of Nelson, who thought Jonah was badass, and who wanted to be like Jonah in every way. Nelson had quickly developed into a kind of mini-Beck, except he wore canvas slip-ons instead of leather boots, had no tattoos, and burned easily in the sun, of which there was plenty to be had in Wyoming.

"So you gonna do it?" asked Beck, leaning forward, so close Jonah could see the moisture lining his teeth.

"Do what?" It didn't matter if in a normal conversation between two people that Jonah sometimes got distracted by his own thoughts, because Beck was pretty hard to derail and would always bring Jonah back on point. Like it was his fucking job or some shit.

"Let me know when you get there, and maybe a heads up if the coast is clear," said Beck, finally leaning back, a satisfied smile brightening his face. "I'll come get you and bring you home to Denver."

Frankly, Jonah knew he didn't belong in Denver any more than he'd ever belonged in his prison cell. He'd been behind bars long enough that the faint dream of returning to work with Beck in a garage just off Colfax for the rest of his life wasn't quite hitting the pleasure buttons that it used to. None of which was Beck's fault.

As to what might replace the garage and Beck and ghost plates, he didn't know. It, however, was for sure that with the tattoo and his prison record, not to mention his wild hair, now gray-streaked among the black, along with his aversion to wearing a suit and a tie or any kind of uniform imposed by someone else, he would be disastrously unemployable.

All of this would only encourage Beck to insist that they double down on their efforts to find another way to do what they always did, which was steal cars, strip them, and allow the drivers of Denver to go about their merry way, getting away with speeding, running red lights, and driving some badass, tricked up cars.

"I don't have a cellphone," said Jonah, remembering how his had gotten smashed when they'd patted him down while standing at the roadside of I-25, probably hoping that he had a weapon of some sort on him. And while, yes, he'd had a boot knife tucked inside his right boot, and while he'd not really resisted when they put the cuffs on him, he might have, yes, told the officer to *fuck off* and *quit handling my balls so fondly* in a very loud voice. Which had endeared him to exactly nobody.

"For fuck's sake, why?" asked Beck. Now he was half standing up, drawing way too much attention to himself, and thus to Jonah. "You should have told me. I could have brought a burner phone up till we replaced your real one."

To Beck, the concept of a burner phone had probably been hammered into his brain by all the cops-and-robbers shows he liked to watch on Netflix, the supreme way to communicate without getting caught. Generously, Beck would have brought Jonah a burner phone, or a legit cellphone, if Jonah had asked for it. And though Jonah had considered asking Beck, or he could have gotten his own by doing some wheeling and dealing while inside Wyoming Correctional, he'd never done so.

Not that the prison was ever a quiet place, but without the phone it was more peaceful, and he was more disconnected from his old life that had, yes, over time, grown more stale. Without the phone, without Beck around all the time, he could just float and be and imagine what his life might be like had he been someone else.

Now all of that was right back in his face, courtesy of the very intense Beck, his glare and that glitter in his eyes now in full force. Placation needed to happen and fast, otherwise, the lazy-assed and very disinterested guard watching over the visitor's room would become a little less lazy and a bit more interested.

If Jonah wanted to be released the next day for sure, either by lunchtime or very shortly thereafter, he needed Beck to simmer down, and fast.

"Tell you what," said Jonah in that confidential tone he used to get his own way. "Let me get up there and get the lay of the land. There's probably a fence around it that we'll have to negotiate, right?"

"Right." Beck nodded, the glare going out of his eyes, his shoulders down, now that Jonah was going along with Beck's plan.

"I'll get a hot shower, a hot meal, maybe even a peanut butter and jelly sandwich and an orange, and a good night's sleep that's not inside a jail cell with Nelson farting his merry tune all night. Then, in the morning, I'll say I have to call home. I'll call you. And we go from there."

By Beck's smile, it was easy to see that he liked this plan. The left corner of his mouth was curling up as if Jonah had just suggested the most badass act of revenge of all, that of taking advantage of the perks of the program Jonah had told him about, but which he secretly didn't believe, and just leaving the valley in a cloud of dust without doing a single day's work.

"You'll rescue me, won't you, Beck?" asked Jonah, though it was so obviously a done deal, as Beck was now, as he forever had been, a very loyal friend.

"Course I will, Jonah," said Beck, an almost loving warmth in his voice.

Unspoken were the words on Beck's tongue, of adoration and adulation and a flat-out refusal to believe that Jonah could ever be weak or scared or in any way overcome. To Beck, Jonah was a god, and though it was sometimes amusing to play the part, it had become more tiring than fun even before his arrest.

Living up to being a man like that, even standing behind the edges of such a template, the one Beck had in his head, got old and made Jonah feel exhausted. But maybe the valley would have a fence around it, making him feel trapped, and he'd be glad of Beck's help to get the hell out of there.

And maybe he could talk Beck into picking up stakes and moving some place warm, where nobody knew them, and they didn't have to be quite so badass all the time. Where the air was tropical, and coconut drinks cost one American dollar.

There, he could just bask in the sunlight and maybe find someone to share it with, someone who was one hundred percent less predictable than his old life or, really, who was less predictable, even by a little, than Beck's insistence that Jonah should always stay exactly who Jonah was. Forever. Until the sun burned up in the sky. Until time turned backwards.

Forever.

Which was a really really, really long time, and Jonah knew he didn't have the guts or the stamina to keep faking it for that long, not even for Beck.

"Pinky swear, Beck?" he asked, holding out his hand, elbow on the metal table, his pinky curved like he was a fancy English lady drinking a cup of tea.

"No," said Beck. He slammed Jonah's hand to the coolness of the metal tabletop, his mouth curved in a mock-snarl. "And stop that, or you'll have the screws onto us."

"Got it." Jonah rolled his eyes a little bit, but only when Beck looked over his shoulder, as if checking on the bored guard at the end of the room, shoulders hunched like he was on the verge of some kind of skulking endeavor, which only the quietest of catlike tread would enable him to get away with. "I'll find a phone and call you first thing—not tomorrow, but the day after. Which is—"

"Tuesday," said Beck, turning back around, nodding as if he and he alone was capable of keeping track of the calendar. "You'll call me on Tuesday morning."

"You got it."

It was way after soothing Beck for a good long while that visiting hours were over and Beck had to leave.

Jonah was escorted back to his cell, where Nelson was waiting, just vibrating with the need to show Jonah how good he could be, and what pleasures he could deliver on his knees, his mouth open, his hands on Jonah's thighs. But Jonah waved him away and sank to his lower bunk, head in his hands, fingers in his hair.

"Dinner's in five minutes," said Nelson, just about pacing with anxiety, as if, should Jonah be late, it would all be his fault, and maybe he would enjoy it if Jonah punished him.

"Yes, I'm aware."

Dinner would be half-assed, like it always was—white slop and gray slop and some brown slop that might taste okay, if there was a slice or two of white bread to dunk in it. Fake, ersatz ice cream for dessert.

It was also movie night, so the inmates would be shown some old black and white film like *Boys Town*, as though to demonstrate to them all how crime didn't pay. Which most of them wouldn't believe even if they had it proven to them over and over.

It gave Jonah a headache to think of such a life lived as though on repeat, day after day, always the same. Nothing new, nothing to spark interest. Nothing to tell his heart it was okay to keep on living. Which, he wasn't the fellow to slit his own wrists, but it was a slog living this life. A giant, empty, echoing slog.

"Coming?" asked Nelson, suddenly, it seemed, standing right in front of him.

Jonah's ears rang with the dinner bell, and he nodded. "Sure. I'm right behind you."

Which wasn't how it happened, because that was never how it happened. Nelson insisted that Jonah walk a little in front, as if walking behind Jonah spread an invisible cloak of protection over Nelson, which was how he liked it.

Ahead loomed a mediocre dinner, and after that, the half-lit darkness and all the weird sounds that came when prison night fell. In the morning, at least, was something unknown, and while it might not turn out to be like a spring morning where everything seemed possible, it would be different and that was enough to be going on with.

CHAPTER 2
ROYCE

The fortunate thing, of course, was the tent to which Royce had been assigned, because it was perfect. Not only was it perfectly situated, the second tent in the row assigned to team leads, he had it all to himself.

The tents were on platforms and there was plenty of shade overhead, pine trees clustered close. That meant that should he chance to sit on the front deck area, and should the sun happen to be low in the sky, the pine trees would provide enough shade to keep him from being sunburned.

Royce got up from his cot to check how many tubes of SPF 45 sunscreen he had, and that the same number of tubes of aloe vera were on hand. And that he had enough coffee pods for his mini-Keurig coffee maker, which, after much dithering, he'd selected in the pale green Oasis color because it looked cool and calming and indeed, looked very nice sitting on the top shelf that currently had replaced the second cot in his tent.

It's not a picnic, Gabe had said when he came by to check on how Royce was settling in and saw the array of amenities that Royce had brought with him. *Or a hotel.*

Gabe was smart and sturdy and steady, and Royce respected him as much as he respected any man, but Gabe had little in the way of imagination, and seemed not to require very many niceties. Like he was the kind of guy who could walk off into the wilderness with three matches and a handful of salt and survive the elements just fine.

Well, Royce was not like that and had never pretended to be, and if he purchased two of every shirt in case one of them got stained, that was his own business and nobody else's. Besides, he liked looking nice and clean and trim for the guests who came to stay at the ranch, so why should he devote any less attention to his person simply because he was going to be surrounded by ex-cons? Ex-cons, who were now parolees, deserved to see Royce at his very best as he set an example of how good life could be.

He'd set up the tent exactly how he liked it. In addition to the mini coffee maker, the box of pods, packets of sugar and little sealed cups of half-n-half, he had his toiletry kit, his books, his glass nail file from Czechoslovakia, and his little jewelry box, which contained only his turquoise scarf slide and his little pinkie ring with a very small hunk of turquoise in it.

He also had a boot polishing kit, and his stack of scarves—everything he might need. Because, really, simply because he was living in a tent didn't mean he had to go without his creature comforts. And damn anyone who thought otherwise.

Next to the shelf was a little dresser where he kept his folded clothes, and over that was a small rod that he'd hung from the support beam of the tent, which was held to the side by two small bits of rope that kept the rod hanging over the dresser. Over that was a very small mirror, because it was important to look good, again, even if one was working around ex-cons all day.

Doing his best to catch his breath, Royce debated whether making himself a quick cup of coffee would do the trick, or if he should polish his second-best pair of boots one more time while he waited for his lunch to settle in his stomach, and waited till he got the text saying that the prison van containing the parolees Royce would have charge of for the summer had arrived. Maybe he should get out his *Birds of*

Wyoming book and flip through that to see if it would help his hard-beating heart.

Not that he was worried that his new adventure would turn out badly, but he was overwhelmed with a whole basket of not knowing. Not knowing who would be on his team. Whether he could relate to them. Whether they'd be interested in what he had to teach them.

Gabe had pointed out, perhaps more than once, that however tame an ex-con might seem, none of them were docile. Well, what Gabe had said exactly was, *Never turn your back on them until you know you can trust them.* Then he usually went on to tell the tale of how one parolee, Kurt, had tried to kill another parolee, Blaze, by shoving him in the wood chipper, which never failed to send shivers up Royce's spine.

Violence was never Royce's idea of a good time, but he wouldn't mind a little adventure to spice up his summer and keep him from having dark thoughts about his divorce from Sandra.

That divorce had happened well over a year ago, so it shouldn't keep pinching his heart anymore. But it sometimes did, and was why, last summer, he'd left the family ranch in Montana and come down to Farthingdale Ranch for a change of scenery.

He had also needed a little bit of a break from the family who, although they loved him and wished him all the best, had never quite understood how bitter it had become between him and Sandra.

In his family's eyes, Sandra was a lovely girl who came to the marriage with land and money and a horse-breeding family background, much like Royce's background. Why couldn't he be happy with her, they'd wanted to know, and Royce had never been able to give them an answer that would satisfy.

The biggest problem had been that he and Sandra had nothing in common besides both coming from ranching families. He'd sensed that from the beginning, when they'd met in college, but the perfection of the match, according to everyone he knew, had blinded him to that until it was too late.

He'd married her despite his misgivings because of the tragedy that had befallen the Thackery family. On Christmas Eve, five years before, they'd lost Royce's parents and grandmother in a pileup on I-

94. Once the eighteen-wheelers started sliding across an icy bridge, there'd been no stopping the devastation that followed.

Hence, in their mutual grief, he and Sandra had married. And hence, three years later, childless, unhappy, bored, even, they'd divorced. He'd taken the job at Farthingdale Ranch not long after.

Come home any time, Grandad Thackery had said whenever Royce called him, love lacing his voice. *The Thackery Ranch will be here when you're ready for it. In the meantime, Leland Tate's a good man and runs a good outfit, from what I hear. You'll be fine.*

It had been fine working on the guest ranch, every day a new opportunity to share what he knew about birds with the guests, and to use his lifetime of experience with horses and cattle to contribute to the guests' experience during their six-night stay. The people he worked with for those five or six months last year had been hard working, honest, and knowledgeable.

Some of Royce's coworkers, like Quint, the ranch's trail boss, had been taciturn and gruff, while others, like Kit, who worked in the kitchen and in the barn, and been sweet and kind. Still others, like Ellis and Jasper, didn't have much to say to Royce when he brought horses to them to be shod, but they, too, were hard workers. Perhaps his coworkers thought of him as overly fussy, a bit of a clothes horse, simply because after he did his laundry, without fail he took out his portable steam iron and made sure his snap-button shirts were wrinkle free before he put them on, but they never said anything about it.

Maybe he wore rose-colored glasses to imagine that having no wrinkles in his shirt made the least bit of difference. And maybe nobody else he knew had a favorite poem that was about a bird. And maybe nobody at the guest ranch had a first-best pair of boots that he only wore dancing, and summer pajamas as well as winter ones.

His closet in his room at the guest ranch had been full to bursting; the little dresser in his canvas tent in the valley, perhaps smaller, was no less stuffed.

And there, on the top of the dresser, was his tin of hair pomade, which he used, not to create a pompadour, but to keep his thick gold

THE COWBOY AND THE HOODLUM

hair neat and tidy while wearing a cowboy hat. To keep his wavy hair from running riot all over his head when he took that hat off.

He was tempted to check his look in the mirror one more time, but he'd already taken care of his appearance and needed to let it be. Otherwise, he'd have to jog over to the showers, wet his hair, and start all over again, and he didn't think he had time before the van arrived. So he only ran his fingers through it to loosen the wave over his forehead, and then decided, in the end, to make that cup of coffee and take several deep breaths.

The pale green Keurig made very good coffee and, in under two minutes, he had his special coffee mug, white with a black ink drawing of a pair of cowboys riding together through the desert, full of the best brew.

It wasn't a very colorful mug, but it held almost twenty ounces, and the drawing, evocative on its own, sent an echo through his heart, reminding him that there were still adventures to be had. In addition, he had four diner style, thick white china mugs, in case he should have any visitors.

Making himself sit back on the cot, regular black coffee with two little plastic cups of half-n-half and three sugar packets in hand, he inhaled the dark scent of the coffee, and watched the swirl of cream go round and round, taking deep slow breaths.

As he took a sip, he sighed and looked out of the front opening of his tent to the wooded area made up of tall, sturdy pine trees that left a spicy scent in the air, stronger when the weather was warm, more distant when the breeze moved through the branches.

He was lucky indeed to have a job that let him live like this, in a tent with so much fresh air that he could hardly get enough of it. Plus, there was a rustic tone to let him pretend he was living in the Wild West, and enough creature comforts that he didn't have to do without.

When he was halfway through his coffee, and thinking he'd make himself a second cup, Gabe stopped by. He paused to wipe his boots on the little welcome mat Royce had put out, and knocked on the tent pole.

"Can I come in?" Gabe asked politely, as he always did. But then his mannerisms were always that way, cowboy considerate, as though Gabe imagined he was John Wayne in *War of the Wildcats*, every second on the verge of telling a young lady that he wanted to build her a house at the bend of the river where the cottonwoods grow.

Well, not only were there not that many cottonwoods in the valley, Gabe had very clearly set his eye on a young *man*. And while he did seem the kind of guy to promise a house like a vow of fealty to that young man, they all had the rest of the summer to get through before a single bit of foundation could be laid.

"Yes, please," said Royce. "I'm just trying to catch my breath."

Gabe stepped inside with a duck of his head, his cowboy hat in his hand. From head to toe, he displayed the kind of manly ruggedness that Royce very much admired, but could never adopt, at least not fully and completely. Gabe had hands roughened by weather, and the back of his neck was dark from the sun, like he had never considered hand cream or sunscreen or even a well-draped scarf.

"Are you ready?" asked Gabe. "Don't forget, at any time, I'm available for questions. And Maddy said to remind you to always wear your walkie talkie, in case of an emergency."

Maddy was the admin at the guest ranch, and she was the brains and energy behind how things were organized in the valley. Leland Tate, the ranch's foreman, always said that he couldn't do without her, and though Royce agreed that she was very good at what she did, he found Maddy a little bossy sometimes.

"I've got it right here," said Royce, patting the cot beside him. "And my notes all tidy and filed in my notebook."

He winced a little, taking a sip of his coffee because he didn't dare tell Gabe the truth. That while staying at the Holiday Inn in Torrington, he'd enjoyed a brief dip in the hotel's hot tub and somehow, from some wayward germ, had caught a cold. Which meant that while, yes, he'd enjoyed the tour of Wyoming Correctional, and while, yes, he'd collected every single handout they'd given him, he'd been too doped up on cold medicine to really attend to the courses and had never asked questions nor taken many notes.

Which wasn't like him, not at all, but the course had been over by the time his cold was gone, and besides, he was better in person, and would soon figure out the best way to interact with the parolees. Not that he was going to tell Gabe that, because Gabe was a rule follower and might insist that Royce's participation in the program be delayed until he'd properly gone through training, and knew all the rules and guidelines.

"That's a pretty color," said Gabe.

Royce looked where he was pointing, at the little pale green Keurig on the top of his shelf, right next to his little Berkey water filter. He needed both if he was going to get a decent cup of coffee every day, though he'd heard it on good authority that Dean and Neal were excellent cooks and made very good coffee, besides.

"Yes, thank you," said Royce. He got up to rinse out his coffee mug with a bit of water from the Berkey and put the mug back in its proper place. He took his pinkie ring from his little jewelry box and put it on, then he turned to Gabe, smiling, spreading his hands wide. "This is the point where I get terrified of something new and regret having signed up, but I follow your lead and do my best to help these guys take advantage of their opportunity. Now." He rubbed his hands together. "Let's go see if my charcuterie board got set up for the parolees' first afternoon snack."

"Your *what* now?" asked Gabe, but Royce just waved the question away because of *course* Gabe was kidding. He attached his walkie talkie to his belt, adjusted the knot in his scarf, and nodded that he was ready. Ready as he ever could be for the upcoming adventure.

CHAPTER 3
JONAH

The white prison van dropped four ex-cons off in a gravel parking lot in the middle of the woods. As Jonah looked around him, the ever-present breeze through the trees felt chilly, though he figured that was because he was no longer standing behind the protection of prison walls.

Next to him in line was Gordy, a B&E man he'd seen a few times, in the yard during breaks, or in the dining hall. Gordy was sweet and innocent looking, with big eyes in a pale face, but he also didn't seem like a pushover.

On the other side of Gordy were two rough-looking fellows, Duane and Tyson, who had short-cropped hair, shoulders made broad by prison yard workouts, and deceptively complicated tattoos on the left side of their necks that were, quite simply, indications of what gang they'd hung with before they'd been arrested.

Jonah had never seen a more rag-tag bunch of inmates looking around them like they'd been dropped off at the end of the world. But before he could decide to make a run for it, a stern-looking kind of guy came out and led them further into the woods. And, within moments, they were sitting very still at a long table inside what looked like a tent that was only used for eating in.

Jonah turned his face to the breeze coming in through the wide opening at one end. At the other end was what looked like a buffet, now silent between meals, and along one wall there was what looked like a little library or an office or maybe both. Sitting on top of a low bookshelf was an old-fashioned landline phone.

Jonah hadn't seen one like that in years, certainly not since his grandparents had died, but he couldn't figure out why it was there. That was, unless it was meant to replicate the phone situation inside of a prison, where calls were monitored and timed and recorded and a landline was the easiest way to do that.

"When do you think things will get started?" asked an anxious voice at his elbow.

Jonah looked down at Gordy, who had the biggest green eyes, round with a frantic expression in them that made him seem quite young, though he was a talented scam artist and pickpocket and all round B&E guy. So maybe not that talented, since he'd ended up in jail.

Better still, he wasn't Nelson, and while he seemed to look up at Jonah, perhaps for direction, he seemed the kind of guy who had other goals in life than merely getting on his knees in front of Jonah to curry favor.

They were out of prison and now that they were both waiting for the next chapter of their lives to begin, Gordy seemed to be merely checking in with Jonah, looking for the tiniest bit of assurance that everything was going to work out okay.

"At least there's no fence," said Jonah conversationally as his eyes drifted over the other ex-cons, two guys he didn't know and had never met before. They looked harmless enough, so he refocused his attention on Gordy.

"No, what?" asked Gordy. "No fence?" He, too, looked around him as if the answer to the puzzle Jonah presented would suddenly jump up and show itself. "What do you mean, no fence?"

"There's no fence." Jonah shrugged as if to belie that the issue had ever worried him in the slightest. "You know. Like the chain-link fence at Wyoming Correctional. Topped with razor wire and all sorts of alarms. No fence. We could just walk out of here."

When Jonah had been in the van driving the parolees into the valley, he'd stared hard out of the windows, scanning the horizon, trying to peer through the trees for any detail he could store away for when he called Beck, his roommate, his cohort in crime, his best friend, to come get him.

There was the landline right there, so as soon as he got permission, or a time slot to make a call, or however it would happen, he was going to call Beck. Right? Yes, sure he was.

"We could," said Gordy, blinking fast, like he was thinking it over and, simultaneously, wondering whether Jonah was considering making a break for it or if he himself would do the same. "But we passed a lot of open nothingness on the way here, so I wouldn't have the faintest idea which way to go."

"Cheyenne is south of here," said Jonah, pointing in the direction, by the pine tree shadows outside of the tent, where south was. "But it's maybe a hundred miles or more. You might die of thirst getting there."

Jonah laughed at Gordy's expression of panic, at least on the inside, and turned his attention to the two men in aprons, the cooks, he imagined, as they placed a plastic cutting board in the middle of the table, and stepped away, wiping their hands on clean white cloths. The board held an array of meats and cheeses, crackers, and dried fruit, what looked like a dish of honey, and another of figs. And there, at the very end, sitting almost forlornly by itself, was a little plate of orange slices.

Jonah's mouth watered. Inside of Wyoming Correctional, there was no such thing as fresh fruit. All fruit was dried or came in little tubs of sugared water to preserve it and tasted of sugar and mostly nothing else. Never had he seen a fresh orange behind prison walls, not once.

There were strawberries on the board as well, but his eye was on the oranges. He could almost taste that burst of light in his mouth. Hopefully he'd get to those slices before anyone else did, and he tightened his fist in preparation for slamming the first person who tried.

JACKIE NORTH

Except nobody reached for what was on the cutting board, and Jonah supposed it was because they were all so newly released. Only yesterday, they were eating off plastic trays and working their way around the underdone green beans swimming in their own bath of lukewarm salt water, and hoping the little bell would get rung so they could go up for seconds of the dinner rolls, which were usually pretty good. Now, in the face of such lushness, not one of them felt comfortable to start without permission, it seemed.

"Is he coming?" asked one of the cooks.

"He's late," said the other cook. His head was turned sideways as if his words were only meant for the other cook, but Jonah heard the words quite clearly. "He's probably doing his hair for the tenth time and retying that scarf he always wears."

"It's not the same scarf, you know," said the first cook. "He's got dozens of them."

"Don't worry," said the second cook. "All we have to do is feed him three times a day. And frankly, he might seem fussy, but at least he appreciates the proper way to cook a steak."

A shadow appeared at the opening of the tent and Jonah's attention was drawn away from the whispered conversation of the cooks, and even from the delectable orange slices on the plastic cutting board to a man wore an outfit that would have, inside of two seconds in the prison yard, gotten him torn to pieces and then locked up in solitary for his own protection.

As the man stepped between shadows from the pines and slices of light, his hair caught a sunbeam and reflected it, making Jonah blink. He'd never seen anyone look like that, dress like that, stepping into a room like a breath of fresh air. He was the prettiest man Jonah had ever seen.

It was easy to see that this was the fussy man the cooks had been referring to for although he wore an outfit that looked vaguely western, with a scarf around his neck, a silver belt buckle, and a pair of shiny cowboy boots, he looked like he was about to step on stage to film a western movie, rather than doing any actual work on a ranch.

This Jonah knew even without knowing it because even from this distance, those clothes looked too finely made to withstand the usual wear and tear. Certainly they wouldn't have lasted five minutes in Jonah's garage back home.

"Hello, everyone," he said with a wide gesture of both hands. "I'm Royce Thackery, your new team lead, and I'm here to welcome you to Farthingdale Valley—"

Royce paused and came closer to the table where Jonah and his fellow ex-cons were seated.

"Why aren't you eating? I had this charcuterie board prepared especially for you to enjoy on your first day in the valley."

Nobody moved, so he came even closer, placing his hands, fingers spread, on the table. Jonah could smell his cologne but couldn't place it.

"Really, it's all right. Help yourselves to whatever catches your fancy. I love a good snack in the afternoon myself."

To Jonah's private horror, Royce reached down and plucked one of the orange slices from the white plate and popped it in his mouth. He then proceeded to chew with much relish, as if to show them all how to really enjoy the food.

Jonah had to curl and uncurl his fist several times, and made himself wait while Gordy bravely reached for some crackers and cheese and began nibbling them as the Duane and Tyson grabbed some of the slices of meat and stuffed their gobs with the meat and some of the almonds, which looked sugared. Then, because Jonah hadn't taken anything yet, Royce eyed him, tipping his head to one side like a curious dog that only wanted to be friends.

"What about you there, in black?" Royce gestured to the board again. "Please help yourself," he said. "Or all this food and the cooks' efforts will just go to waste."

All eyes in the tent were on Jonah, making him feel hot, like they'd pulled him closer to an invisible flame. Like they wanted him to join in the fun and might get irate if he did not. Royce took a cracker, slowly, and placed a slice of some kind of sausage on it, and chomped through both, his eyes on Jonah the whole time.

"It's all very good," he said.

Jonah knew he had to give in or his reluctance might show as defiance, and he very much needed not to be in any spotlight while he waited for his chance at that phone and for Beck to come and rescue him, which suddenly seemed like a very good idea.

"Sure," he said and, with a shrug, as if it didn't matter to him what he ate, he reached across the board for the orange.

He took two slices and told himself his hand wasn't shaking as he stuffed both in his mouth.

The traces of sunlight on his tongue were pure and sweet and, for a moment, he was a very long way from where he was, getting looked at like he was an object lesson about to happen.

"Do you like oranges?" asked Royce, which meant that still all the attention was focused on Jonah.

"I don't know. Yeah." Beneath his black t-shirt, Jonah's skin was prickling like it itched, but he didn't dare move a muscle because every eye was on him. Then he shrugged and did his best to trace the sweetness of the orange with his tongue, but the flavor was fading fast.

"Well, I'll make sure the cooks include more than just the one next time, okay?"

Royce's smile was bright, but Jonah couldn't trust the overwhelming friendliness there, because that was never wise. Someone who smiled like that was either an undercover cop or a tourist who'd started on the 17th Street Mall and somehow ended up crossing over into Five Points and simply didn't know any better.

"Now, eat up," said Royce. He sat across the table from Jonah and Gordy, next to Duane and Tyson, who looked as shocked as Jonah felt at the casual makes-no-never-mind-to-me-that-you're-criminals air that Royce gave off. "I've got your files here, but I've not read them," he said, placing a stack of manilla folders on the table. "I don't know who you are, but I want to learn that from you rather than a piece of paper, so would you each tell me your name and the crime you committed?"

The silence around the table landed like a large boulder in the center of the half-devoured charcuterie board, and it was obvious that

Royce didn't know that kind of information, at least outside of the warden's office, was on a volunteer basis only.

A prisoner could ask a fellow prisoner what they were in for, but the information was never forced, unlike in the warden's office, where they already knew.

Who was this guy, anyway? So cavalier with his request, with his gift of food, wearing that fancy shirt so crisp around the edges, it had to have recently seen an iron.

"I'll go first," said Gordy with a slight shudder, as if he didn't want to step on any toes but couldn't stand the silence lingering all around them, that, and the hopeful look in Royce's blue eyes. "I'm Gordy, short for Gordon. I'm a B&E man. That's it. B&E and maybe picking pockets. Light finger stuff. Nothing violent."

"Very good, Gordy, thank you."

Royce waited, then with a little *tsk tsk* beneath his breath, he managed to wrangle names and crimes from the two other ex-cons, Tyson and Duane, who admitted that they'd worked in the drug trade, making deliveries, and had, upon occasion, dealt directly with customers, and not in a nice way.

"Thank you, gentlemen. Which leaves us only—"

The expression Royce landed on Jonah was full of hope and expectation, a small smile around his mouth as if he meant to encourage Jonah by getting Jonah to think that anything he had to say would be kindly received. As well, Jonah was the last one to participate in this odd roll call, and if he didn't comply, then, once again, he would stand out, even more than he already was.

"I'm Jonah," he said, tightening his shoulders as if it was of no nevermind to him whether anyone cared. "I steal cars, strip the parts, sell those to the highest bidder. And I can fix any engine. *Any* engine."

"That'll come in handy," said Royce. "Thank you, Jonah. Now, everybody, help yourselves to whatever's on the board, then I'll take you for a short tour. I'll show you your tents, inside of which you will find clothing and necessary articles for your comfort. If something doesn't fit, let me know and we can change it out, and if there's something that you need and don't have, let me know and we can get it for you. In the meantime, I'm waiting on the delivery of little maps I've had drawn for you to help you find your way around the place which is going to be your home for the next five months. Any questions?"

Again, there was an enormous pause, and Jonah felt the effect of it, a weight settling on him all glinting like the inside of a silver bell.

He didn't feel sorry for Royce in that silence, because any guy dumb enough not to study up on the ex-cons who would soon be surrounding him kind of deserved what he got. Silence. A lack of response. A balking stubbornness as if not one of them believed he was for real. Which he couldn't be. Not with that shining gold hair and ridiculous outfit. Or the kindness that shone out of his blue eyes, which had to be the most fake thing of all.

CHAPTER 4
JONAH

Jonah had lived all of his life in Denver, most of it in the area just north of Colfax. The farthest north he'd ever gone had been the Wyoming border, and then up to Torrington, where Wyoming Correctional was. He was good with his hands and quick on his feet, but this fact, however true, was no longer true now that he was in new territory.

Which should have surprised him more, except when he'd been incarcerated, it had taken him a good month to learn his way around, to figure out the rules, both written and unwritten. So yes, no surprise that, as Royce led them all around the main part of the camp, Jonah felt a little dizzy.

This sense of unbalance must have begun when Royce explained the rules about landline usage, which was that you could use it as long as you wanted and whenever you needed to. Which was crazy talk.

The rules about the shower were crazy too, because while they were still standing in the mess tent, as Royce called it, and they were all staring at the old-fashioned landline, which had basically no rules surrounding it, Royce handed them each a small baggie of tokens and told them to live it up in the showers.

Well, what he said was something about never-ending hot water, unlimited time, but please be considerate, and so on. As if each man was in charge of himself. Which was how Jonah used to live, before his stint in jail, so he knew how it worked.

But to have Royce, with his butter-wouldn't-melt-in-his-mouth face, tell four ex-cons to have at it with the shower *and* the phone was on the edge of insanity town, if not actually stepping over the border.

Or maybe it was the tall pine trees looming over them at every turn that made him dizzy. Or that even as they were walking on what looked like a wide, newly made path, the trees were so thick that Jonah, as hard as he peered, couldn't quite see where they were or what was on the other side.

By the time they arrived at what Royce called the facilities, Jonah was completely lost. Not that he was going to admit it.

They all gathered inside the shower side of the facilities, where Royce pointed out the rain-shower shower heads and the array of shelves to put your soap and shampoo on, and suddenly Jonah started, involuntarily, thinking that since the afternoon snack had been fancy, and Royce seemed pretty fancy, for a cowboy guy, that was, then the soap would be fancy, too.

If there was one thing that Jonah had longed for during his many, many months behind prison bars, it was good soap.

Soap inside of Wyoming Correctional was off-brand lye soap which could clean mold out of grout and strip the skin off any man inside of five minutes if not rinsed off quickly and completely. It also smelled like chemicals and made Jonah's skin so dry, he would often have to spend all his commissary credits on off-brand skin lotion, which helped, but only for a few hours.

Skin itch was a thing, a *real* thing, and it took everything Jonah had not to ask: *What kind of soap do you guys have?* Because if he did ask, he'd get that look from Royce and that oh-you-poor-thing expression and again all eyes would be upon him. He'd be fine with stirring the pot once he got his feet on the ground and his brain wrapped around the lay of the land, both physically and rule-wise, but until then he needed to lie low and stay out of the spotlight.

"So you're saying we can shower for as long as we want?" asked

THE COWBOY AND THE HOODLUM

Gordy, who had no compunctions whatsoever, that or a spine made of iron.

"As long as you like," said Royce with a nod. "In your tents you'll find, oh, let's see—" Royce rubbed his jaw for a minute and squinted up at the tin roof of the shower facilities. "In your kit, there are several bars of Ivory soap, and the shampoo and conditioner is Jergens, I think. But, again, if you need something else, just ask and we can get it for you. Within reason, of course."

Back in prison, Jonah would have given his left *nut* for a bar of Ivory soap, but he had never found anyone who could smuggle it in for him, not even Beck with his mad skills. And here he'd be given it for free? He didn't ask for confirmation, just clamped his mouth closed and followed Royce and the others out of the shower and into where the toilets were.

As he understood it from his interview for the program, everything was meant to look rustic. Except he could see that the stalls had doors on them, the toilets had lids, and there was a pile of magazines to read, if you wanted. And yes, there was brand-name quilted toilet paper stacked up high on a little wooden beam above the toilet.

Was this real? Or was he going quite, quite crazy?

"Do you have a question, Jonah?" asked Royce, suddenly at Jonah's side, touching Jonah's arm with fingers that, as Jonah looked down at them, shock rippling through him that Royce had come so close without Jonah noticing it, were all manicured. Did he do his own nails every day?

Jonah had no idea, as he'd never been inside a nail salon in his life, but he'd seen certain prisoners doing their nails as carefully as if they were going to be part of a fashion parade.

"Me?" he asked, making a face of dismissal as if he had no interest, none whatsoever, in the type of soap they were going to be allowed to use, that the toilet paper type—two-ply!—was of no nevermind to him. But it was hard, because his skin, as if sensing a new, itchless future awaited it, rippled like someone was rubbing sandpaper over it. "No, not me."

Up close, Royce smelled nice. It wasn't just the cologne he was wearing, though there was that, spicy and interesting, it was the essence of his scent beneath that, a trace of the soap he used, probably not merely Ivory, and sweat from the day.

In fact, he smelled delicious, and the glimpse of throat that Jonah caught from beneath Royce's multicolor scarf was pale and tender looking and all of a sudden Jonah's breath was trapped in his chest.

"Seriously, not me," he said. He tried to move away, but Royce moved with him, like they were liquid, underwater, together within the ocean's tide.

Unsteady on his feet, he grabbed Royce's forearm, totally by accident, and was shocked when Royce gripped him right back, all under the guise, or so it would seem, of keeping Jonah on his feet rather than letting him tumble ass-over-elbows to the ground.

"I know it must be an adjustment getting out of prison," said Royce kindly. "I've never been in prison myself, but I, too, am going through an adjustment. When I came to the ranch last year from Montana, it took me weeks to find my bearings." Royce paused and looked at the other ex-cons, who were silent, blinking as they watched Royce and Jonah just about holding hands, for fuck's sake, and though Jonah wanted to let go of Royce, he simply could not. "I know it's the same for all of you, but believe me, you'll get there. We'll help each other out to make the adjustment. Won't we?"

Royce really looked like he wanted an answer, but nobody was answering. That brilliant smile was just beginning to fade when Jonah made a gesture at Gordy, Tyson, *and* Duane. He didn't care how hardened they were, or how many crimes they'd committed at whatever level of violence. It was simply pathetic how much Royce seemed to care that they agreed with him, that they were with him in this.

"Sure," said Jonah, glaring at the others. "We sure will."

"We sure will," said Gordy, Tyson, and Duane. They even nodded at Royce. Which, to Jonah's pleasure, made that smile come back in full force, as if Royce felt he'd just made an important breakthrough.

Royce then took them out of the facilities and through the woods along the path to the lake, which stretched out for a forever blue distance, perfectly calm and serene in the bowl of the green valley.

THE COWBOY AND THE HOODLUM

To the west, the valley rose up from the lake in a series of low humps and hills, thick with pine and some other trees as well. Above that was a sharp-edged ridge of gray stone.

In the midst of a slight pause in the breeze, silence, like a giant bell, settled around them, and Jonah took his first full breath of the day. It was as if the valley wanted to tame him through the peacefulness of itself.

To the south, curing to the east, the lake spread out with wide banks, and though Jonah couldn't see all the way to the end of the lake, he figured it had to end somewhere. And, to his surprise, there was a long line of fence that looked like it was made out of three strands of cloth, though he really didn't know.

Close to what looked like a gate was a pile of wood and several cardboard boxes. Next to that was a pile of hay covered by a canvas tarp.

"We're going to be building a series of shelters for the herd," said Royce. "We'll also be helping with the care of the horses, and I'm doing my best to arrange for riding lessons, basic ones, of course. Just to make you more familiar with the joy of horses."

"Riding lessons?" asked Gordy, sounding quite shocked. "I don't see any horses."

"I think they've just increased the size of the pasture," said Royce. "Gabe's team—he's only got two ex-cons at the moment, poor guy—have probably gone out there to guide the horses to the far end of it. To avoid overgrazing near the lake and the river beyond, you see." After a pause, Royce added, "You met Gabe earlier. He's the fellow who brought you all into the mess tent when you arrived."

Again Royce focused on their response, anticipation in his eyes as he waited for their interest, their interaction.

"How many—" Jonah paused, searching for what he wanted to ask because he honestly didn't care. "How many teams and, er, horses?"

"Ah." Royce just about clapped his hands with pleasure. "At the moment, we've only got two teams, Gabe's and mine. Gabe's got two ex-cons, Blaze and Wayne. As for horses, right now we have about twenty? And they will be sold or donated once they are cleaned up

33

JACKIE NORTH

and checked over by a vet. We'll get more horses this week, I think, so we'll need to focus on building that shed, and then—oh wait."

Royce looked up, his focus on something overhead. His mouth was open as though he'd been struck by awe and pleasure all at once and didn't quite know what to do with himself.

Jonah looked up, too. In fact, all the ex-cons looked up, but he couldn't see what Royce was focused on. What the big deal was.

"Do you see?" asked Royce, pointing to one of the pine trees. "It's a goldfinch. A pair of them. Perhaps they're mating. I wish I'd brought my binoculars with me."

He turned to them, his smile bright and beaming, his blue eyes lighting up like he'd just won a million dollars. A shaft of sunlight through the tall pine trees chose just that minute to reflect off his hair, and the slight breeze tumbled a single gold curl onto his forehead.

Normally, Jonah would have been put off by lectures about birds and whatnot, but he was drawn, in spite of himself. He shrugged and, oh, so casually asked, "When do we get to see our tents?"

"Oh." Royce's face fell for a second, but he seemed to straighten up and push his shoulders back. "Right this way, gentlemen," he said. "You can get settled in, even take a shower if you like. Then, when the dinner bell rings, come to the mess tent. Any questions?"

As Jonah let himself be led back through the woods along the path, he studied the back of Royce's blond head and thought that the tour, such as it was, lacked edges because Royce hadn't told them any rules. Other than shower as long as you like, but be considerate, and use the phone on your off-hours all you like, but be considerate.

Surely there were more rules than that? Or was Royce going to turn out to be a dick and spring the rules on them only when they were broken, the way some of the guards at Wyoming Correctional had a tendency to do?

"Jonah and Gordy, this is you. Tent number five," said Royce, pausing beside a canvas tent, the kind Jonah had only seen in pictures. The tent sat on a wooden platform that extended beyond the edges of the tent, and though the interior was currently shadowed, he had a sudden inexplicable bubble of curiosity explode inside of him.

"This is for two men?" he asked without meaning to, for the tent had to be at least twice the size of a standard-issue prison cell. Plus, in light of the quality of toilet paper in the facilities, the tent was likely to contain a level of comfort that Jonah would very much like to become accustomed to.

"Yes, indeed," said Royce brightly, as if pleased by Jonah's surprise. "I'll take Duane and Tyson to their tent, and then I'll swing by to answer any questions you have."

With a cheery wave, Royce was in motion again, striding away, Duane and Tyson following behind him like two obedient ducklings. Which left Jonah and Gordy standing next to the wooden platform, staring at each other.

"It probably won't suck," said Gordy with a little, nervous shrug. "It couldn't be bad, right?"

"I don't know," said Jonah. "Let's find out."

Stepping onto the platform brought a cool breeze wafting over him. Another few steps and he was in the shade, staring at two cots, and two white shelves between the cots. On top of the cots were a number of boxes of various sizes.

"Which one is yours?" asked Gordy, coming up behind Jonah, almost bumping into him.

In prison, Jonah would have swatted Gordy away from him in irritation because, while Gordy wasn't as clingy as Nelson, you couldn't be seen to be gentle with prisoners lower on the ladder than you. But he didn't.

As to why he didn't, maybe in the back of his head the realization that he was no longer in prison was beginning to take root, small tendrils growing up the back of his skull whispering to him that maybe he no longer needed to play top dog all the time.

"Open the boxes," said Jonah, pointing. "Look, those are shoe boxes."

Studiously, like a good boy following directions, Gordy went to the left-hand cot and opened the shoe box. Then he held it out to Jonah.

"This is yours. It's a size twelve and I take a size ten."

"Huh."

Frowning, like the whole mystery of a box that big holding a pair of shoes was of absolutely no interest to him, Jonah took the box and flipped open the lid. Inside was a pair of boots, soft creamy yellow suede. The laces were made of thick brown cloth and the soles looked sturdy enough to wear over the sharpest rocks.

"Huh," he said again because though his mouth was watering, he was already wearing the toughest, blackest boots ever known to man.

They were his favorite boots and not just because Beck gave them to him. It was because they fit perfectly and he'd broken them in just right and there was no way he was going to cast them off just for a pair of new boots, no matter how soft-looking.

He put the box on the bed and started to copy Gordy, who was opening every box on his cot, the right-hand one, pulling things out and tossing them down even as he pulled something else out.

The boxes held everything they might need, as Royce had said, though Jonah didn't see the sense in some of the things, like a little sewing kit or the plastic box with a snap-lock lid that held nothing. But he did pick up the cellophane-wrapped collection of three bars of Ivory soap and held it to his nose before he realized he wouldn't be able to smell anything that way.

In the next second, he'd peeled away the plastic and the paper around the soap, and held it to his nose. As he inhaled the clean, white, fresh smell, his skin sighed with anticipated relief, or maybe his whole body did, but his trance-like state was interrupted by a jab to his elbow by Gordy.

"Lookit," said Gordy, flipping a blade right in front of Jonah's face.

Jonah grabbed his elbow to hold him still. Gordy held a Swiss Army knife, pretty basic with just four blades, but it was nice, and shiny, and new. And Jonah, who'd not gotten his own boot knife back when he'd been released from prison, wanted it for his own.

"I'll bet you've got one just like it," said Gordy, as if he recognized the greed and desire in Jonah's eyes. "Check your box."

There was so much stuff in the box, some things wrapped in

brown paper, others in cellophane, that it took Jonah way too long to find the slender cardboard box that held his Swiss Army knife.

The box it came in was slick, but he managed to open it without dropping the whole thing and in less than a heartbeat he held it in his hand, perhaps the smallest knife he'd ever owned. The outside was glossy red, and the inside held four blades, each of a different length.

The knife was marvelous and eye-catching, though he chuckled as he held it up because his old boot knife was twice as sharp and a hundred times more dangerous. Still, at least he had a knife again, and he would have shown it to Beck, making Beck wish he had one like it for his own.

He looked at the mountainous pile on Gordy's cot and looked at all the stuff he had yet to unwrap and discover. Air chuffed out of his lungs, and it might have been out of annoyance or a sense of being overwhelmed, but he didn't have time to mull it over before he heard footsteps on the wooden platform outside the tent.

"Can I come in?" asked Royce's upbeat voice, which was accompanied by a light knock on the wooden tent pole.

"Sure," said Jonah. "I don't care."

Royce stepped in, lifting the tent flap away with his elbow. His entrance had the same effect on Jonah as before, as if a sweet breeze had just graced them with its presence.

Royce's whole face beamed when he looked at Gordy's cot, as if vicariously joining in the fun of opening so many new things. But when he looked at Jonah's cot, the smile fell.

Jonah tried to back away from the sense that he ought to do something to return that smile to Royce's face, only he didn't know what that would be.

"Don't you like your new boots?" asked Royce. He gestured to the bed where Jonah had tossed the box, the lid half crushed beneath the box, the pair of yellow suede boots sitting there like unwanted children. "I've got a pair myself, though they're a little less yellow now. More tan than anything."

On Royce's face was that same expression of expectation, as though he was suffused with an earnest desire that Jonah fall in love with the boots even before putting them on. But, in an effort to put some distance between himself and Royce's happiness, which was surely not his responsibility, Jonah shook his head.

"I've got boots," he said. "I don't need new ones."

"Oh, but you do," said Royce. He came right up to Jonah, picked up the box, and showed it to him. "These are special. They might look soft, but they're waterproof, from the bottom of the sole to the top. The laces are waterproof, too, plus they've got steel toes in them, which will come in handy when a horse tries to step on you or if you drop a tool on your foot. Your feet will be protected when you wear them, and I just hate to think—"

The distressed wrinkles on Royce's forehead were too much to resist, and Jonah didn't have the energy, anyway. So he sat down and tugged off his badass black boots, which looked limp and old next to the yellow boots, which were more gold than yellow, and slid onto his feet with barely any effort at all.

The laces were thick in his fingers, and when he stood up, it was as if he'd stepped from a shaky platform made of plywood onto a rock-solid granite place which would never move or shudder beneath him.

"Now, that's better, isn't it?" Royce asked, his head a little forward on his shoulders, like he meant to wait forever until Jonah agreed with him.

Since agreeing offered the easier path with less effort, plus everything Royce had said about the boots was true, Jonah nodded and shrugged. "Sure. They're great. Brand new and all."

Royce blinked, like he was trying to untangle the real meaning behind what Jonah had just said, but Jonah curled his fingers into fists at his sides and refused to help him. What did he care that Royce didn't understand him? What did he care? He didn't.

"Well, thanks," said Jonah. He meant it as dismissal, and in prison any convict would have known what he meant. *I'm done with you now, so go away.*

However, Royce wasn't now nor ever had been a prisoner in any life, it seemed, because he touched Jonah's arm. Touched it quite gently, and smiled.

THE COWBOY AND THE HOODLUM

"Excellent. They suit you, you know. Now." Royce finally stopped touching Jonah and clapped his hands together as if he'd announced something marvelous. "Unpack your things. Take a break. Have a shower, even, and I'll see you at dinner. All right?"

"All right," said Gordy, as Jonah nodded his head.

The second Royce was gone, Gordy sat down on his cot with a whoosh sound coming out of his mouth.

"That man," said Gordy.

Jonah nodded again, silently agreeing, though his brain was struggling to wrap itself around all the things that *man* represented. Energy. A sunbeam smile. Gold hair and blue, blue eyes, as blue as frozen crystal. That gentle touch, unlike anything Jonah had experienced in his whole life.

"I'm taking a shower," said Jonah. He turned to his cot and started pawing through boxes for what he needed, arranging it all in a little pile, turning to find Gordy at his shoulder.

"Look," said Gordy, breathless excitement stretching the word thin. "There's even a carryall to carry it in."

He held out a little box which, had it been made of steel, could have hauled around tools from his own garage. Only here, the toolbox was made of pale green plastic, and though it was a quarter of the size of Jonah's tool box back home, it was just the right size to hold, at the very least, a bar of Ivory soap. Jergens shampoo *and* conditioner *and* a bottle of lotion to put on his skin afterwards. A disposable razor *and* a can of shaving cream. A toothbrush *and* brand name toothpaste.

All these things, piled together in the soft green-colored plastic carrying case, looked like a bonanza delivery from some unknown Santa Claus who, suddenly and quite inexplicably, had determined that a bunch of ex-cons were to be gifted with a whole lot of self-care products that Jonah hadn't even known he'd needed. All without Jonah having to spend any of his commissary money. Which, as he'd been about to leave Wyoming Correctional behind, he'd bequeathed to Nelson, who would probably make short work of it, most likely on bottles of off-brand lotion for him to jerk off with.

Jonah grabbed the rolled-up towel, paused, grabbed the other one and the washcloth, then, gripping the green carryall hard in his fist, he bolted for the shower, with Gordy close on his heels.

He'd forgotten his baggie of tokens, but swore he'd take care of it later, because now he could strip to the skin, turn on the shower to its hottest level and stand naked beneath it. With his head back, his ankles feeling a soft breeze, the water pelted down just like a warm rain shower would somewhere in the South Pacific, he was sure of it.

His skin sighed and his shoulders unclenched, and he gripped that bar of Ivory Soap like it was a life preserver. The second the bar touched his skin, right above his belly button where he held it so close, he knew that, somehow, quite unexpectedly, he'd managed to arrive in heaven.

CHAPTER 5
ROYCE

At dinner they all sat together in the mess tent at one long table as the cooks, Neal and Dean, served them bowls of chili. In the middle of the table were smaller bowls of green onions and shredded cheddar cheese and sour cream, but the pièce de résistance, at least in Royce's mind, was the platter of cornbread, fresh out of the oven, steam rising off it gently and smelling heavenly.

"We're going to start up the buffet tomorrow," said Neal. "But since this is the first night for some of you, we thought we'd make it special."

Unsaid, of course, or at the very least unrepeated, was the conversation that Royce had had with Neal and Dean earlier that day about how to celebrate the first night for the newest members of their team.

Dean had argued that as more teams came in, they would have to start using the buffet setup, regardless of what day of the week it was, to make everything streamlined. Luckily, he and Neal had been unable to resist Royce's insistent pressure, and the first meal for the newly arrived members of his team was as elegant as it ought to be.

Well, real elegance would have been a porterhouse steak properly served, and a just-opened bottle of Cabernet Sauvignon. But the ranch's chili was excellent, just the same, and he was extra pleased at the sighs of appreciation he heard from everyone at the table, including Gabe and his team of two, Blaze and Wayne.

Really, though, the meal would have tasted just as good had they served themselves from steamers in a buffet line, so all in all, Royce was happy with how things were going. Except for the fact that Jonah, sitting right across from Royce, was glaring at his dinner, teeth half bared as if on the verge of growling. This wouldn't have been so bad or so troubling, if, in fact, this expression had made him in any way unattractive.

Of all the training Royce had gotten, the only part he remembered was what Gabe had told him: *Ex-cons might seem tame, but they are not docile.*

Royce knew that, he really did. However, it would really, really help if Jonah, having showered and shaved as well, it seemed, as evidenced by his smooth jawline and that tumble of glossy-shot-with-silver hair, didn't look like he failed to believe every good thing that had happened to him that day. In fact, he was wearing the same outfit as from before, including those disreputable black boots with the worn heels, as if he couldn't quite bring himself to wear new clothes.

All the ex-cons, when they showed up, received the same basic clothes and gear. Gordy, the youngest ex-con on Royce's team, had big, dark eyes and a heart-shaped face, and he was constantly touching the pearl snap-buttons on his shirt, as if amazed at their silky texture.

The other two ex-cons on his team, Duane and Tyson, were dutifully attired in their new gear. They were both sturdily built, muscled individuals with short cropped hair, tattoos on their necks, and heart-and-dagger tattoos on their forearms, and they were sitting a bit stiffly, like two kids in new Sunday school outfits they didn't want to mess up.

Satisfied those three were off to a good start, Royce's attention was drawn back to Jonah. It was all he could do not to suggest to Jonah that he would look extremely good in a snap-button shirt of the palest lavender. Which was silly to think about because, of course, the ex-cons were not given lavender shirts, pale or otherwise. The three snap-button shirts that each ex-con received were blue, white, and dark blue, good sensible colors in long-wearing fabric.

But Royce, in spite of his disappointment that Jonah wasn't wearing any of his new clothes, rather liked Jonah in his black t-shirt that clung very tightly to his biceps, showing, of all things, a tattoo of a blue heron, its wings spread in anticipation of flight.

Royce didn't know a lot about tattoos, but this one did not look like the work of an amateur, but instead that of a true artist. The fact that it was a bird was even more intriguing, and why a heron rather than something else?

He liked the strong line of Jonah's neck where it disappeared into the black t-shirt, and he liked the way Jonah's dark hair, on the long side, curled behind his ears and tumbled about as if looking for an escape route. And he liked the way Jonah's dark brown eyes flicked up at him as if Jonah had realized, just then, that Royce was staring at him. Yes, staring. And he could not seem to stop.

At no point, not in school, not in college, not while married to Sandra, or even after, during the divorce proceedings, had Royce ever imagined feeling gobsmacked by his reaction to another man.

Women were what his heart was drawn to, right? Women with their soft curves and clever minds, their gentle touches and hard-hearted stubbornness, many of the qualities Sandra had. Kissable lips, round bosoms, the tender, sensitive skin between their legs, all of which added up to a good time in bed, and around the dinner table, and wherever they might find themselves.

So what was drawing him to this dark-haired, dark-eyed man? The answer to that question was edged with confusion, because nobody in their right mind would want to get close to someone with a criminal past, who stalked around in his bad boy clothes, tight black t-shirt and those blue jeans that looked like they had grease stains down the thighs from strong, capable hands being wiped upon them time and again.

The rest of the ex-cons on his team had changed into their valley-appropriate attire, each one looking fresh and clean and ready to go to work. Work that Royce was sure his team would find fulfilling and satisfying. But not Jonah. He looked ready to enter a rough bar and kick someone off their stool at a bar because it was where Jonah wanted to sit. He was also still glowering at his chili.

"Is it not to your liking?" asked Royce, politely as he could. "We could get you something else, if you'd prefer. Like a ham sandwich?"

Jonah's glower deepened beneath dark eyebrows, and Royce got the feeling that Jonah did not like being the center of attention in this way, with everyone at the table staring at him while they enjoyed their chili.

"Try the cornbread," Royce urged, gesturing that someone should pass the platter to him so he could hold it out to Jonah. "It's very good, and for dessert there is chocolate cake with homemade frosting. Unless you'd prefer an orange?"

Watching quite closely, Royce did not miss the flicker of interest that crossed Jonah's face, the one he was not quite able to hide, or maybe he didn't realize what Royce could see. The wash of want in those eyes. The way Jonah's mouth parted, the glimmer of sharp white teeth. Then Jonah caught him looking, and it seemed he tried to wash away the want, only it was too late, and Royce nodded, satisfied.

"Neal, could we get some fresh fruit on the table, please?" he asked. "Oranges if you have them."

Neal delivered the oranges so quickly, Royce knew he'd have to do something nice for him in return. In particular, there was a big, truly orange, orange, still dappled with moisture from being freshly washed, and this Royce placed in front of Jonah. Who looked at it with that quasi disinterested shrug of his, only Royce knew better, for Jonah had shown his tell.

Royce picked up the second orange and brought it to his nose, deeply inhaling the bright sparkle of citrus scent, the way the color orange seemed to turn into a deeper smell beneath that.

"Oh, these are perfect, Neal, just right for eating." Royce put his orange on the table, lifting his chin because what did he care that everybody was staring at him now instead of Jonah? "I'll save mine for after dinner, and after my dessert. Like a treat."

He smiled at Jonah, who didn't smile in return, but who, though he touched the orange, finally, with stiff fingers, left it where it was and started to eat his dinner, starting with a cube of cornbread which he took from the platter. Royce nodded, well satisfied, though his heart was doing a strange little dance, like it had recognized something in Jonah's expression and wanted more of what it saw.

"It's better than in prison," said Jonah, almost mumbling this as he scrubbed at his mouth with the back of his hand.

Which then solved the puzzle in Royce's mind. In prison, the chili probably wasn't of the best quality, so he could easily imagine Jonah had thought the ranch's chili would be equally bad. But rather than say this out loud, he lifted his bowl.

"Neal, could I get second helpings?" he asked to show Jonah and all the new ex-cons that they could have as much as they wanted of anything. "Or maybe I should save room for dessert?"

"I'd save it," said Neal. "Those pieces of chocolate cake are very big."

Jonah finished off his chili and his cornbread, then tore into the orange as rabidly as a man on a desert island, stranded for weeks, who has suddenly come across a cache of fresh food. As he licked the moisture of the orange from his lips, Jonah once again caught Royce looking.

Royce didn't look away. There was no shame in wanting something, no shame in enjoying that something once acquired. Did Jonah know that? Maybe Royce could teach him if he did not.

The chocolate cake, when it arrived, was delicious, and Royce enjoyed every bite. More than that, he enjoyed his little group of ex-cons enjoying their dessert as well. Especially Jonah, who scraped the plate with his fork and then licked the fork with his red tongue, at which point Royce had to look the other way to collect himself, which took a moment.

"It might rain later tonight," said Royce, to the table in general. He looked at Gabe, who nodded that this was so. Then he said to his team, "But I thought you could finish unpacking and putting your stuff away, and then you could join me at the fire pit, where we could build a fire and make s'mores? If you're interested?"

Admittedly, he sat up just a little too straight, unable to stem his anticipatory pleasure at such a simple event. But, in his mind, if ex-cons were invited to do gentle things, that might gentle them, at least a little bit.

"I have ghost stories to read," he said, wanting to entice them even more. But the faces around the table were blank, except for Gabe's, Wayne's, and Blaze's. "There's chocolate involved," he said. "And I could bring more oranges. Anyone?"

At this point, perhaps too sated with food to be demure, Jonah's eyes went wide and dark and deep. Royce wanted to fall into them and had to jerk himself back to where he was, sitting at one of the long tables in the mess tent with a group of ex-cons and Gabe.

"Well, then." Royce wiped his mouth with his napkin and stood up, drawing the attention of everyone at the table. "I'll get the makings for the s'mores and get the fire started. Gabe, could you make sure there are enough skewers and sticks for roasting?"

"Sure can," said Gabe, ever amenable, ever at the ready, friendly and supportive as always.

"Will any of you be joining, do you think?" asked Royce, looking around the table, just about to be disappointed because while Gabe's team looked willing, Royce's did not. And then Jonah surprised him.

"We'll be there," said Jonah. He cast a stern look at Gordy, Tyson, and Duane. "Won't we, guys."

It was not a question, and the rest of Royce's team nodded their heads.

"Good," said Royce, well satisfied now and grateful for Jonah's intervention. He guessed it was that bad boy charm keeping the other three in line, and it was very hard not to thank Jonah out loud because now Jonah had stood up and was looking anywhere but at Royce. "I'll see you fellows there, yes?"

Royce marched to his tent, though what he really needed to do was clear his place at the table and discuss the evening's s'more supplies with the cooks. After which he needed to go to the fire pit and build that fire, and light it, so it'd burn down to nice s'more making coals as the sun went down. And he needed to find his book of ghost stories, too, but once at his tent, he sat on his cot and tried to catch his breath.

What in the world was going on in his head? What was he supposed to do with the sparks flying around in his belly?

And how was he supposed to manage his team when all he could see was Jonah, the bad boy? The dark-haired, dark-eyed criminal with his masculine jaw, and those gestures of long-fingered hands. The most dangerous looking ex-con, the most eye-catching. Least expected and hard-edged, stalking through Royce's thoughts like he knew exactly where he was going and why.

What Royce was feeling should go no further than this moment. That much was true. He also knew it would be better if he could simply not feel this way.

The problem was, all he wanted to do was—what? Walk away? Ignore? No. He wanted to fling himself at Jonah and say, *You're the most exciting thing that's ever happened to me* and *Let me be with you and bask in the shadow of your bad boy-ness.*

He was a fool. All kinds of a fool, and all he wanted to do now, knees knocking together as he stood up, was to get ready for bed and crawl between the sheets. Except he'd promised his team a good night by the campfire, and so he would have to deliver. But carefully. He wouldn't look at Jonah. Not once.

He could manage that for a few hours, couldn't he?

CHAPTER 6

JONAH

When Jonah had been a kid, so long ago, it seemed, he'd known some boys participated in scouting and knew how to build fires and weave baskets and whatever, but he'd never really understood the attraction there. All the same, after he and Gordy had gone back to their tents, pawed through their boxes, and put everything away, they'd put on their lined denim jacket, and trudged back to the fire pit to make s'mores.

Gordy wore his new Carhartt boots, stomping along the trail like he was a giant of some kind, and Jonah did his best not to fret because who cared if he was still wearing his own black boots when, yes, everyone else at the fire pit were wearing those soft golden boots, looking like they belonged.

What did Jonah care? He did not. Besides, he was distracted by the sight of Royce, on his hands and knees in front of the fire, which was smoking in the damp night air. Gabe was standing next to him, flashlight in hand, like that was going to help.

"You got it?" asked Gabe, looking ready to get down on his hands and knees, too.

"I've got it," said Royce. Then he looked over his shoulder at Jonah

JACKIE NORTH

and smiled that bright sunburst smile just as the logs started burning, the silver-gold flames leaping up from the top of the logs where they were leaned against each other. "It just needed a little encouragement to get going, you see."

Standing up, Royce dusted his hands and spread them wide, as if to welcome everyone to something very special. Though all Jonah could see were wooden chairs around the fire pit, a pile of slender metal skewers and metal sticks, and a brown paper bag that might hold supplies for s'mores, whatever those were.

It wasn't very special. And it might just be on the verge of raining. And the night was growing very dark beyond the trees because, of course, there were no streetlights, not anywhere that Jonah could see.

He lifted the collar of his jacket and tried to shrug deeper inside of it, a chill on the back of his neck, his hands, on his face.

"Come closer to the fire, you two," said Royce. He gestured to one of the empty chairs. "You can sit there, Gordy. And as for you, Jonah—" Royce paused, his brow wrinkling as if he didn't know what to make of Jonah, even though he'd moved quite close, close enough to reach up and touch the collar of Jonah's jacket. "Are you cold? That jacket looks like it doesn't quite fit, so we might have to get you a bigger one. In the meantime, here."

Royce reached to his neck, opened the top button, and began to pull the scarf he'd been wearing from around his neck. He did this quite slowly, in a mesmerizing way, drawing the scarf away from him and handing it to Jonah with a flourish.

Jonah didn't know what else to do, so he took the scarf. Everyone was watching, of course, in the light of the campfire, flashes of gold and pale yellow warming the flagstones all around it.

He couldn't help but trace the pattern on the scarf with his fingers, feel the softness of the fabric. Then he jerked it away from himself, just on the verge of handing it back to Royce, because what did he need with a scarf? If he took it, wouldn't Royce's neck get cold?

"Go on," Royce said. "I'm quite warm from my efforts to light the fire, so put it on."

THE COWBOY AND THE HOODLUM

Hesitating, Jonah felt like he'd been caught in the spotlight of Royce's blue eyes.

"It's got a jackalope on it," said Royce. He took the scarf from Jonah's hand and lifted it to curl around the back of Jonah's neck. Then he did something fussy, looping it around and tying a small knot, and now the scarf was snug and made Jonah's neck warm, surrounded by the delicious softness of the scarf.

Jonah had no idea what a jackalope was. Should he ask?

"Jackalopes aren't real, of course," said Royce, cupping his hand to Jonah's neck as if to make sure of the fit of the scarf. "But now you'll be warm."

"Is it silk?" asked Jonah, suddenly confused as to why he would even *care*. But Royce was looking at him with a small, delighted smile, and the two of them were standing there as if every pair of eyes wasn't staring, so what else was he supposed to do but pretend he cared the least little bit about what the scarf was made of.

"It's satin and silk," said Royce, finally, *finally* stepping away. "A blend of the two, so the bright colors can stay fast, and it's less slippery than just silk on its own."

Jonah's neck was quite warm now as he stepped away, as well, and fumbled his way to the empty chair next to Gordy. The chairs were made of sturdy wood and had nice, wide arm rests, but the backs went way back so Jonah ended up propped at the edge of the seat, leaning forward, elbows on his knees, secretly running his fingers up and down the length of scarf where it trailed from his neck.

He took a metal skewer with a marshmallow on it and copied what the others were doing, then assembled his s'more and ate it in two huge sticky bites. Then, finally, sat back as Royce, drawing a log near the fire to sit on, opened a paperback book and began to read ghost stories to them.

Jonah was too old to have someone reading aloud to him, but he was kind of stuck. And, at the same time, it was kind of nice to just float on Royce's voice, deep and soft and slow, sugar rushing through his system as he looked up, up through the pine trees to the bright handfuls of stars that glittered amidst smoky dark blotches of clouds.

In what seemed the blink of a moment, everyone was standing up, helping Royce and Gabe clean up from the s'more making. Then he and Gordy headed back to their tent, stumbling behind Gabe, who was the only one who had a flashlight.

Gordy, evidently freaked out by all the ghosts in the stories, clung to Jonah's elbow the whole way. While normally, Jonah would have batted him away and maybe punched him for good measure, he let Gordy cling and babble on about how freaked he was, though that was only because it was really dark in the woods and nobody could see what was going on.

"This is your tent," said Gabe, pointing the flashlight at the tent. "I'll wait till you turn on your light and find your own flashlight, okay?"

Jonah pulled on the chain to turn on the overhead light, then scrambled to get his flashlight, a blue metal one. He did this as fast as he could because the last thing he wanted to do was have Gabe standing there for hours when all Jonah wanted to do was get under the covers and get his thoughts under control before they spiraled further away from him.

Before that could happen, he and Gordy braved the dampness in the air to use the facilities. When Jonah got back to the tent, he untied the scarf and shook it out. The softness floated in the air, almost touching his face, except then he couldn't retie it, so he gathered it in his hand, and held it in his fist under the pillow as he fell asleep.

He woke in the morning to the patter of something on the canvas overhead. The air was chilly, and as he looked over at Gordy in the pale gray morning light seeping into the tent, he drew up the covers under his chin.

"They're going to make us work in the rain," said Gordy. "It's going to be awful, I just know it."

But it wasn't awful, not at all. And it was nothing like prison, either, or the garage. The day turned out to be its own thing, because while they were eating breakfast, Jonah noticed that both Gabe and Royce had bits of straw or something in their hair. When Gordy asked

THE COWBOY AND THE HOODLUM

about it, they explained that they'd gotten up early to take care of the horses in the pasture. In the rain.

In fact, there were drops of rain on the side of Royce's face, and it was all Jonah could do not to reach out and wipe them away. He didn't, because that would draw attention to the fact he'd be touching Royce. This might remind Royce that he'd loaned Jonah his scarf, and then he might ask for it back.

Jonah wasn't giving the scarf back, though. He was keeping it.

The rain let up after breakfast, and Royce took his team out to the pasture to show what they'd done that morning, how much hay to distribute in the feed bins, how to fill the water tanks from the faucets over each one. Easy stuff.

"Later, we'll need to clear this end of the pasture of manure, since this is where the horses congregate the most," said Royce. "As you see, I've covered the wood for the shelters for the horses with a bit of canvas. We'll just have to wait till the rain clears and the wood dries a little bit, and then we'll start building."

From behind them, Gabe and Blaze came up. They had on straw cowboy hats and cowboy boots on their feet, and they looked like they were going someplace nice. Only Gabe was swinging a key fob around his finger and looked a tad disgruntled.

"Were you heading out?" asked Royce. "The feed will still be at the granary tomorrow, right?"

"Yes, but today is the perfect day to go get it, since work's at a halt because of the rain," said Gabe. "Only I don't know what's wrong with the truck, so I'm about to call Jasper to come fix it."

"I could—" Jonah clamped his mouth shut because the last thing he needed to do was be super helpful. But Royce looked at him, eyebrows raised expectantly, moisture glittering along his skin. It was utterly hopeless. "I could take a look. I know a thing or two about engines."

Both Royce and Gabe knew why Jonah had been arrested, and maybe they were shocked and maybe they weren't. What Jonah knew, as everyone walked to the little dirt track behind the tents where the two silver trucks were parked, was that he didn't like all the attention.

Except for Royce. He did enjoy Royce watching him as he popped the hood and lifted himself up onto the frame of the truck to peer at the engine.

The engine, oddly, was pretty spotless, but then maybe that was the kind of place this was, to be so fussy about a hunk of metal. The truck was a Ford F150, and pretty straightforward, so it was easy to spot that the battery had become disconnected.

Using his bare fingers, he twisted the cap up, resettled the wire clamp, then twisted the cap back down. Dusting his hands, he climbed back down and shut the hood by lowering it, then pushing hard at the end to lock it.

When he turned, everyone gave him a little round of applause. Royce, especially, was smiling broadly as if what Jonah had just done was a miracle. Gabe and Blaze climbed into the truck, Gabe started the engine, and the truck slowly backed up, then headed along the dirt track.

"Well done, Jonah," said Royce. "Now, I think it's going to rain again, so here's what I suggest. I'm going to set myself up in the mess tent with a little space heater, a few of my favorite books, and then I'm going to borrow the large French press from the kitchen and make coffee to drink while I read. How does that sound?"

"What about the logs that need chopping?" asked Wayne, jerking his thumb over his shoulder.

"It's too damp, I'm afraid," said Royce. "Those tools will be too slippery to be safe to use. Besides, the mess tent will be nice and cozy, I promise."

And it was cozy, though a little odd to sit at the long table in the mess tent in the middle of the morning with nowhere to go and nothing to do except watch as Royce bustled about like a host at a very swanky party. It was most definitely not a party because it was raining and the air smelled damp, and overhead parts of the tent looked like they were sagging a bit.

Royce went out and did something to the tent, then went off and came back in with a box of books, which he placed on the table, and

THE COWBOY AND THE HOODLUM

then he went into the kitchen and announced that he was making coffee.

"And I discovered a box of donuts," he sang out.

Gordy and Jonah looked at each other, each half shrugging, and then Wayne pulled out a pack of cards and got Duane and Tyson to join him in a bit of gin rummy.

"I'm going to join," said Gordy. "Okay?"

"Sure," said Jonah, because what did he care? He didn't, especially when Royce came in from the kitchen with the giant French press and a half dozen white coffee mugs, plus a carton of half-n-half and a plastic tub of sugar with a spoon sticking out of it.

"Oh, I need teaspoons," said Royce, then, as he was about to rush off again, he pointed at the French press. "Don't let anyone push this plunger down till I get back, okay?" He looked pointedly at Jonah. "I'm counting on you."

Jonah shrugged because it didn't matter to him, since he'd never seen anyone make coffee in a French press before. When Royce came back with a fistful of teaspoons and a box of donuts, both of which he placed on the table, he sat right next to Jonah and seemed to be counting as he unpacked the box of books.

"We need to wait two more minutes," he said as he arranged the books in two stacks. "Here, look at this one. It's about the constellations in the northern hemisphere. And this one is a field guide to Wyoming birds. And this one—let's see. We've got horses, a book of Sudoku puzzles, one of crosswords, a first aid book. Do you see any you like?"

Jonah wasn't much of a reader, unless he counted his subscriptions to *Car and Driver* and *Muscle Machines*, which he sometimes read and sometimes would just toss because he was usually too busy to read them. Besides, sitting still to just read, other than while on the toilet, sounded too boring.

But again, Royce was looking at him, his mouth curved in anticipation of a smile as if it was his dearest wish that Jonah pore over the pile to pick out a book that he might enjoy spending time with.

"Uh," he said, blindly groping, his fingers tightening on the first spine they came to.

"Oh, that's a good one," said Royce. "Though it's not light reading, that's for sure."

Jonah looked at what he had in his hands, a thick white book with blue lettering that looked like it was five hundred pages long. It was very heavy and for crying out loud, who in the world would want to waste their time writing five hundred pages about birds?

Evidently Royce was delighted that Jonah looked like he was about to try reading the thing, for he patted the back of Jonah's hand and paused, looking up at Jonah with a bright light in his blue eyes, like Jonah had just handed him a treasure.

"I'll pour you a cup of coffee," he said, which he did, deftly, into one of the white mugs. He pulled the sugar and half-n-half closer, and the box of donuts, and poured coffee into the white mugs and distributed them to the others. After a moment, he put two donuts on a plate and placed it at Jonah's elbow, then sent the box down along the table for the card players to enjoy.

Putting sugar, probably too much, and half-n-half in his coffee, Jonah took a sip of what turned out to be the most amazing coffee he'd ever tasted. Perfectly sweet, perfectly perfect, unlike the coffee Jonah usually drank back home from the bodega on the corner of 22nd and Dayton, which was black and bitter and woke him up instantly.

While Royce's attention was on the others, Jonah chomped into the donut, which turned out to be filled with raspberry jelly. As he licked his lips free of sugar, with one hand on the book like he meant to read it any second, he found himself looking at the old-fashioned landline on the long table along the edge of the tent.

He'd meant to call Beck the second he'd arrived, but he'd been distracted by everything, and especially Royce. It was a whole day later than when he should have called, only now what was he supposed to do?

What was he *going* to do, was the better question, because never in Jonah's life had he done what he was supposed to do. He always followed his own direction, and to hell with what the rest of the world thought.

If he called Beck, he'd just tell him the truth. Which was better gotten over with sooner rather than later, because, upon hearing that Jonah neither wanted nor needed to be rescued, at least not at the moment, Beck was going to be unhappy about it.

Only now Gordy, who'd obviously decided he didn't like losing at cards to a bunch of cheating ex-cons, was on the phone, speaking loudly while he called someone on the other end *babe* and *honey* and *sweetie*.

Who that was, Jonah didn't know, nor did he care. But what he liked, especially well, was when Royce came back and sat next to him, doctored his own mug of coffee, and started slurping in a dainty way, elbowing Jonah, as if encouraging Jonah to laugh at his rudeness.

Royce grabbed a donut and bit into it. Then, like he knew exactly what he was doing to Jonah, he licked the red smear of raspberry from his lips, and sucked on his lower lip to erase it of sugar.

All the while, Jonah's insides tumbled up and over, and he sighed at the sight, Royce with his moist lips, and that pink flush on his cheeks, his gold hair tumbling over his forehead, curling in the damp weather. And the smile on Royce's face, the beam of joy in his eyes.

"This is the life, isn't it?" asked Royce.

"Yeah, I guess so," said Jonah, since it looked like Royce was waiting for an answer. "Bit boring, though," he added, even though he wasn't bored at all.

"Ah," said Royce. "This is just the bit in-between. This is when we rest, so we'll be more ready for work in the morning."

Since Jonah had never really rested or taken a vacation, he hadn't experienced what Royce was talking about. But the way Royce said it, his mouth stretching over the words, the satisfied air about him, made Jonah want to find out. Meanwhile, he pushed the five-hundred page book in Royce's direction.

"Do you have a thinner bird book?" he asked, as meekly as he could.

"Yes," said Royce. He reached into the box and pulled out a book called *Birds of Wyoming*, which looked way thinner and shorter. He took back the thick bird book and gave Jonah the smaller one, all the while smiling, his eyes alight, pleasure in every gesture. "You'll like this one, I think. It's got some marvelous photographs."

"And the goldfinch," said Jonah, thinking of the bird in the sky, quite invisible to Jonah, that Royce had gawped at the day before. "Is the goldfinch in here?"

"Yes, it is," said Royce. He took the book and flipped right to the page that had a bright yellow bird on it. "They're not just native to Wyoming, where they like to breed, but have the whole country as their back yard."

Lifting his chin, Jonah meant to say something like *yeah, so what* or *yeah, so who cares* because who the hell was interested in birds? Well, evidently Royce was, so Jonah nodded and said, "Is that so?"

Royce answered this by giving a little lecture on birds of Wyoming, and their breeding zones, and the amazing proliferation of birds along riverbanks and bodies of water, such as their very own Horse Creek and Half Moon Lake.

While it was obvious that Royce knew a lot and loved to share it, what Jonah enjoyed was the flush on Royce's cheeks and the brightness in his eyes. The way he casually shoved his golden curls away from his forehead, and rubbed his nose, and patted Jonah's hand as if he was afraid that he'd lose Jonah's attention.

Which he wasn't going to do because Jonah found dark places inside of himself filling up like bottomless tanks that had finally found a source of water.

"What are the—" Jonah paused, making something up on the spot, figuring there were brown birds somewhere. "What are the brown birds in the pine trees?"

"It could be anything," said Royce, his face lighting up more, if that was even possible. "It could be a mourning dove or a pine siskin or a chipping sparrow. You'll have to point it out to me the next time you see one."

"All right," said Jonah, shrugging to make sure that Royce knew it was nothing to him, he was just being polite.

"We also have robins, though I expect you know what those are." Royce turned the pages in the book and began pointing out different bright-winged birds as if he might be bored by brown birds, or thought Jonah might be.

As for Jonah, he leaned in close, and took in a lungful of Royce's scent, the soap beneath that cologne, still unidentified, and the soft skin on the inside of his wrists, and wondered why he found this man so enticing.

CHAPTER 7
ROYCE

In the morning, it was drizzling but, ignoring his wild, out-of-control hair, Royce got dressed and went down to the pasture, there to join Gabe and Blaze in taking care of the horses.

That was part of his job just as leading a team of ex-cons was part of his job and he couldn't shirk it even if the weather was less than optimal. So he plonked his straw cowboy hat on his head, pulled on his boots and snuggled into his sherpa-lined denim jacket, grabbing his leather gloves at the last minute before he stalked down the damp path to the pasture.

The generator was off so the fence wasn't charged, so he joined Gabe and Blaze in lining the wooden feeders with hay, and checking the water troughs, of which there were three, widely spaced, which required a lot of walking in the dew-dappled grasses, which dampened his jeans up to his thighs.

As they worked, they discussed the need to build a wooden fence at the end closest to the camp, so they wouldn't have to worry about the electric charge in the fence. Then, if next summer, guests wanted to come and linger and look at the horses, they could lean on the fence and relax a bit.

"I'm sure Leland would agree," said Gabe, casting his gaze over the pasture till he stopped and said, "Oh, look who's here."

Royce pushed his hat back on his head and looked too, and there, wearing their denim jackets but no hats, something that needed to be rectified, were Gordy and Jonah. They had dutifully gotten up before breakfast to trudge through the damp morning to come take a look at what was going on. And maybe to help.

Royce was pleased beyond reason. And dismayed to see that Jonah's jacket fit him as badly as it had the night before, reminding him that he needed to contact Maddy and get a bigger jacket. The Quonset hut held supplies that did not, alas, include extra denim jackets.

Making a mental note, he went over to them, waving, joy rising inside of him.

"Did you come to help?" he asked. "We're about to give the area a bit of a rake to clean up the manure around where we want to build the shelters. Which we will when the weather dries up a bit."

There was something in the way Jonah looked at him, the way those dark eyes focused on him. Behind those eyes seemed to stir all kinds of thoughts, as if Jonah was having them for the first time and didn't quite know what to do with them.

It was all Royce could manage not to start asking questions, like *Do you like it here? Is it better than prison? Of course it is, but I want you to tell me how.* And, perhaps most pressing of all, *Do you like me?* It was not a question Royce had ever thought to ask another man, but there it was. He wanted Jonah to like him, ex-con or not, because what did Royce care about other people's rules?

"Yeah," said Jonah, breaking into Royce's runaway brain. "That's why we're here. Isn't it, Gordy?"

He gave Gordy a taste of his elbow, and Gordy straightened up, nodding. But of course he was agreeing with Jonah. There wasn't anything else he could do, not when Jonah was the scariest looking ex-con of the lot. Not that Royce was afraid of him.

Royce opened the gate and let them in, closing the gate behind, just as the small herd of horses, around ten or so, had determined to bestir themselves from the far field and come in to have some breakfast, so kindly provided for them.

As Gabe and Blaze were bringing over wheelbarrows, Royce had just given Gordy and Jonah a rake each when the horses came close enough, grouped together like they were, still sleepy and rain-silvered along their backs, the tips of their manes.

Royce paused to give the closest horse a pet along its damp neck, which caused the next one to move forward on slow hooves, each horse demanding its due. It was only after Royce had petted the five closest horses that he realized both Jonah and Gordy were backing slowly away.

"Don't be afraid," he said. "They won't hurt you, they just enjoy the petting."

The two ex-cons did not look like they believed Royce, not for one minute. Gordy looked like he was on the verge of setting his rake down and escaping to the mess tent. As for Jonah, he was looking at the horses, his dark brows drawn, the dampness of the air sparkling on his cheeks.

He had his hands around the long handle of the rake, twisting back and forth, veins standing up as if he was gripping the handle rather harder than he needed to. Then he took a short breath, handed his rake to Gordy, and came up to Royce, a little grim about the eyes, but determined.

"Like this," said Royce.

He took Jonah's hand and uncurled his fingers, and drew Jonah by his hand to stand close to the nearest horse. She was a sweet little bay mare with a ragged-edged mane, but who had liquid-dark eyes.

When she saw that Jonah's hand was coming close to her neck, she moved into the gesture. Which caused her front hooves to come quite close to Jonah's feet in those disreputable black boots, and Jonah jumped back, right into Royce's arms.

The sensation of it was beyond delicious. Jonah's body was hard as a rock all up and down, the curve of his bottom fitting inside the curve of Royce's hips as though they'd been one body, disconnected, and were now reunited.

To keep from stumbling, Royce slung his arm around Jonah's waist, a dense but trim girth. A delighted thrill ran through him until Jonah trod on his foot and then sprang off it, turning in Royce's arms and then pulling away.

"Sorry," Jonah said, his voice gruff, and then one of the horses, perhaps looking for a treat, put its muzzle over Jonah's shoulder, startling him with a low chuffing sound and a snort from its nostrils. It was all Royce could do to cover his mouth to try to hide his laughter.

"You're all right," said Royce, gently easing the horse's muzzle away. "And you didn't hurt me because, remember, my boots have steel toes."

Jonah looked down at where Royce was pointing, a worried dance of confusion and relief in his dark brown eyes.

Dampness had collected on his hair and now dripped from the ends like it was from the manes of the horses all around. For a moment they stood there together in the circle of damp and water and air, and then there was a flutter of wings overhead and Royce pointed.

"Look," he said to Jonah, and Jonah only. "It's a mourning dove. They'll be building their nests in the eaves of the shelters, once we build those, so we'll probably see more of them."

Jonah looked up, wiping moisture from his forehead with the back of his hand, searching for the bird. Royce knew the moment Jonah found it, for those dark eyes widened and focused, his mouth falling open a little. When he looked back at Royce, he smiled with those white teeth of his.

"A morning dove," he said. "So they don't come in the afternoon?"

"It's *mourning*, as in sadness or grief," Royce explained gently. "Like when someone you know has died and you mourn." Then he added, "It's also known as a rain dove."

"Oh."

Jonah's brow cleared of its confusion and he looked at the sky for a moment before focusing his attention back on Royce. Then he held out his hand and Royce took it and guided Jonah's hand with his own as they stroked the neck of the nearest horse, and then the flat plane

THE COWBOY AND THE HOODLUM

of its jaw. All the while, they stood quite close to each other in the whispery silence of the misty morning.

When Royce finally noticed, there was a circle of horses all around them, each waiting for their turn for attention as patiently as if they'd waited forever, as if nobody had ever petted them. This he knew to be false, because Gabe and Blaze had been coated with horse hair the day before from doing this very thing.

"We'd better get to work," he said into Jonah's ear, his breath moving Jonah's dark, wavy hair just the tiniest bit.

"Okay," said Jonah, the puff of air from his voice moving the mane of the horse closest to him, just the tiniest bit.

Royce backed up and moved the horses away, then took the rake from Gordy and handed it to Jonah. Then got to work shoveling piles of manure into the wheelbarrows as Gordy and Jonah raked.

They soon finished up and Gabe announced that it was time for breakfast, so they hauled the manure to a pile near the gate where someone would be assigned or asked to take it away for people's gardens. Then they latched the gate behind them and Blaze turned on the generator, and together they walked to have breakfast.

It was sometime after breakfast, about mid-morning, that the sun came out. It quickly grew quite warm, and dew sparkled on every branch and blade of grass. A delightfully cool breeze skittered around the camp, bringing with it the fresh smell of pine and the purest air from the tops of the foothills.

Gabe used his walkie talkie to call up to the ranch for some extra help. Soon, a few ranch hands came down to help them dig the holes and fill them with cylinders of cement upon which the supporting posts of the shelter could be built.

While the supports set, they assembled the pieces of the shelter. Royce enjoyed this kind of work just as much as he enjoyed any other, but his pleasure came in teaching Jonah and his team of ex-cons how to use a hammer and nails, how to measure twice and cut once.

What he especially enjoyed was how, during the iced tea and cheese and crackers break that Royce insisted on, Jonah told Gordy and Duane and Tyrone all about the mourning dove and the goldfinch. Then, when the break was over, how he made them get back to work, with a dark scowl and a small gesture that ended with a quick snap of those fingers.

If Royce had ever seen any man eagerly hop back to work, it could never be as fast as his team of ex-cons got back to work, not when Jonah nipped at their heels the way he did.

It was after lunch that Royce determined that the issue of the ill-fitting denim jacket could be put off no longer, besides which, the weather app on his phone told him in no uncertain terms that it was going to rain on and off all week, so they'd need hats as well, sooner as in now, rather than waiting for Saturday.

A delighted shiver ran up his spine at the thought of Jonah in cowboy boots, the length of his legs from the stacked heels. The look of his glowering eyes from beneath the brim of a cowboy hat.

Though ex-cons needed work boots and jackets, they didn't really need cowboy boots and hats, but those were the perks of working in the valley, as Leland had determined from the first to give the project high gloss production values, even if nobody was looking.

But Royce would look, yes, he would, and hang anybody who thought he shouldn't. Because couldn't a man admire another man for simply looking beautiful, much in the way he did the same for a woman or any other aesthetically pleasing individual?

To his dismay, the outing to get Jonah the new jacket Royce had determined he needed turned into a group outing, as it was raining again. No work could be done, so Gabe decided to make an afternoon of it. They all piled into the two F-150 trucks, Royce driving one, with Jonah in the passenger seat, and Gabe driving the other, with everybody else piled in.

With the trucks' hoods gleaming silver with rain, they drove up the switchbacks and through the dense pine trees to the top of the hill, past the lone cabin, and then to the ranch's main parking lot, where the ranch's store was. Then they all spilled out of the truck and tumbled noisily into the store, much to the surprise of the store's clerk and Maddy, who had a clipboard in her hand as though she and the clerk had been going over backorders.

THE COWBOY AND THE HOODLUM

"I just got the text from Leland that you were on your way," she said, waving the clipboard at them all. "The delivery of boots is late, so we might not have everything you want." Then she paused, flipping her gray braid over her shoulder, looking them over with a slight nod of her head. "But we'll get you fixed up as best we can, if you're patient, and help each other out."

As Gabe led the group of ex-cons to the wall of boot boxes, Maddy gestured to Royce with a crook of her finger. "I've got the jacket you need." To Jonah, as Maddy gripped a bit of Jonah's black t-shirt, she said, "I'm sorry about the mixup with the sizes."

Jonah only looked at her, dark brows scowling as though he was confused as to why she was speaking directly to him, rather than addressing Royce, who was not a criminal and an ex-con. And, as well, Jonah seemed to be silently asking why a short, round-bottom woman would deign to tug on his sleeve.

"It's all right," he said with that defensive shrug of his.

Royce understood only in that moment that the shrug was meant to indicate that Jonah didn't give a rat's ass about whatever it was when indeed, on the inside, he cared a great deal. This part of him, newly come to light, made Royce want to be extra gentle with this hard-edged man, so he patted Jonah's shoulder and nodded to show he agreed with Maddy.

"A good fitting jacket will keep you warm in this wet weather," he said. "Maddy takes it as a point of pride to get each man fitted properly. Don't you, Maddy?"

"I do," she said, gesturing them over to a small, free-standing rack that had three sherpa-lined denim jackets.

This made Royce laugh, even if only in his own mind. It was like a small game of which porridge would taste just right, but Royce could already see that the jacket on the very end was going to be big enough.

Jonah went unerringly to that jacket and took off his own and pulled on the new jacket. It settled on his broad shoulders with ease, though Royce frowned because Jonah was still wearing the same black t-shirt and the same, grease-stained jeans and his same old black boots, which looked quite damp as he stood there on the strip of carpet that covered the store's wooden floors.

Royce didn't say anything, not wanting to make Jonah feel ashamed of what he was wearing. They were obviously his own clothes, after all, and he probably felt more comfortable in them, and wanted to wear them in a place that was still new and strange to him.

"This looks nice on you," Royce said, tugging on the soft lapels of the jacket, watching the cloth wrap snugly around Jonah's broad shoulders. "Does it feel nice? Like it fits better?"

Once again, the world went away and Maddy seemed to melt into the woodwork and the cacophony of voices of excited ex-cons trying on boots and hats faded into a low murmur as he and Jonah looked at each other.

As Jonah looked at him, those dark eyes were so warm and soft, perhaps with gratitude or a shy joy at being the focus of Royce's attention. Royce didn't know, only that he could melt into those eyes, and warm himself inside that bank of warmth and stillness and watchfulness.

"Yeah," said Jonah, a strange softness to his mouth as it curved around the word.

"You look rather handsome in it," said Royce because he couldn't, simply could not, contain the compliment, nor hide the feelings behind it, pushed from inside of him. If he could have wrapped the words in a red ribbon and presented them that way, he would have.

Jonah smiled, just the same, a small, low curve of his mouth as he looked away, a faint rose stain to his cheeks as though overcome by the compliment. Then the shared moment, as moments always do, faded away and the excited talk over new boots and hats came into focus.

Royce knew he needed to step back and allow Jonah to pick out a pair of boots that he liked, and determined that he probably should let Maddy measure Jonah's head for the hat, rather than reaching out and taking over as he wanted to, as his hands itched to do.

It was not easy to stand still, on the sidelines, but it was worth it in the end, when, with his new denim jacket laid on one of the chairs,

Jonah was fitted. He pulled on the boots and tucking the damp-edged hem of his jeans over those boots and, finally, *finally*, stood up straight to look at himself in the mirror.

Royce's breath left him as though he'd been punched in the gut rather hard. Jonah, dark and handsome and interesting before, looked ten feet tall in those boots with the stacked heels and, with the jaunty, pale cream straw cowboy hat perched on his dark curls, was now a mouthwatering temptation.

The black t-shirt pulled against his chest, and the blue of the blue heron tattoo on his left bicep matched the faded blue of his grease-streaked blue jeans. His neck and forearms stood out in hard lines as if someone had sketched them. As for the backs of his thighs where they met the curve of his lovely behind, the jeans, faded and worn, the cloth tucked in interesting ways, drew Royce's eyes to that spot, over and over.

Jonah had been looking at himself in the mirror, but when he caught Royce's gaze in that mirror, he winked with a little just-for-Royce grin. Then he made a click sound with his teeth and Royce found himself laughing, right out loud in that perfect moment, the delicious thrill of it, sharing that look, that lingered gaze, he and Jonah, at the same moment.

It was as though Jonah was trying to tell Royce that he wanted what Royce wanted, which was—what? He'd never been with a man the way he'd been with a woman. He'd never kissed a man, or touched him in tender ways, hands slipping beneath the outer shell of clothes to the vulnerable places beneath.

Would Jonah let him if he asked? And would he dare ask?

It was hard to breathe, hard to catch his breath, but Royce did his best, backing up a little, giving Jonah a little space to catch his breath as well because, yes, Jonah's chest beneath that tight black, three-day-worn t-shirt was rising and falling quite quickly. Proving to Royce that his little private dream could become, while still private, the way Royce liked it, something more than a dream. More visceral. More alive. More real.

He perhaps had a responsibility that, amidst a nodding acquaintance to basic ethics, to own up to the fact that he was planning something unethical, something he ought to discuss with Gabe. But then, Gabe was in a relationship with one of the men who worked for him and that seemed to be working out all right, so why couldn't Royce at least explore a similar relationship with a man on his team?

He swallowed hard and looked away at the rest of the ex-cons as they assembled their boxes of cowboy boots, their new straw cowboy hats on their heads. They were jaunty and happy and alive, every single one of them, and a damn improvement as to how they'd presented themselves only days ago, when they'd gotten out of the prison van.

Clothes did not make a man, that was true. But they could go a long way to making a man feel differently about himself. And that Royce knew for a fact.

CHAPTER 8
JONAH

It rained on and off all afternoon, and they spent the time together in the mess tent, drinking hot coffee made in the large French press, and eating chocolate cookies the cooks had made, just for the occasion.

Royce brought out a map of the valley, and showed his team where they were in relation to the end of the lake, the places where bridges or walkways of wood might be built, and how there were plans to build three viewing towers high on the hill so people could go up and watch for birds and look at the view.

"I had smaller maps made that you could have with you," said Royce with a little moan, as if he'd let them all down. "But Maddy sent the job out to a print shop in Cheyenne and it's not come back yet."

Jonah wanted to get up and comfort Royce, put his arms around those lovely shoulders and give him a pep talk, but Royce was busy giving one of his cute little lectures. It was something about Russian olive trees, which ought to be chopped down as soon as you saw one. That, or let Royce know and he'd mark it on the map for future removal because they were a blight on the landscape and not native to Wyoming besides.

When the dinner hour came around, they cleared away the maps and the playing cards and the books, and sat down to a meal of BBQ spare ribs and corn pudding, which was amazing, and miles better than anything Jonah'd eaten in prison. But then, that could be said for any meal shared at that long table in the mess tent.

Except this time, he'd somehow gotten BBQ sauce in his hair, and there was a streak of it on his left forearm. In prison, nobody would have cared, and here, nobody did either. Except when Jonah looked across the table and saw that Royce, in his sparkling white snap button shirt, a paper towel tucked into the neck of that shirt like a bib, other than a streak or two of sauce on the paper towel, was spotless.

Royce pointed to his own cheek, and then to Jonah's, and Jonah reached up and his fingers came away with yet more sauce.

It wasn't like him to wonder what another man thought of him, at least not in the way he was wondering now. Which was whether Royce was put off by the mess Jonah had made of himself. While eating a normal meal, Jonah was fine, but something about eating spareribs with his fingers had made him enjoy his meal with a kind of abandon.

As dinner was winding down, he stood up.

"I'll just go—" he began, but then every eye was upon him, that fucking spotlight of attention that he never needed or enjoyed but which always seemed to be aimed at him at the least perfect moment.

So he didn't say what he wanted to say, but strode out of the tent, into the damp of the evening's growing darkness, and went to his tent to grab his little green carryall. Then he grabbed some of his new, never-worn clothes, wrapped them in a towel and marched himself to the shower.

He wasn't quite used to how good the experience of showering in the valley was, though he hoped nobody was listening to his groans of pleasure. When he was done, after he'd dried off in the little dressing area and put on his new clothes, he groaned again. Everything fit, snug on his arms and limbs, everywhere, and was clean against his skin, a delight and a pleasure at the same time.

Then, finally, he pulled on new socks, and laced his feet inside those yellow boots that looked soft, but which had thick soles, sturdy

THE COWBOY AND THE HOODLUM

beneath him as he stood up, and steel toes that made him feel like he could walk through anything.

And no, he wasn't looking for Royce so he could watch Royce's face light up with approval at the sight of Jonah in his new duds. He was walking to the mess tent to find Royce so he could get the thumbs up that he now was appropriately dressed for all the work he'd signed up to do, at least once it stopped raining, which he wouldn't mind in the least if it never did. But not for any kind of compliment from Royce, of course not!

Once he arrived at the mess tent, however, though the lights were on inside, nobody was there. The cooks had finished their cleanup work and departed to wherever they went. Jonah had no idea and didn't really care. Only that Royce was nowhere to be found.

Royce had mentioned once where his tent was located, but Jonah wasn't sure where that was, so, miffed and put off from his secret pleasure at finally wearing his new clothes, he marched, heavy-footed, to the old-fashioned landline, plunked himself down in the folding chair and dialed Beck's number.

"Hey, Beck," he said when Beck finally answered.

"What the hell, Jonah," said Beck, starting right in, his words sharp-edged. "You were supposed to call me days ago."

"It's only Wednesday, Beck," said Jonah. He meant to calm Beck down, but was somehow winding him up.

"Well, I need you back at the shop," said Beck, softening a bit because he wanted something from Jonah and was going to do, it seemed, a bit of groveling to get what he wanted. "The orders are piling up and we just got a stack of Hondas in here that need stripping down."

As to what constituted a *stack* in Beck's mind didn't matter because if there was an emergency at the shop, it felt very distant from where Jonah was, sitting in a canvas tent in the middle of nowhere, stark shadows from the lightbulbs overhead spreading themselves all around while a cool wind stirred in his hair.

He would have sworn he'd never been out-of-doors in all of his

73

life, not until now. But it made a nice change, even if this was nothing he could put into words to help Beck understand.

"I'm good here for a while," said Jonah. He curled his fingers in the coils of the cord leading from the handset to the blocky, pale tan phone.

"What do you mean, good for a while?" asked Beck. "I'm coming to get you. I'll be up tomorrow. The question is, do you want me to wait until dark? Or be bold as brass in the middle of the day."

"I'm telling you not to come and get me," said Jonah. "Not yet, anyway. I'm liking it here too much to leave."

"What could there possibly be up there that you can't get down here?" Now Beck was well and truly boiling in his shirt, by the sounds of it.

"Plenty of rest, good food," said Jonah, trying to calm his passionate friend. "Not to mention the finest hot showers I've ever had the pleasure to experience."

He didn't mention Royce and, smiling, Jonah ducked his chin and counted the seconds until Beck's next reason for Jonah coming home. But it didn't happen.

Instead, Beck was breathing hard, as if he was grinding his teeth together in an effort not to explode. Not to come undone. Which was about to happen, as evidenced by the growl Jonah heard on the other end of the line.

"I can't keep going like this, Jonah," said Beck, more plaintive now, following the growl with something more sweet. "It's been two years. When are you coming home?"

"You're doing a great job," said Jonah, meaning it because he knew it was true, and besides, it was the appropriate time to unwind Beck a bit and get him to calm down. "Why don't you come up on Sunday? That's visiting day. We can hang out, and I'll even feed you, if you come before lunchtime. But I don't think I'm leaving soon, and I just wanted you to know that."

On the other end of the line was silence, not pure, because Jonah could hear Beck's heavy, unhappy breathing. Which made him realize, as he let Beck stew, how exhausting it was, interacting with Beck over the phone.

Usually the two of them talked in person, in the shop, while they worked, and Jonah could cut Beck off by simply focusing on his work, or drinking some coffee while he thought about what to have for lunch. Talking over the phone, like they were doing now, made it harder to communicate.

"Sunday lunch?" asked Beck, more evenly now, as if having lunch at the same time and at the same table as Jonah was a prize worth hoping for.

"Yeah."

Straightening up, Jonah smiled into the phone, putting the smile in his voice, because while it was true Beck was being a bit clingy, he was also the only person who had visited him in prison, coming a couple times a month, always putting money into Jonah's commissary account.

It suddenly occurred to him that maybe Beck deserved better than Jonah. He'd been so unsettled for most of the last year before he'd gone into prison and sometimes had taken it out on Beck. Beck deserved someone who would appreciate his intense devotion and loyalty, that was for sure.

"Say the word and I'll text you the directions, cause it's kind of hidden."

Jonah would have to borrow someone's cellphone to make that happen, but maybe Royce wouldn't mind if Jonah texted a friend. Speaking of which—

"I have to go," said Jonah. "They've got early lights out and bed checks and all that stuff. But plan for Sunday, okay?"

"Okay," said Beck, seemingly a little forlorn, as if the promise of Jonah-time was ahead of him, only it was too far in the future to be gotten through easily.

"See you Sunday," said Jonah, and then he hung up and stood up, and looked out at the darkness beyond the tent, to see Royce, standing on the edge of the platform, gesturing to Jonah to come closer.

Gleefully, more gleefully than he'd thought possible, Jonah slipped past the tables to where Royce was, just beyond the opening to the mess tent.

"That sounded like an intense conversation," said Royce. "Not that I was listening in, of course, but I waited because I didn't want to interrupt you."

"It was my good friend, Beck," said Jonah. "We work at my auto repair shop together. Or we did. Beck is holding down the fort at the moment."

"Oh, you own a garage," said Royce in a kind, interested sort of way, without the least bit of forced politeness such as Jonah had sometimes heard.

"Yeah."

For a long moment, Royce looked at him as if studying him. Parts of Jonah wanted to squirm but other parts stood up and wanted to know if Royce liked how fine Jonah looked in his new duds, all manly and strong, ready to chop down the biggest tree in the forest or whatever it was Royce wanted him to do.

"You're not wearing the scarf I loaned you," said Royce, reaching out to Jonah's neck and then drawing back.

The scarf. That soft bit of fabric with all the colors in it, like jewels against a soft white, and in the middle of it a crazy multi-colored jackalope. It smelled like Royce, to boot, so there was no way, absolutely no way, Jonah was giving that scarf back. It was currently beneath his pillow, and that was where it was going to stay.

"I lost it," Jonah said.

"You lost it?" asked Royce, his voice rising to a pitch, as though the scarf was his favorite thing in all the world. "How did you manage that?"

"Don't know." Jonah shrugged, extra hard to prove the point that the scarf was now gone and only Jonah knew where it had gone to. "Damn shame."

"Oh, I see."

With a forlorn sigh, Royce reached in to turn off the lights, which left Jonah in darkness, and only reaching out to grab Royce's shoulder allowed him to step off the wooden platform without tripping.

THE COWBOY AND THE HOODLUM

It was pitch dark now, with only little spots appearing between the trees to show where the other tents were. Overhead, the wind tugged the clouds to the edges of the pine trees, leaving large dark areas where stars shone.

Royce led them both into the middle of the clearing, where the sky above them spread out into a deep black blanket. There, Royce stopped, reaching out to tug on Jonah's sleeve, as if to get him to stop as well. Which Jonah did, digging his heels in the dirt because he did not want Royce, not for one minute, thinking that Jonah wasn't interested in whatever Royce was up to.

But he had to know.

"What are we doing out here?" he asked, keeping his voice to a low whisper in case anyone was listening who shouldn't be.

"We're bat watching," said Royce, and maybe it was Jonah's imagination or maybe he was starting to see in the dark, for he sensed Royce was smiling at him. "I went on a quick errand into town and as I came back, I realized that because of all the rain, there'd be a lot of insects about, and thus, a great many bats flying around."

"Bats?" asked Jonah, completely mystified. It was dark, so how could they see anything, let alone bats?

"The big brown bat or *Myotis volans*, to be more precise," said Royce. "I've seen three of them already, or maybe it was the long-legged bat, *Eptesicus fuscus*. Those are a little bit wider in the wing, though *Myotis* has a longer tibia bone. It's hard to tell when they are on the wing."

None of this, absolutely none of it, made any sense to Jonah.

"The *what* now?" he asked, leaning forward, ears perked for Royce's next utterance, any utterance. He had to be the most mystifying and fascinating man Jonah had ever met, and that was saying something because all kinds came into the garage, looking for spare parts, or wanting a car they'd stolen to be stripped down. "Mylo vulcans?"

"*Myotis volans*," said Royce, quite slowly, and he was leaning back, leaning close to Jonah as if he, too, didn't want anyone to share in their private conversation for two. "I just love the Latin names for things, don't you? They have such a thrilling ring to them."

"*Myotis volans,*" said Jonah, whispering it under his breath, feeling the shape of it on his tongue.

"At least I think that's what most of these are," said Royce. He paused, his shoulder rubbing with Jonah's shoulder. There they stood in the multi-layered darkness, the trees tall dark lines against the blue-black sky beyond. "If we listen, we can hear them."

Standing stark still in the middle of a clearing in the woods with darkness all around, waiting for the sound of a bat, was not something Jonah ever imagined he'd be doing. But he was, and it was the presence of the man standing next to him that made it even more unique and freakishly memorable.

A bit of starlight caught itself in Royce's golden hair, making it turn almost silver, and more of that starlight sparked in Royce's blue eyes as he looked at Jonah.

Jonah was leaning so hard that he sensed his forehead could almost brush those golden curls, and maybe he'd move in and inhale the scent of clean skin, the touch of Royce's cologne diving into his lungs. And maybe Royce was leaning right back, as well, for he felt Royce's breath brush his cheek.

They could almost be kissing, on the verge of it, just about ready to tumble them both into sensation and warmth when Royce grabbed his arm, hard, and Jonah froze.

"Do you hear it?" asked Royce, whispering, his words a rush of air across Jonah's face. "That squeak there, sharp and high."

Sighing, desperate to hear what Royce was hearing, Jonah straightened up, though he didn't move away, and did his best to listen for the bat. All to respond to Royce's request, doing that rather than what he'd wanted to do, which was tug Royce close and kiss him, quite softly perhaps, and then maybe a bit harder after that.

Longing filled him, a bereft sense of something lost but waiting to be found in the darkness of the woods all around them.

"You look rather nice in your new gear," said Royce, softly in the silence that followed some high-pitched, irregular sounds. "The cowboy look suits you. And I'll bet those boots will serve you well."

"Yeah," said Jonah. "Maybe."

He didn't think he looked at all like a cowboy, but he didn't want to tell Royce he was wrong about that. And, at the same time, he was warmer, and his feet were dryer in his new, soft, steel-toed boots.

Best of all, he liked the way Royce's voice curled around him in the darkness, liked the way that softness landed on his shoulders and seemed to sink beneath his clothes and into his skin, down to his very bones. He'd never met anyone who made him feel the way Royce did with just a few words.

"Not maybe," said Royce. "Definitely."

There was a touch to his jacket, a tug on the sherpa-lined collar, and then it was gone, leaving Jonah with an even deeper sense of longing. And what the hell was he supposed to do with that? Hold himself back? Hell, yes.

Not because Royce was his boss, but because surely Royce wouldn't be interested in someone who didn't know the Latin names of things. Or maybe he would be. Anything was possible.

It was this last thought, hope stirring inside of him, that let him let Royce say his goodnights and walk off in the darkness without Jonah stopping him. His was the long game, as it always had been, and he always played to win.

CHAPTER 9

ROYCE

The sun was out and shining with all of its might the day they dug the post holes for the wooden enclosure at the edge of the pasture. Royce was glad for his thick gloves and wide-brimmed straw hat, though he'd had to dig for an appropriate scarf to soak the sweat from his neck.

In his pocket he had a small tube of sunscreen, so he could reapply it when he needed to. The ex-cons stared at him when he paused the first time to do this, but then he made them stop and take up a plastic bottle of water and hydrate themselves. He also encouraged them to have some cheese and apple slices, which were also in the small cooler that Royce'd had the cooks make up for them.

"It's important to take breaks," he said to all of them, but especially to Jonah, who paused, the plastic bottle halfway to his mouth, as he listened to Royce.

Which he tended to do, fully and completely. Those dark eyes looked at him with such intensity, it was as if he and Jonah were alone beneath the big blue sky, and it was just the two of them digging those post holes or measuring the beams that would support the slender roofs of the shelters for the horses.

Royce enjoyed that focus, so much that it was distracting him, and he almost stabbed his foot with the posthole digger and left his gloves off for a good hour, which gave him blisters and made him a tad irritated. But then, he'd see Jonah, standing only a few feet away, which continued to put him in better spirits all morning long.

There was so much work that needed doing, all at the same time, that Gabe had mentioned a few of the hands from the guest ranch would be down to help, and though Royce wanted to balk at this, he could see the sense of it, too. Many hands make light work and all that, so when the ranch hands arrived, Royce welcomed them with a wide gesture at all the supplies neatly lined up and waiting for them.

"Your choice, gentlemen," he told them. "We need shelters built, which will require getting up on ladders, or we need the wooden fence put up, which will require mixing cement and perhaps getting it all over you."

Jonah raised his hand to help build shelters. Royce would have joined him, but there were fewer on the task of building the fence, so Royce girded his loins and continued to help dig post holes and then to mix cement to secure the fence posts and hold the end of the wood so Gabe could nail the top cross-rails into place.

He liked watching Gabe work because he was strong and rolled up his shirtsleeves to bare his manly forearms. He also sweated in a pretty way, almost artfully.

Had Jonah not shown up in the valley, then watching Gabe might have been good enough for Royce. Only he was looking over his shoulder half the time, watching Jonah on the ladder as he hammered nails into crossbeams and shimmied up there to guide the laths for the sheets of corrugated metal roof.

Jonah was wearing a white shirt, an image that screamed in Royce's mind even when his eyes were closed. A *white* shirt, stark against the dusky tan of his skin, the sleeves rolled up to show those strong, corded forearms, though the tattoo of the blue heron taking flight was hidden from view. Which was fine because Royce was rather fond of that tattoo and didn't want to share it. Which was foolish, because it wasn't his tattoo, was it.

Jonah wasn't wearing his hat, so the sun shone on his dark curls, laced with a bit of gray. His face was serious as he stood on the crossbeams of the roof, bent over to use the nail gun to drive thick, strong nails through the metal strips to hold the roof down, yes, down as much as up, for Wyoming winds were strong and would want to race down the foothills to scoop up under the roof and pull it off that way.

When Royce whistled for everyone to take a break, and Jonah came close, the sight of him, sweat lacing his neck, almost took his breath away. And when Jonah took a bottle of water and poured it over his head, causing the white shirt to stick to him in places, the curve of his chest showing in darker shadow beneath the wet, white cloth, Royce almost choked on his mouthful of water.

Jonah's dark hair was silvered with water, glossy dark beneath the sparkling sun, and once again, as had happened many times the night before when Royce had been in his tent all alone, his brain went scampering off in its own direction, multiple directions really, as if it couldn't bear to stand in one place and figure everything out.

First of all, Jonah had lied about having lost the jackalope scarf. Royce knew this for a fact because Jonah's whole body had stiffened up when he lied, followed by that casual shrug, which was supposed to have been dismissive. Perhaps, in the past, this had been an effective way for Jonah to disarm anyone listening, but Royce was on to him and knew this particular tell quite well by now.

As to why Jonah had lied, that was a mystery unto itself. What did a man like Jonah, who owned and worked in a garage, and who wore black head to toe, including those disreputable black leather boots Royce was relieved to see him out of, want with a multi-color, satin-silk scarf?

He remembered tying the scarf around Jonah's neck while Jonah held as still as a mighty oak tree. His brows had lowered, and he'd glowered a bit, like a confused horse who wasn't quite sure what would happen once the bridle went on. But he'd worn the scarf, stroking it with his strong fingers from time to time, as if to make sure it was still in place. Like he enjoyed the softness around his neck.

The mystery of the scarf was something Royce very much wanted to solve.

Second, there had been the *leaning*, which Royce knew the meaning of, having seen more than one romance movie, though he'd not experienced it, like, ever.

Sandra had not been very much into leaning, or soft touches, or gentle intimacy, unless that intimacy led to happy fun times in bed. She'd been practical that way, practical and straightforward and just so boring that Royce had stopped wanting to try.

That part was on him, and one of the reasons they'd gotten divorced. Even in that, Sandra had been calm and implacable, telling the judge that irreconcilable differences were the cause for the divorce, though to Royce she'd said, *I just don't want to live this way anymore. I deserve to be happy and so do you, only we can't do that together.*

From what he'd heard about divorces, all the fighting and bitterness that occurred, he was grateful to Sandra who, though unhappy, hadn't taken it out on Royce or the judge or their respective lawyers. Only now, having been married for three years and divorced for a year and a half, Royce honestly had no idea anymore how to court someone. How to court Jonah.

He wanted there to be more leaning, more scent of Jonah in the darkness, and more almost-kisses. And then kisses for real.

He wanted the knowledge of what it would feel like to have those strong fingers touch his skin, and feel the whisper of Jonah's breath on his cheek, and the kind of closeness that seemed to line up with the tumble of desire and confusion in Royce's belly, which was constantly there, now. Like a bright dream that feared it would never see the dawn.

He had no idea how to begin. How to make that connection, how to let Jonah know what he wanted.

In the back of Royce's mind was the echo of Leland Tate's rule about non-fraternization. Well, the rule was more of a guideline. It wasn't even a very powerful one, at least not since Leland had hooked up with a drifter who'd shown up on the property last year, so Royce wasn't too worried about wanting what he wanted, or rather, whom he wanted.

Nor was Royce worried about the fact that since he was, technically, Jonah's boss, there'd be an imbalance of power. Seriously, if Jonah wanted to take off, he could have, at any moment.

Plus, not for a single second could Royce imagine that Jonah ever did what he didn't want to do. And yet, at Royce's encouragement, Jonah had changed into work-sturdy clothes, and he was wearing boots that would keep his feet safe and dry, also at Royce's urging.

And he'd stolen, yes, *stolen*, Royce's favorite scarf, and if that wasn't something a criminal would do, then Royce didn't know what it was. Wouldn't know. Unless he asked.

"Time to take a break, I think," said Royce aloud, his gloved hands on the post hole digger, which had grown quite heavy and cumbersome, the realization finally breaking through into his daydreams. "Break time!"

On the roof, he saw Jonah making that snap-finger gesture to get the ex-cons to put down their tools and join Royce near the second unopened cooler that he'd arranged to have delivered mid-morning. Even the cooks stayed as he opened it, for inside were not just plastic bottles of cool water, but also baggies of gorp trail mix, and little packets of peanut butter crackers and fudge bars and ice cream sandwiches and oh, yes, orange sherbet pushups.

It was a tad warm for the frozen treats, but it was too late to worry about that now, as everyone crowded around and dug in. With smiles on their faces as they enjoyed the treats with as much abandon as if they'd suddenly turned ten and school had just let out for the summer.

As for Jonah, he went straight for the orange pushups, his eyes focused on peeling the paper away and using the stick to push the orange sherbet up through the paper tube. Then, eyes half closed, he circled the sherbet with his tongue, flicking his gaze up at the last minute to focus on Royce.

As to what Royce was supposed to do with his body's reaction was another matter, so he just let it happen. The shiver across his skin that dove inside of him, the twinges up and down his spine, like little bits of silver fire. The way his cock tightened, which had to be a good sign, didn't it? That if his body wanted Jonah, maybe it was okay to want Jonah with his heart? Only, did Jonah want him in the same way?

The last thing Royce wanted to do was throw himself at someone who would shove him away. Not to mention, such an attempt might make Jonah hate him, and then Jonah might get surly and disrupt Leland's pet project. Or that he would no longer call the ex-cons to attention and keep them in line. He wouldn't have Royce's back.

Worse still, he wouldn't want to stand in the misty evenings and watch for bats or birds either. Let alone take Royce's hand one day and, with binoculars strung around their necks, hike up to the ridge above the valley to watch for falcons and, when they spotted one, which they surely would, Royce could tell Jonah his favorite poem, hoping in his heart that Jonah would want to hear it.

Across the cooler, Jonah licked his lips quite slowly, leaving behind a glisten of moisture on those lips of his, lush, parted, as if with invitation.

If that wasn't a come-hither gesture, Royce didn't know what it was. Or maybe he really didn't know what it was and his mind was running away with him, spinning out dreams like a daydream cape, furling in the wind, majestic under the bright blue sky.

He needed to settle his brain so he could figure out what he needed to do, and not just that. What he wanted to do because *who* he wanted was Jonah. Pure and simple.

It was a faraway dream at the moment, and there was still work to be done, so Royce gathered up wrappers and sticks and put the empty plastic bottles in a blue recycling bag. Gordy helped him, which was nice, but then Jonah called and Gordy climbed back up onto the roof with Jonah, and they began banging at nails again.

Royce wasn't jealous of Gordy being with Jonah because that was foolish and unnecessary. Besides, from where Royce was, he could better see Jonah, curved over his work, his long bejeaned legs holding him steady, a nail or two in his mouth as he held the panel of corrugated roofing steady. Yes, it was better to be where he was, holding a fence pole steady for Gabe to bang away at, and watch, hopefully covertly, the majesty that was Jonah at work.

CHAPTER 10
JONAH

There'd been no way for Jonah to miss the flare of bright desire in Royce's eyes when he'd licked that orange sherbet pushup. And when Jonah had been on the roof of the first shelter, manfully pounding in nails, he'd felt Royce watching him and not even pretending not to watch, no. Royce had been full out staring, though perhaps he'd not realized it at the time.

With those indicators and Royce's attention falling on him time and again, Jonah would have bet real money that they'd end up in bed together that night. So, before dinner, he'd hit the showers, relishing the sweet, gentle Ivory soap all over his body, and the Jergens that followed. He'd also shaved, quite close, using a brand new blade, even.

There were no hair styling products in his kit of goodies, so he had dried his hair till it spiraled everywhere, out of control, like a wayward beast. When he'd looked at himself in the mirror, he'd thought *I look okay.*

He didn't ask himself the question whether Royce thought he looked okay because, from Royce's behavior, it was obvious that the answer was yes, he did. And that Royce wanted him.

Jonah even wore his new cowboy boots, the leather tight on his feet, the right heel squeaking slightly as he marched along the path in the woods to the mess tent.

Everybody was already seated, so he was the last one. He had to sit at the end of the long table, far away from Royce and next to Duane, who grunted as he reached for the garlic bread, and thumped Jonah in the chest with his elbow as he leaned back when one of the cooks put a plate of spaghetti in front of him.

"It's camp spaghetti," said the cook as he placed a plate of it in front of Jonah.

Confused as to how this was different from any other kind of spaghetti, Jonah looked down the table to where Royce was sitting, thinking he'd shout out his question and get his answer that way and perhaps draw out a smile or two, and maybe even a twinkle in those blue eyes.

At the far end of the table, too far away for Jonah's liking, sat Royce, his shoulders rolled forward. There was a flush to his cheeks, his eyes were on his plate, and he was eating without a whole lot of interest, which wasn't like Royce at all.

As for the flush, it didn't look like it had come from pleasure or laughter, though Jonah couldn't be sure because he was, quite simply, too fucking far away. And the anticipatory joy he'd felt earlier in the day turned to worry.

Jonah was not a guy who fussed over other guys. If Beck had a hangover, Jonah usually laughed and thumped around the apartment just to see how loud he could make Beck groan, and he certainly didn't deliver any sympathy or anything.

But Royce was another matter, and Jonah wanted to help. If he could. The question was how.

The spaghetti was good and Jonah ate as fast as he could, getting up from the table when Royce did, scrubbing his mouth with the back of his hand as he slid among the tables to the wooden platform, reaching out for a bit of Royce's sleeve, but missing.

"Damn it," he hissed, and froze stock still when Royce turned around, looking even more pale in the long blaze of electric light.

"I'm sorry," said Royce, his mouth down-curved, his blue eyes looking flat, his whole face drawn in unhappiness.

"What?" asked Jonah, his mind racing, turning on its heel to look backward, searching every interaction between them, every conversation, looking for anything that Royce felt he needed to apologize for.

Someone bumped him from behind. Duane again. Tugging on Royce's sleeve while wanting very much to snake his arm around Royce's waist, Jonah led them a little to one side of the mess tent, then ducked his chin to peer into Royce's eyes.

"What?" he asked again, less demanding, more gently this time.

"I have a headache," said Royce, lifting his head as he settled his shoulders, as if he was about to face a firing squad and was very much afraid of what would follow the volley of shots. "And a sunburn, in spite of my best efforts. And though I was going to—"

Royce sucked in a breath, his eyes dark and serious.

"I was going to do a whole *lot* of things tonight," he said now, without explaining what those things were. "Only I feel dreadful, and I just need to take some Tylenol and drink some lavender tea—"

"They make tea out of lavender?" asked Jonah, mystified.

"*Lavendula angustifolia* has been used as a medicine since ancient times," said Royce. "It always calms me, so maybe what I ought to do is get some water for my kettle and brew me some and then lay down—"

"I'll get you water for your kettle," said Jonah, grateful for the opportunity to help.

He was a bit worried that this might be a delay tactic, as various guys and gals sometimes did. Having to shampoo their hair on thus-and-such night, or needing to visit their sick aunt in the hospital. Or the most classic of all tactics: a headache.

If that was true, then maybe Royce didn't want Jonah like Jonah wanted Royce. In which case he was going to have to put the brakes on his own desire and just resign himself to being Royce's very good friend and nothing else, because the last thing he wanted to do was force himself on Royce, because Jonah was not that kind of guy.

But maybe, quite simply, Royce had intentions similar to Jonah's.

"Would you?" asked Royce, his eyes wide as he looked at Jonah, as if Jonah had just offered him the world on a silver platter. "The kitchen has pitchers you can fill up at the sink—"

"I'll do it," said Jonah. He curled his fingers around Royce's upper arm and felt Royce lean into the touch, so maybe all was not lost. In the growing darkness, a bit of warmth grew between them, which made Jonah feel a little bit better. "Which way is your tent?" he asked, finally making himself let go.

"I'm the second one along," said Royce, gesturing vaguely over his shoulder, as if he assumed Jonah could find his way in the darkness, and this Jonah was determined to do. "I'll have the light on for you."

"I'll meet you there," he said. "Is there anything else I can get you?"

"You're sweet," said Royce, perhaps unaware that was the first time anyone had said anything like that about Jonah to Jonah's face. Usually, he was an asshole and a hoodlum and everything bad, but to Royce, he was *sweet*. "I'm all set except for water for the kettle."

Jonah, poised to rush back through the mess tent to where the kitchen was, paused to touch Royce quite gently on the cheek, which earned him a smile and made everything seem better. Then he was off, boots clomping on the wooden floor of the mess tent, making his way around the buffet table, crossing from the tent to the wooden structure that was the kitchen.

The cooks looked up at him with some surprise, but one of them wiped his hands on his apron, and nodded a greeting at Jonah.

"Is there something I can get you?" he asked.

"Royce needs water for his kettle, so can I get a pitcher?" He looked around. "And could I get a cold cloth?"

"We have bar towels," said the other cook. "They're a bit bigger than a washcloth, but they're soft and clean."

"That'll do."

Jonah waited, not tapping his fingers on the metal table in the middle of the kitchen, then nodded his thanks when he was handed a pitcher and a bar towel. He rushed through the darkness, headed toward the second tent along, from which blazed a beam of yellow light. Which turned out to be two small overhead bulbs, each with a little yellow cone of paper around it.

At the last minute, Jonah poured some of the water over the bar towel and wrung it out with one hand.

"I'm here," he said, stepping onto the platform and into the tent.

He was greeted by the sight of a forlorn Royce in yellow pajama bottoms and a pale blue t-shirt, which stopped Jonah in his tracks a little bit because what grown man wore pajamas? Well, evidently Royce did, and he looked rather sweet and kissable in them, but Jonah restrained himself.

In one hand, Royce held a bottle of Tylenol and in the other, he had a tube of ointment, though Jonah didn't know what kind. The back of Royce's neck was pink with sunburn.

"I suppose you think me an overly fussy fool," said Royce, shaking his head, as though at his own foolishness. "I wore sunscreen and a scarf, and I hydrated every other minute, and it still wasn't enough."

"Well," said Jonah, doing his best not to laugh as he placed the pitcher on top of a white shelf that took up half of one side of the tent. "You are a delicate flower, that much is certain. But here."

Sitting on the cot next to Royce, Jonah took the bottle of pills from Royce's hands and held up the damp bar towel before placing it in Royce's empty hands. He raised that hand to Royce's cheek for a long moment, to cool Royce's face in the hopes of making him seem less flushed and agitated.

Not for one minute was Jonah going to hold it against Royce that he wasn't feeling very well or had overexerted himself on the first sunny day they'd had in a while. But he didn't know what to say either, having never been one for handing out words of comfort.

"I have a drinking mug there," said Royce, pointing at the shelf which seemed to hold everything anybody would ever need. "And the kettle is the pink metal thing on the bottom shelf."

Jonah got up and poured a little water into the mug so Royce could take his pills. Then he poured water into the kettle, plugged it into the power strip, and flipped on the switch.

Right away came a rumbling sound as if the thing were gearing up to take flight, which seemed to be what it was supposed to sound like, as Royce didn't look the least bit alarmed when Jonah turned back around and sat back on the cot next to Royce.

"What's that there?" asked Jonah, pointing to the tube of ointment in Royce's other hand.

"It's coconut oil mixed with aloe vera for my sunburn." Royce's head hung low, as if he were completely at fault for letting himself get to his current state and unable to manage his way out of it. "But I pulled something in my shoulder while digging holes and now I can't lift my arm to put it on."

The expression on Royce's face was the most wretched, most woebegone, just about rivaling Beck's expression when Jonah went out on a Saturday night without him.

"Here," he said, holding out his hand for the tube. "Let me."

When Royce handed him the tube of ointment, Jonah gently took the damp washcloth from him as well and placed it carefully on the back of Royce's neck to draw the heat away. After a long, still moment with Royce looking at him somewhat anxiously, he gave the cloth back to Royce.

Jonah squeezed the tube, and applied a thin layer of ointment on Royce's sunburn, and then another, giving the first layer time to sink in before he applied the second.

The muscles beneath the skin along Royce's neck seemed overly tight, but Jonah knew better than to rub over a sunburn, so he simply rubbed Royce's back, long, warm, slow strokes. Those strokes felt good on a bone-deep level to him, and he hoped to Royce, as well, but again, he wasn't usually a caregiver.

Sure, he'd helped Beck with a hangover, or driven him to the emergency clinic when he'd sliced his thigh open when a fender had sprung loose and dug into his leg. But it had never been like this.

With Royce, it was different. It *felt* different. It was Jonah who hopped up and followed Royce's pointing finger to where the box of lavender tea sachets were, and it was he who poured the hot water, and was about to wait while it soaked or whatever it was that tea did, only Royce told him it had to steep for ten minutes and could he just bring it over.

"Sure."

He took the mug over and placed it on the top of the shelf, then took his place at Royce's side, gratefully, once more. He picked up the damp bar towel from where it had fallen on the pale blue counterpane and, one at a time, wiped Royce's hands, cooling them, *tsk tsking* over a little blister that had formed on the inside of Royce's right thumb.

"Feeling a little less like shit?" he asked when he saw Royce's shoulders relax as the pills kicked in. "Maybe building the shelters with me and Gordy would have been easier."

"I'd rather be on the ground where I was," said Royce with a sweet little pink blush rising in his cheeks. "That way I could watch *you* working, which was my treat for the day."

"Watch me?" Jonah shook his head, flustered, though he knew full and well that they'd been playing watching-me-watching-you pretty much all day. Though Jonah had had hopes that the day would end differently, more horizontally, it was still satisfying, in an odd, new way, to be playing nursemaid to a fully grown man who, while fully capable in so many ways, nevertheless had crumpled like paper beneath too much sun.

"You know I was," said Royce, his voice somber and low, like smoke slipping around Jonah's defenses. "You know I was."

"Drink your tea," said Jonah, doing his best to focus on something practical, rather than the way his insides started racing around at the way those blue eyes glinted at him and the tiny, sweet uptick at the corner of Royce's pink mouth. "Do you have bandaids and stuff?"

With his mug, Royce pointed at the second shelf, and Jonah leaped to grab the small plastic box and snapped open the lid, pulling out a bandaid. Carefully, he moved the mug to Royce's left hand. Then, taking Royce's right hand, he put a little of the ointment on it, and then wrapped the bandage carefully around the blister.

"Never pop a blister," he said, giving Royce's thumb a little kiss before letting it go. "Let it heal into a callus, otherwise, just leave it be."

"Yes, Jonah," said Royce, obediently, that mouth curving fully into a smile now.

This was almost too much for Jonah to bear, for he wanted to kiss that mouth and tumble Royce to the cot and show him, carefully and slowly, how much he wanted him. Except, as Royce drank his tea, his body became more and more relaxed, until it was quite obvious to Jonah that the only thing Royce needed to do was crawl into bed and let Jonah turn out the light for him.

"What's it called again?" asked Jonah. "*Laven-something angus-something?*"

"*Lavendula angustifolia*," said Royce, laughing a little as he drank what was left in his mug. "Some people, you know, it wakes up rather than relaxes. Sandra was one of those. She drank some once and was up for two days."

"Who's Sandra?" asked Jonah with a surge of jealousy so strong he wanted something, or someone, to punch.

"My ex." Royce put the now-empty mug on the shelf between the cot and the other shelf. "We divorced a year and a half ago. Sometimes I wonder how we lasted the three years of our marriage, but we did. I came to the ranch last season to get away from the memories." He looked at Jonah with some seriousness. "Our families wanted us to marry, and our ranches in Montana were right next to each other, so it seemed the sensible thing to do. Only it wasn't very sensible in the end. Just sad."

"Montana?" asked Jonah, amazed at how far away from home Royce had traveled just to get away from memories.

"I grew up there, on our ranch." Royce ducked his chin, then looked up at Jonah with a little smile. "We raise paint ponies there."

"Oh."

Jonah couldn't imagine his own family getting that involved in his life. They only cared that he was independent and self-sufficient and that whatever he got up to was his own business.

His family didn't care whom he fucked or whom he loved or whom he hated, and here Royce was, suffering from having scampered about, trying to please people who weren't even there to put ointment on his neck and get water for his lavender tea. But Jonah was here, he certainly was, so he was going to take care of Royce like it was his fucking job and enjoy every minute of it.

"Time you were in bed," he said, testing the words on his tongue, trying it out, looking out for someone else's best interest.

"Bossy," said Royce, but he obediently got up, just reaching for the light switch, when Jonah stopped him.

"Get into bed, and I'll take care of that," he said, patting the cot, then he stood up.

He made sure Royce was comfortable, his head on the pillow, before he tugged up the sheet and pale blue blanket. Then he gave into the urge and sat back down again, leaning forward, clasping Royce's peacefully smiling face, and bent forward to kiss him on the forehead.

"You rest," he said.

"But the light," said Royce, a little fretfully, it must be admitted.

"I'll get it."

Jonah stood up and flicked off the light, then walked out of the tent, zipping it closed behind him. Now he was in pitch darkness, without a flashlight, but maybe the stars, shining brightly overhead, would show him the way to his own tent, though he very much wanted to stay with Royce.

"Another night, perhaps," Jonah said. Then, with a little laugh, completely talking to himself, he said, "Another night, for sure."

CHAPTER 11
JONAH

Inside of him, Jonah found a newfound love for looking out for Royce while he recovered from his bout of frailty.

The whole next day, feeling powerful and guardian-like, he watched Royce like a hawk, half of his attention on his own work, finishing up those post holes and helping to complete the little paddock, and the rest of it fully on Royce. Who wore his hat, sensibly, all day, stopped to drink water often, and whistled while he painted the wooden fence a nice deep rich red stain that he referred to as Redwood, which he said was a classic.

Jonah had to believe him about that because when he painted stolen cars, he knew full well and good that nondescript colors were the easiest way to keep those cars from being spotted as stolen. Knowing what those colors were and how to apply them were skills he was very proud of.

He made sure that Royce went to bed early, and then took himself and his tokens and his pale green plastic carrying case to the shower. There, he stood beneath an ice-cold shower for a good five minutes before deciding he didn't need to punish himself for wanting Royce. He just needed to keep himself patient until he could *have* Royce.

So he turned the shower on full bore, at just the right hotness, and jerked off not once, but twice, and then dried off and slathered himself with Jergens all over and sighed at the blissful glory of having skin that didn't itch, and being able to dry between his toes, one at a time, slowly, without being hassled by another prisoner, and without having to worry about getting another bout of athlete's foot from badly cleaned shower stalls.

If this wasn't heaven, he didn't know what was.

That night, he slept like a baby because he was playing the long game. And maybe he didn't even have to play it for very long. And maybe all of his efforts weren't for play play. Maybe this was for real. Or maybe it was all a dream, and he'd wake up on his hard bed in his cell at Wyoming Correctional.

Saturday dawned with a clear blue sky, not a cloud in sight. Not that Jonah normally noticed those sorts of things, usually being focused on the next car that needed to be stripped and parts sold, or, while being in jail, how not to die of boredom while, at the same time, keeping his back to the wall, and Nelson on his knees. Beck happy over the phone. The usual.

In the valley, it felt different and maybe he'd put off realizing that for so long because, once used to it—this glorious, itch-free, fear-free, well-fed, well-rested life with Royce as his very good friend and soon hopefully more than that—how the fuck was he supposed to go back to his old life? Living over his garage with Beck, with no prospects for a different life?

Beck deserved better than to have Jonah take his frustration out on Beck, simply because he, Jonah, couldn't figure out what he really wanted that was different from what he already had.

Never mind Beck because it was after lunch and there was a cool breeze through the pine trees and Royce was marching up to him with a purpose, his step light, a smile on his face. Those blue eyes glinting with diamonds.

"Jonah," said Royce, his voice rising to an excited pitch. "I've found you."

"Yeah," said Jonah with a shrug, like he usually did, doing his best to present it like he didn't give a damn. But that was how he'd been

THE COWBOY AND THE HOODLUM

before Royce, so he added a smile, feeling the joy rushing through him, the newness of it, the simple pleasure of smiling back at Royce. "You found me," he said, his voice low and soft in a way that was totally unlike him, but which seemed to fit really, really well when he was talking to Royce.

"Gabe says there's a bit of an emergency at present."

"What's that?" asked Jonah. It couldn't be anything really bad, like the cops suddenly showing up because they decided to arrest Jonah all over again, as Royce's smile stayed in place.

"There are not one, but two truckloads—flatbeds, really—of flagstones showing up, and we need to unload them really, really fast because over a certain time limit for each delivery, they charge by the hour."

"Dicks," said Jonah, meaning it.

"It'll be just you and me, I'm afraid," said Royce, not looking at all afraid.

"Not a problem," said Jonah, meaning that, too.

"Thank you, but where are your gloves? And your hat?"

The warmth that was beneath his skin at the very thought of Royce worrying about him blossomed into something rich and pure and deep. Because who the fuck was this thoughtful? There was nobody in Jonah's regular world who was this nice, and Beck didn't count because they'd been friends forever.

Royce gave because that was who Royce was, it seemed, and the whole idea of giving just to give exploded in Jonah's mind to the point where he almost missed that Royce had come up close to tug on Jonah's sleeve.

"I like you in pale blue," Royce said, blue eyes shining, his voice low like he was sharing a secret.

"I'm running out of shirts," said Jonah, dismissing the compliment as soon as it was spoken, but cringing on the inside because what he should have said was, quite simply, thank you. The way Royce would have done.

"There's a little laundromat next to the kitchen," said Royce. "I spoke about it that first day, but maybe I was talking too fast? I sometimes do that when I get excited, and it was very exciting when you and your friends arrived."

The ex-cons Jonah arrived with weren't his friends, not really, though Gordy might be on his way to becoming a friend? Jonah didn't know because how he was with Gordy was totally different from the way he was with Beck. And Nelson. And, especially, Royce. What did the word friend even mean? Maybe he didn't really have any friends other than Beck before this, only now he did.

"I'll check out that laundromat," he said. "But first, those flagstones. I'll grab my hat and gloves and meet you where?"

"Just beyond the fire pit, where the picnic area is going to be."

"Got it."

Jonah trotted to his tent, made sure his boots were laced up tight, grabbed his straw hat and leather gloves, and trotted back through the woods, along the path, beyond the fire pit, to the open area next to the lake where, it was alleged, several picnic tables were to be built.

And there was Royce, his eyes reflecting the blue of the lake, his gold hair tousled beneath his straw hat, and a look of mock panic on his face as he pointed to the two flatbed trucks, currently chuffing dark smoke into the air.

Royce waved the air in front of his face, and perhaps he meant it as a joke, but the diesel fumes stank, and might ruin their afternoon together, lingering amidst the sweet-spicy smelling pines.

"Turn those engines off," said Jonah, striding up to the driver's side of one of the trucks.

"We won't be here that long," said the driver, surly, turning his head away as if Jonah wasn't worth his time.

Grabbing the long grab handle, Jonah opened the driver's side door, and swung himself up into the cab, planting his forearms across the guy's neck, pinning him to his seat.

"When I say turn off the engine," growled Jonah, low enough so Royce wouldn't hear him, but loud enough so the driver knew he meant business. "I mean turn off the engine. Got it?"

Wide-eyed, the driver nodded, and Jonah let him go to turn off the engine, but before he shut the door, he bared his teeth and gave the driver a good punch in the arm so there'd be no question who was boss, and it wasn't the driver. Then he slammed the door nice and hard and stepped back, brushing invisible dirt from his hands as he came around the front of the truck, where Royce was.

"We can get to work now," Jonah said with a satisfied nod.

"I see," said Royce, sounding a little breathless. He was also a little wide-eyed, and perhaps had overheard that conversation after all. Well, he had to understand that sometimes a little force was necessary to get a job done.

"They'll be fine," said Jonah, a flare of unease at Royce's reaction making him rethink the whole conversation with the driver of the truck, but it was too late now to do anything but go balls-out. "They're truckers. They're tough."

CHAPTER 12
JONAH

They made short work of unloading those flagstones and that was because both drivers got out to help them, which maybe wasn't how things usually worked, but fuck it. More help meant that they could lay the flagstones out in three tidy lines, with a little pile at the end, and they could stand and wave at the drivers as they pulled back out from the shelter of the trees.

Well, Royce waved, and Jonah gave them the finger, laughing a bit under his breath at how quickly the trucks were out of sight.

When the flagstones were stacked in several hefty rows, the sun was truly warm overhead, the breeze pushing that warmth around like a distractible child who didn't know exactly what game they were trying to play.

Jonah was glad to break for lunch, to wash up for lunch like everybody else was doing, though he might have overdone it, overzealous at the sink in the restroom, getting his shirt soaked down the front, water trickling along his breastbone because he was in too much of a hurry through the windy woods to get to the mess tent for lunch.

Once there, a hard glare at just about everyone cleared the way for him to be at Royce's side in the buffet line. Or rather behind him, close on his heels, where Jonah could soak in everything about him.

Royce had also washed up and had changed into a clean pale blue snap button shirt, not crisp and new like the kind all the ex-cons wore, but something that looked like it was from his own personal closet. The collar lay soft against his neck, smooth along his shoulders, and his golden curls were long enough to brush against it. The way he'd folded up the sleeves gave him the air of a man who was just about to settle into a chair and read a good book.

Knowing Royce, learning to know Royce, Jonah figured that book would be about birds or bats or some interesting shit like that. Maybe he'd let Jonah watch him while he read, like some dumb schmuck who would wait forever, it seemed, for the tiniest crumb from a beggar's banquet.

Falling in love was for idiots, or at least so Jonah had always thought. But looking at Royce, talking to him, being with him, was making something squeeze at Jonah's insides, his heart, in ways that felt totally weird, but nice at the same time.

"Hey," he said, tugging on the soft sleeve of that blue shirt. "Hey?"

Royce turned to look over his shoulder, and instantly that sunshine smile was in place. And while he'd probably not meant that smile to be so flirty, or for the slight crinkles in the corners of his blue eyes to be so blindingly fetching, it was and they were, and for a moment, Jonah could barely catch his breath.

"What's for lunch?" he asked, grasping for something to say. Something tame that would give him a moment to make his heart slow down. "Looks like shrimp and rice."

"It's jambalaya," said Royce brightly. "It can be quite spicy, though I expect the cooks have toned it down some from what I had last winter in New Orleans."

Jonah blinked. He'd never been anywhere much, not really anywhere at all, outside the confines of Denver and the surrounding area. He'd never even been on a plane, which to a guy like Royce might seem backward, so he didn't quite want to admit it. Nor that Wyoming was the only other place he'd ever been and that had been to commit a crime.

"New Orleans," Jonah said, and then wracked his brain, looking

THE COWBOY AND THE HOODLUM

through everything he'd ever learned and unlearned about geography. "Louisiana, right?"

"That's right," said Royce, dipping his chin as he picked up his silverware and tray. "I needed a break during the winter, and the food there is amazing, so off I went. My family usually stays at the Place d'Armes, which luckily had a room available."

"The pla-de-what?" asked Jonah, scrambling to keep up as he peered over Royce's shoulder while he filled a bowl with jambalaya and placed it on his tray.

"It's French," said Royce, tossing the words oh-so-casually over his shoulder, like it wasn't the most amazing thing in the world that he could speak in a whole other language. "It means, I believe, a military parade ground, or the point where troops assemble." Then he laughed, and that smile was back, aimed only at Jonah. "Funny name for a hotel, right?"

"A little." Concentrating on filling his plate with whatever was at hand, Jonah grabbed his tray and followed Royce to one of the long tables like an obsessed pup.

"I think they meant it to celebrate the idea of a parade, which New Orleans is known for. Mardi Gras parades, funeral processions, that sort of thing."

"Mardi Gras." Jonah knew what that was, but only in passing. The more important thing was the realization that there was a brain under all that golden hair, followed by the question as to why Jonah was so turned on by it. He'd been impressed by Beck's brain on a regular basis, but this was on a whole 'nother level.

"I've never been during that time of year," said Royce, calmly eating his lunch. "Way too noisy for me."

Which was a good thing, in retrospect, because now Jonah wouldn't have to go either. But that begged the question, why, if Royce did go, would Jonah even assume he'd be invited along?

Was he latching on to imaginary future plans now? Dreaming and aspiring to things that could never be, all because he liked to stare at a pretty face? A pretty fabulous face, all things considered, with a brain to match, and a sweet, smiling mouth, and hips inside of crisp blue jeans that seemed to call out to Jonah every other minute, saying *Grab me, grab me!*

Things were so wild up in his brain and in his crotch that he shifted in his seat and made himself pay attention to his lunch, just to get the ideas in his head to back the fuck off. At least for now. Not forever, right? Eventually he'd be able to figure this out, rather than being led by insistent desires that did not seem to want to be called to heel.

It was after lunch that the day darkened all around him as Royce casually mentioned that the mess tent was going to be set up for a Saturday group counseling session, and that he'd love it if everybody on his team attended.

"It's not mandatory," Royce assured them as he gestured for Gordy, Duane, Tyson, and Jonah to wait with him on the platform in front of the mess tent, inside of which Blaze and Wayne were pushing back tables and setting up chairs.

The session might not be mandatory, but Jonah could see in those China-blue eyes that Royce would like it if they all went. That, in fact, he'd be disappointed in them if they didn't.

"Counseling is for schmucks," said Jonah, trying it on for size anyway, giving Royce his best I-don't-care shrug as the others walked away, perhaps to gird their loins for the coming stupidity. "I never went in prison," he added, which was a lie, so he flung another lie on top of that. "Nobody I knew did." Nelson had a time or two because usually they served sugar cookies.

"Sometimes, I think it's important to try new things," said Royce. He patted Jonah on the arm, those warm fingers lingering. "If you go, I'll have a special treat for you this afternoon."

"Just me?" Jonah knew he was glowering, brows lowered, but he couldn't help it. It was not a trick, not if it was coming from Royce, but it meant that Royce really wanted him to go and was prepared to reward him for it.

Just spending any time alone with Royce was reward enough, but if a treat was added—and what treat? What did Royce consider a

THE COWBOY AND THE HOODLUM

treat?—then Jonah knew he had just signed himself up for an hour of utter boredom and stupidity.

"All right," he said, then shrugged again. "I guess. Whatever."

"I'll meet you at your tent after, okay?"

"Okay."

Royce's smile was blinding, soaking all through every part of Jonah, and it was on this floating cloud of goodness that he managed to make himself show up at the appointed time on Saturday afternoon, stuck in a stuffy tent along with a group of ex-cons all glowering at the counselor who made them sit in a stupid circle so they could all stare at each other.

The counselor was a reedy looking guy with fancy glasses, going by the name of Brett or Buster or some shit.

Jonah didn't really care. They'd had counseling sessions in Wyoming Correctional offered on a regular basis, but only losers went to those. Or ex-cons who just wanted a chance to sit for fifty-two minutes without any chance of getting shivved or smacked around by another ex-con. There was always a guard at the door at those things.

Jonah *had* gone once or twice, just for shits and grins, but after sitting in a room, feeling the anger and the sadness and the grief and despair rise all around them like an impending bomb about to go off, he never wanted to go back. Too much sniveling. Too much sharing and caring, or pretending to care.

This particular counseling session was turning out much the same, and if he'd had a watch, he'd be able to tell how many terrible, wrenching minutes he had left to suffer through it all. His only consolation, a prize that felt extremely out of reach at the moment, was that he'd get to go back to work in the bright sunshine once more.

And wasn't that a laugh. That his biggest reward, the thing he was hoping for, counting down the seconds for, was to get blisters on his hands and horseshit on his bright yellow boots, because the reward for doing *that* was a smile from Royce. Surely worth everything he was currently going through.

More importantly, he had a treat coming, though the image of him begging for it like a dog, which he would do, if he had to, made him laugh wryly under his breath, which, unfortunately, brought the attention of Buster or Bob or whoever the fuck he was.

"Is there something you'd like to share with the group, Jonah?" asked Brett/Buster/Bart.

Having had this question, or one like it, asked of him over the years from teachers in school, Jonah knew the exact right and properly breezy response.

"Just happy to be here," he said, shrugging as if overwhelmed with happiness and delight at his current situation. "Just hope I can help the ball club."

The little movie joke went over most of the guys' heads, and it went over the counselor's head, too. The only guy who chuffed a laugh was Blaze, his hippie hair slipping over his eyes as he tried to stifle the sound. But it came out like a bark drawing the counselor's attention to him, so hurray for the art of stealth pay-attention-to-somebody-else!

Eventually, after a miserable fifty-two minutes, thankfully, blissfully, Brett/Buster/Bart let them go, attempting to give each and every one of them his business card. Jonah took one because the counselor, with his library-pale skin, had eyes that simply begged for one of them to let him help them, and wasn't that the most pathetic thing ever.

He stuffed the card in his pocket and slouched away along the path to his tent, where he intended to catch his fucking breath and wait for Royce.

Should he change? Or should he just pretend he didn't care? Of course he cared.

That answered the second question, but the first question left him all twitter-pated like a numbskull, so he sat on his cot with a gasp and leaned back on his hands and stared up at the ceiling of his green tent and took a deep breath while the warmth and stillness, the slight glow of yellow sun beyond the green, soaked into him.

CHAPTER 13
ROYCE

Satisfied that Jonah had opened himself up to something new, something as useful as *counseling* could be, Royce stepped off the platform of the mess tent and nearly into Gabe's arms. Which was a much more pleasant encounter than Royce could have imagined, at least since he'd met Jonah.

Before he'd met Jonah, he'd looked at men, but in an abstract way, in an attempt to determine whether that man was aesthetically pleasing to him or not. Not that he'd ever discussed this with his ex-wife, not that the idea of it had ever floated to the top of the pile of thoughts in his head.

Only now, as his face got smooshed into the curve of Gabe's neck, Gabe's arms coming around him as he inhaled Gabe's scent, it was different. As he pulled himself back, steadying himself on his feet, it was easily and perfectly clear that Gabe smelled amazing. His muttered apology was endearing—

Thus, the idea that Royce liked men as much as, perhaps even more than, women, could now be firmly entrenched. Now Royce knew.

As to what to do with it all, this new awareness as it tumbled with the spark of desire—not for Gabe, but for men, a man, a man like Jonah—the prospect of possibilities was almost blinding.

"Sorry about that," said Royce. "I had my mind on other things."

"Not a problem," said Gabe, in his typically polite if slightly grave way. "I was going to bring up a suggestion. Now's as good a time as any. I think you and I and whatever team leads we get through the summer should have a team meeting. Like, on Saturdays, when the group counseling session is going on."

"Now?" asked Royce, his voice rising in a way that punctured through the peace of the woods. He had plans to get Jonah's treat together. He had to scramble to rein his dismay in, mind racing, as he realized that Gabe's suggestion was a good one.

"Nothing formal, unless it needs to be," said Gabe, spreading his corded forearms as if he wanted to emphasize how very not-formal the meetings would be. "I figure we touch base, we reallocate manpower, we talk about issues, share solutions. That sort of thing." He laughed a bit, his expression lightening. "We never did that in the army. We just followed orders, but I always thought an informal chat might have helped things a bit."

"I agree," said Royce firmly, because he did agree. It wasn't Gabe's fault that his timing was terrible. "Shall we chat now, then?"

"Sure," said Gabe.

"I can make us coffee in my tent," Royce said. "As we acquire more team leads, we could scout out a different location, but for now, it's quiet, and it's out of the sun."

Royce led Gabe to his tent, which, though right next to Gabe's, was separated by trees and hidden, like a secret cave of green canvas. Certainly, when Gabe stepped inside, he gave a little gasp, as if surprised by the way Royce had set things up.

Gabe was terribly manly, so Royce prepared himself to be mocked for how soft the cot was as Gabe sat on it, due to the plush mattress pad, or the way the two shelves were full of things meant to increase Royce's comfort level at every single turn: the Keurig coffee maker, the array of different types of sunscreen, the squat jar of pomade, which was right out in plain sight.

THE COWBOY AND THE HOODLUM

But maybe he was remembering how Sandra sometimes viewed his need for creature comforts because Leland Tate didn't hire jerks in the first place, and Gabe most definitely wasn't a jerk. Leland certainly wouldn't have picked anyone other than the most perfect person to head up his new pet parolee program.

"Oh, my," said Gabe, his tanned fingers spreading on the pale green coverlet beneath his thighs. "This is nice. Just as comfortable as a house." He paused to smile up at Royce. "Except it's in a tent."

"My home away from home," said Royce, pleased at Gabe's reaction, squirreling away notes as to how he'd share his pleasure at Gabe's pleasure with Jonah later. "A little more breezy," he added as he started his electric kettle up, and arranged his cowboy mug and a single white china mug and his French press on the top of the shelf. "But I like it."

Cozily, over two cups of the finest Breakfast Blend, the little impromptu soon-to-be-a-permanent part of the weekly schedule moved apace. Gabe was a good leader, and so had a short, efficient list that he wanted to go over, stuff like his upcoming meeting with Leland, and how he'd pass along the information to Royce, unless Royce wanted to come along?

"Too many meetings for me, I'm afraid," said Royce, smiling over his coffee. "I'll trust you to convey our ideas to him."

Gabe's other talking points were about balancing work allocation, being more specific about who was tasked with horse care, feeding, and maintenance, etc. Royce nodded at each turn, paying attention as best he could, only his thoughts were on Jonah. On how his face had looked when he'd tried to shrug off the importance of the counseling sessions, how stupid he thought the whole idea of it was.

The counselor, Brendan, wasn't to blame for this preconceived notion. He was a very earnest young man, fresh out of the psychology master's program up at UNC in Greeley, filled with the desire to help, to develop his career, to be of use. *I think this is an exciting program Mr. Tate's got set up*, he'd said to Royce when he'd met him earlier that summer, at Leland's request. *I just want to help.*

Well, sitting in a circle with other ex-cons while sharing feelings might not be anyone's idea of fun, let alone Jonah's, but it would be good for him, even if he only went a few times. Then perhaps that dark, brow-lowered glower would be replaced by the calm, brown-eyed gaze and slow warm smile Royce was coming to adore.

Finally, with the meeting over, Royce bid Gabe farewell, and turned to the task of making iced coffee for Jonah, his reward for being willing to try new things. Only, was it so much of a reward for Jonah, who might not like iced coffee? Or was it only in Royce's mind that what he had planned would be something an ex-con would enjoy?

Quelling his doubts, he set about making that iced coffee, getting the Yeti mugs out, looking in the mirror at least three times before deciding ruthlessly that his hair had enough pomade and if he tried to add any more, he'd just be ruining everything.

He needed ice, so ran to the kitchen to get it.

He took another shower, so raced through that.

He changed his shirt, then changed it back again.

By the time the counseling session was over, the afternoon was warm, the wind a bit breezy, but not too much—as perfect an afternoon as if he'd ordered it—and he was ready. Sweaty, but ready.

As to what his hopes were for the result of so much effort, more of a pleasure than an effort, really, he didn't quite truly know. Only that he was more excited about having coffee in the sunshine with Jonah than he'd been in a long time.

Even the summer he'd gotten a painted horse named Posey for his twenty-first birthday, nine years before, could not compete. It was pretty much a perfect day, and the prospect of joy spun all around him as he stepped out of his tent with a Yeti mug in each hand, one pale green, one purple.

CHAPTER 14
JONAH

J onah had waited obediently at his tent until Royce showed up, looking a little flustered, but smiling just the same.

"It's time for your treat, as promised," said Royce, clomping onto the wooden platform.

"Okay," said Jonah as he got up.

Previously, he would have shrugged and made a face to show how much he didn't care. It was plain in his voice as he asked, "What's the treat?" that he very much *did* care.

"Follow me," said Royce, somewhat mysteriously.

It was a treat from Royce, after all, so Jonah followed Royce obediently along the path to the rows of flagstones sitting in the clearing. When Royce pointed, he sat down on the topmost flagstone on the little pile at the end and waved as Royce trotted off through the woods.

"I'll be right back, so just stay where you are."

Nodding to show Royce how obedient he could be, Jonah relaxed, slumping his back and kicking his heels against the stones lower in the pile. After a time, he took off his gloves and tucked them into his belt, the way he'd seen Gabe doing.

He doffed his hat and ran his hands through his hair, lifting his

JACKIE NORTH

chin to catch the small breeze coming from across the lake. Which, when he turned around, was a beautiful blue, stretching out for what seemed miles and miles, and just about the color of Royce's eyes.

Shifting on the stone, he wondered, if he'd not met Royce, whether he'd actually be appreciating this kind of view, the long slope of trees to the west, coming right down to the water, the reflection of a few puffy clouds in the mirror-like blue surface. Or even, come to that, whether he would have stuck around long enough to know there was a lake there so close by.

More than likely, he would have *borrowed* the first vehicle he'd clapped eyes on and hauled ass down the highway, homebound for Denver. Home to the garage, to the apartment over the garage, and to Beck, who would have been impatiently waiting for him to return.

It was warm beneath the sunlight, though he was cooler without the hat and gloves, so he rolled up his shirtsleeves and slouched back, resting his weight on his hands. Just chilling. Just hanging out. Neither of which he remembered doing very often. But he was doing it now, doing a lot of things that he'd never done before, and all because of Royce.

"Oh, this is lovely, this is perfect."

Turning his head, Jonah spotted Royce coming through the pine trees, carrying two somethings in his hands that Jonah couldn't identify, even if he squinted. Which he did, until Royce came close enough to show him that what he was carrying were two thermoses of some kind, one pale green and one dark purple.

"What you got there?" asked Jonah as Royce came around to the other side of the pile of flagstones and plopped the thermoses next to Jonah's hip. Both thermoses said *Yeti* on them in silver letters.

"Your treat," said Royce as he plopped himself down on the pile of flagstones, easily within hand's reach of Jonah. "But first you must take off your boots and socks."

"My what now?"

"Do as you're told," said Royce, pertly, sitting up straight like a teacher about to give Jonah a good scolding.

"All right, yes, okay."

THE COWBOY AND THE HOODLUM

With a huff of a laugh, Jonah undid the sturdy laces and pulled off his boots and socks, stuffing the socks inside, while Royce did the same.

Royce had the whitest feet Jonah had ever seen, perfectly smooth, with the pinkest undersides to his toes. In comparison, Jonah's feet were scruffy and dull looking, with hair on his big toes.

"Put your feet there," said Royce, pointing to an outcrop of flagstone. "On the rock, and let the sun warm them. And take this."

Jonah took the purple thermos, turning it around in his hands as he figured out how to open it without exploding the contents everywhere. Then Royce showed him how to push the little black thingy back.

"Like this. Now, take a sip."

Taking a sip, being absolutely good and obedient, was like stepping into a ray of gold when he received Royce's smile. Then he tasted the contents, iced coffee, perfectly sweet and strong, sliding down his throat, a pure, cool blessing. Added to that, the warmth on the bottom of his feet from the sun warmed flagstone, he shivered with pleasure and knew that Royce was the best thing that ever happened to him.

"Good, eh?" asked Royce, eyebrows raised, an anticipatory smile playing around his mouth. "I love the contrast of warmth and cool. It's amazing. Makes everything taste better, feel better."

"This is great." Of course, Jonah wanted to say more than that, wanted to rave at how good it was, but he'd been so casual for so long, so dismissive, so bored, that it was hard to express the way he felt. So he tried again, leaning close to where he could almost touch Royce's forehead with his own. "This is perfect. Just perfect."

"I thought you'd like it," said Royce, and then Jonah interrupted him with a tiny kiss that allowed him to taste the sweet, cold coffee on Royce's lips.

"How'd you like that, then?" asked Jonah, pulling back, tilting his head back, an arch to his neck, a thrill coursing through him that he'd finally, finally done what he'd been wanting to do for days.

Seeing that Royce was smiling, blushing hot pink along his cheeks, made him want to give himself an award for being so brave. And one to Royce as well, for being so clever and amazing and fascinating pretty much all the time. For changing Jonah's world so hard and so completely from the way it had been that he knew it would be almost impossible for him to return to it.

Not that he minded. Not when he had this view, this coffee, and this beautiful man sitting next to him on a perfect blue-sky sunny day.

"I liked it," said Royce, simply, taking another swig of coffee as he focused his view on the lake. "I like being here with you."

He scooted closer on the warm flagstone, and Jonah scooted closer, too, until they were hip to hip and could drink their coffee nearly in tandem while they soaked up the sun's rays and drank in the view and just sat. Together. In the brightness of the day.

CHAPTER 15
JONAH

Still pleasantly reeling from the simple pleasure of iced coffee, sun warmed flagstone, and a sweet kiss, Jonah woke up on Sunday morning, knowing he needed to send Beck directions to the valley.

After breakfast, Royce had asked Jonah to go on a hike with him to see falcons on the ridge. It had almost killed Jonah to say no, but he was spending time with Beck that day.

Then, not wanting to bother Royce about borrowing his cellphone, Jonah had done his best by giving Beck verbal directions on the landline, and Beck was smart enough to figure it out from there. Nevertheless, he found himself waiting for a good ten minutes in the parking lot, too excited to pretend he wasn't glad to see Beck while outside of prison walls for the first time in two years.

Beck visiting him in prison had been an unhappy Beck, and the prison lighting, an odd mix of nasty green and yellow, had made him look cadaverous and halfway to being sick. Now, at last, he'd be able to be with Beck without the taint of prison walls, lighting, sounds, and smells.

Beck lived an indoor life and liked his creature comforts and his black leather jacket. He was also scrupulously punctual and honest about the accounts when he'd brought them to show to Jonah.

Jonah knew Beck had been waiting for Jonah's return to work at Good Deal Auto Repair, and the return of their working relationship, and how they were in the apartment over the garage.

They might not fit together exactly the same way anymore, because not only had it been two years that they'd been apart, now there was Royce in the picture. As to how Jonah was supposed to explain Royce to Beck and vice versa, Jonah didn't know, but perhaps the best thing was just to let them figure it out for themselves.

Over the tops of the pine trees swaying in the low breeze, Jonah heard the rumble of Beck's car, a beautiful Pontiac 1968 GTO, the engine rebuilt from a stolen V-8 engine, the paint job, a glossy olive green copied from a picture in a *MotorTrend* article.

Beck had spent all of his spare time on that car, and drove it with pride, and now he was coming down the dirt road, a sparkle of chrome amidst the trunks of trees. Finally there was an explosion of silver and green as Beck drove into the parking lot, hand hanging out of the open window on the driver's side, his dark hair a mess from the open-window driving all the way here from wherever.

His wave, as he got out of the car, sent a shard of tenderness through Jonah's chest. Beck was a good friend, and he'd been true to Jonah the whole time, not giving the cops any information they didn't already have, and taking care of the shop when Jonah couldn't. Visiting Jonah in prison month after month, typically twice a month, putting money in Jonah's commissary account any time he could.

How was Jonah supposed to repay him for that?

"Jonah," said Beck, half growling, half laughing, throwing his arms around Jonah with abandon, hugging him tight, almost too tight for Jonah to breathe.

Jonah hugged him and pounded his back, his gladness at seeing Beck mixing with a sudden inexplicable wish that Beck had left the visit for the next week, or the week after that, or maybe even never.

"Beck," said Jonah, in return, pushing away his misgivings to throw his arm around Beck's shoulder, waving at the parking lot, and the

THE COWBOY AND THE HOODLUM

mess tent and all the trees. "Let me show you around and then we can have lunch."

"Lunch?" Beck froze, gripping onto Jonah's arm just a bit too tightly. "I thought you were just saying that in case someone was listening. I thought you'd be packed and then we'd drive out of this hellhole, just you and me."

"Fuck that," said Jonah with a shrug, stepping into his old pre-prison irritation. "There's no reason to leave—"

"But there aren't any fences," said Beck, astonished, flinging his arm out to show Jonah the exact nature of his free passage out of the valley. "Not for miles. I checked. Sure, there's a gate, but it's not even locked."

"If I can leave at any time," said Jonah, being extra patient to show Beck what an idiot he was. "Then I can stay however long I want. Besides, I've got a comfortable place to sleep, the grub's good, and I don't have to work very hard, so there's almost no point in going."

"So what are those blisters?"

Beck pointed at Jonah's hands, and for the first time Jonah could remember, he didn't have a retort handy

When he looked down, he could see that there was a line of blisters along the inside of each thumb. The blisters were quite small and on their way to becoming callouses, but trust Beck to notice the smallest detail about Jonah.

"Pay more attention to your own fucking hands," said Jonah, shoving off Beck's grip. "I've been building shelters and moving flagstone around, just because they asked me to, and I felt like doing it. So what?"

"So what?" Beck was just about geared up enough to show his teeth. "What about being able to calibrate an engine so it purrs like a cat? What about being able to match the paint on a Jag without anyone being able to spot it? That's the kind of work you should be doing, not this shit."

Beck didn't know the other half of the shit Jonah had been up to, part of which was laying down sand in the newly built paddock, or taking a rake to the near end of the pasture to clean up horse manure.

Beck also didn't know that Jonah had been *this* close to going on a hike to see falcons with a fussy-mannered, golden-haired angel and had turned it down for him, for Beck.

Opening his mouth to tell Beck exactly all of this, he saw Royce coming from the mess tent and snapped it shut. Beck would figure out soon enough what was between Royce and Jonah, for however annoying he might be, he most certainly was not stupid.

"That's my boss," said Jonah with a shrug to show Beck he didn't care that Royce was in charge of him because he would never bow to any man's will. "Royce Thackery. Owns horses up north or some shit."

"The boss man, eh?" said Beck as Royce came close enough to hear, not a question, but a sneer of words to show Royce exactly what he thought of him.

"Hello," said Royce, in that happy breezy way Jonah was coming to love, as if every day was the perfect day and he was just happy to be alive. "It's nice to meet you, Beck. I'm Royce."

"That's Beckett to you," said Beck with a snap.

Royce blinked, and however badly Jonah wanted to jump in and mend the fences that were already being torn down, he didn't let himself. Better that Royce and Beck did not like each other very much. Better that they not know each other at all, so Jonah could keep the two worlds apart for as long as possible.

"It's nice to meet you, Beckett," said Royce, holding out his hand for Beck to shake, and Beck did, though it was with half a jerk before snatching his hand away. "You're here for lunch, as I understand it?"

"Maybe more than that," said Beck, doing his best impression of being a man of mystery, though Royce couldn't possibly know this and just looked hurt that his overtures of friendship were being refused.

It stabbed at Jonah's heart to be even remotely involved with making Royce look like that, but other than punching Beck right then and there, the only thing to do was pretend it hadn't happened.

"Weren't you going on a hike to see birds?" asked Jonah, jerking up his chin to show just how much he wasn't interested in anything Royce was up to.

THE COWBOY AND THE HOODLUM

"I was," said Royce, his voice low, shadows appearing around his eyes in a strange way as he looked at Jonah. "But it's not safe to go up there alone and besides, I'm here to help you entertain your guest."

"Entertaining's the last thing I need," said Beck in his most utterly bored voice. "I'm just here to see Jonah."

Looking like he'd just been slapped, Royce blinked hard, several times, and a new expression slid over his face, one that made Jonah feel queasy in his belly because it looked like Beck had gotten to Royce and now Royce was retreating. And just what was it Jonah wanted? For Royce and Beck to fight over him?

Regardless, Royce was just about to turn on his heel, though he paused to say, "I hope you have a lovely time and I'll see you at lunch."

"Good riddance," said Beck, not at all under his breath, though he made an *oof* sound when Jonah shoved an elbow into his ribs. "What's your problem?"

"Don't be a dick," said Jonah, giving Beck his hardest, darkest scowl. "I've got it easy here and I don't want you screwing it up."

"Fine."

But Beck was not fine, for he seemed to be simmering under the surface of his skin the whole time Jonah was showing him around. He wasn't impressed by the fancy shower heads, nor the seemingly rustic looking but very posh toilets. He wasn't impressed by Jonah's tent, either, even though it was the lap of luxury compared to Jonah's prison cell. Though, to be fair, Beck had never seen that.

"Who do you share with?" asked Beck, looking at the other cot, his arms crossed over his chest.

"Gordy," said Jonah, giving Gordy's clothes on the floor a good kick just to show Beck how little he cared for his tent mate, though he was growing rather fond of Gordy, simply because Gordy had balls and said exactly what he thought without pussy footing around.

"Did you know him in prison?" asked Beck. "And that's why you're sharing a tent?"

"No," said Jonah. "Saw him across the yard once or twice, but never met him. Anyway, that's the tent. Let's go have lunch."

Introducing everybody to Beck in the mess tent went a bit easier,

JACKIE NORTH

perhaps because the hardest introduction was over, and Jonah didn't care who else Beck knew. Besides, the cooks had outdone themselves, serving up steak and baked potatoes, saying that they'd be starting up the buffet system for good come Monday. Not that Jonah cared about that, he didn't care where his food came from, only that it was good.

"Nice to meet you," said Gordy with a flirty bit of a smile, digging into his lunch.

"Likewise," said Beck, as if he didn't give a rat's fart in a high wind, though at the same time, his gaze lingered on Gordy, and why wouldn't it. Gordy had big eyes, and a cute mouth, and might have been Beck's type, except for his focus on Jonah.

"You guys going up on the ridge with Royce this afternoon?" asked Gabe, as though wise to the tension Beck had brought with him, doing his best to create conversation.

"I wouldn't hike up there if you paid me," said Beck without any consideration at all. "Besides, aren't there mountain lions or bears up there?"

Gabe laughed under his breath and shook his head, and then turned his conversation to Blaze, like he didn't give a fuck who Beck was and wasn't going to play games with him. Which took Jonah's respect for him up another notch.

Then there was Royce at the far end of the table, eating his meal without any pleasure at all, and it was then that Jonah decided to get Beck as far away from Royce as possible.

"Let's go look at the horses after lunch," said Jonah, putting a tone in his voice so Beck would know it wasn't up for discussion. "Take in a view of the lake."

"Fuck the lake," said Beck, casually, because what did he care and, of course, he didn't see the raised eyebrows of every man there.

It was then Jonah realized that he'd not heard a single swear word all week, except for the ones in his own head, though, only a little while ago, he'd said *shit* to Royce, just to show Beck how much he didn't care about Royce. Had it worked? He had no idea.

"We're going to the lake," said Jonah, putting all of his sternness

THE COWBOY AND THE HOODLUM

into each word. "You'll like it. It's pretty," he added, even though he knew well and good that Beck did not care about nature at all.

Neither did Jonah, that was, he didn't use to, until he came here and Royce started pointing out things to him like goldfinches and bats. Maybe Beck would be changed by his visit, or maybe he wouldn't.

"C'mon," said Jonah, getting up from the table, scrubbing his mouth with his fingers. "Let's go."

Leading the way through woods, following the main path, Jonah wondered at Beck's silence, that was until Beck tripped over something in the tall grasses, and landed on Jonah like a hard, slamming punch.

"All these fucking trees," grunted Beck, his scowl telling Jonah everything he wasn't saying—That he hated the valley, that he hated the woods, and that he'd just about reached his last nerve as far as this visit was concerned.

The next thing Beck was going to say would be about going back to Jonah's tent to pack up his things so they could get the hell out of there, and in all honesty Jonah should just leave. Right? He could do his parole another way, so why was he staying?

Looking over Beck's shoulder, Jonah saw a flash of blonde hair, heard the faint edge of happy laughter, and knew the reason why he was staying. Only he couldn't let on to Beck, or he'd never hear the end of it.

"Easy, Beck," said Jonah, giving Beck's shoulders a brief pet as he waited for Beck to steady himself.

"Show me the lake and let's get this over with," said Beck with a growl.

"Once you see it, you'll understand."

The lake hove into view once they went down the little slope from the new, unpainted picnic tables. But rather than being smooth as glass, reflecting the tree-covered foothills and the ridge to the west, the surface was frothy, speckled with white in the building breeze from the mountains. The colors of the water—dark blue, deep green

—made the water look haunted, as if it had sunken stories to tell, and shapeless ghosts to tell them, just below the surface.

Royce would know why the water looked like that. And, and if Jonah were to tell him about the ghosts, he was sure Royce would be right there with him, drawn into the fanciful, stray thoughts Jonah wanted to share with him. He certainly couldn't share them with Beck, who was scowling hard at the lake as if it had personally offended him somehow.

"What do you think?" Jonah gestured to where the far end of the lake disappeared behind a curve of trees standing tall on a jut of land.

"It looks freezing," was all Beck had to say. "Is that snow on the mountains?"

Jonah looked up.

"Just a bit of rain, I think," he said. Royce would know why the weather looked so changeable, and Jonah planned to ask him just as soon as he saw him next.

Beck didn't seem to care about the small herd of horses, some assembled beneath the shelters, others spread among the grasses, their heads down as they grazed, looking all picturesque, their tails swept by the wind.

Nor did Beck care about the neat pile of flagstones or the lovely path that Royce and his team had made of them all the way up to the marsh. But Jonah made him walk the path anyway, up to the point where they'd stopped working, on account of the water from Horse Creek crossed the path where it drained into the lake.

"You ruined your hands doing *this*?"

Pointing at the path with a jerk of his chin, Beck seemed focused on the way the path suddenly ended at the marsh, as if wondering why they'd not just shoved on through.

Which was like Beck to not understand the needs of what Royce had called riparian intricacies. Nor would he have cared had Jonah known enough to explain it to him, because, to Beck, if it didn't have to do with cars, the shop, or Jonah, he simply wasn't interested. Which was so boring. Why did Beck have to be so boring?

"I didn't ruin them, Beck," said Jonah, scrubbing his hands

THE COWBOY AND THE HOODLUM

together, a sudden worry spiking through him at the thought of not being able to work on cars because he had a few blisters. Maybe Beck was just fucking with him. Or maybe Beck wanted Jonah to only work on cars and not mess around with any other kind of manual labor. "Anyway, that's been my week so far."

"It all looks like a waste of time to me," was all Beck had to say as they trudged back to Jonah's tent.

There, Gordy was lounging on his cot, flipping through what looked like a book about stars that Jonah was sure he'd seen on Royce's bookshelf, and what the hell was Gordy doing with one of Royce's books? Jonah was about to go off, when Gordy showed them the book, and kind of shimmied on the bed.

"Look who's getting educated," he said, as if delighted with himself. "The boss loaned it to me."

"What would you need to know about stars for?" asked Beck, teeth bared, as if he'd meant to smile to soften the words, only he'd forgotten how to smile.

"Oh, for fuck's sake, Beck." Jonah was ready to come to Gordy's defense. Only Gordy, true to his own self, winked at Beck as if he didn't care what Beck thought of him.

Beck blinked hard, as if he'd been struck. Which might have been an appropriate time to plant the seed that maybe Beck could look at fresher horizons, and that maybe he'd have to look no further than Gordy.

"I guess I'll get out of this shithole," said Beck. "If—and I mean if—I come back, do you want me to bring you anything?"

Jonah thought about all the things he might need or want, but couldn't think of a damn thing. Except for the boot knife, which the prison had failed to return to him.

"I need another boot knife," he said. "If you come across one," he added, knowing full well and good that Beck would scour the earth looking for just the right one, an exact copy of Jonah's old boot knife, if possible.

That was just how Beck was. He might bitch and moan and be an all around dickhead, but he was a good friend, and that was the truth of it.

"Can I come any other day than Sunday?" asked Beck as Jonah walked him back to his car. "Or is there some law against coming on a different day?"

"Just Sundays," said Jonah with a shrug.

With a hard hug and a slap to the back, they bid each other farewell in the parking lot, and Jonah breathed a sigh of relief as the glossy, olive green Pontiac wended its way back up the hill and out of sight.

As the last bit of chrome flashed amidst the tree trunks, he sprinted to the mess tent to see if Royce was there. He was not, and when he asked Wayne, who was on the landline, Wayne just shrugged and then muttered something about Royce taking the truck into town.

Great. So not only did he have to put up with Beck's disapproval, he'd missed out on a hike with Royce, and now Royce had gone somewhere without him. *Without* him. Making it a shitty day from start to finish.

CHAPTER 16

ROYCE

Royce came away from lunch, shaking his head, doing his best not to roll his eyes. Beck had rubbed him the wrong way, acting like an impudent teenager who had been told to keep it down in the library. His eyes had spit sparks at Royce, and that sneer had gone on for days. And for what? Because the valley was a peaceful place and Beck didn't know how to conduct himself?

There had to be a reason that Jonah was friends with Beck, had to be a reason that Beck had come all the way from Denver to visit his friend, only to act as though everything about the valley, from the green pine trees sweetly scenting the air, to the gray edge of Guipago Ridge, to the bowl of blue sky above, was an affront to his sensibilities.

More, he seemed to view Royce as some kind of opponent, giving Royce nothing but hard glares during their brief introduction by Jonah. Did Beck—*Beckett*—view Royce as his enemy, simply because they both valued Jonah's company?

It wasn't in Royce's makeup to belittle another man's choices in friends, but he might have to alter that opinion, having met Beck. At the very least, he knew that a man could be elevated by the company he kept around him, or lowered by the same. Beck had rough edges.

JACKIE NORTH

There was no doubt about that, but was it up to Royce to decide for Jonah who his friends were?

No. Royce would have to move on from that, and hope that once Beck left that he might never come back so Royce could have Jonah all to himself. In the meantime, he needed to occupy himself on a Sunday afternoon where he'd hoped, once upon a time, to have Jonah come with him to do a little bird watching.

That would have to wait also because Gordy, Duane and Tyson, the other ex-cons he was responsible for, were looking at him with hangdog expressions, hoping for a treat, or at the very least, some direction.

"So, gentlemen," he asked them, putting on a smile that he hoped, quite soon, would start to feel more real. "What are your plans for today?"

"Plans?" they asked, just about in unison.

"Yes, plans," Royce said. "You have the whole day off to rest and relax, catch up on your reading."

Duane shrugged, and perhaps he was the bolder of the two, for he said, "We got nothing."

"I see." Royce thought a minute, and did not look around him to see if he could catch a glimpse of Jonah. "Well, I'm headed into Cheyenne to pick up a few things. You could come with me if you want."

"Sure," said Duane, and Tyson nodded his agreement.

They were both more excited by the prospect, it seemed, than Royce would have thought. But then again, they'd been stuck behind prison walls for years, and perhaps missed the simple pleasures of an afternoon doing errands.

He didn't need to tell them he'd broken the flask himself while puttering in his tent in an exorbitant effort to distract himself from the fact that not only would he not get to spend his Sunday on a hike with Jonah, Jonah was busy with someone else.

Nor did he need to tell them how hard it was not to stomp and pout and complain about it all, because it wouldn't make any difference to Gordy, Duane, or Tyson. Nor would it make any difference

THE COWBOY AND THE HOODLUM

to how his whole Sunday was turning out. Which was a giant disaster.

He didn't tell them because they wouldn't care and it didn't matter because Jonah deserved to spend time with his friend Beck. Also, they didn't really need, nor probably cared, about Royce's opinion of Beck, not to mention his even larger, somewhat darker opinion of Jonah's relationship *with* Beck.

"Let's go then," said Royce, checking for his wallet. Five minutes later, without sight or sound of Jonah to be found anywhere, they were in the truck, and headed along the foothills along Highway 121.

There were clouds building up above the ridge, puffy rolls of blue-edged white cotton that looked like they wanted to become a storm, only they weren't quite sure how.

"Shall we stop at Wal-Mart on the way back, guys?" asked Royce.

"Sure," they all said, Duane from the passenger seat, and Gordy and Tyson from the back, gripping Duane's headrest as they both peered out from between the seats.

"Sure," they both said again, though they seemed so excited about the outing, he probably could have suggested they take the truck through the nearest carwash and they would have been equally enthused.

According to Royce's web search, the Forge Cafe was a little place just inside the local mall at the northeast edge of Cheyenne. It had a great selection of loose, freshly ground coffee, and a variety of things to make coffee with, including spare glass beakers for French presses.

He made his selection quickly, including two bags of coarsely ground coffee, Vienna Roast and Breakfast Blend, hurrying through paying because his team were getting antsy, even with paper cups of some very fine vanilla lattes in their hands.

They seemed happier at Wal-Mart, snickering and shoving each other like a couple of kids at recess while looking at men's briefs until Royce had to shush them and promise them a candy bar at checkout if they were good.

They were, and Royce made a mental note to tell Gabe that he was needlessly being overly cautious about not ever turning his back on an ex-con because, as far as Royce could see, ex-cons just wanted an opportunity at a taste of how good life could be and, once they had it, they would never go back to lives of crime.

"Can we get McDonalds?" asked Duane as they piled back in the truck, proving Royce's opinion once more.

"It'll rot your guts," said Royce, wanting to say no, but already scanning both sides of the street for golden arches. He pulled through the drive-through rather than going in, because he couldn't stand the stench of fast-food, though in the truck, with the windows down it wasn't so bad as Duane and Royce plowed through their Big Macs and French fries, and Gordy nibbled on his McChicken nuggets.

"Take your trash," he told them as he parked along the dirt road behind the kitchen, then he followed them, his new flask and bags of ground coffee tucked under his arm.

It started to rain, faint drops at first, but he'd been ignoring the clouds forming above the ridge this whole time because he wanted to, quite simply, find Jonah. When he did, he'd ask how his visit with Beck was and he'd do his best not to act like a jealous fool.

It was full on raining by the time he got to his tent, the patter of raindrops on canvas lulling him as he unpacked his flask and plugged in his kettle, puttering about, assembling the French press, pouring the ground coffee into two small metal containers with airtight lids. Then he sat on his cot and listened to the rain until the kettle boiled. He made himself some coffee, curled his hands around his cowboy mug and told himself he was happier than he was.

It was only a little while till dinner, though he wasn't hungry, his stomach still sour from the smell of McDonald's all the way back from Cheyenne. And, to be fair, while he was petulant about missing his hike with Jonah, he shouldn't be so upset, should he?

It was only one afternoon, after all, and there were plenty of Sundays left in the summer and surely Beck wouldn't come visit Jonah on each and every one of them? Still, Jonah and Beck seemed rather close, so it was a possibility, which sent him further down a spiral of dejection, indicating a need for more coffee, this time with extra sugar, and maybe one of those chocolate-covered cookies he

THE COWBOY AND THE HOODLUM

had stored away. There was plenty of water in the kettle, after all, so why not.

The kettle, halfway through boiling, was making a pleasant rumbling sound in harmony with the rain on the canvas, when Royce, alerted by a sudden, sharp movement, looked up to see Jonah standing on the platform of the tent as he looked at Royce but didn't come any closer.

He'd been in the rain for some time, by the looks of it, his dark hair plastered to his head, his chin ducked to his chest like a dog who has rolled in the mud after being freshly bathed and knows it has been bad but just wanted to come inside where it was warm so he could dry off.

As to why Jonah looked that way, Royce couldn't fathom, as his visit with Beck looked like it had been going very well at lunchtime. But Royce got up and lifted the tent flap all the way, so Jonah would know he was welcome.

As Jonah marched in rather wetly, wearing his old black t-shirt and those horrible, flat-heeled black boots, Royce didn't say anything, but reached for a towel, freshly laundered and folded, from the bottom shelf.

"Here," he said. "Dry off as best you can. I'm making coffee. Would you care for some?"

Royce laid a towel on the cot so Jonah could sit down. When he didn't, Royce placed a hand on each of Jonah's damp shoulders and gently eased him down.

Jonah obliged him, looking up at Royce with the biggest, saddest brown eyes, all round and worried to the point where Royce hardly knew what to think. Only that it felt natural to take the towel from Jonah, and finish drying Jonah's hair, though more gently than Jonah had been doing it, less scrubbing and more petting.

"Take that shirt off," said Royce, deciding at that moment that it was too chilly to sit around as Jonah was, as if determined to dry his clothes with the warmth of his body. "And those jeans. Honestly, you act like you need a governess."

He handed Jonah a gray sweatshirt, and a pair of blue jeans that might fit, and turned his back on Jonah, fiddling with the coffee so Jonah could have his privacy while changing clothes.

By the time he turned back around, a mug of coffee in each hand, Jonah was dressed in Royce's clothes, and if the clothes, the sweatshirt gaping a bit from Jonah's neck, the blue jeans tight across his hips, made him look a little vulnerable and sweet, well, Royce wasn't going to complain.

Best of all, Jonah was now barefoot, having doffed the black boots and horrible black socks, and had one foot resting on top of the other, as if he was trying to warm them. His dark hair, now on the way to being dry, was standing up in waves around his forehead, and rude, pert curls behind his ears.

"Here." Royce handed Jonah a cup of coffee, doctored the way he'd seen Jonah do it at breakfast, with plenty of sugar and a healthy dollop of milk. "That'll warm you from the inside, at least. Would you like to borrow a pair of socks?"

"No, I'm good." Jonah took a drink from his white china mug and sighed. "I never go barefoot," he said, shaking his head with a little laugh. His cheeks flushed as the coffee warmed him up. "Because of the shop, you know. You can't walk around without your boots on or you'll find a metal spike coming up through your foot."

He laughed again, though Royce couldn't understand why the idea of having your foot punctured was in any way funny.

"So you've never waded in a creek in the summertime, or watched dust puff up between your toes?"

Opening the box of cookies, Royce held it out to Jonah, and was gratified to see that Jonah took two cookies and then had to wait while Jonah crunched happily through the first one before taking another sip of his coffee.

"Or even padded around barefoot while indoors?"

"No, never." Jonah shook his head, then devoured the other cookie in two huge bites.

"Well, now is your chance," said Royce. "Remember the sun on the flagstones when we were sitting there? You were barefoot then."

"Yeah." Jonah buried his nose in his coffee mug as if to hide the flush on his cheeks and the sparkle of memory in his eyes. Which, at the very least, had taken away that earlier mournful light in them. "Not something I ever thought I'd be doing."

"I believe it's good to feel the earth beneath your feet every once in a while," said Royce. "You know? Your body draws energy from the earth, which only makes sense, because the earth is like a giant battery."

"A giant *what* now?" asked Jonah, his eyebrows going up. "You mean like a car battery?"

"Sort of," said Royce, smiling as he scanned his little bookshelf.

He didn't have a book on the chemistry of the earth, so he explained about heavy elements and light elements, and how electrons hopped from one to the other, creating a kind of electricity, keeping it simple because he didn't want the light, newly lit, in Jonah's dark brown eyes to fade because of boredom.

But they never did. Instead, they sparkled with interest and Jonah was still asking questions when the dinner bell rang. So after Jonah slid on his wet boots, they trudged through the damp grasses and the drops of rain from the overhead pine needles.

Soothed by their little bit of time together, Royce was tempted, when they got to the mess tent, to keep talking about the earth as a battery, he knew none of the others were like Jonah and would have little patience for Royce's natterings, so he didn't. Instead, he talked about the fact that the painting of the shelters and the picnic tables would have to wait until Monday afternoon, if then, because all that wood would need a chance to dry off a little.

"It shouldn't rain for much longer tonight," he said, digging into his bowl of beef stew. "At least I hope it won't."

"We'll get that shipment of paint tomorrow, at least," said Gabe. "And once the wood is dry enough, we can make a painting party of it. Doing it together, your team and mine."

Royce nodded, because that made the most sense, and was very much the way Gabe thought. There was a brain under all that dark hair, but just as he was thinking it, he saw that Jonah was looking at him, eyebrows lowered in a glower, so he quickly turned his attention away from Gabe and back to Jonah, because the last thing he wanted Jonah to think was that he had a thing for Gabe.

After dinner, he stepped quite slowly off the platform just to make sure Jonah could keep up, then tugged on the sleeve of the borrowed sweatshirt.

"You should come back to my tent," he said. "Your things won't be dry, but you could toss them in the dryer."

What he meant to say was for Jonah to come back to his tent and that he didn't give a damn how wet and dripping Jonah was. He just wanted to be with Jonah, a surge of want and hope growing in his chest as Jonah tugged Royce's sleeve right back, sticking close at Royce's heels all the way to Royce's tent.

"I have some brilliant lavender tea," he said, reaching for the kettle, then he paused.

Maybe Jonah would want to take his stuff and go back to his own tent so he could wear his own clothes. After all, all Royce had to offer was hot tea made from flower buds and all the thoughts in his head. Surely nothing to tempt Jonah, who'd just spent the better part of the day with his oldest friend.

"I remember," said Jonah, standing so close to Royce that Royce just about tripped over him. Only Jonah's arms came up around Royce's waist and held onto him until Royce had steadied himself. "But maybe the tea can wait."

The tea could wait. It could wait forever, if Jonah's kiss on Royce's ear, his cheek, his mouth, was an indication of things to come. Up close, holding Royce to him, Jonah proved just how warm he was, even on such a damp evening, the tent flap open, showing the slow fog misting among the tree trunks.

The calls of birds flying, bats lunging for insects midair, the soft clatter of the upper branches as the trees swayed in the slight wind— all of this was a gentle music in Royce's ears as he kissed Jonah back, and hooked his fingers through the belt loops of Jonah's borrowed blue jeans.

"I'm going to zip that," said Jonah, the words soft along Royce's neck where Jonah was kissing him, and that was fine with Royce. He

THE COWBOY AND THE HOODLUM

never liked an audience and anyway, the tent would be warmer when shut. Quieter, the evening coming down like a soft song, the scent of rain all around, as his hands let Jonah go to close the tent against the night.

When Jonah came back, his arms went around Royce's waist again, the muscled length of Jonah hard against him, the warmth of his body soaking into Royce as all of Royce's thoughts and his concerns of the day, questions about Beck and his friendship with Jonah, simply evaporated like mist in full sunshine.

"Take those boots off," said Royce, trying for his best stern voice. "Let me warm your feet for you."

Breathtakingly obedient, Jonah let Royce go and landed on the cot even as his hands reached for first his left boot and then his right. He wore no socks, as those were still hanging on the end of the cot. Which meant that as Royce sat down on the cot as well and reached for Jonah's foot, he found it was ice cold in his hands.

"Scoot," he said. "Sit all the way on the bed and lean back on the pillows."

Jonah again did as he was told, which meant that Royce could take one of Jonah's feet to tuck it beneath his thigh, and hold the other one on his lap. Watching Jonah's face, he pulled his shirt out of his jeans, and tucked Jonah's foot against his belly.

"No, don't."

"Yes," said Royce, extra stern as he held onto Jonah's ankle and kept his foot right where it was. "Mind me, now."

"Yes, Royce," said Jonah, his chin tucking to his chest so he was looking up at Royce through his flirty dark eyelashes.

He held the sole of Jonah's foot against his belly, and rubbed Jonah's silky ankles, tweaked the few strands of hair on the top of Jonah's big toe, making Jonah smile. Perhaps nobody had ever fondled Jonah's feet before or paid attention to him like Royce was, stroking and petting, lifting Jonah's foot to cup his hands around it, drawing it to his mouth so he could blow warm air along it.

Jonah's foot quickly warmed, and when it did, Royce changed it out for the other one. When that one was warm, he put Jonah's foot down, both feet now cradled in his lap as Jonah eyed him through dark, shy lashes.

"Everything all right?" Royce asked, his voice low, his fingers curled around the outsides of Jonah's bare feet.

"I should go," said Jonah, and this response, completely unexpected, lanced through Royce with a shock.

"But why?"

He didn't want to let go of Jonah's feet any more than he wanted Jonah to disappear into the growing darkness. But Jonah was already sitting up, slipping on his boots, still sockless and, grabbing his damp socks and clothes, did exactly that, unzipping the tent flap and slipping through the space like a magician doing his best conjuring trick.

Royce could hear footsteps crunching away through the wet grasses. Then, when that faded, was left with only the patter of raindrops falling from pine needles. That, and his own excited breath, struggling to slow down.

CHAPTER 17
JONAH

Monday felt like a clusterfuck, for all kinds of reasons. The most important of which was the fact that Jonah felt the weight of realizing that leaving Royce's tent—leaving Royce—had been due to his own fear. Fear of getting too close, too fast. Fear of the intensity between them. Simple cowardly fear.

But what could he do about that? Man up and talk to Royce, of course. But then say what?

He had no idea.

Worse, it had stopped raining but was still too damp to paint, plus the paint had yet to arrive.

Worse still, it came to light that having only two washers and two dryers in the little outbuilding behind the kitchen building meant that there wasn't enough space for everybody's laundry. Which meant that before breakfast, Royce and Gabe hopped in the truck to take their laundry up to the ranch, while the ex-cons played endless games of poker for crackers and stick pretzels, while all of their laundry cycled through.

Thus Jonah suffered, Royceless, and pretended he didn't give a shit that he was losing, which was mostly on account of the little movie playing over and over in his head, his feet in Royce's lap, being warmed by those delicious, soft hands, those blue eyes fully on him every second.

He'd been hard. He'd gotten so hard he couldn't imagine how Royce didn't notice, only he didn't. That or he had noticed, but had been studiously ignoring the quivers in Jonah's legs, or the tumble inside his belly, the heat along the back of his neck.

Jonah's interest in that glorious mind covered by angelic blond hair had turned into want, which, at the merest touch of Royce's hands cupping his feet, had turned into full-blown need.

Jonah had never needed anyone. Ever. Like, really, ever.

Oh, sure, in a Saturday-night-and-we're-both-a-little-drunk-and-your-body-is-warm-and-close-here-we-go kind of way. But never like this, with Jonah wanting to charge like a bull hopped up on steroids.

Royce, while not acting like a fussy virginal miss, still, nevertheless, had looked at Jonah with blue eyes so wide, like a pool of endless, deep blue water.

Jonah had wanted to fall into those eyes, but he'd held himself back out of fear of crushing everything growing between them.

He'd already decided he'd play the long game. Jumping Royce at that moment would have cut everything short. It was not a game, it most definitely wasn't, at least not anymore.

It all meant too much.

He needed to be patient. Needed to wait for the right moment.

Or maybe Jonah was reading all this so wrong, squinting at the signs he thought he'd seen, only to realize, too late, that he needed glasses and Royce wasn't into men at all—

Fuck everything. Fuck all of it.

"Two aces," he said, slamming down his cards, then scooping all the pretzel sticks toward him, proceeding to crunch through two of them at the same time, as if to prove to everyone at the table that he simply didn't care.

"Dryer's free," said Wayne, marching into the tent with his arms full of laundry.

He proceeded to plop his laundry on a nearby table, close to where the poker game was being dealt once more, as if folding and fussing, like a content little housewife, amidst a group of poker playing ex-cons, had always been his dearest wish.

It was growing quite domestic with all of them hanging out like this, but maybe it wasn't all bad. At least Jonah could keep winning crackers and pretzels—and yes, store-bought chocolate chip cookies, which one of the cooks plopped down in the middle of the table.

By the time lunchtime rolled around, Jonah almost wasn't hungry, but everybody's laundry was done, and as they lined up for the buffet, every single ex-con seemed to be smiling to himself, content with his lot.

Jonah knew that he himself was not domesticated, but as he got in the buffet line, he told himself that he was not looking around for Royce.

Gabe and Royce only showed up after everybody had been seated, telling the exploits of how, after they'd finished their laundry at the ranch, they'd rushed out to Chugwater, because the paint had mysteriously been delivered to the Dairy Queen there.

"We'll be able to paint this afternoon, I think," said Gabe, as he began to eat his lunch.

At his side, practically rubbing shoulders with Gabe, getting all chummy that way, was Royce. Who, while he didn't avoid Jonah's gaze, nevertheless was paying as much attention to his lunch as he was to everybody else at the table. Which meant less of that attention for Jonah, who knew he needed to behave less like a fucking teenager and more like the grown man who wanted who he wanted. Who hadn't just messed everything up by running away like a scared kid.

Okay, so fucking teenagers who had a thing for somebody sometimes did stare without a word to say, and didn't mean any harm by it. Tripping over their own tongues, overwhelmed by signals their bodies were telling them. Even if Jonah was fully grown, maybe it was okay to feel all mixed up this way. To stumble through a courtship from time to time. He just needed to fix what he'd messed up.

"I've got Leland coming down this afternoon," said Royce. "To talk about the wooden walkways and such."

"Well, join us when you can," said Gabe, ever pragmatic.

Lunch was over far too quickly, along with Jonah's opportunity to look at Royce to his heart's content, to absorb every movement, every breath.

Plus, work that afternoon was work, real *fucking* work beneath the sun blazing through the trees and onto the open areas of the pasture. Gabe made everybody help paint the four horse shelters, two coats each, the smell of the paint hanging in the still, warm air.

Then they painted the Adirondack chairs around the fire pit, and *all* the picnic tables along the lake's edge. Jonah had paint in his hair, and streaked along his bare chest, because he had stripped to the waist in order not to stain his new shirts, something he wouldn't have worried about back home in his garage, as he had an endless supply of black t-shirts or cheap white ones from the thrift store on Clinton Street.

At one point, Gabe handed Jonah a cloth to wipe cedar-colored paint from his tattoo of a blue heron on the wing. Yes, that got attention focused their way, but Jonah had glowered and kept working just to get it over with because painting was the worst job *ever*. And it had been Gabe to hand him the cloth, not Royce. So yeah, Monday could just end already.

CHAPTER 18

ROYCE

Maybe it had been something Royce had done or said that sent Jonah racing from his tent. Had he been too forward, petting Jonah's feet as if he had every right to? Had he been too forward? Had he simply been too much for Jonah, because, yes, sometimes he knew he overwhelmed people.

He would find out as soon as he could and get things resolved between him and Jonah, so they could, at the very least, be friends, and hopefully more than friends.

In the meantime, he would focus on work, which was the surest cure he knew for a case of the jitters.

Leland Tate had come down to the valley right after lunch, and together he and Royce walked through the compound, discussing how it was going, and what still needed doing. They looked at the shelters and discussed a need for a shed of some sort to hold grooming gear, salt blocks, halters, and other supplies.

Then Royce took Leland to where the men were painting, being very careful not to stare at Jonah, who had taken off his shirt and now, bare chested, was manfully slopping cedar-colored paint on tables and chairs with a brush.

JACKIE NORTH

It was enough to make Royce feel warm all over, so he made himself look away, fast.

"Let's go to the tributary next," he suggested, and at Leland's nod, he led the way along the path through the woods to the tributary where it led into the lake.

Royce described his potential solution, which Leland had heard before, over the phone. Except now, standing in the sunshine as the clouds built over the ridge to the west, it was easy to see that the mental picture Royce had formed of a wooden walkway wasn't going to be enough.

"You can't go straight across without support in the middle, not across something that wide, and that's a fact," said Leland in his slow, methodical way, turning his straw cowboy hat in his hands. "It doesn't matter how shallow or deep the water, the bridge'd sag first time someone walked across it."

"What if we laid a wooden walkway to that stone in the middle, there?" Royce pointed. "Zigged up to it and then zagged over to the other bank. We'd build abutments on both banks, and the stone would help support it in the middle. The triangle shape of it would add interest and give people time to pause and reflect. Make them slow down a little."

"I like it," said Leland. "And thank you for asking me down here. I've been so busy at the ranch that I haven't been able to see how much was getting done."

"My pleasure," said Royce as he walked Leland halfway back to the parking lot, then turned back, as he'd caught the flutter of wings across the tributary and wanted another look. Yes, as he'd suspected, it was an American kestrel, a male, from the shimmer of orange and gray-blue feathers, something to note in his copy of the *Wyoming Book of Birds*.

What would be even more exciting than seeing a kestrel up close would be to go up to the ridge with his binoculars and see if the birds floating on the updraft were, in fact, peregrine falcons. And should he try again to ask Jonah to come with him? And would that be like going on a date?

THE COWBOY AND THE HOODLUM

Yes, it would be the perfect solution. A hike like that, one that was private, with just the two of them, would be the best time for a talk. For him to give Jonah a chance to say what he was filling, rather than Royce making stuff up about what had happened.

He'd have to wait to ask Jonah about the hike, because work called, and he hustled to change into a rattier t-shirt and blue jeans to help with the painting.

That task lasted all afternoon until the dinner bell rang, at which point Royce was so wrung out, he worried about his ability to hike up the ridge, if he got the chance. At dinner, the mess tent was quiet, as though a bell of silence had descended over the tables, the conversation desultory, energy low, with elbows on tables and slumped shoulders.

He'd not managed to get a seat near Jonah, but had to sit at the end, catty corner and across, so while he was able to look, he couldn't engage. Though, it might have been better to ask Jonah when they were alone if he was interested in that hike. Royce was learning that his little team was up for just about anything, and if Gordy, Tyson, and Duane were to get wind of the plan, they'd want to join.

Royce most definitely did not want them to join. Not this time, especially.

As for Jonah, he seemed to disappear right after dinner, and though Royce walked slowly through the woods, pretending he was reconnoitering, just checking out the compound in general, his head was on a swivel. But Jonah was nowhere to be found.

So, all right, he was on his own. He'd been on his own before, many times, and quite liked it. He should plan for himself, as he usually did. A hot shower, a good book, a cup of lavender tea. An early night. He'd plan for that hike in his head, and how he would ask Jonah to go with him, and he would make sure to bring his best binoculars so they could get closeup views of any birds they saw together.

By the time he'd circled back to his own tent, it was almost too dark to see to turn on the light. But he managed it, shucking his work boots at the entrance and, padding across to his shelves sock-footed, made a mental note to get a little broom and dustpan, to help keep the floor of the tent tidy. So much grit got brought in, however unintentionally, it verged on being like what he imagined walking on cornmeal would feel like.

Also, he needed a new blade for his razor, needed to find that extra tub of pomade he'd brought with him, and he needed to calm down or his heart was going to jump right out of his chest. How had he gotten this worked up over nothing? Usually he was the calm sort, steady, almost ploddingly thoughtful about everything.

Now he had to stop and take a deep breath, his hand on his chest as he stood beneath the bright bulb and surveyed the little world of his tent. He told himself that he did not imagine that Jonah would come striding onto the tent's platform, out of the woods like a shadowy form, ready to step into one of Royce's fantasies, already forming in his head.

Jonah would come. There would be leaning, and warmth between them, growing, a ribbon tying them close to each other. He'd sit on Royce's cot, long limbs, sun warmed skin, that come-hither look in his deep brown eyes.

They'd talk it over. Then, what exactly what was it that Royce was expecting would happen? Kisses hopefully.

He'd never been with a man, but found himself drawn to this one, who seemed to delight in his company and looked at Royce as though marveling at the most beautiful sunrise he'd ever seen. As though Royce lit up his whole world.

Royce had never made anybody feel that way, not that he was aware of. Though as to why he felt bold enough to imagine that was how Jonah felt—it was foolish, quite foolish, but very hard to resist. Especially when every time Jonah looked at him, just about, Royce felt the same. Felt warmed through, as though the very rays of the sun were reaching out to enfold him, glinting off deep water and bringing it to life.

It was a good feeling, and continually reached deep inside of him, but Jonah did not come to the tent, no matter how hard Royce puttered. In due course, Royce gathered his shower things, and, taking his flashlight, strode along the path through the woods, imagining

THE COWBOY AND THE HOODLUM

that he might come upon Jonah headed to do the very same thing. Or that he would be headed to his own tent, after hanging out with the other ex-cons in the mess tent. Or that he was, hope upon hope, looking for Royce.

But Royce met no one, and the woods seemed incredibly empty, and he was glad to reach the facilities and tuck himself inside one of the showers, pulling the curtain closed, and stripping himself to the skin. Reaching in, he turned on the water to just about as hot as it would go, then stepped into the spray.

Looking down at himself as the rainwater rolled along his skin, hands splayed across his belly, he sighed. Being active on the ranch, and now in the valley, kept him trim and strong, but the amount of sugar he loved in his tea made his belly soft.

His skin was good, and perhaps he was a tad vain about it, but his constant use of sunscreen made him appear pale beneath the water, pale in comparison to the hale and hearty Jonah. With his sun-warmed skin and that tumble of dark, gray-shot hair, he was so much more interesting than Royce's blondness, plus he probably never had to use pomade, not even once. Or maybe, what was more likely, he didn't care that his hair tumbled under its own power; Jonah's hair was a bad boy, just like he was.

He closed his eyes. Beneath the stream of water, steam roiled up all around him, pounding gently on his head. Showers like this were meant to be lost in, so Royce lost himself, letting the little movie of him and Jonah on a hike in the sunshine play over and over in his head.

Sometimes he changed the camera angle to where he was looking at Jonah or Jonah was looking at him, but mostly, he panned back so he could see the two of them together, scrambling over the rocks, stopping to point out birds to each other. Jonah leaning close while Royce scouted for falcons through the binoculars.

While it might be a bit fussy to think that masturbating in a shower used by others was rude, Royce abstained for that very reason, focusing instead on lathering his hair with shampoo that smelled like the ocean, using his loofa all over, except for his soft bits, rinsing and creaming until his whole body fairly slithered beneath his hands.

Maybe he should be more relaxed about it, not so uptight. And maybe if Jonah were with him in the shower, and certainly there was enough room for the both of them, he'd be okay with it, especially if Jonah led the way.

Or maybe he should just give it a go, now that he was rinsed off and clean, now that his body, all heightened senses and erect cock, was giving him signals that it was quite, quite ready for some randy pleasure.

Images of Jonah stripped to the waist, tanned shoulders and strong arms steadily painting in the bright sunshine were just about all it took. Royce had quickly gathered every other image he had stored away, but that one, the painting one, was it.

He'd no sooner taken his cock in his hand, the wet drench of the shower coming down steadily, that he flicked to that image, eyes closed. His body took over, electric with pleasure.

His cock jumped beneath his touch. Jonah's smile, that wide, warm smile in his mind, was directed only at him, those brown eyes a little sly, a little teasing.

He was done for, pulsing hard into his palm, the rain-shower rinsing his spend from his skin, which tingled with his release, shivering like a shy-skinned horse, his sigh echoing beneath the thunder of the shower, while steam rose around his head as he opened his eyes.

He was smitten, that much was certain. Taken in by not just a charming mien, but by a warm spirit, a brown-eyed gaze that told Royce that Jonah did not give a damn what the world thought of him, but went by his own rules and nobody else's. A free spirit winging into Royce's life like a sharp-taloned hawk had come down from the heavens and speared Royce's heart.

As to what he should do about it, well, he shouldn't simply wait for Jonah to come to him, he needed to act, to reach out, not just wait idly by. Which meant that the hike in his mind would become reality. Not because he'd asked permission, or dropped his proverbial handkerchief, fluttering his eyelashes in the hope that Jonah would notice and stoop to pick it up, handing it back to Royce with a flourish, no. He was going to man up and propose the hike and give it his all, throw himself into the adventure, and court Jonah as best he could.

As to what would come of it, only good things, surely.

He clung to that hope as he dried off, rubbed a little treatment oil into his hair, and shrugged into his boxers and the t-shirt he saved for sleeping. He'd forgotten his flip-flops, so he had to put his bare feet back into his work boots, and then, laces flopping, he hauled his shower stuff through the woods, back to his tent.

He'd left the light blazing, gold lines amidst the black night, and for a moment he paused, turning his back on the tent, eyes scanning the woods for the little dots of light that told him where the other tents were. Then he looked up to the blanket of night sky, stars speckled like silver thrown by a careless hand.

His heart filled with the potential of it all, the space, the whispering sounds of the forest all around him. Life was good, it surely was, and he was lucky to be in the valley, a bit more untamed than the ranch had ever been, a bit more indulgent of dreams, a gateway to something new.

With a happy sigh, he stepped up to the platform and went into his tent, zipping it closed behind him to keep the bugs out. Now that he was home, he put his shower things away and scanned his blue jeans, looking for just the right pair, his shirts for just the right snap-button one to bring out his eyes. Maybe a little scarf, perhaps not as bright and colorful as his old jackalope one, which Jonah still had, but a silk blue one, to reflect the sky. Or would that be too fussy?

There was a flicker of a thought that he might call Grandad Thackery to talk it out, to share his heart and his troubles. But he already knew what Grandad would say. Quite gently, he would tell Royce to man up and have the conversation that needed to be had. Also he would say, *Wear your best scarf, for sure.*

Royce made a little pile of clothing and brewed some lavender tea while he carefully cleaned the lenses of his binoculars, content to anticipate all the potential the next day would bring.

CHAPTER 19

JONAH

They finished up the painting on Wednesday, and Jonah swore off ever painting like that again, though he imagined the plans in the valley would involve more painting at some point. He'd just have to make sure he was elsewhere.

He was able to grab a quick shower before lunch, only to find that Royce was anxiously looking for him when he arrived at the mess tent. It was as if Royce was psychic and knew that Jonah had been searching for just the right moment for them to meet up.

"There you are." Royce's fingers curled around Jonah's bicep in a way that felt familiar, like Royce had been doing that for years instead of only for a short while. As though Royce, and only Royce, had the right to touch him that way. "I've got good news."

"Do tell," said Jonah, lining up with his tray at the newly set up buffet line.

It might have been nice to have still been served one at a time while waiting at the table, sort of posh and strange all at the same time, but it was a good deal nicer to stand in line with Royce, their heads ducked together as they looked over the choices on the two long steam tables.

Here, Jonah could take as much as he wanted of the creamed corn

JACKIE NORTH

and none of the spinach, could have two bread rolls with extra butter, and could copy Royce when he took two slices of roast turkey, plus crispy bits of skin, all in all a more satisfactory experience.

Plus, he could sit next to Royce at the end of the table, rather than hoping there would be a free seat he could grab, and if there wasn't, having to stare across the table at Royce. This way, he could rub shoulders with Royce and snicker when Royce's iced tea spilled, and hop up to grab extra napkins to clean it up before Neal shooed him away, bringing a bar towel to wipe up the mess and a fresh iced tea for Royce, besides.

"Thank you, Neal," said Royce as he took a sip and sighed. "Now, about my good news," he said, tucking his chin, turning to look at Jonah like he had a secret to share.

"What's that?" asked Jonah, and he was all ears because Royce had never shared a secret with him before.

"It's going to be a beautiful afternoon," Royce said, his smile already bright with joy at the prospect. "And I've told Gabe that you and I need to do some recon on the ridge so I can see a bird's-eye view of the tributary to help determine where a particular walkway might go. We'll bring snacks and binoculars and maybe we'll see some falcons." That smile grew brighter. "It'll be just you and me. What do you say? Care to join me?"

"Of course." Jonah was on the verge of half-shrugging to demonstrate that he really didn't care one way or another, but he really *did* care.

Royce had mentioned wanting to see the falcons on the ridge, and Jonah was totally willing to go with him, especially after a shitty morning spent elbows deep in cedar colored paint. So he leaned toward Royce, their shoulders brushing, and said, low, "I'd love to."

Back at the garage, Jonah had seldom taken the day off, and only when there were no customers in the front shop or stolen cars in the back shop, needing to be stripped down. He'd even worked holidays because who gave a fuck about those?

One time, Beck had bought some scalped tickets to a Rockies baseball game at Coors Field, and though the seats had been amazing, just to the left of home plate and only two rows up. The brats and beer delicious, and afterward, he'd taken Beck to eat sushi on the 16th Street Mall, even though sushi was disgusting and he'd never liked it. At least that had cheered Beck up.

This hike would be the perfect, very private opportunity for Jonah to apologize for being a dumb fuck. He would just have to wait for the right moment to speak up.

After lunch, Royce got a backpack from his tent and filled it with sunscreen and binoculars and a guide book, of course, and then got two large, wool-coated canteens of water and a couple sticks of beef jerky and a large plastic Ziploc bag full of what he called gorp, which turned out to be a collection of chocolate candies, peanuts, and raisins.

"Why is it called gorp?" asked Jonah as they walked through the woods toward the switchback road in order to cross over Horse Creek, where it was narrow. There was even a little wooden bridge Jonah was surprised to see, a bit of civilization in the middle of a forest, but it was better than wading and messing up his beautiful golden boots.

"It stands for good ole raisins and peanuts, so they say," said Royce, marching ahead, his head turning this way and that, already on the lookout for whatever he might see, his golden curls peeking out from his straw cowboy hat.

"No Latin name?" asked Jonah, trotting to keep up.

"Alas, no," said Royce, his laugh ringing sweetly through the trees.

Could it be better than this? As they walked through the woods along the faint path, their footsteps each an echo of the other's, Jonah didn't think so.

Each time Royce looked up at Jonah, face flushed with the warmth of the day, the brisk walk, his eyes as blue as the sky, he knew the answer was no. Because nobody was as interesting, no, screw that. Nobody was as *fascinating* as Royce was, the way his brain worked, the way he knew all kinds of shit that Jonah didn't know and how he was as interested in what Jonah knew as he enjoyed telling Jonah the definition of things, the Latin name first, always, and the regular name for regular people second.

"*Pinus ponderosa var. scopulorum*," said Royce with a wave of his hand at the whole valley as they took the narrow path up the rocky hillside. "Or, to you and me, Rocky Mountain Ponderosa pine."

To Jonah, one pine tree looked like another, and maybe Royce realized that, for he explained the difference in the length of needles, the shape of the pinecones, still forming mid-May. The way some trees liked it lower down, and others liked higher altitude.

"Here's a beauty," said Royce, coming to a pause beneath a small collection of thin, spindly trees with narrow white trunks.

"What is it?" asked Jonah, dutifully coming to a stop right next to Royce, taking a drink from his canteen, gasping at the delicious taste of the cool water.

"*Populus tremuloides*," said Royce, touching a collection of pale green leaves with gentle fingers. "Otherwise known as trembling aspen, from the way they tremble in the wind."

The tree was pretty, shaking its leaves gently in the low breeze, but what was even prettier, and drew Jonah's attention, was Royce's sweet smile, as though he was quite alone and sharing the moment with only himself. Except Jonah was there, wasn't he, so he moved forward to circle his arms around Royce's waist so he could kiss him and kiss him again.

"What a brain you have under all that hair," said Jonah, going for casual, as if he weren't impressed at all, except he was and he could hear in his own voice how impressed he was.

"I just read a lot is all," said Royce, blushing in his adorable way, leaning into Jonah's kisses as if he couldn't get enough of them. Then, with a sigh, he pulled away and bent to lift Jonah's canteen so Jonah could take another drink. "We need to get a move on, if we're to see any falcons before the clouds move in."

"What do we care?" asked Jonah, encouraging Royce to drink likewise, settling the backpack from Royce's shoulders onto his own. "We won't melt in the rain."

"We won't," said Royce, agreeing, taking his straw hat off to scrape

THE COWBOY AND THE HOODLUM

his curls away from his temples before settling his hat back on his head. "But you wouldn't want to be up here if the storm turns to thunder and lightning. You'd get electrocuted."

"We don't want that," said Jonah, doing his best not to roll his eyes as he stepped in line behind Royce as they marched up the rocky path where it led up onto the ridge. But really, there were two, maybe three puffball clouds over the hills beyond the ridge, so what did they have to worry about?

After a good hour of what felt walking straight uphill, they came to the south end of the ridge and stopped.

Overhead the sky was so blue against the gray-blue, lichen-dappled rocks, Jonah had to blink at it, grateful for the brim of his straw cowboy hat and the cool drink of water that Royce reminded him to take. Below, the blueness of Half Moon Lake reflected the sky, a perfect mirror, surrounded on all sides and along its long length with green pine trees. Far beyond, Jonah could see the land stretching out in green and gray and blue, until he could see the horizon.

"Amazing, isn't it?" asked Royce, though he must have known that the answer to that was yes.

"Yeah," said Jonah, hooking his thumbs through the straps of the backpack. Never in a million years would he ever have imagined being where he was, on a hike, for fuck's sake, drinking from a canteen and eating gorp with the most beautiful, most interesting man in the whole wide world.

"Look along the ridge there," said Royce, pointing.

When Jonah looked along it, he could see flat places amidst the rocks, and how the rocks sloped up to more rocks, and high above that, three dots circling each other.

"What are those?" Jonah asked because he wanted to know and, mostly, because he knew Royce wanted to tell him.

"*Falco peregrinus*," said Royce without hesitation, sounding so confident and sexy that Jonah wanted to kiss him, but he restrained himself because, undoubtedly, Royce had more to say on the subject. "Peregrine falcon," he said now. "You can't see from here, but they've got yellow beaks and talons and their feathers have a blue tinge to them. And they're the fastest animal on the planet."

"What about cheetahs?" asked Jonah, knowing from somewhere that cheetahs were fast.

"Cheetahs can run up to seventy-five miles per hour," said Royce, looking very serious as he pulled out his binoculars, fiddling with the strap so he could put it over his neck, and he was so tangled that Jonah had to help him. "But when a falcon dives for its dinner, it can go up to two hundred miles an hour."

"That's fast," said Jonah, stopping himself from kissing Royce right then and there because Royce had placed the binoculars to his eyes and was adjusting the focus.

"It is," said Royce, baring his teeth a bit as he focused the binoculars and then froze. "Got them!"

Instantly, he took the strap off from around his neck and handed the binoculars to Jonah, keeping hold of them until Jonah's hands were steady around them.

"Look up and then over to the right, more toward the mountains than the prairie," said Royce. "A little to the right. To the right. And there—do you see them?"

Jonah froze, concentrating hard. He could see them, three falcons circling around and around, on a draft of wind that held them aloft. They were just playing up there, as near as he could figure, and then one of the falcons, as if noticing that Jonah was below, seemed to look right at him with its yellow-rimmed eyes as if Jonah was next on the bird's dinner menu.

Royce's smile was broad when Jonah handed the binoculars back, and when Royce started fumbling in the backpack and drew out the *Wyoming Guide to Birds*, Jonah waited, simply waited, warm beneath the sun as Royce read the bookish description out loud. Which was marvelous and clever and so much more interesting than school had ever been.

While Royce talked out loud about the wooden walkways that were needed, they munched on gorp and drank water from the canteen and watched the falcons circling, circling, until the clouds glowered over the mountains, no longer white and puffy and innocent, but dark and threatening.

They stayed as long as they could until, finally, they had to stuff everything in the backpack and race down the path to get out of the storm's way.

Rain caught them at the bottom of the slope, where the path entered the woods, and there was lightning on the rocks that glittered in Royce's eyes, as they stood out of danger, but just on the edge of it.

"Amazing," said Royce, taking in the storm, the hard rain that came down, the way the trees bent and danced. "Just amazing."

"Yeah, it is," said Jonah, but he was looking at Royce when he said it.

"But here's the thing," said Royce in a rather serious voice, which made Jonah's heart pound over the roar of thunder. Was Royce about to tell Jonah to stay away?

"What is it?" said Jonah, swallowing hard. Being brave.

For a moment, Royce looked at Jonah with wide blue eyes, as if he was about to walk across hot coals and would rather not. Then he swallowed hard, like Jonah had just done.

"I want to be with you," said Royce, carefully and clearly. "So I don't want any misunderstandings—I don't know why you left so quickly on Sunday. Did I do something wrong?"

Royce thought it was his fault, only it totally and absolutely wasn't. Jonah needed to make that very clear, very fast.

"No," he said. "It was me. My fault. I freaked out. Right? It was too much."

"I'm too much?" asked Royce, placing his hand over his heart, his eyes looking so wounded that Jonah wanted to kick himself for not explaining it right.

"You?" asked Jonah, a shake in his voice, his hands trembling as he reached out to curl his fingers around Royce's palm. "You are amazing—no, it was me. I got overwhelmed. Didn't know which way was up. You make me dizzy, but it's a good dizzy. You know?"

"I make you dizzy?" asked Royce, the wounded look replaced by one of pleasure. "That's good, right?"

"So good," said Jonah, leaning close, planting a kiss on Royce's forehead. "Better than good."

Royce smiled at him, rain-mist sparkling on his hair and eyelashes, and Jonah knew he was a lucky, lucky man to get a second chance with such a beautiful, big-hearted man.

CHAPTER 20
ROYCE

The rain stayed on the ridge, but they'd brought the taste of rain with them, the wind shifting all about. It was time for dinner, as well, so they headed back to camp, walking side by side through the woods.

This got Royce more worked up than he knew what to do with, so he excused himself to check on the condition of his tent to make sure it was ready for guests. Then he showered and shaved, and by the time they got to the mess tent, he was breathless. But, luckily, Jonah had saved a seat for him, his smile warm, dark eyes glittering in the overhead light.

As they ate their dinner of cheeseburgers, salad, and some really good French fries that Royce knew had to be from fresh potatoes, hand cut, and twice-fried in peanut oil, he attempted to mentally bolster his own courage, conscious of Jonah's shoulder brushing his, though by the time dinner was over, his courage was still in tatters and he was practically shaking when he stood up and followed Jonah outside the mess tent.

"Would you—" said Royce, half gulping, half stammering. "Would you like to come back to my tent and look at my book about bats?"

He was pathetic. His question was as bad as the old chestnut that men used to use where they'd ask if someone wanted to come up to their apartment to look at their etchings. Only there were no etchings, just the expectation of some wild, hot, headboard-banging-against-the-wall sex. Or maybe not.

Royce had a headboard, the metal one of his cot, but he didn't have a wall. Nor had he any idea how to go about starting up a night of sex. Especially with a man. But he wanted Jonah and was ready to learn.

When he'd been married to Sandra, and even before that with the few partners he'd had in college, he'd learned to appreciate the way women were built, the softness of their skin. He knew what to do, and how to do it. How to stroke, how hard or soft, and, most importantly, where most women liked to be touched.

Sandra'd had a round bosom and a curvy bottom and a trim little waist, simply luscious all the way around. But Jonah was all angles and corded muscles, his strong neck that maybe wanted Royce's arms around it. He'd showered before dinner, like Royce had showered, and was wearing his dark blue denim snap-button shirt, the sleeves rolled up to show his corded forearms, a little nick along his jaw that showed just how fast he'd shaved, ostensibly for Royce.

In contrast, Royce had added too much pomade until his hair was simply a disaster, hot around his ears. He was a pathetic mess and should just stick to his lane, but still—

"It's just the one book," he said, trying not to wring his hands. Failing, so he shoved his hands into the pockets of his jeans and rocked a bit back and forth on his toes. "But there are several pictures of each type of bat—"

"Does this book have Latin names for things?" asked Jonah, moving not farther away, not bored by Royce's ramblings, it seemed, but instead moving closer until they were boot to boot.

"Why, yes," said Royce, a little startled. "The Latin is in italics, so it's easy to spot—"

"I'm in," said Jonah.

"What?"

"I said I'm in," said Jonah. He paused to use the back of his pinkie to brush the thick swirl of forelock from Royce's overly hot forehead, making Royce degrees cooler and more nervous than ever, all at once. "Lead the way."

Royce knew that Jonah knew the way to his tent, but it was nice of him to pretend that Royce had any control over what was happening. It was as if his internal desire had somehow been set free, and he had no way, none at all, of bringing it to heel. And so, like a wild, out-of-control animal, he led the way, stumbling along the path to his tent, and unzipped the opening with unsteady hands.

All the while Jonah was at his side, patient, silent, looking at Royce with brown eyes, round and wise and watching.

Making himself step inside and turn on the light, Royce blindly searched for *Bats: An Illustrated Guide*, which was unique not just for the number of crisp, clear photographs of each kind of bat, but also for the unusual printing of white text on a black background, making it impossible to read for long stretches of time.

It was absolutely indispensable as a distraction. Or a shield, which it seemed to be as he tried to hand it to Jonah, standing there, so patiently, looking ten feet tall, his head almost brushing the main tent pole.

With his eyes always on Royce, Jonah gently took the book and put it back on the shelf. Royce's head was ringing and sweat built up around the collar of his shirt and beneath his arms.

Should he tell Jonah he'd never been with a man? Or should he just fake his way through the whole thing? While the latter idea might have been the easy way out, his heart was pounding, telling him, no, no, no, he needed to be honest with Jonah, especially this time, their first time.

"I'm—" he gasped, gesturing to himself with both hands, palms spread, fingers wide. "I'm a virgin. I mean, with a man. I've been with women, with Sandra—"

"Not to worry," said Jonah, his voice low, a burr in his chest that sent waves and waves of comfort in Royce's direction. He repeated the gesture of pushing Royce's hair back from his flushed face, only this time he used a twist of his fingers while Royce shivered, his mouth falling open. "I'll just have to be extra gentle with you."

There was a promise in Jonah's velvet-soft voice and in his serious brown eyes, a promise of gentleness, yes, and of strength. That Jonah seemed so calm as he reached for the snap buttons on Royce's shirt also told Royce that Jonah had been with men before, and perhaps knew all kinds of things that Royce didn't know and couldn't even guess at.

"I'm not afraid you'll hurt me." Royce's voice was a whisper, almost a squeak. "I'm just *afraid—*"

"Of me?" asked Jonah, a dark glower forming across his face as if Royce had just told him some gravely bad news. "I wouldn't hurt you for the world. Not for anything."

Royce opened his mouth to say *I know*, or some other platitude, anything to cover the pounding of his heart, the roar of an ocean in his ears.

Instead, quite suddenly, quite gently, Jonah clasped Royce's face in his warm, steady hands and kissed him. It felt rather like when he'd kissed him as they'd been having iced coffee together, but instead of being cool and brief and light, this kiss was warm, soft from the softness of Jonah's lips, but hard and overwhelming, a swipe of Jonah's tongue along the inside of Royce's lip that left him trembling and gulping for air.

"All right?" asked Jonah. "Do you mind if I zip the tent closed?"

Wildly shaking his head, Royce watched as Jonah zipped the tent closed, then sat on the cot, bending to take off his cowboy boots while patting the place beside him at the same time.

"C'mon then," he said, pausing to look up at Royce.

Royce felt frozen in place. In spite of that, the newness of it all, parts of him were shimmering beneath his skin, a newfound electricity. All at once, he turned on the little bedside lamp, and drew his fingers down the dimmer, so it was a faint yellow glow coming from the side, spreading itself across the tent, softly, so softly, it was as round and gentle as a candle's light.

"Ah, that's perfect."

Jonah's voice was a low burr, soothing and enticing. Royce turned toward Jonah, spinning on his boot heel. Then he stopped, realizing

THE COWBOY AND THE HOODLUM

that he was going to have to get undressed down to his bare skin and that the comparison of Jonah's hale to Royce's pale was going to leave him feeling even more naked than he thought he could bear.

Jonah was looking up at him, dark curls tumbled around his ears, dark eyes glinting golden in the low light, the light passing through those eyes as if, just behind that light, was a doorway into Jonah, if only Royce was brave enough. Well, he was, damn it, and he'd come this far to be with this utterly fascinating man who made him feel more excited about life than he had been in a long time.

Again Jonah patted the cot beside him, so Royce took a breath and flung himself down, sitting shoulder to shoulder with Jonah, until Jonah turned and kissed him again. Leaning in, pressing on Royce with those broad shoulders, the bulk of his body.

Shuddering, Royce leaned back, but his hands reached out and clutched at Jonah's arms, fingers gripping tight. Which made Jonah pause, his hands coming up to clasp Royce's hands as he looked up at Royce with a flick of those dark eyelashes and those shimmering brown eyes.

"Come with me," said Jonah and before Royce could even take a breath to ask what he meant, Jonah leaned back and pulled Royce with him, spreading his bejeaned thighs to tug Royce on top of him as he sank back onto Royce's three plush pillows.

"Better?" asked Jonah, his voice a murmur in the low glow of the dimmed lamp.

Jonah's chest was hard and hot beneath the spread of Royce's palms, and the scent of him, salt and warmth, curled around Royce, and he sighed.

"Yes," he said, though it came out a whisper that was swallowed by Jonah's next kiss and the sensation of Jonah's strong thighs on either side of his hips, and the warmth of Jonah's groin, the hardness of his cock through his blue jeans—all of this surrounded him, a warm tumble of sensation, the newness of it, and the familiarity, as well, because Jonah was a man, and Royce was a man, so he well knew how the pleasure rising in his body was echoing in Jonah's.

A mirror of warmth and delight and the tumble in his belly as he lay on the strong body beneath him. Jonah. Whose hands came up to card through Royce's hair, combing through the messy disaster Royce had left behind by overdoing it with the pomade.

"Your hair is gold," said Jonah, lifting his chin for another kiss, which Royce gave to him. "I love the way it shines."

Royce's brow furrowed, but he didn't want to hear any more about his troublesome hair. He only wanted more kisses, and the warmth of Jonah's palm on his cheek, and the rumble of a laugh rising up from Jonah's chest. And more of that heat between Jonah's thighs, the sensation of shivers building inside of him as he undid the first snap button on Jonah's shirt.

He paused, holding his breath, and then Jonah nodded at him, slowly, understanding in his eyes.

"Go on, then," he said, a gentle murmur. "You lead the way. We'll have a bit of a tumble, then we can look at the bat book, okay?"

Laughing, Royce ducked his chin and kissed the first bare place on Jonah's chest that he came to, soft lips on hard muscle. Suddenly he wasn't afraid anymore and could do those things he'd imagined in his mind, undoing those snap buttons and sliding his hands along Jonah's ribs then, squirming a bit to reach.

Resting his cheek on Jonah's mostly bare chest, he watched his own fingers as he undid Jonah's jeans, and wondered at his own daring, joyous in the rising warmth in his belly, the heat of Jonah's belly as he slid his hand beneath the waistband of Jonah's briefs.

"Want to take me in your mouth?" asked Jonah. "Get it over with?"

"I don't want to get it over with." His voice shook as he ducked down to kiss Jonah's belly button. "I want to remember this for a long, long time."

"Let's just make out for now," said Jonah, quite kindly as he traced Royce's jaw with gentle fingers. "We can get to other things later."

Jonah curled his fingers around the back of Royce's neck, tugging him upwards. A bit relieved, a bit disappointed in himself and his own verve, Royce crawled up from between the sprawl of Jonah's come-hither thighs, pulling himself up Jonah's body until he was flush on top of him and could kiss Jonah's chin, his cheeks, rising up to kiss his eyebrows even.

All the while, his fingers were snug beneath the elastic waistband of Jonah's briefs, stirring in thick, wiry hair, scooting down, bit by bit, until he could circle Jonah's very erect cock, and cradle it in the palm of his hand.

The silky skin there was quite warm to the touch, softness over hard, but it was Jonah's sigh, his eyes closing over a low guttural sound that came from his belly, that surprised Royce. Nobody he'd ever been with, and quite a low number that was anyway, had ever made a sound like that when he'd touched them. Nobody had ever closed their eyes as if absorbing every bit of Royce's touch.

And when his hand stilled, and Jonah opened his deep brown eyes, Royce held his breath.

"I'm lost in you," said Jonah, low. "Lost in you."

Royce carried on, pleasuring Jonah with as much tenderness as was in his whole body, stroking Jonah long and quick, long and slow, until Jonah came in his palm, mouth damp, rounded in surprise, his eyes flicking up to capture Royce in that gaze.

"And now I've found you," said Royce, low and satisfied. "You are found."

Had there ever been joy like this in his life? No. But there was now.

CHAPTER 21
JONAH

Jonah had made his way through the darkness, back to his own tent. He would have stayed with Royce, but Royce was fast asleep and Jonah hadn't wanted to wake him. So he kissed Royce's sweet forehead, turned off the lamp, and made his way out of the tent, carrying his cowboy boots.

Sitting on the edge of the platform, he put on his cowboy boots in the still cool air, pitch black all around him except for pinpoints of light amongst the trees that he assumed were other tents. It looked as though a sky full of stars had settled low to the ground, flickering between the branches, a little star party.

Now, if that wasn't the kind of whimsy that Royce would appreciate, he didn't know what was.

It did feel a tad strange to be thinking that way, as if Royce had influenced him through gentle touches and sweet kisses, his shyness turning to boldness as he'd undone Jonah's clothes and half-stripped him to admire him. To touch and to kiss, with his mouth and his pink tongue. Taking Jonah someplace new, a shared intimacy, wave upon wave, with none of the aggression that Jonah had shared with Beck, or any of his other partners, in the past.

And when Royce had finally taken Jonah's cock in his mouth, there'd been zero hesitation over that, absolutely zero. He'd licked and sucked in all kinds of delicious, spine-melting ways, not like he'd been doing it for years, but with the kind of abandon Jonah had never experienced. For the simple joy of giving pleasure, it seemed, also something new for Jonah, as his partners, whoever they might have been, seemed to have done it to earn Jonah's attention, his approval.

As to why they all thought they had to be that way, he had no idea, none at all. But he did know that being with Royce was the most amazing thing, and that beyond the newness, there seemed to be a vast ocean of things to discover about Royce.

Starting with bats, and evidently, also with horses and falcons and wolves. Royce had at least one book on each kind of animal, had taken notes in the margins, highlighted bits in yellow or pink. *There's so much to know,* Royce had said earnestly, as they'd drowsed in the bed after putting some of their clothes back on and drawing the sheets on Royce's bed up to their chests.

Royce had propped himself up on his three pillows and Jonah had propped himself up on Royce so Royce could flip through the pages of the bat book. Which kind of gave Jonah a headache on account of the pages being black and the print white. But that was okay because soon Royce had told Jonah to grab the next book on the shelf, one about what he called painted ponies, but which turned out to be horses that were splotched with black or brown or white, some combination that made them eye-catching and sleek.

"We raise these kinds of horses on my family's ranch back home," said Royce, pointing at the page, his arm slung over Jonah's naked shoulder, casual and warm.

"Is there a Latin name for them?" asked Jonah, half laughing, half wanting to know.

"Of course there is," said Royce, with a laugh. "It's *Equus caballus*, if you want to be really poetic about it, but mostly it's *Equus*. Only the names of paint horses are in Spanish, you see."

Then Royce trotted out a whole string of Spanish words that

THE COWBOY AND THE HOODLUM

described, in seemingly minute detail, the variations of color and splotches, reeling in Jonah's head, with the only thing he could remember was that a pinto horse was a kind of paint horse, and not the other way around.

"How do you keep all that straight?" asked Jonah, kissing the curve of Royce's elbow, tracing the line of muscle with soft fingers.

"I don't really know." Royce kissed the top of Jonah's head and sighed. "I've always had my nose in a book, except when I was riding my horse, Posey."

When Jonah lifted his head in interest, Royce talked about Posey, his little pinto mare, who was now living a life of leisure, giving rides to his brothers' kids from time to time, back home on the family ranch, Thackery Acres.

"Thackery?" asked Jonah.

"The ranch is named after my family," said Royce. "I'm Royce Thackery, youngest of five brothers."

"I see."

Royce's voice glowed as he talked about the ranch, so Jonah tilted his body sideways so he could see that glow in Royce's eyes, the way the blue in them sparkled like diamonds, and wondered if he'd ever meet them, the way people met each other's families in movies. There was no one Jonah wanted to introduce Royce to, relative or acquaintance, but that didn't mean he couldn't meet Royce's people, right?

Maybe it was best to let that idea go altogether, as they were very likely to part company once summer ended, or sooner than that, if Beck had his way and dragged Jonah back to Denver.

Royce had made a valiant attempt to open the book about wolves and just keep going, as if he meant to teach Jonah straight on till morning. Only his eyes had kept shutting, his chin nodding forward on his chest, until finally, Jonah had bitten the bullet and gotten up and tucked Royce in properly, so he could sleep without a crick in his neck.

While it was nice, once again, to be the caregiver, he was glad for the little bit of space and silence as he walked back to his own tent in the darkness, where he stripped to the skin, slipped between the sheets and, pulling the jackalope scarf beneath his cheek, fell asleep instantly.

In the morning, he struggled to wake up, though he'd slept deeper than he had in probably years. When he rushed to the showers to clean up and shave, he was met by a wide-awake and bright-eyed Royce Thackery who, upon seeing Jonah in a rush, tugged on the fold of his towel.

"We'll hold breakfast for you," he said, with a sweet kiss, right on Jonah's mouth.

And if that wasn't the nicest way to be greeted in the morning, Jonah didn't know what was.

It was only later, as he was dumping his things in his tent, that he realized he'd accidentally included the jackalope scarf in a fold of towels. What Royce had actually been doing was tucking the scarf back into his things, so Royce knew full and well he had it and hadn't asked for it back.

As to why Royce hadn't mentioned it, Jonah had no idea, only that it made him smile and feel well-pleased with himself. The scarf was his, which meant he could keep Royce with him all the time.

Work the rest of that week involved laying sand beds along the main cleared path that went from the fire pit and up along the lake to a clearing in the woods. Then came the backbreaking work of placing flagstones in the sandy bed, to make a path.

As to why they didn't just lay cement sidewalks, Jonah had no idea, but Royce was throwing himself into the work, so Jonah did, as well, making sure that Duane, Tyson, and Gordy all did their bit, and that at no point was Royce ever left to lever a flagstone into place on his own.

"We're doing it by hand, you see," said Royce as he made them sit beneath the pine trees to drink bottled water and eat crackers and cheese. "If we brought a truck or big, heavy tools through here, we'd mash these marvelous tall grasses."

Jonah nodded as he sucked salt from his thumb, staring but trying not to stare at Royce, who, in the shade, had taken off his hat. His gold hair was wild all over his head, and though he seemed to be fussing at it, trying to curve it behind his ears, it was all over the place and, in Jonah's mind, adorable.

When Jonah noticed that Gordy was watching him watching Royce, he gave Gordy a good jab with his elbow to get him to mind his own business, but Gordy just jabbed him back as if to say *You're not the boss of me* and *I see what I'm seeing, and you can't tell me differently.* Well, as long as Gordy kept his mouth shut, that'd be fine by Jonah.

When they finished the main part of the path, at the north end of the lake, they had to splash through some water that Royce said was a tributary of Horse Creek. He moaned about ruining what he called the riparian purity, but he seemed to cheer himself up at the sight of a dense stand of what looked like green saplings on the other side of the water.

"It'll be hot through here, through those willow bushes," he said, pointing, then he stopped, mouth open. "D'you see that yellow bird there?" he asked, pointing even harder.

"Is it a goldfinch?" asked Jonah, though he couldn't really see anything, and the only yellow bird he knew, the only *bird* he knew, was the goldfinch.

"Close," said Royce with a bright flash of a smile at Jonah. "It's *Cardellina pusilla*, or Wilson's warbler. Can you hear it?"

Jonah listened as hard as he could. He snapped his fingers at the others to make sure they were listening, too, but he couldn't distinguish one sound from the other, from the almost-silent rush of water to the wind through the trees. When he looked at Royce, he shook his head faintly, not wanting to disappoint this sweet man.

"Just be still," said Royce. "And listen for the way it sings the same note, over and over."

They listened, and when Jonah thought he heard it, a repetitious, high-pitched sound, he looked at Royce, his eyebrows raised. He was pleased with himself when Royce nodded, his smile lighting up his face, as though Jonah's new discovery had been his own.

In the end, they decided to stack as many flagstones at the edge of the tributary as possible and wait for a walkway to be built over the water so they didn't mash the grasses or disturb the birds' feeding areas. The willows beyond, dense and yellow-green, would have to wait, though Jonah didn't miss the longing in Royce's eyes to keep going.

"It really is best to wait," said Royce, though he seemed to be speaking mostly to himself.

Jonah wanted to grab some boards from leftover scraps from building the horse shelters, to build that walkway across the water right then and there, just to bring that smile back to Royce's face. And he would have volunteered, except Royce was leading them back to the clearing, where they stacked the bags of sand and picked up flagstone chips. It involved a lot of bending, too much bending, but it gave him a chance to admire Royce's lovely ass, and to pick up his straw hat and hand it back to him when a sudden curl of wind blew it off his head.

"My hair is a mess," said Royce with a flush to his cheeks as he put the hat on.

"I like it a mess," said Jonah, ducking his chin so he could share a secret smile with Royce and only Royce.

He did catch Gordy looking and snarled at him to mind his own business. Gordy, who'd seemed a little fearful of Jonah that first night in the tent, just tossed back his head and laughed silently for his own amusement.

Maybe Gordy needed to be taught a lesson or maybe it didn't matter, for who was to care? As Jonah well knew, people were mostly focused on themselves, which was what made it easy to steal cars in broad daylight. Not to mention this world was miles away, literally and figuratively, from his old world, so why shouldn't Jonah have a sweetheart to call his own?

No reason. No reason at all. Only being with someone else felt so different and new, gentler, somehow, than what he was used to. It was as if a part of Royce had invaded Jonah's soul, softly, like a silk scarf, and he'd have to wait and see if his heart rejected that invasion or accepted it. And from there, then what?

Well, fuck it. No sense obsessing when everything would come to an end when the summer was over and the parole program disbanded. That was how things usually turned out, anyhow. In pieces. Tatters. Over and done with.

CHAPTER 22
ROYCE

Royce had been so bold Wednesday night, asking Jonah back to his tent, as though it was something he did every day, his knees knocking the entire time, with Jonah so strong and powerful, overpowering everything in the tent simply by being there, standing between the cot and the shelf.

Even the simple kiss they'd shared while sitting on the cot had seemed too much and Royce was on the verge of bolting, especially when Jonah had zipped the tent closed, and the whole evening had begun moving at a terribly rapid pace before he was ready.

Then Jonah had pulled Royce's whole body between his strong thighs, as if on top, so to speak, Royce had control of the whole proceedings. Jonah had made it so easy for him that he'd been able to simply enjoy being taken up, floating away, surrounded by touch, taste, and feeling.

Jonah had made it very easy, tipping his chin back, sprawled beneath Royce, half-naked chest, the rest of him seemingly ready to be all the way naked. Exhibiting exactly no shame as he'd helped Royce undo his jeans, guiding Royce's not-quite-steady hand to the waistband of his briefs. Drawing Royce's fingers beneath that waistband, and then gesturing with the sweep of one hand, as if to say, *Have at it*.

Jonah's belly had been warm and taut, almost concave, a long vein streaking down along each side of his hips. Royce didn't have time to wonder whether his own somewhat less taut belly would make Jonah turn away, when the sensation of being between Jonah's legs was so overwhelming.

He scooted down a bit, until the line of Jonah's cock in his briefs was just beneath his hand, his mouth. The scent of Jonah, the thrilling wave of adventure that raced through him cut through the rest of his inhibitions, and he mouthed at the hard curve beneath cotton, his fingers tracing the line of one leg hole, touching that warmth, feeling Jonah's urgency, though he was holding himself back.

"Is this all right?" asked Royce, pausing to look up at Jonah.

Who, dusky against the white sheets in the low gold glimmer, looked back at him with half-lidded, almost sleepy brown eyes, as if he had all the time in the world for Royce to take his time. Then he nodded, closing his eyes, the way a cat might wink a kiss.

Royce knew it was all right for sure, and ducked his head and let his mouth do what it wanted to do, let his fingers pull and tug at that elastic band to take Jonah's cock in his mouth, like a shameless thing, tasting the wash of salt, feeling the firmness, the hard pulse of blood beneath tender skin.

And then it was all right, it felt natural like breathing as he sucked on Jonah's cock, and tugged and tugged until Jonah's jeans and briefs were halfway down his thighs, making him laugh under his breath as Jonah struggled a bit until Royce helped him all the way off with all of his clothes. Then he was sleek and long and wild on Royce's cot, reaching to help Royce off with his clothes and once they were both naked, it was as if he'd been given wings and set free.

All modesty was gone as Jonah's bare arms came around his bare back, and they could kiss and tumble together, Jonah stroking Royce's cock, his fingers stroking between Royce's legs in wonderfully new ways, sending zigs and zags of pleasure up Royce's spine, shooting him into a mental stratosphere. He was so high, he lost his breath, and only knew it when Jonah was stroking his chest, saying, *Breathe, breathe*, over and over.

Sighing as he collapsed against Jonah's chest, damp with speckles of sweat, he asked, breathless, "Do you want to fuck me now?"

Imagining that would be the next step, he had no idea how to go about it, only that Sandra liked being fucked quite gently. Maybe Jonah liked it hard, and wouldn't it be better to get it over with sooner rather than later, so he didn't have time to mull it over till it tumbled almost painfully in his brain.

"Or you could fuck me," said Jonah, quite casually, his arm curved around Royce's shoulders. "But next time. Right now, I need to come and you need to help me."

There was a laugh in Jonah's voice, so Royce looked up and there it was in those brown eyes as well.

Jonah was being bossy just for fun, but there was no way Royce would make him wait, so he curled down, and sucked and kissed Jonah's cock, slow and then fast, licking the long cord of vein on the underside, doing all the things, doing more of those things that made Jonah's belly jump, pulled long, gut-uttered moans out of him. The way you did when you wanted to please someone and make them happy.

Well, Royce was making Jonah happy, it seemed in all kinds of ways, for when Jonah came, hard, milky pulses across Royce's smile, his head was tossed back, eyes tightly closed as if overcome, overcome with pleasure and delight.

"And that is how I roll," said Royce, overcome with pleasure and confidence as he scooted up Jonah's hard-breathing chest to plant kisses everywhere, everywhere.

Strong arms came around him, hugging him tight, almost too tight, a shudder passing through Jonah's body as if what they'd shared had almost been too much for him, as well.

Flicking his gaze up, he saw Jonah's brown eyes, impossibly deep and rich, like newly dug earth, flecks of raw gold so tenderly revealed, looking at him as if Royce was his treasure, newly found, and held quite dear. There were no words in Royce's brain just then, only the response, primal and swift, as he kissed Jonah, hard, and held him close, as if Jonah were the one who needed comfort and reassurance.

Another glance and it seemed that Jonah was almost too overcome, so Royce drew the top sheet and light cotton blanket over them both and reached for the bat book, and then the one about wolves.

Dreamily, he spilled his knowledge into the night air, until he felt Jonah put the book away, and together they drowsed on the three pillows. They listened to the sounds beyond the canvas tent, imagining bats and nightjars on the wing, beaks wide to devour insects, and how he would tell Jonah about them as soon as he could keep his eyes open long enough.

But he'd fallen asleep and woke Thursday morning to find himself so neatly and sweetly tucked in that he lingered in bed for a good ten minutes, before realizing that he needed a shower, desperately, and he wanted to be fresh and clean when he saw Jonah again.

When he scampered to the showers, he was on his own, as if all the ex-cons had chosen the same morning to sleep in, or perhaps, having experienced the gentleness of the valley, had determined it didn't matter when they got up or started work. Well, it did matter, but perhaps the ex-cons deserved a bit of a lie-in, so Royce plonked his tokens into the box, and used every ounce of the never-ending hot water.

He shaved faster than he'd ever shaved in his life and got dressed, rushing out of the showers just as Jonah was coming in, looking a bed-tousled delight in Royce's eyes, his dark, gray-shot hair tumbling over his eyes, beardgrowth fully evident, those brown eyes half closed, and sleepy.

Dangling from one hand was his plastic carrying case, and amidst the fold of towel was Royce's jackalope scarf. Which, not having been lost, was evidence that Jonah had kept it. For his own purposes, to be sure, but maybe Royce could imagine that Jonah had wanted a token of Royce to take with him. Even to the showers.

"We'll hold breakfast for you," said Royce, using the still moment between them to tuck the jackalope scarf safely away, so maybe Jonah would never know that Royce had seen it and knew that Jonah had it.

He might tease him about it later, but now feeling shy, knowing his face was flushed, he dashed off to the mess tent where he planned to grab a mug of the cook's hot, almost bitter coffee and allow himself time to wake up while the ex-cons tumbled from their cots and chose to join him.

Which they eventually did, one by one, freshly showered and shaved, coming to join Royce, getting cups of coffee from the silver urn that the cooks kept filled with fresh coffee, until they were all around the table together as the cooks served breakfast. Though, alas, Royce was at one end and Jonah was at the other, sharing glances and secret smiles that he was sure nobody else noticed.

The rest of the week sped by as they cleared paths and laid sand and flagstones to create gentle paths through the woods. By Sunday, Royce was ready for more one-on-one time with Jonah, rather than single, clandestine kisses when they thought nobody was looking. At breakfast, his nose buried in a coffee mug, he mentally outlined his hopes for repeat hike, and a repeat of what had come after the last hike. That is, if Jonah agreed.

"What's on the agenda today, boss?" asked Blaze, sitting across from Royce, scraping his long, dark hair back from his face.

"It's Sunday, m'friend," said Gabe, affection showing plainly in his voice and his eyes. "Tomorrow, as long as it doesn't get too hot or too wet, we can paint the shelters for the horses and finish that up, but today is a day of rest." Gabe looked at Royce. "Do we need more paint?"

"We might," said Royce. "If we do, I'll check with Maddy." He looked around the table at the ex-cons in his care. "You fellows are at your leisure. You can call home, play cards, read, nap, do your laundry. Whatever you like."

"Do we really get *every* Sunday off?" asked Gordy, eyebrows raised like he thought Royce was playing a trick on him.

"Yes, every Sunday," said Royce, nodding. "Consider it like a little weekly vacation." His team was still looking at him as if he'd gone quite mad, including Jonah, and he considered that in prison, convicts didn't get any days off, so this would be something new for them. "I was thinking of getting a packed lunch, and taking my binoculars up on the ridge to look for falcons, if anyone would care to join me?"

As he expected, most of the ex-cons were shaking their heads, as if a bit of fresh air and exercise was simply not on their agenda. Which meant that he and Jonah would get to go alone. That is, if Jonah agreed to go with him.

"What do you have planned, Jonah?" asked Royce, a sudden worry that Jonah was already regretting what they'd shared between them. But he didn't have to worry long, for Jonah winked at him, and gave him a secret smile.

"I thought Beck was coming, but I guess he isn't," he said. "I haven't heard from him anyway, so I'm free as a bird."

"What kind of bird?" asked Royce before he could stop himself, worried because it sounded like he'd been flirting out loud.

"The fastest, of course," said Jonah. Then he licked his lower lip and scowled a bit, concentrating. *"Falco peregrinus."* Smiling, he asked, "Did I say it right?"

"Exactly right," said Royce, joy and pride bubbling up inside of him. "We can leave right after lunch."

"Maybe I want to come with you," said Gordy, piping up from the end of the table. "I shook my head before, but now I want to go."

Royce froze. He was a team lead, so he couldn't hardly say no to one of his own team members. But Gordy saved him.

"Oh, never mind. It sounds too much like hard work."

Looking up, Royce could see that Jonah was scowling extra hard at Gordy, which explained why Gordy suddenly didn't want to go.

"We can do more hikes this summer," said Royce, polite and secretly pleased. "Plenty of times for you to join. For anyone to join."

Hikes, kisses, and more hikes? How could he ever have dreamed of such bliss as this?

CHAPTER 23
JONAH

The cozy cocoon of morning enfolded Jonah, and it took him a moment to realize where he was. Not in his room over the garage. Not in prison. Not in his own cot, with Gordy snoring gently across the small distance between their two cots. Instead, he was in Royce's cot being, of all things, the little spoon.

Jonah had never been the little spoon in his whole entire life, not even as a joke. Yet here he was, curled forward like a pill bug, chin tucked to his chest, knees drawn up, his ankles tangled in Royce's ankles. He was purely naked, as well, as was Royce, his ass tucked into the warm curve of Royce's hips.

He wanted the moment to last forever and ever, the warmth, the blissful simplicity of their two bodies connecting in comfort and closeness without anything else needing to happen.

Maybe the morning—Monday morning, he realized—would last for hours and they could stay like this until nightfall, when Jonah would most assuredly turn in Royce's arms and give him a taste of those feelings curling around inside of Jonah. That this was wonderful and so new that he almost didn't know what to do with it. That his feelings for Royce, whom he'd only known for a short while, had taken flight like a goldfinch in sunshine, or a bat in the moonlit dark.

He'd never felt this way before about anyone, not even Beck, where good feelings spun themselves into warm, deeper ones, and he no longer knew how to be coy or cool about it. And why should he be? Royce was never coy or cool, no. Instead, his heart was on his sleeve, his joy about every moment of life shining from his face, his smile.

How had he ended up in this delicious position? Oh yes, he and Royce had gone for a hike up to the ridge to look for birds and to hold hands and to sit on the rocks together, looking out over the valley below. And in spite of having taken that same trail just days before, the experience had been totally different, the views under the sunny skies as new as if he'd never seen them before. The wind had been different, the glint of sun on the rocks different.

And, as for him and Royce, they were in sync, their footsteps taken in tandem. Their eyes meeting, smiles echoing the pleasure in their hearts.

Coming back, they'd just missed the rain, scampering to Royce's tent. There, Royce had dried Jonah's hair and neck with as much care as if Jonah had been made of bone china. Then he'd drawn off Jonah's clothes and ransacked him with his mouth, his hands, sending Jonah into a series of pleasure spirals he never wanted to come down from.

Afterward, it had been easy, so easy, to pull Royce beneath him and love on him all over, kisses everywhere he could reach, tucking Royce's hands in his so he would be still while Jonah took Royce's cock in his mouth and pulled him right into pleasure. And then another time after that, watching Royce's eyes roll back in his head, a sight which would never grow old.

All of this had been done in the bright glow of the overhead bulb, as if there was no shame to be found in the whole universe, and especially not in Royce's tent. Then Royce had decided it was time for lavender tea, and while the kettle was boiling for that, he made Jonah get up and stand stark naked while he tidied the cot, which, after all of that, was quite comfortable to get back into.

Who in Jonah's world did anything like that, for fuck's sake? Nobody, that's who. Only Royce.

While they drank their tea, Royce was talking about the next hike he wanted to go on, maybe high enough to discover some pronghorn in the valley beyond the ridge. That sounded a whole lot more adventurous that he was ready for, but for Royce, he would go.

He was on the verge of saying yes, but he'd been so tired, so worn through, deliciously so, that he barely remembered Royce taking his empty mug, and urging him to scoot down in the cot so Royce could tuck him in. Maybe he'd fallen asleep when Royce had finally gotten under the covers as well, having turned off the overhead light, and together, in the sweet darkness, Jonah had finally fallen asleep.

Now it was morning, and he was awake. He was the little spoon, and wondering why in the world he'd never wanted to be one before this.

"Morning, my sweet," said Royce, whispering the words along Jonah's spine with a kiss. "It's time to get up or we'll miss breakfast."

Jonah would be willing to miss all the meals 'til the end of time if it could always be like this. At the very least, he'd be willing to pay someone good money to have the rest of the day canceled. But no, the sun was shining and yesterday there'd been a discussion about more painting, and the tasks of the day loomed.

Except behind him, Royce shimmied his hips, pressing his groin, the hardness of his cock, against the curve of Jonah's ass, and the warmth of this spread all the way through him. Screw it, work could wait, breakfast could wait.

Jonah turned in Royce's arms, almost spinning, until he had Royce in his arms, their hips pressed together, bodies joined in a delicious warmth, the coolness of the morning air settling over Jonah's shoulders.

Royce reached behind him and pulled the sheet and cotton blanket up, covering Jonah, tucking him in all over again.

"I think we've got time for a delay," said Jonah, holding himself quite still.

When Royce looked at him, that sweet mouth opening as if to ask a question, Jonah kissed him, quick.

"Oh, no." Royce covered his mouth and mumbled, "I've got morning breath."

"Screw that," said Jonah, most definitively. Then he kissed Royce again, licking into his mouth, murmuring softness against Royce's cheek, relishing every moment of this slow, slow morning that he would drag to a standstill if he could. The world could wait because Jonah had better things to do.

He ravaged Royce, kissing him breathless, reaching between their bodies to circle his fingers around Royce's cock, stroking him almost roughly to get him to spill into Jonah's hand.

He quieted Royce by stroking his belly and trailing kisses along his neck, then started all over again, this time more slowly. Slowly, which meant kisses to Royce's ear, tracing those pink curves with his tongue, sending Royce into shudders, a half-moan as he turned his head into his pillows, his cheeks flushed in the low light, tinted with a bit of green from the way the sunlight was pushing through the green canvas.

"D'you like that?" asked Jonah, his voice more raw than he'd expected, making him feel exposed, more naked, even if he'd been fully dressed. "D'you want that?"

Settling his head back on the pillow, Royce looked up at him with eyes so blue they were an ocean Jonah wanted to drown in.

"I want you," said Royce, quite clearly. "Just you."

Now it was Jonah who shivered. His whole body lit up from the inside, every word, every thought vanished into thin air. He scooted down beneath the bedclothes, pushing Royce's hands away, kissing his way down Royce's chest and sweet, round belly to between Royce's legs, the warmth of Royce's groin against his cheek as he took Royce's cock into his mouth. It was soft, tasting of salt, and he held and simply tongued it, round and round, feeling the low pulse of blood beneath the satin skin, the hard beneath the tender.

With each heartbeat, Royce's cock grew taut, the new hardness enticing Jonah to the point where he rose up on his knees, fingers curled around Royce's balls, twirling and twirling, his tongue echoing the motions around the top of Royce's cock. Then he reached down with his fingers, stroking Royce's hole, tender touches, but quick, which sent a cry from Royce's mouth, open, eyes half closed, as he seemed to lose himself in Jonah's ministrations, not being able to tell one touch from the other.

"D'you like that?" asked Jonah again, this time, his voice a low rumble from his chest. "I could make it better, if you want."

Royce's response was a low, quick moan, his cheek on the pillow again, which Jonah took as a yes. He popped his fingers in his mouth to lick them hard, then pushed between Royce's parted thighs again, stroking Royce's hole, sending more shivers up Royce's body before pushing in with a finger and pulling out. In and out.

Royce's eyes opened, slices of deep blue, pink mouth opened, and everything went still.

Had Jonah pushed it too far, gone too fast? He wasn't used to remembering that his bed partner was new to sex with another man. And Royce was too sweet to be used so hard, as hard as Jonah used some of his bed partners, so he relaxed his hands and leaned forward, kissing his way up Royce's chest, a kiss to his chin, a tender kiss on his beautiful mouth.

"Too much?" he asked. "D'you want me to stop?" He swallowed, his whole body screaming at him at this pause in what it wanted. His knees shook, his cock weeping against his belly. "To slow down?"

"Slow." Royce's eyes were wide, with surprise, maybe, or anticipation.

Jonah needed to focus on not doing what he might have done with someone else, which would be to slick himself up with his hand and just push right in, shoving to his own release. This was Royce, sweet, joyful, tender-eyed Royce, and Jonah wanted to do this the way that Royce needed it done.

"Slow it is, sweetheart." Ducking his head, Jonah took Royce's cock in his mouth and tickled Royce's hole with damp fingers, settling between Royce's quivering thighs. "I've got you," he whispered, pausing to kiss the crook of Royce's thigh, each side of Royce's tight balls, giving them a lick in between. Then he slunk down, all the way down, until he could trace the lines of Royce's anus with his tongue, tender licks that made Royce go absolutely still.

Jonah paused, waiting, waiting for hands to circle his wrists to get him to back off or to stop. But Royce only laid his fingers on top of Jonah's wrists, a slight pet, and then stillness.

Then Jonah did what he loved to do, his tongue on that silky skin as he licked, sending Royce wriggling, sweet, soft moans escaping his parted mouth. When Royce came, Jonah backed off, pressing his thumb, the curve of his wrist, against his mouth, smiling as he rested along the inside of Royce's warm thigh.

"Yeah?" he asked, though he already knew the answer.

"Yeah," said Royce, his voice guttural and low, pleasure making rich music of his panted breaths.

Sweeter still was to crawl up Royce's body to collect him close, tugging the sheet over both of them so they could doze a bit, Royce curled in Jonah's arms.

The reward for finally getting up and hustling to breakfast was that Jonah got to look at Royce over the rim of his mug, barely tasting the dark brew as he waggled his eyebrows at Royce just to watch him blush. Nobody noticed.

Well, maybe Gordy did, his eyebrows going up. Gordy wasn't stupid, and obviously he'd been fully aware that Jonah had not come back to the tent the night before. Add that to Royce"s pink face and his overly serious expression as he concentrated on his breakfast, and well. The world probably knew, only nobody probably gave a good God damn, as long as the work got done.

CHAPTER 24
ROYCE

It rained off and on for the next two days, which meant that by Wednesday, everything was damp, too damp to work. They finished each day early, covered their tools with sheets of tarp, and scurried off to the mess tent, there to lollygag, play cards, use the landline, and basically wait for dinner. The smells coming from the kitchen in the back of the mess tent were amazing, as was Jonah's laugh when he lost at a game of Old Maid.

"We should be playing poker," said Jonah, shuffling the cards in his deft hands as the rain pattered overhead on the green canvas tent. "This is just a kid's game."

"I cry when I lose at poker," said Royce, shaking his head, making a mournful face as if this were actually true, even though it wasn't. The fact of the matter was that poker required a different skill set than he wanted to use at the moment, and would detract from a fine time of Jonah-watching. Then, on the other hand, if they played poker, he could figure out what Jonah's card-playing tell was, which he'd been unable to do during three rounds of Old Maid. "But, okay. Let's play for pennies."

They bullied the others into donating their pennies, and Royce was just shuffling to deal out two hands, when Jonah lifted up in his seat and looked toward the opening of the mess tent, where a sheet of rain was coming down like a gray curtain.

"What the fuck?" he asked of nobody in particular, and Royce found himself looking in the same direction.

Maybe he heard the rumble of a faraway engine coming closer, or maybe that was just the sound of thunder along the ridge. He couldn't be sure. Only that Jonah jumped up and raced to the platform, standing just out of the rain as he looked out.

A moment later he was waving, shouting "Beck!" with a hard bark, laughing as Beck tumbled into the tent.

Beck shook himself the way a half-drowned dog might. Water from his dark hair went everywhere as he hugged Jonah tight and laughed, baring his teeth.

"Jesus Christ," said Beck, stepping back, wiping his eyebrows with a black-gloved hand. "I almost went off that fucking switchback coming down. You guys should pave it." Turning, Beck greeted everyone with a chin jerk, his eyes resting on Gordy, who was at the far end of the table, amusing himself with a child's puzzle, aged three to five. "Otherwise you're going to kill some customers before you can make any money."

"The customers don't come till next summer," said Gabe, which kind of made it sound as though Gabe didn't care about the ex-cons who might come to danger on that road. "And typically we don't allow visitors mid-week, but welcome, just the same."

"Why didn't you come on Sunday?" asked Jonah. "I called and called."

Ignoring Gabe, Beck pulled something out of his black leather jacket and slapped it against Jonah's chest.

"Because I was buying this for you," he said with a hard pat to the object. "Best I could find. It's not like your old one. It's better."

"Oh," said Jonah, his voice curling in the air with pleasure. "My boot knife!"

With one deft hand, Jonah pulled the blade out of its sheath, letting the silver edge sparkle in the air.

Royce knew about boot knives, but had never seen one as stealthy, as wickedly sharp as this one. Jonah probably knew his way around a dangerous blade, but Royce couldn't help a quick indrawn breath as the blade glittered while Jonah twirled the handle before slipping it back in its sheath.

Was there a rule about bringing boot knives as gifts? Probably not, as Leland mostly likely hadn't anticipated anything like this. Nor had Royce anticipated having his plans for a nice romp with Jonah in his tent so abruptly canceled.

"Will there be one more for dinner?" asked Royce as he got up. His goal was to be polite, though he dearly hoped that Beck would say no and head back up the deadly switchback road, back to Denver and far away from the valley.

"Yeah, if that's okay," said Beck with a casual shrug and a bit of a sneer.

Royce interpreted the double gesture as meaning that Beck didn't give a damn if it wasn't all right, he'd arrived in time for dinner, and was also planning on sitting in Royce's place right next to Jonah and he didn't care who objected. All this with a simple movement and facial expression, and Royce was already heartily sick of him.

"I'll tell the cooks," he said.

When he came back from his errand in the kitchen, where Dean told him there was plenty to go around and to stop apologizing, everybody was sitting at the same table, leaning toward Beck, who was in the midst of a story, it seemed like.

Royce took a seat at the very end of the table, on the other side of Gabe, who looked over his shoulder at him to make sure he had enough room.

"All right?" asked Gabe.

"Yes, thank you," replied Royce, keeping his voice low so as not to interrupt the story.

Which, evidently, amidst much hand waving and loud barks of laughter, was about not one, not two, but three high-speed chases Beck and Jonah had been involved in.

"They tried to use those fucking road spikes on Havana Street," said Beck, just about spitting as he laughed at how dumb cops were.

"But Jonah just drove up on the sidewalk, you see, and bypassed them completely."

"The cops were chasing you?" asked Royce, unable to keep his mouth shut, even if he knew he was being a stick-in-the-mud. "Why didn't you pull over?"

The ex-cons, every single one of them, laughed at Royce, and though they didn't point and jeer, it felt just about as bad as it could. He didn't want to be on the outs with his team, didn't want them to make him the butt of their joke, but he couldn't possibly approve of such gratuitous flouting of the law.

"Why didn't you pull over?" he asked again.

Steeling himself and, fully expecting to hear something along the lines of *we would have been arrested if they stopped us*, he was surprised at Jonah's answer.

"Because it was more fun to keep running," he said, bright sparks in his deep brown eyes, a fond smile for Beck, and a general grin for everybody else at the table, including, it seemed, Royce.

"It'd be years in prison for both of us if they caught us," said Beck. "The Jaguar was stolen, you see."

"Not by us," said Jonah, rolling his eyes and making a hand-waving gesture as if his part in this particular crime was completely and utterly defensible.

"It was an XJS saloon," said Beck, as if this detail was the most important fact of all. "A light gray-blue, I think, wasn't it, Jonah?"

"We made a mint, selling it for parts," replied Jonah with a grin that didn't look quite right and made the hairs on the back of Royce's neck stand up. He didn't know cars, not really, but he did know that Jaguars were expensive, well-tuned machines that should not be stripped down for parts.

"There was one time you did get arrested for speeding," said Beck, echoing the leer of Jonah's smile. "When you were driving with a shit ton of those ghost plates."

"Damn Wyoming," said Jonah with a laugh, looking around the table in a way that seemed he meant everyone to join in his mirth about the state. "There was nowhere to hide, and too many miles between exits, and so, ta-da!" He held out his wrists as though they had been cuffed. "Two years in the joint."

The story was meant to be funny. Even Royce could see that. But it wasn't funny, just a sheet of smoke and mirrors to disguise the fact that two years of Jonah's life had been taken away on account of his recklessness, and what was funny about that?

He didn't open his mouth to deliver a lecture, because it would mostly land on deaf ears. As well, Jonah suddenly flicked a glance his way, a dark, sorrow-eyed apology for him being this way. Then, a second later, he was slapping Beck on the back and howling at something Beck had said, which Royce had missed.

Only he didn't care that he'd missed it. He just knew that he didn't like who Jonah was when Beck was around. He didn't need more visits from Beck or more time spent in Beck's company to figure that out. Not that he was jealous, he simply wasn't impressed.

"Shall we get some dinner, guys?" asked Royce as he stood up.

Neal and Dean had long since turned on the steam tables and were now bringing out deep metal trays to place in the slots.

Everything smelled good, as it usually did, but Royce didn't have much of an appetite. In spite of that, he grabbed his tray and was at the head of the line, smiling to pretend everything was all right when it very much wasn't.

He needed to decide what he would say to Jonah once Beck had departed after showing up unannounced on a day not officially designated for visitors. They were all very busy at the valley and didn't need interlopers who laughed too loud and sat too close to Jonah and brought him sharp knives—

Royce pulled himself up straight. He was a grown man and so was Jonah, who had the right to be friends with anybody he liked. Still, visits needed to be restricted to Sundays, unless prior arrangements were made.

When he sat down, it was in a seat where he was within eyeshot of Jonah, but didn't have to see Beck talk or eat, and oh, yes, he was still blathering about other near-arrests that Jonah and he had been involved in that didn't involve a high-speed car chase.

Each and every near miss was considered a high victory, something to be celebrated, which they did with much laughter and waving of forks. They even had all the other ex-cons laughing too, which didn't really surprise Royce because these men had been in prison for a reason, which meant they had the same mindset that Jonah and Beck did.

Then Royce noticed that Gabe wasn't laughing and Blaze wasn't either, and that Gordy was rolling his eyes, as if he was completely unimpressed.

"He wouldn't have lasted a minute in a prison yard," said Gordy, suddenly, leaning across the table to whisper this to Royce.

"Excuse me?" asked Royce, his glass of iced tea halfway to his mouth. "Why not?"

"He's a dick who thinks he's king of the hill, that's why, and just about any con worth his salt would be itching to take him down."

Gordy rolled his eyes and pursed his mouth, as if that would help enforce his point. Then his gaze seemed to linger on Beck, and the annoyance melted away from his expression to be replaced by something Royce could not define.

"Don't worry," Gordy added now. "I think Jonah likes you better than he likes him, anyway, in spite of the stories."

Not knowing quite what to say to this, it took Royce a full minute to answer. He pretended that his iced tea had gone down the wrong way and that he needed a minute to breathe normally, his fist in front of his mouth. All the while Gordy watched him, sweetly, patiently, as if he meant for Royce to understand what was going on and had to point it out to him because Royce was too stupid to know any better.

"He can like who he likes," said Royce, focusing on his dinner and not the bright glare of Gordy's inspection of him.

He didn't add *It's of no nevermind to me* because, of course, he *did* mind, only he wasn't going to let it show. Maybe Beck wouldn't come back on the next Sunday, or maybe he would. Between now and then, Royce needed to get his head on straight and his heart in order.

Liking Jonah, caring about him a great deal, in fact, did not mean that Jonah had to stop caring for his friend, and who would Royce be to insist that he did? Another kind of dick altogether.

"I'm sure he can," said Gordy, somewhat cryptically. "And I'm sure he does." Then, with an arched eyebrow, he said, "Could you pass the salt, please?"

"Sure." Royce passed Gordy the salt and concentrated on his dinner and did his best not to care as much as he did. Only he was failing, and miserably.

CHAPTER 25

JONAH

After dinner, Jonah took Beck along the path through the damp grass down to the lake, not just because the view fascinated him, because it did, but also so they could test out Jonah's new boot knife with a quick game of mumblety-peg. Beck thought it would be more fun to stand on the picnic tables while they did this, but Jonah shook his head.

"I just spent hours painting those," he said. "You have no idea. It was gross and sweaty, and Royce even says they might need another coat."

"You sure seem fucking devoted," said Beck, frowning, but then he shrugged. "We can do it over here." He pointed to the very edge of the lake where the ground sloped down and was soft enough so it wouldn't damage the blades too much.

They started by doing casual throws, flicking their knives from their palms, their wrists, then their shoulders, between a thumb and forefinger. Then, when they were warmed up, they stood a bit apart, legs spread, and did Rock Paper Scissors to see who would go first. Beck won and, with a laugh, gestured that Jonah should be ready.

Jonah steadied himself and didn't flinch when Beck's knife landed only an inch away from the inside of his left foot, almost cutting into his still-new yellow boots. Beck's aim had always been deadly, but it seemed in the two years Jonah had been away that Beck had been practicing.

"Damn," said Jonah, not too proud to give Beck his due. Then he had a go, flipping his knife between Beck's spread legs, snickering when he got close to Beck's foot, and shaking his head as if to say, *I'll never be as good at this as you are.*

Of course, he couldn't say it out loud, as it wouldn't do to give Beck a swelled head and an overly large sense of his own skills. Or maybe he should say it out loud, because maybe that's what Royce would do. "You've gotten better," he said after a low whistle. Then he added, "I mean, seriously, dude!"

There was a faint flush of pleasure on Beck's cheeks that made Jonah feel good inside. Beck deserved to be acknowledged for his skill with the knife, and Jonah knew he'd done very little of that in the year before he'd gotten arrested.

He was glad to make up for lost time with compliments, but there was still a game to be won, so Jonah threw himself into mumblety-peg, checking his aim, making sure his new boot knife was well-balanced before each throw. Getting closer to Beck's foot each time, both his right foot and his left foot. Getting close to Beck's right foot was harder because Jonah was right-handed.

Beck, on the other hand, was ambidextrous, which Jonah had forgotten, and in possession of some mad skills, coming so close to Jonah's feet inside those boots that he began to worry about the new leather.

When the sun was going down, they called it a draw, though Jonah was sure Beck should be the winner, though he didn't say this out loud. He walked Beck to the parking lot where the olive green Pontiac was gleaming beneath the pine trees, and gave Beck a quick hug.

"I was going to come to Cheyenne for a car show this Saturday," said Beck, his hands lingering on Jonah's arms as if he couldn't bear to let go. "Thought I'd come up here after, and we could hang out."

"No," said Jonah, peeling back Beck's fingers. "We've got our little outing on Saturday night to John Henton's Tavern."

THE COWBOY AND THE HOODLUM

"What outing?" asked Beck. "Why didn't you tell me?"

"Because I just remembered," said Jonah. "It's like a little graduation ceremony in the valley. We get to go out, have a beer, and we get cellphones for our very own use. It's for team members only."

Beck was scowling when he got into his car, but Jonah couldn't make himself care, he was too excited about getting a new phone and sharing a beer with Royce.

"See you on Sunday," he shouted over the rumble of the burbling engine. Beck gave him the finger, and he gave Beck the finger right back and, tossing his sheathed boot knife in his hand, turned around and started walking toward the mess tent, intent on finding Royce.

The mess tent was a lively place, with Gordy, Blaze, and two other guys, all who were deep inside a game of gin rummy, it looked like, with Gabe watching, reminding them of the rules. That Wayne guy was on the phone, talking in a loud voice to someone. But Royce wasn't there.

"Hey?" he asked, raising his voice to be heard over Wayne.

Flipping a card on the table and without looking up, Gordy said, "He's in his tent. Something about plans for viewing towers."

"Oh," said Jonah, blinking, wondering how Gordy knew whom he'd he been looking for. "Thanks."

Speeding up to a trot, Jonah made his way in the growing darkness to Royce's tent. He really should have his flashlight on him, but he wasn't used to thinking about that, and besides, what did it matter, when the golden glow of the light from Royce's tent was shining over the platform and into the darkness beyond. It was like following a spotlight, and it felt pretty good to jump up on the platform and knock loudly and obnoxiously on the tent pole of Royce's tent.

"Can I come in?" he asked.

"Sure," said Royce's voice from inside, low and maybe not very welcoming.

When Jonah pushed the tent flap aside, he saw why. Royce was sitting on his cot, the overhead bulb blaring, curled over a thin, curved plank of wood on his lap, a little lap desk. It looked like he was busy drawing something, pencil on paper. Jonah couldn't be sure, so he inched a bit closer.

"What's that you got there?" he asked, growing cautiously aware that Royce's attention wasn't on him even though he was standing right there. "I brought my new knife, if you wanted to see it up close?"

Jonah held out the knife, his mouth open, on the verge of telling Royce all about the amazing game of mumblety-peg he and Beck'd just had, when Royce held up a finger, and then kept on drawing.

Frowning, Jonah shifted his weight, first on one foot and then the other, thinking again how close he'd come to getting his lovely new boots sliced up and how, next time, he'd be sure to change into his old black boots before going up against Beck in a knife fight. And still Royce kept drawing.

"Hey," said Jonah, sitting right down next to Royce on the cot, unable to stand it a second longer. "Show me what you're doing."

Royce seemed to pause, then took a breath as if deciding how much to share with Jonah, which wasn't like Royce at all. Jonah held very still as Royce turned the lap desk so Jonah could see the rough sketch of the ridge and three outlines of what must be the viewing towers Gordy had mentioned.

"What are those?" asked Jonah, pointing, feeling oddly like he was walking on his tiptoes into a dark room, where maybe there were landmines.

"These are viewing towers." Royce tapped the middle drawing with his pencil, which was in fact a very nice looking mechanical pencil. "Leland had hired someone to design these, but they backed out. Since I took drawing lessons when I was a kid and a bit of landscape design and drafting in college, I thought I could help."

Once again, Royce amazed him with how much he knew how to do. It was like beneath all that hair, that beautiful brain couldn't help but absorb everything in the world around it. Which made him pretty much the smartest person Jonah had ever met. And that included Beck, who was pretty smart.

"Are we going to build those?" That was the first thing that came to

THE COWBOY AND THE HOODLUM

his mind: how much work would be involved, how much sweat and effort.

"We might," said Royce. "First, we have to build a bridge across the marsh. There is another way in. The back way, you remember? When we went upstream and crossed that footbridge? That's how we'd bring supplies in, I think. Get the truck loaded up, take the logs and beams as far up the ridge as we can manage, and then carry it the rest of the way. Or carry them in by helicopter, I don't know."

With a sigh, Royce relaxed from his earlier stiff stance, as if talking about a project he was interested in made him feel good. Well, maybe Jonah would never be as interesting as how to build a viewing tower, but he was going to do his best.

"Did you want to see my knife?" he asked, holding it out to Royce. The warmth between their bodies was slight, but it was growing, the cot creaking slightly beneath them. "Handle first, as always."

Royce took the knife, and it was no surprise to Jonah that he held it properly, like he knew the value of a sharp blade, knew how to handle it, handle in his palm, thumb curled around just below the bolster, to steady it.

The blade glittered in the electric light, a dangerous little piece that he was already proud to own. But Royce didn't look at it for long, only re-sheathed the blade, and handed it back to Jonah, handle first.

"That looks like it'd be good in an alley fight," said Royce, pleasantly enough, but his face had the expression that told Jonah that there might be something wrong with not only being involved in a fight in an alley, but being prepared for it, being *good* at it.

"What's in that pretty head of yours, I wonder." Jonah reached up and pushed a golden curl back from Royce's temple, happy to see that at least Royce didn't pull back from the touch, even though there was something in his face that Jonah couldn't quite define. "What is it?"

"I wanted to say," began Royce, then he paused to lay his hands on the pieces of paper on the lap desk to truly look at Jonah, his eyes very blue and serious. "Beck shouldn't have come on Wednesday, as that's not how the program was set up. That is, initially, though I suppose there's always room for change. The thing is, he came unannounced, and the cooks had to scramble to accommodate him. It's rude. They shouldn't have had to do that."

"Rude of Beck?" Jonah's eyebrows shot up in his forehead, and he had to blink, hard, several times, as the idea Royce had just presented to him whirled in his head. "The cooks didn't seem to mind."

"That's because they're pros at what they do." The way Royce was looking at him was almost a stern glare, as though even if Jonah didn't already know this, he should understand it, understand the implications of it.

There'd been plenty of food to go around, and Beck's manners had been no worse than anyone else's. So what if he was constantly mentally sneering at everything in the valley? So what?

"You don't like Beck." It wasn't a question.

"I don't know him well enough not to like him," said Royce. "But I think he's a bad influence on you."

"I'm the bad influence on *him*," said Johan, barking a laugh. "I'm the one who went to prison, remember?"

"That was just bad luck." Royce clicked his mechanical pencil and rearranged the drawings in a tidy stack on his lap desk. "The way you two ran around, it could just as easily have been him who was arrested that day."

"No." Jonah shook his head. He wanted to stand up and shout this fact, but he held himself still, puzzling over what it was that Royce was truly upset about. "I was the one involved in the ghost plates. That's what got me arrested. Not him."

"You don't get it, do you." Now it was Royce standing up, placing his lap desk and papers on the cot. "All of this happened to you, and you still don't seem to understand that being on the wrong end of a police chase is not a humorous anecdote. Did being in prison teach you nothing?"

"No." Jonah stood up too, and now they were almost toe to toe in Royce's tent, the overhead light a glare that seemed to be doing its best to be absorbed by the soft color of the green canvas and failing. "I mean. Not much. They did teach me how to make birdhouses out of old Wyoming license plates, but that skill's not going to do me much good in the real world when I go back to my shop in Denver."

"Is that what you want?" Royce asked, seeming a little sad as he reached out to touch Jonah's face, quite gently, with the tips of his fingers. A soft stroke. Reaching out in a way that Jonah found impossible to resist.

Going back to the shop at the end of the summer would mean living in a world where there was no Royce. Plus, he couldn't imagine, not even for one minute, that Royce would want to live over a garage whose main business was stealing cars and stripping them for parts.

Royce probably wouldn't want to live over *any* garage, because there were no birds where Jonah had lived before prison. Or maybe there had been, but none interesting enough to tempt Royce.

"Is it?"

The sadness in Royce's blue eyes had been replaced by a deep light, through which Jonah could almost feel Royce's concern for him, affection, even love, which surprised him. Love was just a word, or it had been, and even all their tumbles in bed hadn't struck him in the heart, as deeply as this single look from Royce.

"I don't know," he said, as honestly as he could. "Sometimes I think so—"

He paused. His heart was pounding so hard, in a way it never had before, all the memories of his time shared with Royce, looking at the goldfinch, listening to bats winging their way in the darkness. Everything.

His pre-prison life had never included any of the feelings, not any of them, that he'd had since meeting Royce. And maybe that made it worth thinking about his life a little differently. Which, in its own way, was the scariest thing he'd ever considered.

What if he did something differently, only he fucked it up so bad, it ended up being worse than anything he could ever imagine? And what if that fuckup lost him Royce?

"I honestly don't know," he said, meaning it with everything he had. "But I'll tell Beck to at least call first, when he comes to visit, no matter what day it is."

"That's all well and good," said Royce, nodding his approval. "But I'm more concerned about you. With helping you figure out the kind of life that you want."

"Which you want for all the ex-cons," said Jonah, a little laugh in his throat, as he suddenly wanted to drown in Royce's small smile, overcome beyond his ability to cope with the joy and affection he saw in those blue eyes.

"Of course I want good things for all of you," said Royce. His hand came to Jonah's cheek and stayed there. "But you're the only one I've invited into my tent."

Jonah lifted his hand and placed it over Royce's hand, holding the warmth in, drawing Royce closer with a little tug on Royce's waist.

"I don't mean to be pissy about Beck," said Royce, quite low, his chin ducked.

This made Jonah laugh, a rumble in his chest, a helpless giggle in his throat. "That's the way I feel about him half the time."

"Is that the way you should feel about a friend?" asked Royce, suddenly going still. "Is it?"

"It's complicated." And it was, and though Jonah had been able to balance his feelings about Beck in the past, since getting out of prison and coming to the valley, that had changed, along with everything else, every way he looked at the world, reacted to it. Even the way he dressed and went about his day. All because of Royce.

"Sometimes I think I should do better by him. I was so mean to him before I got arrested." He shrugged. "I think I was frustrated. Not with him, but with myself."

"Why was that?" asked Royce, perhaps the first person to ask it, but then, he was the first person to whom Jonah had told how he'd felt at the time.

"It's like I fall back into a kind of black hole." He peered at Royce, feeling the intensity of this idea rising inside of him, feeling helpless, unable to describe it better than that. "You know?"

"I think there are many black holes in life," said Royce somberly, looking as though he wanted to grab one of his many books and look something up. "Which sounds ridiculous when all I want to do is kiss you and have you kiss me back so we can have marvelous makeup sex after our quarrel."

"Did we quarrel?" asked Jonah, thinking of how a little bit of heated discussion in a green canvas tent stacked up against the bitch-fests that used to ensue when Beck discovered that Jonah had drunk all of his favorite beer, and proceeded to lob the empty bottles at his head.

"We did," said Royce, simply, rising up on his toes to kiss Jonah on the mouth. "While we didn't solve everything, we realize we have different ways of looking at things. And as we move forward, we'll figure everything else out. In the meantime, I'd like to get my clothes taken off me, if you please, and to have you help me with that, if you're willing."

"Fuck yeah," said Jonah, though it came out as a gasp, desperate with gratitude that he'd not fucked everything up with Royce, who seemed to still want to be with him, in spite of the company Jonah kept. Though, in reality, Beck was a good friend, and it was up to Jonah to convince Royce of that. "Come here to me now, sweet man."

His hands came around Royce's waist, and he pulled Royce to him so they were hip to hip, warmth growing steadily between them, an eager light in Royce's blue eyes that Jonah had longed to see ever since he'd knocked on Royce's tent post.

"I'll strip you right down to the skin," he said, whispering this in Royce's ear. "But gently. So, so, so gently."

Royce shivered in his arms, tucked his face into Jonah's neck, and sighed, his arms coming around Jonah's waist.

"I've been waiting to hear that all day," he said with a happy sigh. "Just take me to bed, please. And show me how gentle you can be."

In this, Jonah obliged him, feeling that never again would there come a time when he could deny Royce anything.

CHAPTER 26

ROYCE

Royce knew when he was being courted. That was, he knew when he was being courted by *Jonah*, because any flirtation, dating, or anything Royce had experienced in high school and college could not compete with what Jonah was up to. There were no flowers delivered or boxes of Godiva chocolates arriving at his tent. No, nothing as trite as that. Instead, Jonah piled on seemingly whatever he thought Royce would like to see or hear about or experience.

Thus, the very next day, when they were at the edge of the woods near the marsh piling up sawed off hunks of wood for the new footbridges, Jonah came up to him, panting, his eyes wide, arms spread as if to encompass the very exciting thing that he had to tell Royce.

"What is it?" asked Royce, pushing up his safety goggles and lowering his saw.

"It's not a mourning dove," said Jonah. "Or a goldfinch, but it's been hopping around the pile of brush over there, cute as anything. Come see. Come, tell me what it is."

That spoke to Royce's heart in a way he'd not expected, because usually he was hefting his knowledge about birds, bats, wolves, and so forth, without really expecting that anyone would be interested in what he knew. Sure, his brothers and his Grandad were always gracious listeners, but they knew as much as he did, so it was never as much fun.

Jonah made it fun. Even more than that, he made it gratifying, his eyes wide as he listened to Royce explain that what they were looking at were black-capped chickadees, some of the cutest birds in Wyoming.

"I can hear their morning calls from my tent," said Royce, smiling as the pair of birds danced from one low branch to another, lighting there as if they'd followed Jonah as he raced toward Royce.

"Come on, come on," said Jonah, tugging on Royce's sleeve. "What's the Latin for it?"

"*Poecile atricapillus*," said Royce, a smile on his face that went all the way to his bones.

"*Poecile atricapillus*," said Jonah, all but whispering, his mouth moving over the words as if he wasn't just memorizing them, he was absorbing them into his very soul.

This deserved a kiss, which Royce delivered with some swiftness, as there were others nearby, and he really didn't feel like sharing the moment with them, or having them get jealous because he was paying more attention to Jonah than anyone else.

"Let's finish up these walkways," he said, smiling against Jonah's mouth. "Leland is sending some of his ranch hands down this afternoon to help us put them in place. After which, we could take a little hike along the other side of the river to see what we need to do to continue the path."

"And to hold hands," said Jonah, on the verge of a pout like a three-year-old who very much fears he will not be included in a special adventure. "Maybe kiss a little."

"But of course," said Royce, shaking his head as if Jonah were just being silly. Which they both were, in the sweet, innocent quiet of the woods near the marsh. "Come on, then," he said. "Give me a hand with this and we'll be finished in time for lunch."

After lunch, around ten ranch hands showed up, which meant that the project of laying the two walkways over the marsh was an amusing mix of efficiency and the Three Stooges, a reference which almost no one got, except for Quint, of all people, who guffawed a laugh just as one of the ranch hands slipped and fell backwards into the marsh.

They fished the ranch hand out and stabilized the ends of the two walkways, and it was then that Royce could make his first foray into the shade of the growth of dappled willows that lined Half Moon Lake on the far side.

There was a kind of path, but it was narrow, having been made by, he assumed, foxes, rabbits, and other wild critters who would feel safe among the willows. The smell was amazing, spicy and green and damp, and the shade nice and cool.

The trick would be to create a path without ruining the lushness. He'd need to do a longer hike to survey, and then he'd consult with Leland and Gabe before setting his team to the task of building paths.

His satisfaction in his work was amped up by Jonah's constant companionship and the sweetness they shared in his tent when the sun went down. If the summer went on as it had been, he'd be a very happy man.

CHAPTER 27

JONAH

Beck had been told quite clearly that the evening's celebration at John Henton's Tavern did not include him, but as Royce drove his team into Farthing, Jonah kept a sharp lookout, his head practically on a swivel. There was no telling how or when Beck would decide that any rules he didn't like, let alone polite requests, did not apply to him, and he'd crash the party.

That didn't mean Jonah didn't feel bad about saying no to Beck. He did. Beck's expression, hang-dog and sad, had been so sad that Jonah wanted to turn to Royce and ask him if Beck couldn't come anyway, but he knew he'd regret that choice.

If Beck did come, he'd want all of Jonah's attention. He'd want to talk shop and tell funny stories about stealing cars and handing payoffs to the local cops to look the other way. Subjects that Jonah already knew made Royce wince with distaste.

Royce was a law-abiding guy. Beck was not. The farther away Jonah kept the two, the more peaceful his life would be.

"Is this it?" asked Jonah, as he, Gordy, Duane, and Tyson piled out of the silver F-150. Royce had parked on a side street of the sleepiest looking town Jonah had ever been in.

There was no paid parking, not as far as he could see. There was only free parking, and very few cars were parked along the sidewalk, anyway. And, rather than a sense of Saturday night excitement growing, as it did around the apartment in Denver, a pre-twilight sleepiness lingered all around him.

"This is it," said Royce, bright and chipper as he waved them in the direction of the tavern's front door. "We're a bit early for our reservations, I think, but that just means we get to order extra appetizers."

"Reservations," said Jonah, almost under his breath. "Fancy."

Royce flicked a smile at him, holding open the door for the three of them, and Jonah couldn't remember the last time anyone had held a door open for him, or bowed as he walked past, like he was someone special. But then Royce liked these little niceties, and it felt nice, besides, to hold his head up high as the host, a young woman, came up to them with a stack of menus in her hands.

"We're just about to open," she said. "But we're not quite ready yet."

"We're early for our reservation," said Royce, his chin just about brushing Jonah's shoulder as he stood close behind him. "We just wanted to come and sit."

"Reservation for—" She looked them over and then smiled. "Are you from the valley? The rehab program?"

"That's right," said Royce. "That's us."

"Well, let me take you to your table and leave some menus with you."

She gestured that they should follow her, which they did, to a booth along the far wall near the empty dance floor. Reaching out, she picked up the folded card that said *Reserved for our Valley Guests*, and smiled at Royce.

"I'll bring you some waters, and the waitress will be over as soon as she gets here. Shouldn't be long."

"That's fine," Royce said, and she hurried off. "Anybody care to scoot in?"

Duane and Tyson both slid in all the way to the inside of the booth, one on either side, and there was a chair for Gordy at the end.

This left Jonah and Royce to sit across from each other. Which was fine by him, as it meant he could look and look at Royce to his heart's

THE COWBOY AND THE HOODLUM

content and it wouldn't seem strange or out of place. He could even play footsie, if he wanted to.

A busboy came over with five glasses and a pitcher of water, then proceeded to pour the water, making quite a drama out of it, like he was a waiter at a fancy restaurant, rather than a busboy in a tavern in the middle of a small town in the middle of nowhere. A tavern decorated with wagon wheels and red and white gingham-checked curtains and tablecloths, and paintings on the walls of buffalo and antelope.

"Your waiter will be right with you."

Jonah's stomach growled as he pulled the menu toward him, enjoying the glossy pictures of hamburgers piled high with just about everything.

"The onion rings are very good here," said Royce from behind the wall of his menu. "Everything is, really."

Blue eyes peered at Jonah from over the top of the menu that Royce was holding open as reverently as a prayer book, making him look very angelic and utterly kissable. But of course, it was too public to do something like that, so then Jonah had to resist pulling Royce into the nearest dark corner, of which there weren't any.

At such an early hour in the afternoon, the tavern felt more like a family restaurant than the dark hangouts Jonah had gone to before his stint in prison. He almost felt out of place, and he knew Beck would have felt the same.

With a pang at the thought of Beck's sad face, Jonah concentrated on his menu. When the waitress came by with a little sashay and a pat to her apron, they told her they'd need another minute, and then she sashayed away.

"There he is," said Royce, unexpectedly. "Leland, over here," he said loudly, with a big wave.

Leland Tate stood at the door, tall and manly, hat in hand, and a pink plastic carrier bag dangling from his fingers.

Jonah had a sudden flashback of the Zoom meeting he'd had with Leland on a ratty laptop in a wood-paneled room just off the warden's office. Back then, only weeks ago, he'd been dubious about the whole idea of going to a work camp to complete his parole.

He'd been on the verge of saying no and fuck off, imagining the whole thing was a scam, a trick to get ex-cons to sign up for what would amount to being a chain gang, like the ones he'd heard about in Texas and Oklahoma. Where men slept in tents after working from sunup to sun down in one hundred degree heat.

He'd been so sure of it he'd prepared a funny story for Beck when he saw him next visiting day. Only the valley had turned out to be different. Definitely not a chain gang in any way, shape or form, and he'd definitely not suffered. Instead, he'd met the most amazing man, the most *beautiful* man—

"You fellows having a good time?" asked Leland as he came up to them, smiling. "I hear your first two weeks were very productive, and I'm proud of you all."

He nodded at them, each in turn, a warm smile from that handsome face, and it made Jonah blink. He could feel a scowl forming between his brows and wondered at his sudden rush of emotions. Nobody had ever really told him that before, and while it could have been condescending, the way Leland said it sounded like he meant it.

"Thanks for bringing these," said Royce. "I ordered them the first day, but there were so many delays and maybe I didn't fill out the form right—"

He seemed a bit flustered as he took the pink plastic bag from Leland, which was concerning until Jonah realized that, of course, Leland was Royce's boss, and he wanted Leland to approve of him. So Jonah spoke up.

"It was great," said Jonah, bringing everyone's attention to him, a spotlight he regretted creating, but he squared his shoulders and kept going, for Royce's sake. "I thought it would suck. You know." He shrugged, feeling the skin flush along the back of his neck. "That it would be more like a chain gang than what it was."

"Which was?" asked Leland, and he seemed perfectly serious about wanting to hear Jonah's answer. "I've gotten a little bit of feedback about the chain gang angle." He grinned, shaking his head, amusement bright in his eyes. "So what could I tell other potential parolees to help 'em see the truth of it?"

Jonah knew he was gawping. He couldn't help it.

Maybe he was a little in awe of Leland, due to his status as the foreman of the nearby guest ranch and the man in charge of the entire valley. Jonah also hated being put on the spot, but he'd put himself there, good and proper, in defense of Royce, who was looking at Jonah as if utterly charmed by his bravery in speaking up.

"Just say it to them," said Jonah, feeling very bold and clever. "Right out loud."

"Right out loud?" asked Leland. "Like, right out loud as in hey, fellas, it's not a chain gang?"

"They won't believe you," said Tyson, speaking up, making everyone look at him instead of Jonah. "You'd be wasting your breath."

"I guess they'll just have to have faith," said Leland, utterly serious now, and Jonah could see why anybody who'd resisted Leland's plan about having ex-cons develop the retreat would have fallen back, hands up in defeat within two hot minutes. "Just like you fellows did, faith that things can get better, if you're willing to put in the work."

On a normal day, any other day, Jonah would have scoffed and maybe rolled his eyes at the earnestness of this statement, the utter purity of the idea of signing up for anything based on faith. Not today. And certainly not about anything Leland might say or do or think, because it was Leland who'd made the program that Jonah had signed up for and where he'd met his one true love, the angelic-haired Royce.

"Go on, then," said Leland, gesturing to the pink plastic bag. "Hand 'em out, then I'll let you fellows get on with your festivities."

"All right," said Royce, eagerly reaching into the bag. "Thank you again, Leland."

As Leland left, Royce pulled out four white boxes that Jonah recognized immediately. Of course, he knew they were getting phones at the end of two weeks, but he'd forgotten. The sight of those white boxes, delicate looking but heavy, created a flash of realization that now he could call Beck anytime he wanted, and Beck could call him back. Or text, even.

"Can they text?" asked Jonah, rolling the box in his hands before opening it to reveal a quite new-looking Android phone. He knew it was a refurb phone, and that it had six months' worth of data on it. He knew it was all his and that even though it was cheaper than any phone he'd owned, used, it was part of his ticket back into civilization.

"Sure can," said Royce. He waited a minute while they gawped at their phones, then reached out his hand to Jonah. "Come on," he said. "Hand it over."

With a smile, his chest rising as though buoyed up by happiness, Jonah handed his phone to Royce and watched as Royce scrolled and tapped, knowing that what he was getting was direct access to Royce. Forever, or at least until he changed his phone number.

That happiness dimmed a bit as Royce did the same with the other phones and then everyone exchanged numbers. But Jonah's had been the first phone.

"If you need me, you can reach me, even after the program is over," Royce said. "I'll help you all I can." Then he added, "Go on, text me. Let's test it."

Eagerly the four ex-cons bent over their phones like a group of bored teenagers at a museum, thumbs going madly. Royce's phone pinged quickly, four times, but he nodded at Jonah, and Jonah knew he'd been the fastest.

Pleased, Jonah lifted his chin, then updated his contacts to include Royce's number. Almost as an afterthought, and feeling bad about it, he added Beck's information, which he'd not forgotten, and probably never would.

The waitress came over and the ordering began, a not-quite-solemn progression from appetizers to drinks to the main course and, naturally, dessert. The waitress, very good-naturedly, took notes and made suggestions, and then sashayed away to the bar to get them their drinks and onion rings and hot pretzels with mustard.

"Bring me some beer," growled Jonah, mock-ferociously, both fists pounding the table. He'd not had a beer in over two years, but his taste buds were already perking up and crying out for it. "Bring it!"

The waitress brought their drinks, as well as the appetizers, and

THE COWBOY AND THE HOODLUM

they all drank and ate as though they'd been starving. The onion rings were delicious, crispy and juicy at the same time, perfect dipped in ketchup.

Jonah preferred the onion rings to the pretzel bites, but had a few anyway, just to keep his hand in. Plus, it was almost more fun watching Royce moan while he ate his. The most amazing cheeseburgers followed that, followed by brimming bowls of banana pudding, made with real bananas, and tasting like heaven.

"Roll me home, boys," said Royce, licking his spoon, looking at Jonah while he did this.

Jonah kicked him a little under the table because Gordy, Duane, and Tyson were right there, watching, wide-eyed, collapsing into good-natured, beer-gentled guffaws.

They knew. They had to know what was going on between their team lead and fellow ex-con, but there was nothing Jonah could do about it, unless he was willing to take his boot knife and cut out their tongues. At best, all he could do was glare, and his teammates shrugged because, as it was obvious, they didn't give a damn who Jonah was dallying with, now or ever.

"You okay to drive?" asked Jonah, as Royce paid the bill with a crisp new-looking blue credit card.

"I'm good," said Royce. "You're sweet to ask."

The trip back to the valley was short, it was only two miles after all, but Duane had said something about texting his high school sweetheart, which all set them to giggling for some moments, then that stopped with a collective sigh as Royce paused the truck at the top of the hill before the switchback descended into the valley.

"Will you look at those stars," Royce said, turning his head to look directly at Jonah.

"Do you have a book about them?" asked Jonah. "With Latin in it?"

"I used to," said Royce. "I loaned it to my Grandad, and I think he still has it."

"You should get another one," said Jonah, then he amended this, not wanting to seem too eager, but then fuck it, surely Royce already knew how much Jonah adored that brain of his. "We could order it. You know. Together."

"On my laptop," said Royce with a happy sigh. "Let's do it."

He drove them all safely down the dark switchbacks, the truck's headlights cutting through the pitch black darkness like a glowing pair of silver blades.

When he parked, Gordy, Duane, and Tyson scrambled out, giggling as they used their phones as flashlights, square blocks of light jumping about as they hurried to their shared tent. Which left Jonah and Royce sitting in the parked truck while the engine pinged as it cooled.

"Shall we go to your tent and order a book?" asked Jonah. His other suggestion, waiting in the wings, was that they could make out in the truck like a couple of wild youngsters, making the truck rock on its axles until somebody came knocking on the windows, telling them to cut it out. Those were the days.

"And other things," said Royce with a little happy lift of his shoulders, as if those other things were completely innocent, but his wink in Jonah's direction told its own story.

"Yeah," said Jonah, giving a little I-don't-care shrug that he had the sudden feeling had seen better days, and didn't fit with how he really felt, that going back to Royce's tent was the best idea anybody'd ever had. "Let's go. I've got a new phone. We can use it as a flashlight."

They got out of the truck, and Royce left the keys in the ignition because there was, quite simply, nobody interested in stealing it. Then Royce slipped his arm through Jonah's arm and, as if they were heading a procession of couples, paraded happily through the dark woods, lit only by Jonah's phone.

CHAPTER 28

JONAH

On Sunday morning, Jonah called Beck on his new cellphone to make sure he was coming that day. Later, he told Royce and the cooks that *Beck* had called to say he was coming for lunch on Sunday, a very small lie that he knew would slip under the radar because it'd only been him and Beck on that phone call.

Nobody needed to know that Beck wasn't as polite as all that. The only thing that needed to happen was for Royce to believe that Beck was a changed man, enough to the point where he would be considerate enough to call first before visiting Jonah in the valley.

"What time will he be here?" asked Royce at breakfast on Sunday morning, which consisted of French toast and sausages and freshly squeezed orange juice that was sending Jonah's mouth into dances of rapture.

"Around ten, I think," said Jonah, though he didn't really know because he and Beck had not discussed when. "I thought I'd take him up into the willows, give him an appreciation of nature."

"You're going to take him on our path?" asked Royce, his blue eyes going a little bit round and sad.

"Or maybe I'll show him how we feed and groom the horses." Not that Jonah'd had much to do with the horses in the pasture, but he'd done his share of raking manure and getting horsehair all over himself.

"Well, if he's here long enough," said Royce, "you can probably show him everything that you haven't already."

There was an expectant, wide-eyed expression on Royce's face that Jonah could only interpret as Royce wanting to know how long Beck was going to be there that day. And though Jonah knew it was because Royce did not care for Beck, he was also hoping that it was because Royce wanted more time to have Jonah to himself. So maybe Jonah would tell Beck not to come at all next week, if that were the case, because he'd like to have Royce to himself, as well.

"We'll come up with some way to have fun," said Jonah, winking at Royce as he downed his delicious orange juice. And just where the fuck had this orange juice been all his life, anyhow?

Beck showed up, the Pontiac's engine burbling, the sun shining off the chrome bumpers, late in the afternoon. He should have been there for lunch, and Jonah could feel Royce watching him from the mess tent as Jonah hugged Beck and slapped his back, and didn't say anything at all about the fact that the cooks had prepared enough food for lunch to include Beck.

Unsaid by anyone, even Royce, was that the food had gone uneaten and was now stored in the fridge. But who cared about any of that? Beck's smile told Jonah he was in a happy mood, right from the get-go.

They played three good games of mumblety-peg until their shoulders were tired, their fingers laced with small cuts.

"We should wash for dinner," said Jonah, as they put away their knives and shook the dust from their shoulders.

"Fine," said Beck, as if Jonah had compounded error with stupidity. Then, as they washed at the sinks across from the toilets, Beck, while frowning at himself in the mirror, said, "This place is so fucking weird."

"Yeah?" asked Jonah. "How so?" He knew it was weird, but he'd grown used to it, and if Beck had an opinion, then Jonah was happy to hear it because wasn't that what friends did?

"You told me they were going to charge more than four hundred a night, right?"

Jonah nodded, because that was true.

"They got fancy shower heads. You showed me those, and I can see this is fancy soap."

"So?"

"There's a frog in here. I can hear it," said Beck, flapping his hands dry before wiping them on his dark jeans. "Who is going to pay that much when they've got frogs hopping around? Not to mention the bugs everywhere. There's even a fucking millipede."

"That's part of the valley's charm," said Jonah, but there was no way he could explain it better than that because he didn't quite understand it himself, even if he pretended to Royce like he did.

There was something about very rich people pretending they were roughing it, which made no sense. If you could afford the best, why would you sleep in a tent that was lit by only a single bulb, and that was, really, exposed to the elements? Why would you rent a room in the valley if you had to hike through the woods in the dark with your flashlight just to take a whiz?

"That's not what I'd call charming," said Beck with his usual disapproval of things he didn't like, didn't understand.

There was an edge to his voice, as well. The same edge that would appear when Jonah would talk about upgrading the apartment by putting in a new carpet or something. *Everything's fine the way it is*, Beck would say.

The thing was, before being arrested, before prison, before *Royce*, Jonah would have agreed with him, or joked with him about it. But now, the complaints coming out of Beck's mouth sounded lame and, knowing what Royce's reaction would have been, they felt mean.

At dinner, though Beck seemed to be on his best behavior, Jonah could see him giving everything the hairy eyeball until it must have been obvious to everyone around the table that Beck was not having a good time.

Whether it would be wiser to give Beck a verbal poke so he could let off steam or just let him explode, Jonah couldn't decide. Only that if he didn't, Beck was liable to throw something, maybe even at someone, and that wouldn't be the greatest way to finish a meal. If Jonah had been able to handle Beck before prison, now he was woefully out of practice.

"Let's go up and look at the horses after dinner," he said, jabbing Beck with his elbow in a friendly, light way.

"What for?" asked Beck, ignoring the looks he was getting. "You said you went to a tavern. You and I should go there. Like, right now."

Figuring that he needed to get Beck out of there before someone punched him, hard, Jonah nodded as he wiped his hands on his napkin, as if to show he was up for anything Beck wanted to do.

At the same time, his heart went out to Beck, who must feel, as Jonah had once, and sometimes still did, that the valley was strange and new and just plain weird. Who fucking came up with the idea of what pretty much amounted to an adult sleep-away summer camp?

Jonah had never been to summer camp, had never wanted to go. Yet here he was creating one and he'd dragged Beck with him, kicking and screaming.

Plus, Royce was looking at Jonah in a stern way, like a crabby schoolteacher at the end of the year who has just about had enough of Jonah.

It was becoming really fucking hard to try to balance what Beck needed from him against what Royce wanted from him. And maybe Jonah had just about had enough of the struggle for now, so even though there was a promise of homemade ice cream for dessert, he was going to get Beck out of there and maybe have a little fun for once.

"Sure, we'll go," he said. "After we look at the horses."

They tromped together along the path through the woods to where the pasture was. Though Beck wanted to go to the tavern, Jonah wanted Beck to appreciate the place, at least a little, and going to visit the pretty horses was the best way he knew how to do that, especially since the woods and the lake and the blue-edged mountains beyond the foothills hadn't had the least effect on Beck.

"Here," he said with a wide sweep of his hand. "Look at that. I help take care of them. Can you believe it?"

Beck had already seen all of this, but it was important that he appreciated it.

"What I can't believe, and that's at one hundred percent," said Beck, teeth gritted. "Is that you're still here and don't seem to want to be leaving anytime soon."

"C'mon, Beck," said Jonah in his best cheer-the-fuck-up voice. "Don't you want to pet them? Just one?"

Beck had never really been able to resist what Jonah wanted, and it was easy to see that as Jonah came closer to the newly built wooden paddock, recently painted cedar red, courtesy of Jonah and everybody else.

The smell of paint was tart in the air, chemical and stringent against the lower, softer smells of damp grass, dust, horse hair, and hay spilling from the troughs in the shelters. Also newly built. Also smelling like paint, at least on the outside.

"We could go in," said Jonah, doing his best to tempt Beck, his hand on one of the posts.

"Or we could let them out," said Beck. He jerked his chin at the horses who had gathered, curious at the voices and maybe hoping for treats. "Just for a laugh. Because they're prisoners here, just like you are."

This was more like the old days, when one of them would suggest they do crazy shit, and the other would go along with it out of boredom, or just a desire to stir things up.

The memory rose up strong, like a pillar, familiar and sturdy, so Jonah just laughed when Beck started unlatching the wooden gate to the paddock. There was an electronic gate, too, but the horses in the paddock were closer.

At the last minute, just as the first horse shifted on its hooves, as if hardly able to believe that freedom had come at last, Jonah knew it was a stupid idea. The horses might not go far, but they might run off, might get hurt.

Rounding them up would be a real pain in the ass. Not to mention Beck would be banished from the valley for life. Whether that was a good thing or a bad thing, as being around Beck was so confusing sometimes, Jonah didn't wait to figure out.

"Never mind," he said. "This is stupid. Let's just go to the tavern."

"We'll go to the tavern," said Beck, shoving Jonah away from the gate. "After we set these horses free."

"Look," said Jonah, trying to be his most sensible, his brain scrambling to figure out why Beck was being like this. "Knock it off and shut the gate. I'm not for play play here."

Beck, almost smiling, hauled back and punched Jonah in the face, making him rock back on his heels, stunned, lip stinging, jaw aching. Then Jonah punched Beck back. A second later, they were on the ground, rolling, dust in Jonah's eyes making them water, the blood on his tongue bitter-bright and tasting of copper.

"What on earth is going on?" a voice rang in Jonah's ears.

It was Royce, and he lifted Jonah off Beck as Beck scrambled to his feet. Then he was in Beck's face, chin jutted, a hard flush to his cheeks. He showed absolutely zero fear as he stood toe to toe with Beck, who was on the verge of coming apart.

Jonah knew it wasn't just the fight with Jonah or the fact that Royce, who was fifty pounds lighter than him, and far less bulky with muscle, was standing him down. Jonah knew it was everything that had happened between him and Beck from the day he'd planned on dealing in ghost plates.

Beck had said dealing with ghost plates was dumb, and Jonah had gone ahead with it, anyway. From then, their friendship, as solid and satisfying as it had been, had begun to unravel. Beck was fighting back against what life was throwing at him: losing Jonah.

"It's all right," said Jonah, mostly to Beck, but also to Royce.

Which was when Royce turned to face him, blue eyes blazing, golden hair tumbling over his forehead, looking so angelic and furious at the same time, that Jonah couldn't help smiling.

"You think this is funny?" asked Royce, demanding, strident. "It most certainly is not. I saw what Beck was doing. Any one of those horses could have gotten hurt. And you just stood there, going along with it."

"Were you watching us?" asked Jonah, shock flooding through him at the thought that Royce would do such a thing. "Were you—were you *jealous*?"

"No, I'm not." Royce's voice was firm, and he stood his ground, even though Beck had come up behind him. "I was concerned because Beck was obviously unhappy, and I was going to ask if there was anything we could do to make his visit better."

"That's bullshit," said Beck, his hands balled into fists. "This whole place is bullshit. You've got Jonah jumping around like a trained dog. You think you're helping ex-cons? This place is fake, and the fact that you're making Jonah take part in it—"

Jonah had never imagined the day when Beck would raise his fist at someone, and that someone, a bookish, sweet-faced man who had never so much as gotten a speeding ticket, would catch Beck's fist in his hand and hold it tight. Sure, Royce was shaking, but he was standing up to Beck like he was ten feet tall and covered with hair. Fearless. Completely in control.

"You're out of here, Beck," Royce said, calm in spite of the quake in his voice. "You're disruptive, so get in your car and go and don't come back." Royce let Beck's fist go, and stepped back, looking at Jonah over his shoulder, something flickering in his dark eyes as he seemed to reconsider. "You can come back to the valley when you apologize to me. To Jonah. To everyone here. Do you understand?"

"Fuck you," was Beck's reply. He stepped back, swallowing, his gaze flicking to the herd of horses all bunched at the wooden gate to the paddock. "And fuck your valley." To Jonah he said, "You coming?"

In that split second, Jonah knew he had to repair what was broken between him and Beck. Royce would understand that, wouldn't he?

"Sure," he said, as calmly as if, the moment before, the two of them hadn't been grappling on the ground, intent on killing each other. "Let's blow this place."

Royce looked like he'd been slapped, and Jonah regretted agreeing with Beck the moment it had come out of his mouth. But there was nothing else to do but march on out of there, side by side with Beck.

The day had turned to shit so fast, moving into an out-of-control death spiral like a snake spinning around to bite. He was jumbled from the inside, and a nice cool beer and some time with Beck, just like the old days, was what he needed. And not the expression on Royce's face as he watched them stride through the woods to Beck's olive green Pontiac.

CHAPTER 29
JONAH

John Henton's Tavern, even on a quiet Sunday evening, still matched the vibe of the valley. Like a lot of bars Jonah had been in, there was a long bar at one end, booths at the other, pool tables in the back, and in the middle more tables, and a dance floor.

The difference between the tavern and other bars Jonah had been in was that here everything gleamed with care, from the mirror over the bar, to the dance floor, where couples were now dancing to upbeat country/Western music from the retro jukebox. He could see the waitstaff hustling to take care of customers, who all looked happy and were tipping big, if the folded bills placed on round trays were anything to go by.

Until Saturday night, and until that very moment, this wasn't any place Jonah would have gone to before prison, before Royce, for the customers were the type to own the Jags and Mercedes and other cars he would haul into the back of his chop shop. They were the kind of people he stole from, not the kind of people he drank with. Although, looking at Beck across the top of the table in the booth in the back, he knew better than to bring it up.

Class differences had never mattered to him, other than as a useful tool on how to spot a rich guy so he could take from him. For Beck, though, Jonah would be starting another fight by daring to mention that the two of them weren't as good as everybody else in the place, and that was just the mood Beck was in. Looking around, scowling. Not enjoying his fifth beer, not one little bit, not even when some excellent onion rings were plonked on the table by a smiling waitress.

"Thanks," said Jonah, and though he didn't have a five-dollar bill to put on the tray, she seemed perfectly happy to serve him just the same.

"You never were going to leave the valley, were you." It was not a question, and Beck's glare at him told its own story.

"What do you mean?" asked Jonah, doing his best to play innocent for as long as he could, his own fifth beer making him more confident than he should be about the success of this.

"It's because of *him*." Beck slammed down his now empty beer mug, sending a spray of beer foam across the table like a string of tiny pearls. "Isn't it."

"What?"

He was going to desperately cling to not understanding Beck, at least as far as that would take him, which didn't look like it would be long. No, not long at all. Now that he was nice and relaxed—drunk— it was easy, so easy to see that what Beck was afraid of. Which was losing him to Royce.

"I can see what's going on between the two of you." Beck's mouth moved between snarling and trembling, which made Jonah's heart ache. He'd never wanted it to come to this, and yet here they were.

"We're friends, is all," said Jonah. "Like you and I are friends."

"Like you and I?" Beck was all but leaning over the table as if he meant to grab Jonah by the throat and throttle him. "You and I aren't like that. You don't look at me like you look at him. Face it, you're in love with him, and he, in turn, is very, very, very fond of you."

"You think you're so fuckin' smart!" Jonah's voice rose over the general, happy glamor, and the tavern went still, every pair of eyes on him. But the truth of it was, Beck *was* smart enough to have figured out how Jonah felt about Royce, because in only three visits, he'd seen what he needed to see.

THE COWBOY AND THE HOODLUM

Jonah's grip tightened around his beer mug and he finished what was left with a swallow.

"Another beer. *Please*." His voice croaked, like he'd been asking for hours.

"I don't give a damn who you love," said Beck, equally loudly. He gave his beer mug a smack on the table, sending up more pearls of beer foam. "And I don't give a damn who you fuck."

"Just as long as it's you, right?" Now Jonah's glare matched Beck's as he danced on the precipice of knowing, right then and there, that none of this was working, and his friendship with Beck was already in tatters. So why was he trying so hard?

"Just know that you're going to be stuck with a guy who uses fucking pomade in his hair!"

"He needs that pomade, damn you!" Shaking his head, he muttered, but loud enough for Beck to hear, "He's got the hair of an angel. He *needs* that pomade."

"Guys."

Up to the table had come a dark-haired fellow who looked a tad out of place, who looked like he might be up for the challenge of a fight in the nearest alley, and Jonah had not even noticed him. Nor had Beck, who stood up and basically spat at the man's feet.

"Before you throw us out," said Beck. "We. Are. Gone. Coming, Jonah?"

"Yeah," said Jonah, half gasping as he stood up, dizzy on his feet, realizing too late that he'd had too many beers too fast and that he needed to get back to Royce.

"Take me home," he said to Beck as they slipped past the dangerous-looking guy who looked ready to toss them out and then beat the crap out of them both, one handed.

They held their heads high as they marched past the tables in the middle of the tavern, slipping along the edge of the glossy dance floor full of rich people who had no idea, no idea at all, what Jonah was dealing with. And then out to the street, where Beck's Pontiac was carefully parked beneath a streetlight.

"Take me home," he said again.

225

"Get in," said Beck, growling.

Jonah got in, buckled himself tight, and let his head sink back on the headrest, eyes closed, a sigh easing from his chest. He heard the engine burble to life and settled himself in for the quick ride to the valley. Only instead of soon arriving, as he'd expected, the drive seemed to go on and on, the streetlights turning to darkness.

When Jonah opened his eyes, he saw the blackness of empty countryside. He had a glimpse of a blue and red sign with the number twenty-five on it and he knew in a single heartbeat that they were headed toward the highway, and not to the ranch.

"Beck, stop." He sat up, head spinning, one hand on the door handle, the other on Beck's elbow. "I mean it. Stop and let me out."

"You going to puke?" asked Beck, 'cause yeah, that was his main concern, and not the fact that Jonah was the one who was now falling apart, almost shaking with the urgency of getting back to Royce.

"Maybe." Jonah settled his shoulders and took off his seat belt. It was one of those old-fashioned kinds, original to the car, a priceless artifact of days gone by when nobody gave a damn if your head went through the windshield if the driver put on the brakes too fast. They were easy to take off, the metal ends of the buckle thunking against Jonah's thighs. "Stop or I'll throw myself out, so help me, Beck."

For a long moment, as Jonah imagined he could see the lights of Cheyenne, it didn't look like Beck was going to stop. He was doing almost seventy miles an hour on a backcountry two-lane road that only had tiny glow-in-the-dark rectangles on the mile markers to guide drivers.

Deer jumped into the road in places as dark as this. A place so dark, the stars overhead looked like more pearls, spread in an uneven blanket amidst the dark, dark bluish black, furled at the edges with a low, lemon-blue glow that could have been the city or the moon coming up or anything.

Royce would have known what caused that glow and which stars were which and how long it would take Jonah to walk back to the valley in pitch black darkness. And Jonah wanted, very much, to ask him.

THE COWBOY AND THE HOODLUM

"For fuck's sake!" Jonah reached over and grabbed the steering wheel to yank it down with one hand, opening the door with the other.

As he expected, or maybe half hoped, Beck put on the brakes to keep from plowing off the road into the nothingness that was on either side.

Jonah took his chance and threw himself out, standing, shaking, his knee on fire as he gave Beck the bird.

"Fuck you!"

"Fuck you, too!"

Beck gave him the bird right back and put on the gas, the tires screeching as he zoomed into the darkness, his headlights cutting two yellow, dust-glittered swaths into the night as he went.

Which left Jonah on the side of a dark two-lane highway in the middle of nowhere. The only way he knew which way to start walking was because Beck's engine could be heard in one direction, and the silence of the grace of the valley loomed in the other.

He started walking that way, up a slight rise, stumbling once, his knee killing him, making him limp. But he kept going. The going was slow, but he was going home, going home to Royce. It might take him till morning, but what the fuck did that matter, just as long as Royce gave him a chance to explain.

Feeling perfectly sober, but knowing he was miles from that, he half stumbled along the shoulder, following the white line, a faint glow beneath the starlight. There were chunks of gravel, which felt huge beneath the soles of his yellow boots, and there were twigs, which seemed to snap very loudly when he stepped on them. And then there was the wind coming off the foothills, colder than he'd expected, biting into the side of his face, the curve of his neck above his t-shirt.

When he was just about to sit down in the dirt and take a breather, thinking that he might pull out cellphone—except he and Beck had left the valley in too much of a hurry for Jonah to stop at his tent for it—a pair of headlights swept across him, then slowed to a stop. His heart racing, he lifted his hand to cut the glare of the headlights, thinking it might be Royce come to get him, but it wasn't.

One guy got out of the car, bright flashlight focused on Jonah. There was another guy, staying back a few feet, both men operating just as they should if they planned to arrest someone like Jonah. So, not amateurs. Not taking any chances.

"You all right, fella?" asked the first guy, almost gently, as he approached Jonah.

The flashlight was lowered to point at Jonah's middle, which was a sign that the first guy wasn't worried about Jonah getting violent. It was now that Jonah could see he had a brown sheriff's hat and a shiny sheriff's badge. Which meant that he was the local sheriff, which meant that the other guy was his deputy. Which, of course, only made sense because Jonah was in the middle of fucking nowhere. There were no cops for miles, just sheriffs and deputies.

"I'm fine," said Jonah, his voice inexplicably loud in the darkness, starlight blinking overhead.

"I'm Sheriff Lamont, and this is Deputy Munroe," said Sheriff Lamont. "The owners of John Henton's sent us, thinking there might be trouble. You don't look so steady on your feet, there. Is there somewhere we can take you? Somewhere you belong?"

What kind of law enforcement began with polite introductions and an offer of a ride home? Jonah was on the verge of spewing the kind of disdain that Beck would be proud of, but, on the other hand, if he just went along with this farce, he'd get home to Royce a whole lot quicker. Only he didn't want Royce to be angry with him when he got there.

"Valley," he said, waving his hand vaguely in that direction. "Excon, parolee," he added, waving with equal vagueness at himself. "Take me to Royce, but only if he isn't mad at me."

"Royce," said Sheriff Lamont, his gaze flicking to Deputy Sheriff Munroe, who'd come up to share the circle the glow of the flashlight aimed at the ground offered. "Do you mean Royce Thackery?"

"He worked at the guest ranch last summer," said Deputy Sheriff

Munroe. "He's working in the valley now, helping with the Pathway to Freedom, or whatever it's called."

"I think it's the Farthingdale Valley Parole Program in official circles." Sheriff Lamont seemed to laugh at some inside joke. "We can take you there, sir. What's your name?"

"Jo-nah," said Jonah, cursing himself for stumbling on his own name. When Sheriff Lamont put a hand, quite gentle, on his arm, he jerked it out of the sheriff's grasp. "But I'm not going back unless I know he's not mad. I already can't stand the look on his face that I'm gonna see when I see him."

Sheriff Lamont reached for him again.

"I said no!" Jonah swung his arm wide and almost hit the deputy, then, feeling like he was going to puke, he stepped back. "Seriously, guys. Have you seen that face? It should only be happy and sweet and smiling, only it won't be, 'cause we got thrown out of the valley and then out of the bar. Can't go back. Can never go back. Only I want to go back. Back to Royce."

"Okay." Sheriff Lamont took a breath that Jonah knew was meant to be soothing, and it was, at least a little bit. The deputy held up his phone for the sheriff to take. It was already ringing. "We're calling him now. I'll talk to him first and see what he says. You be ready to step up and say what you need to say so we can take you home."

Stunned to his core at the kindness, Jonah felt frozen where he stood as the sheriff talked into the phone and appeared to listen to the voice at the other end.

Jonah could barely hear Royce's voice, so he couldn't tell if Royce was happy or sad or angry or anything because Royce was speaking too softly, even when Jonah strained, his neck stretched out, to hear.

"He wants to talk to you," Sheriff Lamont was saying to Royce. "Only he's worried, like I said. Is it okay if we bring him home to you? Let him know it's okay if we do."

A second later, Sheriff Lamont was holding his phone out to Jonah, which, of course, he was. Everything in the valley, everything that was in the least way connected to the valley, was exactly like this. Where the local law, without any compulsion whatsoever to encourage them to do so, was holding out a personal phone of one of the officers for Jonah to use for his own benefit. If he didn't feel so sick as he took the phone, he'd be laughing until he puked.

He held the phone to his ear.

"Royce?" he said, or at least he tried to. It came out as a gurgle, the result of five beers drunk rather quickly and a belly full of stress. He tried again. "Roy-ce."

"Hey, Jonah," said Royce's voice, soft and musical and low. Jonah wanted to sink into that voice and float away on it till he vanished forever and could pretend that today never happened. "You're stuck on the roadside, I hear," he said, his voice rising in a gentle question.

"Sorry." Jonah gulped, trying to swallow.

His face itched, and when he raised his hand, he felt something sticky there. Tears, then. He was crying in front of two guys he hardly knew, just because Royce, on the other end of the line, didn't seem angry with him. He would have been more embarrassed if he was sober, only he wasn't, so everything came spilling out of him.

"Beck's my friend. You know? We go a long way back, and he's always been there for me."

Jonah licked his lips, which felt incredibly dry, and at that moment, didn't really care that the sheriff and his deputy were listening to him choke on the feelings in his heart.

"It's all tangled now and I've not been very nice to him. He deserves better than me and so do you, only—" He took a huge breath and blurted out the rest. "Only he told me that I was in love with you and I think it's true. I just want to come back. I want to sit on the flagstones in the warm sunshine and we can talk it over. Barefoot. Drinking iced coffee. With you."

"I'd like that." Royce's voice sounded thick, like there was something in his throat that he couldn't swallow past. "You let those officers bring you home to me. I'll meet you in the parking lot and we'll sort everything out in the morning. Please don't cry, you're breaking my heart—"

"Fuck you, I'm not crying." He shoved the phone at the deputy, scowling, his heart beating, scrubbing his face with both hands. Then he dropped his hands and looked at them with a hard glare, the way Beck would have done. "Sorry, fellas," he said. "I won't be any trouble if you could just take me to him. Along the way, I'll let you know if I need to puke."

"Sure thing, Jonah," said Sheriff Lamont, while the deputy put his phone in his back pocket. "Step this way, won't you? Your ride awaits."

CHAPTER 30
ROYCE

The long shadows of evening had seemed to drop so suddenly over the valley that the lake Royce was staring at was an inky black, the surface rippled and dark with the breeze that had kicked up. It might rain or it might not, but the truth was he needed to focus on something else other than the look on Jonah's face, just before he'd turned away to walk off with Beck.

There had been something there, angry, resigned, but unsettled, as if Jonah didn't quite know what he was doing. And maybe he hadn't.

Maybe Jonah only followed Beck, went with him to his car, so the two of them could drive out of the valley together. Each following the other the way they must have been doing that for ages and ages, regardless of the situation. Kind of in the like the situation Grandad had sometimes mentioned, when Royce had been younger, admonishing him never to be a sheep.

If young Timmy jumps off a cliff, does that mean you have to?

No, Grandad, Royce would always say, solemn and large eyed, as he'd been when a child. But maybe neither Jonah nor Beck had had anyone like that, no one to guide them through the storms of growing up, to tell them right from wrong, guidelines that Royce had woven into his very being.

Being bad, breaking the law, wasn't the answer, not ever. Or maybe in cases of life or death, sure. But not to get richer off other people's woes, which surely was what the two of them had been doing while stealing cars and stripping them for parts.

Thinking about any of this wasn't going to help him now, though. And nothing Royce said, did, or felt was going to bring Jonah back any quicker.

What if Jonah stayed away? What if he went back to Denver with Beck? What if, after all Royce and Jonah had shared, it had become too much for Jonah, making his former life, before prison, suddenly glowed brightly as the better option?

Perish the thought. Royce's heart couldn't bear thinking about it, so he turned from the lake to march as steadily as he could to his own tent. He stepped up on the platform in the near dark, intending to unzip the opening, turn on the light, and find something to read. Then he'd take a hot shower and simply get into bed and relax with a good book—

—and though he did all of this, the relaxing never happened. He couldn't relax, nor sleep a wink until Jonah got back.

"He'll come back," said a voice beyond the opening of the tent. Gordy's voice, a little wobble of worry in it that Royce might be annoyed at Gordy giving his opinion unasked for.

Getting up to unzip the tent, Royce held it open, and reached for the light, waiting until Gordy was inside before zipping the tent shut to keep out the bugs.

"I'll make some tea," said Royce, beyond grateful for the distraction of entertaining a guest in his tent. "It's a bit late for black tea, so how about some chamomile?"

"No, it makes me sick," said Gordy with a little shiver. "My nan used to make it, and it reminds me of her. And not in a good way."

"Lavender then," said Royce. He bustled about boiling water, and getting two mugs ready. When they were, he handed one to Gordy and sat next to him on the cot. "I know I shouldn't be worried, but I am." He looked at his phone, flipping it over to see the time. "It's so late."

THE COWBOY AND THE HOODLUM

When his cellphone rang, he wasn't ready for it, and almost dropped it. Answering quickly, regardless of the strange new number that showed up, he almost gasped into the phone. "Jonah?"

"Hey there, is this Mr. Thackery?"

"Yes?"

"This is Sheriff Lamont, county sheriff."

"Oh, hello." Royce's heart froze in his chest, all the air leaving his body as though someone had landed a stout blow to his belly. "Is everything all right?"

"It sure is, Mr. Thackery," said Sheriff Lamont. "I found a friend of yours by the roadside, walking by himself in the dark. I think he's had a little bit too much to drink, he and his friend both. They got kicked out, or were about to be kicked out of John Henton's Tavern, though for some reason they seem to have separated."

"Jonah?" Royce's voice rose so high it almost cracked him apart from the inside. "Is he okay?"

"He's fine. We'd like to bring him to you, but he's worried."

"Yes, please!" said Royce, almost shouting it. "Bring him back to the valley. I'll meet you in the parking lot."

"He wants to talk to you," said Sheriff Lamont. "Only he's worried, like I said. Is it okay if we bring him home to you? And will you let him know it's okay that we do?"

"Put him on," said Royce, as politely as he could manage. Then he relaxed his shoulders and simply listened as hard as he could.

On the other end of the line, Jonah was breathing hard, struggling to speak, and if he was as drunk as the sheriff said, that only made sense. After Jonah went on and on about how badly he felt about how he had treated Beck, when it was obvious that Beck was the culprit, Royce knew it didn't matter what had happened, or who had said what to whom. The only thing that needed to happen was for Jonah to be brought home so Royce could take care of him.

He could hear Jonah crying. It almost broke his heart, but any attempt at reassurance was cut off. He could hear Jonah mumbling something, and then the call was dropped. At any rate, he now had a task ahead of him, something specific that he could do, which was to get Jonah back from the sheriff before he did something that might land him in jail. After that, he'd take each moment as it came.

Waiting in the darkness of the parking lot was its own kind of hell, even with Gordy, who was very kind to wait with him so he wasn't alone.

When the sheriff's car came down the switchback, Royce strained hard to keep track of it as the headlights appeared and disappeared amongst the dark pine trees. When finally the car stopped, and Jonah was helped out, Royce did not hold himself back from reaching out, arms around Jonah's waist, the heavy burden in his arms the best feeling, for now he knew Jonah was safe. Everything else would come with time.

"Thank you, officers," he said, as politely as he could, though all he wanted was for them to go away as fast as possible. The last thing Jonah needed to feel was that he was a criminal. "I'll take it from here."

"Good night, Mr. Thackery," they both said in unison, tipping their hats to him.

"Good night."

Jonah felt heavy in his arms, staggering on his feet even as he tried to walk, and thank goodness for Gordy, leading the way with the flashlight so that Royce had one less thing to worry about. He breathed a sigh of relief as he stepped into his tent, the light still burning, the two cups of tea gone quite cold.

"I really appreciate this," said Royce as he helped Jonah sit down on the cot. "Could you bring me a cloth and some cool water? From the kitchen?"

"I'm on it," said Gordy, and then he was gone.

Which left Royce quite alone with Jonah, as he'd wanted to be. Helping Jonah out of his clothes and between the sheets was no hardship, no hardship at all. Neither was tucking him in and smoothing his tumble of dark hair from his forehead as Jonah stared blearily up at him.

"Am I going to puke?" asked Jonah, coughing around the words like an old man who has been bedridden for a long, long time.

"I don't know, you tell me."

THE COWBOY AND THE HOODLUM

As a precaution, Royce moved his plastic wastebasket closer, and looked up to see Gordy, out of breath, with a plastic pitcher full of water, and a folded kitchen towel. Both of which were perfect.

"Thank you, Gordy," he said, taking the objects from him.

"Do you need my help or anything?" asked Gordy, though from the expression on his face, hanging around with a drunk Jonah was the last thing he wanted to do.

"No, I'm good," said Royce, making a wish that Gordy would just go away without having to be asked. Which he did, and the silence fell in the tent, a peaceful blanket, as Jonah, eyes closed, appeared to doze.

Laying his hand on Jonah's where it rested on his chest, curled into a reluctant fist, Royce took his first full breath of the day, it felt like.

"I'll look out for you," he said to Jonah, remembering the time when Jonah had looked out for him when he'd gotten his unfortunate sunburn.

"I might puke," mumbled Jonah without hardly moving his mouth.

"If you do, there's a wastebasket here," replied Royce, stroking Jonah's forehead with the back of his fingers.

Jonah leaned into the touch, but did not open his eyes. Nor did he puke, which made it easier, all things considered.

Royce spent time wetting the cloth to place on Jonah's forehead, flipping it over from time to time, wishing he had some lavender oil to put on it so it'd smell nice. In spite of this, he dozed sitting up, and when morning came, a burst of yellow and gold into the tent, his neck had a crick in it.

When he looked over at the cot, Jonah's eyes were open, deep brown and staring at him.

"You're staying in bed today, Jonah," said Royce, not even making it an order because there was nothing more sensible than staying in bed when you had a hangover.

"No, I'm not."

"Yes, you are." Royce made it an order, putting force in his voice. "You can get up for dinner, but until then, I want you to rest."

Royce heard a rap on the tent pole and turned to see Gordy with a tray in his hands. Behind him, Duane and Tyson were peering over

Gordy's shoulders as if they expected to see the results of a lurid automobile accident.

"Brought this for you," said Gordy. He came in and set the tray on Royce's knees, awkwardly, except there was no place else to put it. "It's breakfast."

"Get to work, you lazy fucks," said Jonah, with a bit of a glare at the ex-cons at the opening of the tent. "I want to see elbows and assholes. You got it?" To Royce, he said, "Don't let them slack," he muttered, a bit grimly. "Or they'll become slackers."

"Yes, I will," said Royce, doing his best not to laugh at the grumpiness in Jonah's voice. "I mean I won't. Go on, you guys, and let Jonah rest. I'll be out to join you in a minute."

When Royce was alone with Jonah again, he took a deep breath and did his best to relax his shoulders, which felt like they were up around his ears. He put the tray of breakfast on the wooden floor, as he didn't yet feel much like eating.

"If you're going to yell at me," said Jonah, his lips barely moving as he spoke. "Do it now and get it over with."

"I'm not going to yell." Royce nodded, though Jonah's eyes were closed. "But I am concerned."

He meant to go on and explain what it was he was concerned about, but Jonah's face tightened and his eyes opened to slits, as if the gentle morning light, filtered through the green canvas of the tent, was too bright for him to bear.

"Beck is my friend," said Jonah, slowly, swallowing over the words.

"I know." Taking the damp cloth, Royce slowly drew it over Jonah's sweat-damp neck.

"He's my only friend."

"I'm your friend."

The warmth of the morning was filling the tent, and though Royce wanted to get up and push the tent flap back, he also didn't want Jonah exposed to the eyes of the world, or at least whoever would be passing by, peering in to see Jonah come apart.

"We've known each other forever," said Jonah, now. "I don't remember a time before Beck, to be honest."

THE COWBOY AND THE HOODLUM

Placing the cloth back on Jonah's forehead, Royce laid his hand on top of Jonah's hand where it rested on his belly, and waited for the rest of the story. Because there had to be more, there always was.

"Only I've not been very nice to him recently." Jonah swallowed hard, and Royce winced in sympathy because the swallow looked like it hurt. "I pushed and pushed and he just gave and gave, and it used to be funny, only now it just makes me feel like shit. What's happened to me, Royce?"

"They say prison changes a man," said Royce. "Maybe that's what happened." He paused to help Jonah take a few sips of the now-cold lavender tea, and wiped his neck again as Jonah settled back on the pillow. "The two of you—" He paused, looking for the right words, the best words. "When the two of you are together, it doesn't seem like you're having a good time. And you always come away from an encounter with him acting like you don't like yourself very much."

"I don't." Eyes still closed, Jonah nodded firmly. "I don't like myself when I'm around him." Now he opened his eyes and looked at Royce, squinting a bit like the sun was a shining bright beacon behind him, and he could not bear to look away. "Prison, yeah. That made things different. But you, you're the one who made everything different. You're the one who changed everything in my head."

Touching Jonah's face, wishing he could erase all traces of Jonah's hangover, it was easy to remember that Beck had told Jonah he was in love with Royce, and that Jonah had agreed with that statement, or at least mostly. But now was not the time to ask Jonah to repeat that particular proclamation. Now, his only job was to take care of Jonah until Jonah could take care of himself.

"Enough talk now," said Royce, making little *shh shh* noises as he wiped Jonah's face, refolded the cloth, and placed the cooler side on his forehead. "Close your eyes. When you're feeling better, I'll make us a nice thermos of iced coffee, and we'll sit on the flagstones—"

"Bare feet," said Jonah, a little smile curling his mouth. "We must have bare feet so we can feel the warmth of the sun in the stones."

"Absolutely." He tucked a dark curl behind Jonah's ear and smiled at the idea of it. "And we'll talk it over, you and me. All right?"

"Yep."

There was sleepiness in Jonah's response, and maybe a bit of weariness, as well. Royce would help with that, when Jonah was feeling better, and in the meantime, he'd watch over while Jonah slept, and then he'd go and make sure his team was staying on task, and not goofing around. Most of all, he was glad Jonah was home, here with him, and not racing along some highway with that madman Beck at the wheel.

CHAPTER 31

ROYCE

Royce waited until Jonah was fast asleep, snoring gently, curled on his side, before he took the cold cloth away and placed it on the tray with his uneaten breakfast. He pulled back the blanket, in case Jonah got too warm, then smoothed the cotton sheet up around his shoulders. Picking up his cellphone and unplugging it, he tiptoed out of the tent, zipping it gently shut behind him.

The air outside the tent was fresh and cool, the sky above the pine trees and Guipago Ridge a startling, sapphire blue. He knew he should join his team and start working instead of mooning around about his relationship with Jonah, but his feelings, Jonah's feelings, felt more urgent than picking up a saw and putting on a pair of safety goggles. So, instead, he dialed his Grandad's number on his cellphone.

It didn't take but two rings for Grandad to pick up.

"Hey, Grandad," Royce said. "Are you busy?"

"Not too busy for you, m'lad," said Grandad, cheery as always. "I'm just at the feed and grain in Huntley, putting in the order for salt blocks."

"Are we out already?" asked Royce, his mind going to the inventory in the feed barn, even though it'd been a while since he'd had any responsibility for it.

"No, but it's going to be a hot summer according to *The Old Farmer's Almanac*," said Grandad with a little laugh, sounding like he knew he was going to be teased about it.

"You know they never get it right, Grandad," said Royce, shaking his head.

"But they almost do," said Grandad, defending himself. "Besides, the farmers down at the feed and grain all say the same thing: get ready for it to be hot."

"It's been doing nothing but raining here," said Royce, slipping into the familiar conversation about the weather, salt blocks, and whatever Grandad had on his mind as he ran the family ranch. "How's everything? How's Posey doing?"

"Posey's fine," said Grandad, and from somewhere behind him, he heard someone say, *Bye, Roderick*, and a screen door slamming shut. "But you didn't call to ask me all that. I can hear it in your voice that something's up. Everything okay?"

"It is and it isn't," said Royce. He rubbed his thumb along his lower lip as he thought about how to break the news that he'd fallen in love with a criminal. Or, at the very least, that he'd lost his heart to a guy who'd spent a few years in prison and who might or might not want to give up his law-breaking ways. "So, you know. There's this ex-con program, and I'm in charge of these four parolees, right?"

"Yes, I recall," said Grandad, his voice rumbly and low, reassuring in its familiarity. "Are you having trouble? Last time we talked, you said it was going so well."

"I'm not having trouble with my little group," said Royce. "But there's this one ex-con. His name is Jonah. And he likes—"

Pausing to gather his galloping thoughts, images of him and Jonah walking up to the ridge to look at falcons. Him and Jonah drinking iced coffee while warming their feet on sun-drenched flagstones. Him and Jonah—doing everything, it seemed, everything that was pleasurable and fun and interesting, with Jonah hanging on to his every word, even down to wanting to know the Latin names for things. Not to mention the happy, sexy fun times they'd shared.

And what did Royce do that Jonah enjoyed? Certainly not stealing cars or getting thrown out of taverns. And he knew nothing beyond Jonah's first and last name, and what he'd been arrested for, almost nothing about his background.

Except he knew how Jonah made him feel all the time, and that was the most important thing. And then Jonah had said that he might be in love with him, and even if that information had come through Beck's filter, it still did things to his heart to hear it.

"He likes *me*, Grandad, and I like him. Only—" Royce took a breath and dove right in. "He's an ex-con, and I can't forget that. He spent two years in prison for stealing cars and dealing in ghost plates, and I don't think he entirely regrets that."

"Maybe he does," said Grandad quite sensibly. "Have you asked him? Have you talked to him about any of this?"

"Wait a minute." Standing still as a stone, Royce lifted his chin, and drew in a breath of the cool air, tasting the scent of pine on the back of his tongue. "You're not shocked? I just told you I have feelings for a man. I also just told you that man is an ex-con, hardly the type of boyfriend you'd want me bringing home to meet everyone."

"I'm only shocked that you're talking to me instead of him," said Grandad. "Love is love, after all. Sure, I have some questions about his character, but I know you, dear lad. You have a very good sense about human nature, and you wouldn't be drawn to this man if he didn't, underneath it all, have a good heart."

"He does have a good heart, Grandad."

Across the clearing, he could see Gordy and Dale carrying long white poles, and remembered that they were setting up a pavilion for Marston, the team lead who would arrive in the next week and who would be working on creating descriptive signs and placards for all the flora and fauna. Royce had already made a list of the things that needed describing, but it wouldn't hurt to go over it again.

"Does he make you happy?" asked Grandad now.

"Yes, he does." The answer came without hesitation, and Royce knew it was true. Jonah made him feel good inside. Jonah made him feel like he was interesting and fun, and seemed enchanted with him. And the sex couldn't get any better if they tried. In fact, it was so good, he wondered why he'd ever been afraid of having sex with a man. Not that Grandad needed to know that part. "I'm so happy with him, sometimes I feel like I'm floating."

There was silence at the other end of the line. Royce knew that Grandad was thinking before he spoke, which was so like him that Royce felt his eyes grow hot and his throat fill up because where would he be without having Grandad to guide him?

"I'm just worried, on account of his background. He seems to have a tendency to want to continue on with his life as if we'd never met."

"You know we all have high hopes for you to come home and help run the ranch," said Grandad.

"Yes, I know." Royce did know this. The ranch was a part of his history, and he wanted it to be a part of his future, once he'd slaked his desire to see a bit of the world before he settled down.

"There's a lot of money involved at Thackery Ranch," said Grandad thoughtfully. "People's livelihoods are at stake, and all of that depends on the success of what we do and the decisions we make every day."

"Yes." Royce knew this as well. Grandad wasn't telling him anything new, just reminding him.

"But mostly, what I care about is that you are happy. You love who you love, that's the most important thing. This guy? Tell him how you feel. Be honest with him and yourself, and I promise that the weight you're carrying will lift right off your shoulders."

The weight was lifting off so quickly that Royce rubbed his eyes to take away traces of tears, even though he knew Grandad would tell him that tears were nothing to be ashamed of.

"I will tell him," said Royce. "And I'll get him to tell me."

"Do it today," said Grandad. "It's always better to share your heart while you can, before it's too late."

Royce knew Grandad was referring to how they'd lost Royce's parents and his Grandma five years before. "I know, Grandad." His heart was racing, speeding up at the memory, aching at the loss, which still hurt.

Behind him, in the tent, gently snoring, being impossibly cute and grouchy with his hangover, was Jonah. Who might or might not prefer his old life to a new one with Royce.

He'd have to find out if Jonah truly felt the same way he did and whether he might want the kind of life that Royce would eventually go home to, raising painted ponies on five thousand acres in Montana.

The thought that Jonah might not want any part of this made his heart race a little so, blinking fast, he took several deep breaths and focused on the pine trees and the way the wind blew gently through them.

Of course, they couldn't even begin a new life until the summer was over, as Royce had signed the contract and meant to comply with his obligations.

"I'll talk to him," said Royce, firmly making himself that promise, as well as making it to Grandad. "I'll find a quiet moment and just tell him how I feel. Get him to tell me how he feels."

"And that's all you can do, dear boy. Share your heart. Be honest with yourself and with him. It'll turn out for the best, you'll see. Now, I'm blocking Mrs. Henderson and her little girl from getting into the feed and grain, so I must go. But call me and tell me how it goes, yes?"

"Yes, I will, Grandad. Bye for now."

Royce disconnected the call with his thumb and snuck back into the tent to plug his phone back in. Then he sat on the cot, on the very edge of it, his hand on Jonah's shoulder, waiting in the stillness to check on Jonah's breathing. Slow and steady.

He tipped forward until he could brush Jonah's shoulder with his forehead, drawing in the warmth, realizing that Jonah had been wearing one of his black t-shirts, as though he'd donned it especially for Beck's visit. Like he was stepping inside of his old skin for his oldest friend. Only that was Royce's imagination, wasn't it. Beck was a part of Jonah's life, regardless of what he was wearing.

"Royce?" Jonah's voice was sleep-rough, but the extra rest seemed to be doing him some good, as when he looked at Royce over his shoulder, there was a bit of a smile in those dark eyes. "I didn't know I liked being waited on hand and foot till I met you."

"I'll wait on you all day, if you like, but here." Royce helped Jonah sit up, then grabbed a bottle of water from his little fridge, helping Jonah to drink it. "Do you need some ibuprofen?"

"Water's fine," said Jonah, licking his lower lip as he winked at Royce. "I could get up now," he said. "I could get to work rather than slacking off. I know you're thinking I'm a slacker. I can see it in your eyes."

"You're not a slacker," said Royce. "And while I'm glad you're feeling better, can you stay in bed till lunchtime at least? Make me happy and rest?"

"I hear and obey," said Jonah with mock-resignation. He slipped back down, his head on the pillow, dark hair sticking to his temples. Royce brushed the hair back, letting his fingers linger in a soft caress.

"Good," said Royce. "You rest, and then we'll get some lunch together, right?"

Leaning forward, he kissed Jonah's forehead, and then his nose, and then his smiling mouth, pleased to be able to do that, rather than spending the rest of his life regretting that Jonah had driven off with Beck forever, and left Royce behind.

"Maybe I can use some iced coffee first," said Jonah, his eyes still closed, though he opened one to take a peek at Royce.

"Maybe you can," said Royce. "I'll go check on the team and then I'll come back right before lunch with that thermos. Deal?"

"Deal."

He had to make himself stand up and leave Jonah to his nap, when what he really wanted to do was crawl beneath the sheet and take Jonah in his arms and whisper sweet things to him until he fell back asleep. But sweet whispers would have to wait, as he had an obligation to his team.

With another kiss to Jonah's forehead, he let himself out of the tent, zipped the screen mostly closed, and took a deep breath. Grandad was right. He needed to tell Jonah how he felt. But first, work awaited.

CHAPTER 32

JONAH

Standing on the platform of Royce's tent, a Yeti thermos of some amazing iced coffee that Royce had left for him between his cupped hands, his head pounding with the remnants of just about the worst hangover headache he'd ever had—and which he blamed Beck for, completely—Jonah knew there was something he needed to do.

He needed to apologize to Royce for every time Beck had been rude and every time Jonah had let him. And, most especially, for following Beck's lead in taking off for the tavern, drinking too much, and coming home in such an obnoxious way. Dragged to the valley by two local sheriffs, no less, weaving and drunk, and unable to put two words together.

Royce was the best thing that had ever happened to Jonah. He'd opened up a whole wide world of exciting flavors and mind-blowing niceties that Jonah had never even known existed. Take the iced coffee that Jonah now held in his hand. When it came to coffee, Royce was not for play play.

As for the way Royce was with his men, Jonah had never seen anything like it. With that fussy way he had and blond hair arranged just so, Royce looked like butter wouldn't melt in his mouth. And he surely didn't look like he had the balls to lead a team of ex-cons forced to do hard labor. But he made it happen. He made those ex-cons stay on task.

Well, the labor wasn't that hard, and Royce insisted on plenty of breaks and snacks, and basically coddled any parolee he came into contact with. Which, it seemed, made those parolees adore him.

And, especially, he coddled Jonah, which no one, to Jonah's memory, had ever really done. Yes, okay, Beck did, but Beck had never made coffee as good as Royce did.

But it wasn't just the coffee, it was Royce himself. With his straightforward, gentle ways, and how when he looked at Jonah, those blue eyes that would light up as though Jonah was the greatest thing since half-n-half was invented. And the tender sweetness they'd shared in bed that softened the edges of his jangled soul—if Jonah lost that, he didn't know what he would do.

He'd just about fucked it all up with his association with Beck and giving in to Beck's cajoling and getting more drunk than was sensible.

The thing was, he already knew Royce would forgive him, with a bright heart and a sweet smile. The apology needed to be made just the same. It wasn't that he had to go begging on his knees for this; it was just that was the kind of guy Royce was.

Beck, in the same scenario, would have held a grudge, if he so decided, until hell froze over, and Jonah knew he himself could be the same way. But not Royce. Still, that didn't make the prospect of admitting he'd behaved like an ass any easier.

This was all Beck's fault.

No, it wasn't. It was his own fault for allowing himself to be led by Beck.

Beck was still his friend, though. They'd been friends forever, since back before he could remember. Except things had to change. The way they'd been together, the way he'd treated Beck, couldn't go on.

Nobody deserved to be treated that way, though the truth of it was he'd only begun to realize it once he was behind bars, separated from Beck. Able to stand back and see it for what it was. Something so tangled, the only way to untangle it was to slice a knife through it. Painful but necessary.

Wincing at the thought of what that would do to Beck, Jonah took a long swallow of the most beautiful iced coffee ever created. *Ever.* And realized that he'd need to apologize to Beck, too.

But first a shower. Lunch with Royce. A bit of groveling, maybe. And a whole lot of exposing more of himself than he'd ever thought possible back when he was living in an apartment above a garage in the not-so-nice part of town. Drinking shitty coffee from the bodega. Looking for the next stolen car to strip down and sell for parts. The next get-rich-quick scheme. The next way to take something he wanted from somebody who had it. Being an all-round loser, somebody who Royce would never have said hello to on the street.

Jonah was willing to do just about anything to keep from losing what he'd come to hold dear. And he'd punch any dickhead in the face who might even think about laughing at him for it.

Finishing his coffee, he put the Yeti mug on the shelf in Royce's tent, then strode through the woods, inhaling the bright, crisp air, sensing the wind cooling the hangover sweat from the back of his neck.

At his own tent, which felt oddly empty and abandoned, he grabbed his pale green carryall and a towel and hurried to the showers. There, he lingered beneath the rainfall stream and washed his hair twice. Then while the conditioner sat in his hair, he took the Ivory soap and slowly, luxuriously, washed himself all over.

His fingers lingered over skin that was coming to know the pleasures of soap that was gentle, the anticipation of good skin lotion to follow, both of which he'd never appreciated before he'd gotten thrown into prison. Then, slowly, he curled his wet, soapy fingers around his cock and enjoyed a leisurely, slow pleasure, the hot water spilling all around him, visions of Royce's sweet smile in his mind's eye as he came into his hand.

Had life ever been this good before? No, it had not. It was as though, at the Ranchette's Stop 'n Go, he had shed his old skin in preparation for a new one. Only he'd not known it was happening at the time, that it would be good if he was patient.

Well, he'd not known, and he'd not been patient. He'd railed against the prison system, and shouted at and mistreated Beck—if he'd known how good it would turn out, he would have been more patient, especially with Beck.

Sighing, he rinsed himself off, dried with a towel, and applied as much Jergens as his skin wanted, slapping it everywhere with zealous joy, inhaling the plastic cherry scent, and loving it. He'd never use any other brand.

He got dressed in his old clothes, not having brought clean ones with him. At his tent, he changed into his newest, cleanest clothes, taking care to make sure his pearl snap buttons lined up with his belt buckle. That his boots were dust free. That he was ready to grovel.

He headed to the mess tent, as he had no idea where Royce and the team currently were. Only his steps slowed the closer he got as the realization grew that he'd spent the night in Royce's tent—hungover—with Royce—and that everybody in the valley knew it.

Did he give a shit? No. But maybe Royce would, and that would have to be part of what Jonah apologized for. *Sorry, I turned your tent into a hotel. Sorry, I basically texted everyone in the valley that you and I are sleeping together. Hope you're okay with that.*

And what would he do if Royce wasn't okay? Cry like a baby? No. Jonah would grovel. Yes, that was the plan.

The mess tent was empty, the tables set up for lunch, an empty, echoing sound swirling around as the wind moved the tent, making it flap a little. In the back, the two cooks were busy setting up the steam tables, all sweaty-browed and white-aproned.

They ignored Jonah for the most part, except for a little chin jerk in his direction, and that was fine by him. He needed a minute to get his stomach to stop turning, and wished very hard for another iced coffee, served to him with that blue-eyed smile and flop of golden hair.

How in the fuckall had he become so smitten? And what was this going to look like come the end of summer when Royce went back to whatever he did in the winter, and Jonah was given his certificate of completion? Originally, his plan had been to go back to the apartment over the garage, back to Beck, back to his old, comfortable, broken-down, worn-in life. But now?

Fuck. Would his mind not shut the hell up?

Evidently not. In fact, it started competing with his heart as to which was the most rabbity-scared as he heard footsteps coming toward the mess tent. The low laughter and warm chatter. The shadow between the pines, outlines of shoulders and legs that turned into real men, sweat-dappled and smiling.

Leading them to the mess tent was Royce. Who looked like an angel surrounded by lumberjacks, the contrast so startling, so deliciously perfect, that Jonah put his hand over his heart in an effort to soothe it. Which could never be done, not until he'd apologized and begged Royce to forgive him.

"Hey," he said, waving from the front deck of the mess tent, taking a hitching breath to get his damned heart to slow the fuck down. "Did they slack?" he asked.

"No, not at all." Royce's smile as he came up to Jonah was bright and beaming. His hair was a golden mess around his ears, and there was sweat along his lovely neck.

Jonah wanted to eat him alive. But first, lunch. Or maybe the apology should come first, and then lunch.

"I need to talk to you," said Jonah hurriedly, tugging on Royce's sleeve, where it was rolled up elegantly above his elbow.

"Shall we have lunch first?" Royce stayed where he was, at Jonah's side, while the others filed past, eager to get to the steam tables from which the most amazing aromas floated, making Jonah's stomach rumble. "Then later we can have some private time."

"Yeah, okay." He raised his shoulders in a half-shrug, a sure-what-the-fuck-do-I-care shrug that had always been his shorthand to con people into thinking he did not care when he very much did. It was his go-to way of communicating forever and for always. But Royce deserved more and, though it hurt like a bitch, he stopped and tried again. "Yes, that'd be good."

"Good," said Royce, putting his hand over Jonah's hand where it was still tugging, like he was begging for Royce's attention the way Beck always did with him. Only Royce didn't seem to mind and the warm weight of his hand was comforting, making Jonah go quite still, his eyes focused on Royce like a hawk's. "Let's get some lunch."

Making himself settle the fuck down, Jonah stayed close at Royce's side while he sidled along the steam table, taking whatever looked hot and was closest, mostly protein in the form of meatloaf with plenty of ketchup. Which he'd learned long ago was what he needed after a hangover.

They all ate together as a team at one of the long tables, which was how Royce seemed to like it. Jonah did his best to pay attention to the general conversation about what had gotten done that morning, and what was left to do before they could break for dinner.

Jonah didn't really care about the small details. Point him at a tool or a task and he was good to go, whatever. But it was important to know, so that if the looming conversation between him and Royce went sideways, he could always cherry pick from the lunch conversation and keep the connection going between them that way.

Lunch was over before he was ready, and after they all bussed their places, Jonah followed close on Royce's heels to the kitchen building, where, to his surprise, Royce was asking for a container of ice. Then he followed Royce to his tent, where Royce quickly made two iced coffees, poured them into two Yeti mugs, and handed one to Jonah.

"I know you love coffee this way," he said. "Let's go to our rocks and just sit."

At the flagstones, still in stacks, waiting to be placed in the most attractive and useful way possible. The air was brisk, spinning in the bright sunshine, puffy white clouds bouncing along Guipago Ridge. But the rocks, as Jonah sat down on the top of the pile next to Royce, were warm and smooth and solid.

He took off his boots and socks, sighing when the soles of his feet felt the pink stone, and held the Yeti mug in his hands. Like he had when he woke up before lunch.

The worry squirting around in his brain was still there, but at least he had this. Iced coffee in a Yeti mug. Sun-warmed stone beneath bare feet.

Royce, at his side, smiled at him as he stuffed his white socks into yellow boots and, barefooted, took up his Yeti mug, his hands cupped in echo around it. He didn't say a word, just wrapped his energy around Jonah's shoulders, easing the rest of his hangover away, bit by bit.

"I'm sorry for being such an asshole," said Jonah. "Putting the horses in danger. Coming home drunk."

"I know," said Royce, with utter sincerity and the warmth of forgiveness in his eyes.

"And I still have your scarf," said Jonah, as the weight of the truth of it climbed on top of his slowly-going-away headache.

"I know," said Royce.

"It smells like you," said Jonah, his voice feeling raw. "D'you want it back?"

"I'd like you to keep it." Royce's smile was low and secret, almost as if he was sharing a private memory with himself. "Keep it—" He straightened up and looked at Jonah, eyebrows raised, blue eyes wide. "Near your heart?"

"Of course." Jonah couldn't even begin to bluster his way out of how much that simple, heartfelt request meant to him. "Always."

He got a quick kiss then, sweet with coffee, cool with ice. Life was good, turning out much better than Jonah could ever have expected. So much better, it was almost scary.

CHAPTER 33
JONAH

It wasn't until Wednesday, after his brief respite on the flagstones, that Jonah decided he needed to use his new cellphone to call Beck. It wasn't that he was afraid of Beck. No fucking way was he afraid of Beck. It was just that dealing with Beck ever since Jonah had gotten out of prison had been like a landmine he was totally unprepared for.

And after the disaster that followed their outing to John Henton's tavern, he'd simply rather not. But he was going to, anyway.

He had Beck's number, along with Royce's, stored in his phone, but he also knew Beck's number by heart, so it was easy to punch it in, though his heart sped up when Beck answered.

"Beck, here," said Beck.

"Hey," said Jonah, barely saying the word, breathing it.

"Oh, it's you," said Beck, quite clearly, more than breathing it. Barking it. "You left me."

"You left *me*."

Mentally, he gave Beck the same finger he'd given him on Sunday, but then he pulled it back, fingers curling against his palm.

They'd been friends a long time and the truth of it was, he missed Beck. Missed the way they used to be at the beginning, when they'd

JACKIE NORTH

first gotten the space at his uncle's garage and started making money fencing stolen car parts.

Those days, golden and heady and over two years in the past, might never come back. But did he even want them to? It was much nicer in the valley, sweeter and more mellow. The food was better. The beds. The showers. And Royce was here, in the valley, which was the best thing of all.

No, he didn't want those days to come back, but he didn't want to lose Beck over any of it. So he tried again.

"We left each other," he said, speaking more gently to Beck than he had in ages. "Maybe you could come for another visit. Try again. I'll get Royce to agree to it—"

"I don't give a shit what your boyfriend agrees to," said Beck with a snap that Jonah felt all the way to his bones. "And speaking of him, you do know how rich he is, don't you?"

"What?" The conversation had taken a sudden left turn, so sharp that had he been a car, his tires would have been screeching across the concrete.

"I looked him up, your boyfriend." A low, not-so-nice chuckle came from the other end of the line. "He's a rich man. His whole family is. They own acres and acres in Montana, did you know? They raise horses."

"Yeah, I knew." Jonah shrugged, though he knew Beck couldn't see him. "I knew that." Because of course he did. Royce had mentioned the ranch in Montana at least once, and his big family. All the horses. "So what? They have a few ponies. Royce might invite me up sometime. I know all about it."

"You *don't* know all about it." There was a bite to Beck's voice, like he was delivering amazingly horrible news and almost didn't want to, but he was going to plow through like the trooper he was. "You don't know *anything*."

"So fine. Tell me."

Rolling his eyes, casting a gaze around the compound to where Royce was waiting for him in the mess tent, Jonah turned away so he could focus on what Beck was saying and, more importantly, what he

THE COWBOY AND THE HOODLUM

was trying to do. He was fucking with Jonah simply because he could, and that was so like Beck that Jonah wanted to hang up and be done with it.

"He's not just rich," said Beck with a hiss. "He's *fucking* rich."

"*You're* fucking rich." He should cut off this conversation right now—

"No, I'm talking thousands of acres and millions of dollars' worth of horses. His family is so rich it's off the charts." After a hard pause, Beck said again, "I looked him up. I did the research, and you better believe he's too rich for you."

"H-how rich?" Jonah couldn't help asking this simply because of the tone of Beck's voice. He'd never been a liar, nor was he the kind of guy to exaggerate, except when he was talking about his beloved green Pontiac and how fast it could go, or how much he could sell it for, even though Jonah knew that Beck loved that car too much to ever be parted from it.

"Richer than dreams," said Beck. "They've got a few pieces of property up there in Montana, and the property alone is worth a fortune. The houses on those properties start at a million each, and there's typically more than one. As for those horses? You couldn't own one of those so-called ponies for under ten thousand dollars—and they're buying and selling and breeding all year long. Year in and year out. Their lives—"

Beck choked off a breath and Jonah could imagine him gripping the phone just about hard enough to crack the protective case.

"It's a whole 'nother level they live on," said Beck, and if he seemed calmer than he had before, there was more despair in his voice, as if the empty places inside of him had been filled with a hope that would never be realized. To be well off, to never have to worry about money. To not have to do criminal things to fill those spaces.

"So?" Jonah knew why Beck felt the way he did about money, because he'd felt the same way himself. Maybe he still did, but he wouldn't let it divide him from Royce. "So what?"

"So *what?*" asked Beck, spitting the words again. "He's not going to want someone like you. He's never going to take you home and intro-

JACKIE NORTH

duce you to anyone up there. If he's made you that promise, he's lying. Nobody as rich as him could ever love *anybody* like you."

There was no arguing with Beck when he was in a mood like he was, and Jonah had exactly zero energy for this conversation. He disconnected the call, shoved his phone in his back pocket, and marched to the mess tent.

Everybody was already there, shambling peacefully into one line for the buffet, with Royce at the very end, holding out his hand for Jonah. Waiting for him. Like a gift and a blessing, all rolled into one.

"Hey," said Royce with a sweet, soft smile. "Did you get ahold of him?"

"Sure," said Jonah, half-gasping a laugh, as if dismissing the fairy tale that Beck had just told him. Crazy ole Beck, making shit up. Because of course, none of it was true and surely not the staggering amounts Beck had described.

"Are you two still mad at each other?" Royce asked as the line moved forward.

Jonah shook his head, giving a half-shrug because, of course, what was being presented to them at the steam table was far more interesting than whatever Beck was up to. Trying to make Jonah back away from Royce simply because Beck claimed he was a bazillionaire. Beck just wanted Jonah all to himself.

Sitting next to Royce at one of the long tables, Jonah ate his lunch, not really tasting it, only half-able to focus on the conversation around him, or on Royce telling a joke about bats. *What did the bat do when he didn't know the answer to the teacher's question? He winged it.*

Around the table, all the ex-cons were snickering, only half-heartedly trying to hide their laughs.

Had this been a few weeks ago, Jonah knew the reaction would have been quite different, when they didn't know what to make of Royce or the gentleness of the valley. But now, in response to a very terrible dad joke, they were laughing like little kids, as if their innocence had never been stripped away by a stint in prison, or by the idea that breaking the law was a good way to get ahead in life.

That was the way, the innocent way, Jonah and Beck had been, back when they were kids fresh out of high school. Back when life seemed awash with possibilities and all the opportunities their teachers had told them about.

Beck was the smart one, between the two of them, and his grades could have been higher had he not been dragging Jonah behind him, making sure he got through his classes. Or if he'd not been distracted by Jonah's mad escapades, street races, and engine rebuilds that took up all the time they should have been using on their studies.

Setting up a garage to strip cars and sell parts had seemed the best of all possible worlds. Had Jonah not gotten arrested, he and Beck would still be together with grease-stained hands on a Saturday night, munching on leftover Chinese takeout as they discussed who would shower first and which bars they would hit.

And now, Beck was all on his own and he'd never moved on from their old lives together. Hadn't made new friends or figured out his life without Jonah. He was frozen where Jonah had left him on the day he'd gotten arrested.

Jonah looked up when he felt a gentle pat on his hand, and looked down at his mostly full plate, then up again into a pair of the most loving blue eyes. Those were Royce's eyes and that beautiful mouth was pulled into a bit of a concerned frown.

"Lunch is over," said Royce. "Let's go for a walk and you can tell me what's wrong."

Jonah let Royce bus his place for him, and watched as Royce paused to tell Gordy, Duane, and Tyson what they needed to work on that afternoon. He sighed with relief as Royce tugged on his sleeve and pulled him into the woods, along the path that led to the flagstones. There, in front of the assembly of pink-and-tan rocks, in sight of the calm blue water, he paused.

"Tell me what's wrong," said Royce. He reached up and ran his thumb along Jonah's eyebrows as if in smoothing them, he could soothe the wild, unhappy race in Jonah's heart. "I'll help you carry it, whatever it is."

"It's fucking dumb, that's what it is," said Jonah, kicking a small pile of pine needles with his yellow boots.

"Most arguments are," said Royce, quite gently. "Is that what happened? You two had an argument? Tell me about it."

There was no way, simply no fucking way, Jonah would ever be able to resist those eyes, the small curve of Royce's smile, the patient way he stood there, the sun in his golden hair, tufts of it curling behind his ears. Making him even more of an angel than he already was, a kind, listening angel.

So Jonah told him. Everything.

The words spilled out of him as he recounted the story of him and Beck and their friendship, some of which Royce already knew, some of which was new. All of it. Stolen cars, street races, their Saturday nights, or the times they stayed home and wrecked the sheets. But no matter how shocking it all was, Royce didn't seem shocked.

"And the worst of it is," said Jonah, wishing that this conversation was over and everything resolved between him and Beck without him having to climb a hill of nails to get there. "You're too rich for me to even be talking to."

"What do you mean, too rich?" asked Royce.

"You're a bazillionaire," said Jonah, spitting out what he knew, what Beck had just told him, as fast as he could. While he'd told himself had just been saying that to mess with him, he also knew Beck had never lied to him about anything, so, really, he'd believed him the second Beck had started telling him the facts. "You don't want to be with someone like me. A poor man. A criminal."

"What does that matter?" asked Royce, and he honestly seemed puzzled. "I could be anywhere, doing anything, but I'm here with you."

"Well, your family is certainly not going to approve." Jonah barked a laugh, tossing his head back as if it was a supremely funny joke and not the saddest thing in the world, the basic, bare-faced fact that was going to, in the end, break his heart. "They'll cut you off without a cent if you stick with the likes of me."

"Well, that's not true," said Royce with a sweet little laugh, a pink blush to his cheeks. "I've already talked to Grandad about you. He told me to follow my heart, so that's what I'm doing. Following my heart straight to you."

"You didn't."

"I sure did," said Royce with absolute sincerity. "My family is very important to me, so of course I would talk to them about you. I mean, I talked to Grandad, but he probably told everybody else, so the cat is out of the bag, as they say." He shrugged. "I figured we'd go up at the end of summer, after you've gone through the whole program. And maybe—"

Royce paused, the look in his blue eyes a little more serious now. "If you and Beck can patch things up between you, he might like to go with us, so he can still feel he's a part of your life. Because I think that's what the problem is. I mean, I don't know Beck very well, but if I were him and you'd gone off, I might feel left behind, too. I think he misses you."

"I can't believe you just suggested that," said Jonah.

"I did," said Royce. "Why would you think I'm the type of person to tell you not to be friends with who you're friends with?"

"You don't like how he behaves," said Jonah, sticking out his chin.

"Well, that's certainly true," said Royce. "I think his manners could improve, but with your good influence, perhaps they can by the time we all head up to Montana."

"My good influence?" Spreading his palms across his chest, Jonah took a step forward, relief filling him, gratitude like a bubble of pure light. That Royce was like this, somebody so good, so kind—he'd do anything to keep him. "I'll invite him up for Sunday. Is that okay?"

"Have a chat with him when he gets here," said Royce, quite gently. "Make sure to set expectations. That you're with me now, but you still want him in your life. I don't want you to be sad." Royce took a step forward, giving Jonah a quick, light kiss. "Being without him, I think, makes you sad. Or am I wrong about that?"

"You're not wrong," said Jonah. Images of him and Beck through the years, from kids in white t-shirts stained from road grease and Kool-Aid to grown men in white t-shirts stained in road grease and Jack and soda raced through his mind—Beck had always been there for him.

He'd make it up to Beck for treating him so badly, for taking advantage of Beck, when he could, being mean, just *because* he could. "I'll call him."

"Call him now, if you like," said Royce, gesturing along the lake to the horse pasture. "I'll go help Duane and Tyson and the other guys to give you a bit of privacy. And then, join us. And tell me what he said. Okay?"

"Okay."

Jonah pulled out his cellphone as he watched Royce stride away through the tall grasses at the edge of the line of pine trees, the sunlight in his golden hair making it dazzle brightly, like honey. And braced himself to dial Beck's number one more time.

The conversation was simple. *Come up on Sunday,* he'd said. *I need to talk to you.* And Beck, who could never resist anything Jonah ever asked of him, said, *Yes.* And that was it.

Jonah counted the hours to Sunday, in between working hard when it was sunny, and hanging out in the mess tent when it rained. Whispering in Royce's ear come sundown, sweet nothings, all the poetry in his heart.

Royce always responded by turning to Jonah, nestling in the curve of his arms as they lay together on the cot in his tent, sighing at Jonah's poetry and responding with some of his own, including what seemed to be his favorite poem, about a morning's morning minion, whatever the hell that was.

"It's about a falcon," said Royce, going straight into teacher mode. "A beautiful sun-dappled falcon."

CHAPTER 34

JONAH

It was hard to wait until Sunday. But even though, while he waited, he was half-scared, half-eager, he knew that with Royce's support, he could fix his friendship with Beck.

When Sunday came, Jonah had showered and shaved and then debated whether to wear black on black, the way he always used to, or if he should wear his new lilac snap button shirt, and cowboy boots, because, at the very least, this was part of who he was now. He went with the lilac shirt and the cowboy boots, but he wore his old grease-stained blue jeans, freshly laundered, so Beck would know he needed to accept the new Jonah along with the old Jonah.

His heart was pounding as the sun winked off the chrome bumper of Beck's green Pontiac, his heart just about exploding as Beck parked and climbed out, looking freshly shaved and somber.

Jonah had mental notes on what he wanted to say, but the words would wait because the hug he wanted to give Beck wouldn't. He pulled Beck to him and hugged him hard, smiling at Beck's *oof* of surprise, and the way those familiar arms came around him.

"I'm sorry," he said softly in Beck's ear. "For everything. For my stupid ghost plate scheme. For leaving you. For being the worst friend anybody could ever be. Can you forgive me?"

Beck went still, though Jonah could feel the pounding of his heart. The hitch of his breath.

"It just got so fucked up when you were arrested," said Beck. "Fucking ghost plates."

It sounded as if Beck blamed the plates, rather than Jonah's scheme behind them. So, just as he'd confessed to Royce about keeping the scarf, he needed to confess the truth to Beck.

"I was trying to earn some money for your birthday by selling those ghost plates," said Jonah, half choking on the words. "Wanted to get you some whitewall tires for your car."

Beck pulled back, his grip hard on Jonah's arms.

"You fuckin' asshat," said Beck without only a little heat, then his voice rose, twisted with tears. "That's why you left me? Fuck the tires. *Fuck* everything."

Then Beck hugged him hard, kissing Jonah's cheek.

"Just don't ever leave me again. Don't leave me *behind*." Beck's voice fully cracked on the last word, and Jonah's heart cracked at the sound of it.

"No," he said. "I won't ever."

Jonah pulled back a little so he could see Beck's face, his hands still on Beck's upper arms, to keep him close. Then he tipped forward till their foreheads were touching, their eyes locking the way they used to do in the schoolyard when they'd come up with some mad scheme or other that would do nothing more than get them into trouble before the sun went down.

"I love you, man," said Beck, half whisper, half croak.

"I love you, too," he said, then he straightened up, nodding so Beck would know he meant it. "And here's what I think should happen."

Carefully, slowly, he spelled out all the things he felt in his heart, his uncertainty about the future, about the shop, about the valley, about an as-yet unseen ranch in Montana.

"If we behave and don't get up to any shenanigans," he said. "You and me both. Then Royce has invited you and me up to see everything. Maybe we can even ride a painted pony."

THE COWBOY AND THE HOODLUM

"Ha," said Beck, with a hard laugh, but there were tears glittering in his eyes, as well. "Me on a ten thousand dollar horse. That'll be the day."

"That *will* be the day," said Jonah stoutly. "Until then, it's such a long drive from Denver that Royce suggested that you come up for the whole weekend, maybe every weekend for the rest of the summer. That is, if you can shut up the shop. And if you want to. We could stay in one of the spare tents—"

"You and me, you mean?" Beck's eyes flew open, searching Jonah's face.

"Of course, I mean you and me," said Jonah with a laugh, a soft, pleased one. "We can pretend we're at summer camp like we never got to go do when we were kids. Remember how we wanted to and both our parents said no, fuck no, hell no?"

"Yeah." The response came as a sigh, the daydream of yesteryear flickering in Beck's eyes. And devotion alongside that as he smiled the smallest smile. "Royce is okay with this?"

"He suggested it," said Jonah.

"That's big of him," said Beck with a sarcastic half-roll of his eyes.

"He's got a big heart, and he wants me to be happy." Jonah didn't want Beck dismissing the sweetness that was Royce, though he knew it would get better with time if he was patient. And encouraging. "You've got a big heart too," he said now. "Maybe the biggest I've ever known. And it would make me the happiest man on the whole fucking planet if we could all just get along."

The biggest silver tear streaked down Beck's face and as he was attempting to scrub it away with the back of his hand, Jonah stilled that hand, pulled it away, and wiped Beck's tears away himself with gentle touches of his thumb.

Such a soft heart Beck had. Jonah should have realized it before now, only just as he was about to start kicking himself, he saw Royce coming through the woods, bright like the reflection off the chrome bumper of Beck's Pontiac.

"It's lunchtime," he said sensibly, like Beck hadn't just broken down in front of him. He swung his arm around Beck's shoulders and pulled him close for a hug. "I asked the cooks to make your favorite ravioli, but it's not from a can. They make it by hand. Can you fucking believe that? By *hand*. This place. This fucking place." Jonah waved at the woods, the mess tent beyond, at Royce, even, who was coming up to them both. "It's like a dream here, only you never have to wake up cause it just keeps on going."

Before Beck could respond to this wild statement, Royce had reached them, both hands taking Beck's hand to shake it warmly.

"Hello, it's nice to see you again," said Royce, his voice kind, welcoming. "I'll bet the traffic on I-25 was crazy on a day as nice as today. But it looks like you came through without a scratch. Both you and your lovely green wheels."

Royce gestured to the Pontiac, now parked peacefully in the shade, and smiled at Beck.

"I really am glad you're here," he said. "Jonah's simply not himself when you two are at odds, so I'm counting on you to help me keep him happy."

There was a long silence.

Jonah could see it in Beck's eyes that he was trying to figure out what to say. Jonah had just given him a lot to think about. As for Royce, well, he was his own man, a puzzle to figure out, but only if Beck was willing. And Jonah wanted him to be. Oh, he so wanted him to be.

"Sure," said Beck with a casual half-shrug, as if it was of no never-mind to him that Royce had just asked him to share in the caretaking of Jonah. "But is it true that we get to ride painted ponies in Montana at the end of the summer?"

"Only if you're very good," said Royce, shaking his finger at Beck like a schoolteacher trying to keep his young charge in line. "You'll need to take some riding lessons—beginner lessons with the rest of the ex-cons. If you're up for it."

There was a glint of a smile in Beck's eyes now because, though Royce probably didn't realize it, Beck was considered a bad-ass kind of guy, at least back in Denver. Nobody crossed him, especially with

Jonah at his side. People gave them a wide berth on the sidewalk, and they never had to wait in line at the local bodega.

Back home, they were treated with anxious reverence everywhere they went, and here, Royce was scolding Beck and telling him to be a good boy and all for the promise of a pony ride.

Only Jonah knew that Beck was eating this up, like Jonah had eaten it up, almost from the beginning. The high standards. The way Royce never raised his voice, but taught by example. How he had his team of ex-cons eating out of his hands and doing his bidding, simply by asking them nicely.

"Yeah, okay," said Beck, as if the struggles of the last few years were nothing but a feather-edged memory. "Riding lessons, huh? And me an' Jonah sharing a tent every weekend?"

"Of course." Royce nodded like it was a done deal, like he was surprised that Beck could even doubt it. "Jonah works every day of the week except Sunday, so if you're here on a Saturday, maybe you'd like to pitch in? Rather than being bored just hanging around." Royce wrinkled his nose as if to express the distaste for this idea that he was sure Beck would share with him. "We typically have a campfire almost every night and we make s'mores and tell stories, and it's a lot of fun. Does that sound good?"

"Yeah, okay," said Beck, and it was obvious he was trying to be casual about it, but was buoyed up at the prospect of being not just at Jonah's side, but being part of what Jonah was a part of. Being a part of a team, even if that team was mostly made up of B&E guys, thieves, and drug dealers. "I'm in."

As they trudged off to the mess tent, a happy band of three, Jonah had a flicker of concern about what Leland might say to Beck's continued presence in the valley.

Probably Royce had it all figured out, knew how to get permission from Leland, no matter how long after the fact. Maybe nobody would tell him that Beck was planning to be a semi-permanent visitor. Or maybe it just wouldn't matter if, as Royce had instructed, they all behaved themselves.

Which they would, they most certainly would.

Jonah slipped between the two of them, linking arms with each of them, and as they marched up to the mess tent, he was happy. Maybe happier than he'd been in a long time.

Strike that. He was happier than he'd *ever* been.

Than he'd ever *fucking* been.

EPILOGUE - JONAH

Toward the end of summer, the phone call had come that Royce's grandad, Nolan Thackery, had taken a tumble off a new gelding that Thackery Ranch had acquired. According to Royce, Grandad was fine and resting at home with a sprained wrist and a couple of scrapes. Still, Royce was in a state.

"I've just talked to him," said Royce, as they sat on the pile of flagstones, drinking their iced coffee, basking in the sunlight. There was a snap of chill in the air, so they wore their sherpa-lined denim jackets, and their feet were snug inside of their work boots.

The flagstone pile was a new pile, as the other stones had finally been used up on paths and little patios in various parts of the valley. Now, there were two permanent rows of pink and tan stone, one row tall enough to sit on, the second row just the right height to rest feet upon.

Royce had presented the idea to Leland, calling it a Restorative Spot, where guests might come and enjoy the view of the lake and the ridge and, quite simply, just sit, without any expectation of anything else happening. Leland had fallen in love with the idea, and told Royce to make sure the flagstones were the prettiest he could find, and if he needed to cut down any trees to make it happen.

"No tree cutting," said Royce at the time, quite firmly. "That glade is what it is, and the stones will be what they are."

Jonah brushed his shoulder against Royce's and sipped at his delicious coffee, his mind racing as to how he might best help his sweetie. Royce's happiness was all to him, his rising moon, his setting sun, bats aflight in the twilight air, the lone howl of a not-too-distant coyote. Royce's smile filled his heart, and the sparkle in those blue eyes the only jewels he would ever need.

So what did Royce need? He was worried about Grandad Thackery, and so even though Jonah's experience was that old birds like that were quite tough, and the injuries Grandad had sustained weren't life threatening, whatever he did would be for Royce's sake.

"What if we just went up there?" Jonah asked, lifting his purple Yeti mug in the air as though he were casting a vote.

"Go up there?" asked Royce. "Now?"

"Yeah, why not?" Jonah's nod was firm. "How far is it? Not that far, right?"

"Why didn't I think of this?" asked Royce, astonishment in his voice.

"Because you're too worried to think clearly," said Jonah with a nod, knowing he was absolutely right. "Work is winding down. It's almost the end of September. Surely the Big Boss will give us a quick weekend to get up there so you can see Grandad Thackery with your own eyes?"

There was love in Royce's eyes as he turned to look at Jonah, a pure strength in his slow smile.

"I love how thoughtful you are," he announced. "It's only five hundred miles from here to the ranch. We could get there in a day."

"We could leave tomorrow. Early. If Gabe says yes," said Jonah, and then he paused. Tomorrow was Saturday and Beck was due to arrive. That was, if he didn't show up later that night in his eagerness to start his weekend in the valley.

Beck had been coming up for weeks all summer, never missing a weekend. He was always wild to be there, making himself useful in ways Jonah couldn't have predicted, and making himself a part of the

THE COWBOY AND THE HOODLUM

team in ways Jonah could not have predicted, either, even though he should have.

Beck willingly helped rake the horse pasture of manure, making jokes about horseshit the entire time, or took the weed eater, hat on, head down, earbuds in his ears as he jammed out to Black Sabbath, Metallica, and Led Zeppelin. He'd trim the grass to make it tidy around flagstone patios, wooden platforms, along the walkway paths among the trees, keeping them wide and visible.

It'd been his idea to plant little glow lights that absorbed sunlight during the day and released it at night, so the paths were lit with enough light to see by without blaring into the darkness with flashlights and making everything feel all modern and suburban. It'd been his idea to replace the auto lights over the mess tent and the facilities with something a little more soft, reducing light pollution to retain the gentle atmosphere of the valley.

When a mountain lion had started prowling round, Beck had willingly done night patrol duty with Jonah, keeping watch beneath the moonlight with lights and alarms, rifles resting in the crooks of their elbows, the two of them giggling the whole while because the danger didn't seem quite real.

At the end of that weekend, Beck had suggested setting up a series of alarms and lights that would go off automatically if a mountain lion came near, scaring the animal off that way, rather than wasting so much manpower. Royce had done the research along with Beck, pointing out the increased need at dawn and dusk, when the mountain lions were more active, and he and Beck had worked together to set up the entire system.

It was obvious that Beck wanted to get everything right because, somehow, during all his time in the valley, he'd absorbed the idea of the idea of what the valley was meant to be: a safe, calm respite from the world. Something that Beck had never had, but that he was willing to create for perfect strangers.

True, the perfect strangers would be paying five hundred dollars a night, or thereabouts, a fact which still astonished both Jonah and

Beck, but the facts were the facts. The valley was now a much safer place, thanks to Beck's efforts.

In the midst of Jonah's thoughts, memories swirling all around, Royce turned to look at him and asked, "Would he want to sit in the front, do you think?"

"Who?" asked Jonah, his eyebrows going up.

"Beck, silly," said Royce. "He won't need to help me navigate or anything, but I've long thought he's a front seat kind of guy."

For a moment, Jonah was still. The purity of that kind of love still struck him, the generosity of assuming that Beck was, of course, invited to go along on the impromptu road trip and might prefer to sit in the front passenger seat, amazed him, filled him with wonder and joy all at once. Royce knew how much Beck meant to him, how much they'd gone through together, changed together.

When Jonah had asked Royce about that kind of willingness to let Beck be in their lives like that, Royce had said, *You are my one true love, but I don't own you. Beck is your friend. He's a part of your life. A part of you. Why would I deny you that?*

Royce wouldn't deny Jonah that and, in fact, had never denied him anything within his power to give.

In return, Jonah gave Royce everything he had, everything he was, everything he felt. Fierce in this love, protective, until Royce started calling Jonah his wolf with a heart of gold. The thought of this made Jonah smile because as far as he knew, from everything Royce had taught him, wolves were not for play play any more than he was.

Later that day, Beck showed up a short while after dinner was over, his headlights shining through the shadows between the pine trees as he came down the switchbacks, the rumble of the Pontiac's engine low and slow and sure. Jonah met him in the parking lot, gently lit by those solar lights they'd set up at Beck's suggestion earlier in the summer.

"Hey," said Jonah in greeting, the casualness of the word belied by how tightly he hugged Beck to him, the soul-deep pleasure when Beck hugged him back just as tightly. "You're here."

"Yeah," said Beck. "Thought I'd come up early," he said. Which was

THE COWBOY AND THE HOODLUM

what he typically said, because he usually came up early. The idea that the garage would be closed all weekend became less troublesome as time went by, and the fact that guys looking to buy stolen car parts might be going elsewhere had grown into even less of a concern.

"The tent's set up," said Jonah, doing his best to grab Beck's weekend duffle bag, but Beck batted his hand away.

"Shit, man," said Beck with mock-disdain, flipping his dark hair out of his eyes with a jerk of his chin. "I got it."

Together they walked along the path to tent number ten, the one nearest to the facilities, because sometimes Beck needed to get up and pee and he wanted to be close enough so he wouldn't quite have to wake up to do it. The tent was still buried in a copse of woods, like the other tents, and was just as quiet and luxurious.

They both sighed as they stepped onto the wooden platform, then Beck led the way inside, reaching up to turn on the light, then tossing his duffle on the left-hand bed.

"Where's your friend?" asked Beck, as he flumped down on the cot.

In the beforetime, that kind of question would have been dismissive, derisive, indicating quite strongly how little Beck thought of that person. And while it still sounded that way, Jonah knew that, for quite a while now, the question meant something different because Beck truly wanted to know where Royce was.

If Beck showed up on Friday night, Royce would typically show up soon after Beck's arrived, bearing gifts of eats and treats, accompanied by an invitation to the campfire evening or the movie in the mess tent, and then he'd leave them to their own devices. Giving them the privacy of their friendship, an expectation of seeing them at breakfast on Saturday morning.

If Beck showed up on Saturday morning, the few number of times that did happen, Royce would typically make sure the buffet was still running or that food had been kept warm for Beck. Then, while Beck chowed down, Royce would sit across from him in the mess tent, his hands curled elegantly around a china mug of coffee, and present a list of tasks that might need doing.

Beck would eat, a little messily, it must be admitted, listening without a word. Then, equally without a word, he would bus his place, don gloves and a hat, and rake or mow or weed or haul, whatever was needed.

Around mid-morning, his comfort level would rise, and he would jokingly shout, *Wench, wench, where's my drink?* And Royce would come running with a cooler of snacks, always including Beck's favorite sweet tea, made fresh that morning, and cheddar cheese and Ritz crackers.

Oddly, or perhaps it wasn't so odd anymore, Beck was willing to try other types of cheese that Royce had picked out for him, and would say please and thank you and then make jokes about cutting the cheese, just to make Royce and Jonah both laugh out loud.

"We've got a road trip planned in the morning," said Jonah as he flumped down on the other cot.

"Is that so," said Beck, his voice a little hard. "You and Royce?"

Jonah could see it in his eyes that Beck completely expected he'd be left behind to toil in the valley, so Jonah hastened to clarify as quick as he could.

"Oh, yes," Jonah said. "Royce is driving, and you're in the front seat so you can help me absorb all the bird talk and cloud talk and plant talk. You get me?"

"I get you," said Beck, doing his best to sneer as if this task was a weight of untold misery, but in his eyes, he was smiling. He was sitting up, even, to show how ready he was.

"He won't stop talking," said Jonah, pretending to be annoyed at the prospect. "It'll go on and on for five hundred fucking miles. You know this, right?"

"Yes, I'm fully aware of your boyfriend and his proclivities," said Beck with a dismissive wave.

Proclivities was the type of word that Royce would fling around with abandon, as if he expected that everyone around him had an internal dictionary to look the word up. Beck, taking it a step further, had absorbed all the new vocabulary from Royce into his very being, and liked to use as many five-dollar words as he could to show he'd been paying attention.

In another life, had they both been shown that school, or maybe even college, should one care to daydream, was important, Beck would have been at the top of his class. He was that smart, that *fucking* smart, way smarter than Jonah. He'd just needed a chance to show it, to rise up to it. With Royce around, Beck had that chance.

As Beck unpacked enough for one night, Royce came by and announced that movie night was just about to start, and that he'd made salted popcorn, popped in coconut oil, which he knew was Beck's favorite.

"I've got bags of peanut M&M's to put in there as well," said Royce, standing between their two cots as they looked up at him. His golden hair was a mess around his temples, as if he'd been running his fingers through it. "For anyone who might want them."

The twinkle in Royce's blue eyes told Jonah that of course Royce was well aware that the combination of peanut M&M's with freshly made popcorn was a personal favorite of Beck's, and that Royce had arranged for the treat or, more likely, made the popcorn with his own hands.

"Has Jonah told you about our road trip?" asked Royce. "I thought we'd leave promptly at nine in the morning, if that works for you two."

"Royce's grandad's had a fall," said Jonah, almost at the same time as Royce was speaking.

"Oh." Beck's expression, amused, attempting to look bored, mostly out of habit, faded away into genuine concern that he did not bother to hide. "Is he okay? Do we need to leave now? I could drive. I'm good at night driving, just ask Jonah."

"He is," said Jonah. "He's the best at it. Better than me. And yeah, we could go now. Right now."

That Beck would be willing to dash off at a moment's notice for an old guy he never met, and that Jonah would be willing to, as well, showed how far they'd both come. Under the valley's influence, and especially under Royce's gentle leadership, they'd become different men, different friends to each other.

"No, there's no need to rush," said Royce, his smile tender as he looked down at them. "He's doing fine, according to him. I just want to make sure with my own eyes. We'll leave in the morning, stay the night, and drive back on Sunday."

"Or we stay if we need to, okay?" Jonah made his most serious face. "Promise me."

"I promise," said Royce, utterly solemn.

The evening proceeded with its usually stately pace, Gabe setting up the projector in the mess tent, everybody jostling for seats as they folded and pushed aside the long tables, putting metal folding chairs in their place.

Blaze joked about getting a bunch of old couches, which would be a whole lot more comfortable, but the look on Gabe's face told Jonah that the idea of it wasn't a joke, and that if Blaze wanted couches, couches he would get. Jonah imagined they could easily store them to the side on some pallets next to the mess tent and cover them with canvas when not in use, but that was a job for another day.

After the movie, they put the mess tent back in order, stacking the folding chairs, unfolding the tables, and sat around yakking. Jonah knew Royce was worried about Grandad Thackery, but he was being his usual polite host, welcoming Gordy when he came over to sit at the same table where the three of them were sitting.

Gordy was his sweet, sassy self, and Jonah noticed, as he had done several times in the past, how attentive Beck was being to pretty much everything Gordy had to say.

"I think I found some poison ivy along Horse Creek, below the lake," said Gordy, vigorously scratching his forearm. "In an aggressive little patch, just waiting to get at me."

"*Toxicodendron radicans*," said Royce in a soft little voice, almost as though he was speaking to himself, but of course, this just made Jonah want to kiss him all over, he was just that freaking sexy when he went into teacher mode.

"Do we dig it or burn it?" asked Beck, looking quite concerned as he leaned close to examine the bit of rash that Gordy was making a fuss over.

"No," said Royce, sitting up. "All we need to do is pour boiling water over the roots." He laughed under his breath. "The trick is getting boiling water out that far."

"I could rig up a little propane stove," said Beck. "And we could boil water from the lake, right?"

It was lovely to see Royce smiling at Beck, and to see Beck smile in return, after which Beck's attention returned fully to Gordy.

"Hey, Gordy," Jonah said, flicking a glance at Royce, his eyebrows raised, knowing Royce would understand what he meant to do. He got the nod from Royce, and asked, "We're taking a roadtrip to visit Royce's grandad, d'you want to join?"

Gordy said yes right away, which was how it was the four of them, directly after breakfast the next morning, loaded up the F150 with what they'd need for the quick two-day trip, and were headed north to Montana. Beck seemed pleased to be in the front with Royce, and Gordy, wide-eyed and beaming, was happy to sit in the back row with Jonah.

EPILOGUE - ROYCE

Royce knew the way to Thackery Ranch as well as he knew his own face, knew the dips in the highway, the best places to stop for gas, or for sodas and snacks, which wasn't quite as healthy as the fruit and cheese he'd packed in a small cooler, but which was joyfully accepted by everyone else in the truck.

"You're a Bugle man, I see," said Royce, as Beck crunched noisily in the truck's passenger seat.

"That I am, sir," said Beck with good humor. "That I am."

It didn't matter the crumbs were getting everywhere, as that was what car vacuums were for. And it didn't matter that Gordy, behind Royce, was talking nonstop, because it meant that he was having a good time. As well, Royce wasn't missing the fact that when Beck turned in his seat, it wasn't to say something to Jonah, which did happen, but more, it was so he could look at Gordy.

Royce had eyes, yes, he sure did, and he had ears, and the exchange of glances, of words, of energy between Beck and Gordy was sweetness itself. The shining expression on Gordy's heart-shaped face, which Royce could see in his rear-view mirror, told Royce that Beck's attentions were greatly appreciated.

As for Beck, almost totally gone was the surly, dark-eyed, angry young man. Yes, there were sometimes flashes of that, but considering Beck's background, bits of which Jonah had shared with Royce when telling him of his own history, that was to be expected.

Some things stayed with a man, and while Beck had the makings of a true gentleman, the gritty, rough edges of his soul would never truly be smoothed. Which was perhaps what attracted Gordy to him. Which was fine by Royce, because if Beck was happy, Jonah was happy, which made Royce happy as well.

"How much longer?" asked Jonah, leaning forward to peer at the roadsigns as they trundled through the small town of Billings, Montana, and Highway 90 turned into Highway 94.

"Around twenty minutes," said Royce. "Depending on traffic. Then, when we reach Huntley, the ranch is ten minutes north of that."

Tightening his hands on the wheel, then flexing his fingers to relax them, Royce glanced at his passengers, then carefully took Exit 6, slipped up Northern Avenue, then, just past Barkemeyer Park, took Nahmis Avenue north to the ranch.

The small town quickly changed into green farm fields, and then, as they crossed Yellowstone River, the green valley bottom stretched out before him, scattered with a few barns and farmhouses, and it wasn't that he'd meant to be misleading, but it was another twelve miles before they arrived at the broad stone sign with Thackery Ranch carved into it, and a wooden archway that announced the entrance to Thackery Ranch.

"We're here," said Royce, leaning forward, his heart jumping in his throat as if it, too, wanted to be there already, making sure of Grandad Thackery. "Hang on, I'm going to speed."

Dust flew up from the tires as Royce put on the gas, bits of gravel pinging in the wheel wells as he raced along. Had he been younger, he would have gotten a good scolding, but now that he was older, he could get away with it, and it was important to cover that last mile before the main house as fast as possible. And soon enough, the main house hove into view, a large two-story stone-faced building that faced south, the gravel driveway turning into a flat, flagstone-paved

THE COWBOY AND THE HOODLUM

driveway. The main house had two guest buildings, one on either side, so there'd be plenty of room for everyone.

Royce drove right up to the main house, pleased to see that Grandad was standing on the wide porch, but displeased to see that he was using a cane, and that his left arm was in a sling. Royce parked and, forgetting his guests, flung himself out of the truck and up the stairs to gather Grandad in the biggest hug he could manage.

Grandad was wiry and thin, his blonde hair turned to silver gray, his intense blue eyes behind gold spectacles laughing as he pulled back to take a look at Royce. With his plaid shirt and red suspenders, he looked like a farmer, rather than the head of a high-powered ranch that bred expensive painted horses.

"You got sunburned, I see," said Grandad, laughing.

"Just the one time," said Royce, and then he sighed. "I didn't know it was bad enough for you to be using a cane, Grandad."

"It's only to protect my knee," Grandad said. "Just to be safe so I don't have another tumble. The sling is also a safety precaution to remind me not to use my left hand."

"Oh, Grandad," said Royce with a sigh.

"And your guests?" asked Grandad, looking over Royce's shoulder, telling Royce that he didn't want to be fussed over, at least not too much.

Royce turned. Jonah, Beck, and Gordy had all gotten out of the truck and were standing in a row, like the ex-cons in the valley did when they were first dropped off. Their expressions were a little wary, but Royce could understand why.

The stone gate and the wooden arch were understated, to be sure, but the main house was big, and the driveway was fancy flagstone rather than cement, and the guest houses were almost as big as the main house. Beyond were the barn, the blacksmith shop, the front pasture, its white rails shining in the sun. Land was money in Montana, and there was no hiding how far the ranch stretched into the distance.

"Introduce me, if you would," said Grandad, and before he could

JACKIE NORTH

start down the stone steps, Royce hastened to wave the three men up to the covered porch.

"This is Gordy," he said, touching Gordy's shoulder. "Gordy, this is Grandad."

"Hello, Mr. Thackery," said Gordy with a little hunch of his shoulders, a sure sign of nerves.

"Just call me Nolan," said Grandad, shaking Gordy's hand. "We don't stand on ceremony here."

"And this is Beck, Jonah's best friend," said Royce. He'd mentioned Beck to Grandad when they'd talked over the phone, but while he'd said that he and Beck had a rough start, he hadn't belabored the point. Instead, he'd praised Beck's work ethic, his intelligence, his love of classic rock. "Beck, this is Grandad."

"Uh," said Beck as he shook Grandad's hand. "You guys are way the fuck out here, aren't you?"

"We sure are," said Grandad, with a little laugh. "And that's how we like it. Tons of peace and quiet and privacy."

"And this is Jonah," said Royce, saving the best for last. "Jonah, this is Grandad."

"Call me Nolan," said Grandad, his smile widening as he looked Jonah over, head to toe. "I hear you're smitten with my grandson."

"You hear correctly, sir," said Jonah, returning the hearty handshake with a smile. "Totally, completely, and utterly smitten."

"Well, you've got good taste," said Grandad. "But then, maybe I'm biased. Well, come on in. We've got cool drinks ready, and Royce, you're the only one here. All your brothers have already fussed at me till I sent them away so I could have you to myself."

"That's fine, Grandad," said Royce, making gestures so everybody would go inside, because if they sat down, Grandad would sit down, too. Besides, he talked with his brothers all the time, on the phone, or on a Zoom call. He knew they were doing well, and that they loved him. Had they been here, they would have loomed and teased, and Royce preferred it how it was, with only Grandad to introduce Jonah to. That was the most important thing.

The front living room off the main hall was where the pitchers of

THE COWBOY AND THE HOODLUM

iced tea were set up, and where the housekeeper, Judith, a tall, imposing German woman who made it her life's work to feed everyone in sight, waited to greet them.

"You're here, safe and sound," she said, spreading her arms wide for a hug from Royce. "There's ice in the bucket, and cool tea to drink, and cheese and crackers and cookies, if anyone's hungry. Dinner is at six."

As she left, a little silence settled over the group. Royce knew the front living room was a bit overwhelming, but it was designed to impress guests, to woo prospective clients, to appease those who wanted to see evidence of the ranch's success. The room did that and them some, but it meant that the little group from the valley looked a little rag-tag amidst the western splendor, the arrangement of oil paintings of cowboys and horses and the high prairie on the walls, the bronze bust of a cowboy sitting on the sturdy but elegant side table.

The handwoven Navajo rug on the wall was carefully back from any windows so it wouldn't get bleached by the sun, and it was not only enormous but eye-catching and beautiful. Royce had grown up with all of this, but for someone new, someone not in the ranch business, it might be a little overwhelming.

"Help yourselves, everyone," he said. "We don't stand on ceremony here." Well, they did, but only with guests who might turn into clients, guests who liked a bit of pomp and circumstance. These, on the other hand, were his friends, his co-workers and, in the case of Jonah, his one true love. They all needed to understand how welcome they were, and food was the best way he knew to make that happen. "Judith makes the best charcuterie boards, you know. Second to none."

The delicious food instantly eased the conversation until Beck and Grandad, sitting catty corner from each other on the leather couches, were knee deep in a conversation about Grandad's 1932 two-seater Ford coupe. There was trouble with the engine that had been installed, Grandad was saying, a replacement for the original which didn't run quite right, and could Beck help?

Both Jonah and Beck jumped on that, all-out willing to drop everything to work on such a sweet ride, as they called it. Which left

Royce conversing with Gordy who, wide-eyed, had been asking about the art on the walls, the bust, the blanket, everything.

"Where are they going?" asked Gordy as Grandad, Jonah, and Beck all stood up and, without a word, headed down the hallway that led to the back door.

"The only thing that way is the kitchen and then the garage," said Royce. "They must be going to look at the coupe."

"In the old days," Gordy said with a quick laugh. "I would be casing the joint, looking for ways in. Looking for what I could easily carry away." Then he flushed, as if embarrassed to admit this. "Some things stay with you," he added. "But I would never, ever—you know, actually *steal* anything. The valley's been good to me, and so maybe I can see another way to go about things. Besides," he said, pointing at the Navajo blanket. "All of this looks like it belongs here."

"It feels that way to me, too," said Royce as he munched on some very good, thinly sliced Italian mortadella. "Sometimes I wonder why I ever left home."

With a gesture, Royce stood up, and together he and Gordy headed down the hallway, as well, going through the kitchen and out the back door. There was a flagstone path that led to the barns, to the staff quarters and, yes, to the garage. They passed by all of this, the low rumble of the coupe coming out through the open garage doors, and went to the front pasture.

There, the long, white PVC fence stretched off into the distance, and among the lush green late-September grasses, several mares grazed, their tails twitching, their brown-and-white splotches beautiful against the blue sky.

"That's Posey, way off there," said Royce, pointing. He rested one foot along the lowest rail, and Gordy followed suit. "She used to be my horse, but she's older, and I'm heavier, so we save her for special rides for my brother's kids. She'll come if we call. Would you like to meet her?"

With a low whistle, Royce called Posey to him, and she came willingly, nickering and trotting right up to the fence, ducking her soft

THE COWBOY AND THE HOODLUM

muzzle into his hands, flicking her long horsey eyelashes as she looked for a treat.

"I've got none, girl," he said, admiring her dark brown eyes. "But I'll bring you something later, for sure. In the meantime, this is Gordy."

"She's beautiful," said Gordy, gently stroking her strong neck as he looked at the small group in the near pasture of horses grazing, brown horses with white splotches, white horses with brown splotches. "All these horses are."

It was peaceful to stand in the warm September sunshine, elbows on the fence rail, looking out over the grandeur of the valley, lush and still and frankly huge, spreading out forever. Mostly Royce never thought about how big the ranch was, but he was looking at it through Gordy's eyes, now, and knew he'd been lucky to grow up there.

"Hey," came a shout behind them.

When Royce turned, he saw it was Jonah and Beck, striding together, in tandem. As they came closer, Royce could see the streak of grease on Beck's face, and that he held an old grease-streaked cloth in his hands, as if he'd been so deep in the coupe's engine, he'd forgotten to leave it behind when he'd come out of the garage.

"Hey," said Royce, giving Jonah a quick kiss on the cheek. "Did you have fun?"

"Yeah," said Jonah. "That car's a beaut."

"I've never seen a '32 coupe up close like that," said Beck as he tried to clean the grease from his face with the cloth. He failed, so Jonah took the corner of his sleeve and wiped it off for him, not seeming to realize he now had grease on his sleeve.

"Those things run for thousands of dollars," said Gordy, a bit unexpectedly. "I mean, I've never stolen one, but I know these kinds of things. Can't help it."

"Your Grandad's offered me a job," said Beck, his eyes wide, his hands going still. "Said he liked my style. Said I touched his car right, with reverence."

"A job?" asked Royce, his eyebrows going up. He looked to Jonah for confirmation, and maybe for an explanation as to what had happened in that garage in under half an hour.

"They got on like a house on fire," said Jonah, with a shake of his head and a that's-how-it-was shrug. "Beck's got a dab hand with cars, and that's the truth."

Royce looked at Beck, the smear of leftover grease shining on his face, a streak of oil on his blue jeans, that messy dark hair over his eyes, eyes that glittered dark in the sunshine. And knew, then, what had happened.

Grandad was lonely, and Beck was like a tom cat he'd found in the rain, just begging to be taken in and petted and cared for. Beck could never be tamed, but it'd be nice for Grandad to have someone to join him in his garage with his beloved cars. Who could talk cars and engines and tires all day long and never get bored.

"Just wait till he gets an eyeful of your Pontiac," said Royce, because to him, it was a done deal. "Will you accept, do you think?" he asked, as it was still Beck's decision.

Beck looked at him, wide eyed, worrying the stained cloth in his hands. All the things that had happened between them, between Jonah and Beck, between Beck and Royce, flashed in those dark eyes. Jonah and Beck's shared history, Beck's own background, those things could not be denied, but the idea of it, of Beck working on the ranch, seemed the perfect solution.

After the summer ended in the valley, truly ended, Royce's original plan had been to return to the ranch and take up the yoke of responsibility, as his four older brothers had lives, and wives, and families, and their own ranches, located close by. He and Jonah were still talking about how Jonah might fit in, and what would happen with the shop. And if Beck worked in the garage as Grandad's mechanic—

—it could not be that simple, that straightforward. Or perhaps it could be.

"What about the shop?" asked Beck.

"Sell the fuckin' shop," said Jonah with a growl. "The air's fresher here, anyhow."

"What about Olive?" asked Beck.

"Who's Olive?" sked Royce in complete confusion. Was there another person whom both Beck and Jonah knew and they never told him about her?

"That's his car," said Jonah, smiling, his teeth flashing white against his tan. "His Pontiac. Olive green. Olive."

"She'll have her own spot in the garage," said Royce.

"Where will I sleep?" asked Beck.

"There's an apartment above the garage," said Royce.

"Would you want me here?" asked Beck in a small voice, looking at Jonah and Royce, each in turn.

"*Yes*," they both said, in unison.

Beck looked away, working his jaw as he seemed to glare at the white fence, the horses, the stretch of green grass gently shifting and dancing in the low, constant wind. When he looked back at Royce, his eyes glittered.

"I didn't think you'd want me around," he said. "At least, not after the summer was over."

It was as if Beck believed, even after all they'd been through together, that Royce *suffered* through his company, which couldn't be further from the truth.

"This is such a good idea," said Royce. "I wish I'd thought of it. The main thing is, you and Jonah don't have to be apart if you say yes." Royce paused as the certainty of this decision sank in, the perfection of it. "If you're here, Jonah will be happy. Which means that I'll be happy, too."

"What about me?" asked Gordy, and they all turned to look at him. "With you guys all up here, I'll be on my own. It'll be like prison when I had nobody to look after me."

"I would have looked after you," said Beck, quietly, and quickly, too, as if he'd been thinking this thought for a long, long time. And in response, Gordy looked at him and seemed just about to swoon, a flush to his heart-shaped face, his green eyes enormous.

Jonah looked at Royce and Royce looked at him. Royce knew, had almost always known, that their partnership of two was strong enough to include Beck. In a heartbeat he knew that it was also strong enough to absorb Gordy into the fold. Together, the four of them could support each other, keep each other happy.

"But of course," said Royce. "You've made yourself very useful in the valley, so I'm sure it will be the same here. Though—" He paused, focusing his attention on Gordy. "That's not the most important thing about you being here, you know. It's just you. You're wanted. You're a part of who we are—"

He paused again, the words thickening in his throat, the warmth of the idea filling him. In spite of the fact that he and Sandra had divorced, childless, he now had a little family of his own.

Yes, his new family was made up of two ex-cons and Beck, who had not, it must be admitted, led the most law-abiding of lives. But they were his now, his to keep and to care for. And in return, they would love him back, and he would never, ever feel alone to the end of his days.

"Oh my," he said, wiping away the heat from his eyes with splayed fingers. When he opened his eyes, he saw the three of them looking at him, somewhat alarmed, it seemed, at his display of emotion. He needed to fix that, and quickly. "This is what I think."

"What?" they all asked him in unison.

"I know Judith has a steak dinner planned, but if we ask nice, she'll keep it for another day. Then we can go to a bar I know in Huntley. It's got sawdust on the floor and shelled peanuts in tin buckets and it serves the most amazing BBQ you've ever tased. We'll go as a family and bring Grandad and Judith with us and just be together, without the tablecloth and the fancy wine glasses. Could you go for something like that? I know I could."

His ears rang with a chorus of *Of course*, and *Fuck, yeah*, and *I'm in*, which filled his heart with almost more love than he could bear. This was the life he never knew he'd have, and he was going to do his best to deserve it.

The End

Thank you for reading!

If you enjoyed this book, please consider leaving a rating (without a review) or leaving a rating and a review!

Would you like to read more of my m/m cowboy romances? I've got a whole series you can binge on! Start with *The Foreman and the Drifter*, Book #1 in my Farthingdale Ranch series.

JACKIE'S NEWSLETTER

Would you like to sign up for my newsletter?

Subscribers are alway the first to hear about my new books. You'll get behind the scenes information, sales and cover reveal updates, and giveaways.

As my gift for signing up, you will receive two short stories, one sweet, and one steamy!

It's completely free to sign up and you will never be spammed by me; you can opt out easily at any time.

To sign up, visit the following URL:

https://www.subscribepage.com/JackieNorthNewsletter

- facebook.com/jackienorthMM
- twitter.com/JackieNorthMM
- pinterest.com/jackienorthauthor
- bookbub.com/profile/jackie-north
- amazon.com/author/jackienorth
- goodreads.com/Jackie_North
- instagram.com/jackienorth_author

Author's Notes About the Story

From the beginning, I fell in love with the idea of writing a series about a place where ex-cons might come to serve out their parole while doing useful work.

The focus would be on how the work, clean living, clean air, good food, and comfortable accommodations might convert a man used to making his way through the world by committing crimes.

Plus, who doesn't love a good redemption story? Not me, that's who.

In the first story in the Farthingdale Valley series, Blaze is innocent of the crimes he's accused of and arrested for. This makes him a little bitter, but with Gabe's love, he's able to heal.

During the planning stages for this series, it also occurred to me to wonder how a summer in the valley might be experienced by someone who is a criminal, a guy who committed the crime, but doesn't think what he did was all that bad.

Enter Jonah, who can't understand why stealing cars and stripping them for parts is such a bad thing. Enter Royce, the pomade-using cowboy bazillionaire who takes one look at Jonah and can't help but be smitten.

It's an opposites attract pairing that I never knew I wanted. And

AUTHOR'S NOTES ABOUT THE STORY

while I was writing this particular story, I had fun with it, and worked hard to keep Royce fussy and to keep Jonah from becoming too tame.

To me, that was one of the important things about this story - that Jonah remained true to himself. That, unlike Darth Vader and other villains like him, Jonah would never lose his teeth. That he would stay a little wild, stay the bad boy that Royce had fallen in love with.

Enter Beck, who, though a side character, became truly a secret favorite character to me.

His original purpose was to have been a cohort in crime for Jonah. He was to have been kind of vicious and mean to show, by association, just what kind of criminal Jonah was.

Instead of that, however, Beck turned into so much more. He's Jonah's best friend and part of his heart, the second member of a wolf pack made up of only two. These two, Jonah and Beck, love each other so much, it was as if I had discovered the script for a buddy movie that I didn't have time to film.

Just know that, up in Montana, on the outskirts of Huntley, on Thackery Ranch, Jonah and Beck are still getting up to their usual shenanigans, stuff like attempting to ride the horses in the pasture without bridle or saddle. Getting an old junker truck, putting enormous wheels on it, and attempting to drive through the mud on the banks of the Yellowstone River. Seeing who can get more drunk before they go out and howl at the full moon.

They will never change, and I'm sure Royce (and Gordy!) wouldn't want them to.

The book is finished, but my pleasure in writing it will stay with me for a good long time.

ROYCE'S FAVORITE POEM

Royce's favorite poem, about a morning's morning minion, happens to be my favorite poem of all time.

It's by a fellow named Gerard Manley Hopkins (July 1844 - June 1889) who wanted to praise his god through poetry. I think he did it beautifully.

And here, without further ado, is Royce's favorite poem:

The Windhover

I caught this morning morning's minion, king-
    dom of daylight's dauphin, dapple-dawn-drawn Falcon, in his riding
      Of the rolling level underneath him steady air, and striding
High there, how he rung upon the rein of a wimpling wing
In his ecstasy! then off, off forth on swing,
    As a skate's heel sweeps smooth on a bow-bend: the hurl and gliding
      Rebuffed the big wind. My heart in hiding
Stirred for a bird, – the achieve of, the mastery of the thing!

ROYCE'S FAVORITE POEM

Brute beauty and valour and act, oh, air, pride, plume, here
    Buckle! AND the fire that breaks from thee then, a billion
  Times told lovelier, more dangerous, O my chevalier!

  No wonder of it: shéer plód makes plough down sillion
Shine, and blue-bleak embers, ah my dear,
    Fall, gall themselves, and gash gold-vermilion.

Note: If you're keen, there is a very lovely writeup about the poem by Ange Mlinko: https://www.poetryfoundation.org/articles/69191/gerard-manley-hopkins-the-windhover

A Letter from Jackie

Hello, Reader!

Thank you for reading *The Cowboy and the Hoodlum,* the second book in my Farthingdale Valley series.

If you enjoyed the book, I would love it if you would let your friends know so they can experience the romance between Royce and Jonah.

If you leave a review, I'd love to read it! You can send the URL to: Jackienorthauthor@gmail.com

Best Regards,

Jackie

- facebook.com/jackienorthMM
- twitter.com/JackieNorthMM
- instagram.com/jackienorth_author
- pinterest.com/jackienorthauthor
- bookbub.com/profile/jackie-north
- amazon.com/author/jackienorth
- goodreads.com/Jackie_North

About the Author

Jackie North has written since grade school and spent years absorbing mainstream romances. Her dream was to write full time and put her English degree to good use.

As fate would have it, she discovered m/m romance and decided that men falling in love with other men was exactly what she wanted to write about.

Her characters are a bit flawed and broken. Some find themselves on the edge of society, and others are lost. All of them deserve a happily ever after, and she makes sure they get it!

She likes long walks on the beach, the smell of lavender and rainstorms, and enjoys sleeping in on snowy mornings.

In her heart, there is peace to be found everywhere, but since in the real world this isn't always true, Jackie writes for love.

Connect with Jackie:

https://www.jackienorth.com/
jackie@jackienorth.com

facebook.com/jackienorthMM
twitter.com/JackieNorthMM
pinterest.com/jackienorthauthor
bookbub.com/profile/jackie-north
amazon.com/author/jackienorth
goodreads.com/Jackie_North
instagram.com/jackienorth_author